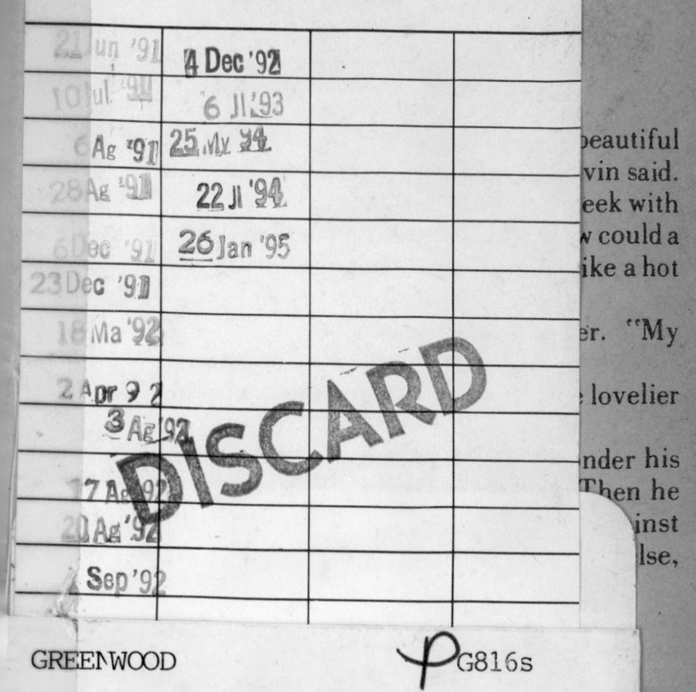

Gy 816 s

ZEBRA BOOKS
KENSINGTON PUBLISHING CORP.

ZEBRA BOOKS

are published by

Kensington Publishing Corp.
475 Park Avenue South
New York, NY 10016

First printing: May, 1991

Printed in the United States of America

Chapter 1

London, November 1745

"I think you only love me for my breasts," Clarice Wynburn said to her young lover, her tone a mixture of petulant rebuke and mounting desire. Gavin Carlisle had bypassed his usual ritual of flattery and the presentation of a gift, and gone straight to the true object of his visit.

"I love all of you," Gavin muttered, as he fondled the warm flesh of his mistress's generous bosom and teased the firming nipples with his fingertips. He was too far under the sway of hot desire to be drawn into an argument over which attribute of the well-endowed widow appealed to him most.

Even though Gavin's virile presence made her tremble with desire, Clarice was not entirely mollified. "Sometimes I don't think you care enough which woman is in your arms to look up," she protested as she halfheartedly attempted to check his passionate advances.

"Are you afraid I might confuse you with someone else?" There was only a faint trace of a Scottish burr in Gavin's deep bass voice, but it was clear he was more interested in planting kisses on the white skin of Clarice's neck than attending to her answer.

"No," she admitted, gazing at her lover out of eyes veiled to hide the caution and speculation in their depths, "but then, I always make sure no one else is about to distract your attention."

"I haven't been with another woman since Cumberland introduced us," Gavin muttered, as his large, strong hand delved into the front of her dress. "I haven't wanted to."

Clarice had intended to make a more substantial complaint, but the effect of Gavin's lips on her breast robbed her of any desire to halt his exploration, however briefly. She had been his mistress for almost three months, but she still had not accustomed herself to the marvelous perfection of his body or the fiery energy of his lovemaking. After marriage to a wealthy squire—who had providentially died before her youthful appeal could fade—Clarice was not about to waste time quarrelling over niceties of manner.

A knock at the door surprised them both, but Gavin didn't pause in his attentions; when the knock came a second time, it was an intolerable irritation; when it came a third time, followed by the entrance of Clarice's terrified maid, it was impossible to ignore. Gavin paused but remained where he was; Clarice sat up abruptly, hastily clutching her crumpled gown to her bosom.

"I have told you never to interrupt me!" she shouted in cold rage. "I'll turn you off for this."

"Please, Madame, I didn't want to, truly I didn't, but there's this gentleman downstairs . . ." The flustered girl stopped, too overcome by her own embarrassment to continue.

"I'm already *with* a gentleman," Clarice said in icy tones, "or do you think I should be the better satisfied with double rations?"

"No, Madame. I never would . . ." The silent laughter which shook Gavin's six-foot length did nothing to improve Clarice's temper.

"Get out and don't bother me again."

"But—"

"And no but's!" screamed Clarice, flinging her discarded slipper at the overwrought maid. "Get out, or leave this house at once." The beleaguered servant hesitated only a moment before closing the door.

"I wonder what that was about," mused Gavin, a half smile on his lips as he resumed his exploration of Clarice's body.

"Damn!" she exclaimed, still seething with anger. "There's nothing to do but get rid of her. She's a stupid creature, poor child, but she's the best maid I ever had."

"Why do you have to turn her off?" Gavin said idly, amusement dancing in his black eyes. "She didn't bother me."

"So I noticed." Clarice's rich chuckle rolled from her effortlessly. "You acted like maids pop in on you all the time."

"Maybe she would like to join us?" Clarice's laughter erupted again despite the shuddering waves of sensual delight that were sweeping over her body.

"If you did to Janet what you're doing to me right now, she would run screaming into the street."

"Then it's a good thing you're the one who's in bed with me," Gavin said as he tugged at her gown.

"I'd murder you if I caught you with Janet," Clarice swore. She ran her fingers through his thick black hair and roughly drew his head to her bosom. His face was clear and smooth, with no rough beard to scratch her sensitive skin.

Gavin pulled Clarice's badly wrinkled gown over her rounded hips.

"You could have waited for me to change." But Clarice's coyly voiced objection failed to conceal her satisfaction at Gavin's impatience.

"I don't mind helping," he murmured, as his marauding lips ranged over her neck and shoulders.

"I think you like taking my clothes off," Clarice whispered, biting his ear. "It makes you feel like a savage, dominating male."

"*You* make me feel savage," Gavin muttered. "I'm a perfect gentleman at all other times."

"I don't want you to be a gentleman with me," Clarice moaned suddenly, her whole being filled with a yearning as urgent as that of the male animal who was about to possess her.

Clarice raked Gavin's strong mouth with her own, glorying in the heavily muscled power and lithe grace of the body that filled her arms. She was eager for him to satisfy the craving that suddenly shook her like the ague, and she clung to him, kissing his face with hot, hungry lips. She knew that no matter how perfect their first consummation, no matter how shattering its results, it was no more than a prelude. Gavin's young, insatiable body demanded much more, and before the night was over, he would completely exhaust her with his demands.

All petulance and artifice gone, her eyes glazed with desire, Clarice abruptly turned toward Gavin, impatient to surrender to him without reservation.

The bedroom door opened again—there was no warning knock—and Clarice sat up with a convulsive start. "Hell and damnation!" swore Gavin, not nearly so sanguine this time.

"I regret the necessity of disturbing you at such a moment," announced a male voice which reverberated with tightly controlled fury, "but I won't take more than a few minutes of your time."

Gavin froze, his eyes not needing to seek the visitor's face to know it was his father, the Earl of Parkhaven. His thrusting, seeking tendrils of desire withered into nothingness, as the Earl advanced toward the center of the room. Clarice cowered behind Gavin, reaching frantically for her discarded gown, but the Earl didn't appear to be in the least disconcerted by the presence of a half-naked woman in his son's arms; in fact, he didn't seem to notice Clarice at all.

"I would never have intruded on you, if you had taken the trouble to answer any one of the several messages I have had sent around to your rooms," the Earl began. "And please don't tell me you were out of town, or that your valet only remembered it when you were stepping out the door," he continued before Gavin could reply. "I'm only too well acquainted with your reluctance to answer any summons from me."

"That's because you never say anything I want to hear," replied Gavin, not the least cowed by his imperious sire. "And your complaints about my style of living have become extremely irksome, not to mention entirely predictable."

"And altogether ignored," replied his father, favoring Clarice with such a fierce glare that the not-so-courageous beauty cowered behind her lover. "I had thought such overripe fruit must have lost its savor by now, but I fear I failed to take into account that though you are old in debauchery, you are young in appetite."

Gavin struggled to keep his temper under control. "Say what you've come to say and get out," he barked. "Your presence is damned inconvenient."

"You have only yourself to blame. I would have much preferred to conduct the interview in less vulgar surroundings."

"It cost me a fortune to have this place done," Clarice exclaimed hotly, goaded into speech in the defense of her lavishly decorated boudoir.

"Be assured it suits you to perfection," sniped the Earl.

"Thank you," she replied, her indignant frown transformed into a gratified smile. "I worried for months over the colors."

"Don't be a simpleton. He's not flattering you," Gavin snapped before turning back to his father. "Stop baiting Clarice, and come to the point. Not even you can believe I would choose a mistress for her taste in hangings."

"Some do, but you are correct in assuming I did not take you to be one of their number."

"Damn you!" Gavin snarled in a harsh whisper. "Will you never let up?" He had no filial feeling whatsoever for this desiccated old aristocrat, but the bastard could always slip past his guard with his damned poisonous tongue.

"It's the rest of your life that I wish to speak with you about."

"You can't mean to do it *now!*"

"It does seem to be an unauspicious moment," the Earl remarked, with a wry glance at a room decorated to give one the feeling of being at the bottom of the sea. "This overabundance of green makes me feel unwell. Perhaps tomorrow morning at ten would suit you better?"

"I already have an engagement. An important one," Gavin added when he saw his father's brows gather.

"Then I suppose it will have to be now."

"You must be joking!"

"This discussion has already been postponed too often. There is a very real danger that even now it may be too late. I'm quite prepared to wait while you weigh your decision."

"That won't be necessary," Gavin said furiously, when he saw his father preparing to settle into one of the several chairs with which the room was provided. "I'll be there at ten, though it's damned inconvenient. My friends will wonder at my standing them up."

"Send them a message, or is writing another of your

laboriously acquired skills which has been put aside in your unending quest for gratification of the flesh?"

"I'll be there!" shouted Gavin. "Now get out. You've already ruined my evening."

"I shouldn't think I have been here long enough for that," drawled his father. "Considering the heights of ecstasy within your mutual grasp, I would say that five minutes ought to be enough to regain any lost ground."

Gavin was nearly speechless with rage, as much from the ruthlessness of his father's speech as from the cruelty of his judgement.

"You needn't bother to accompany me to my carriage," the Earl added with a sardonic smile. "I don't think the watch would understand."

"I'm tempted to do it, just to see your face," replied Gavin with a savage snarl.

"It would not be my face that would draw their attention," his father responded dryly.

"Get out before I break your neck," Gavin said with a reluctant crack of laughter. "I'll be around at ten sharp, soberly dressed like a dutiful son."

"It's your duty I wish to discuss, but I shall save that until tomorrow," the Earl added, as Gavin's brief burst of good humor vanished. "I will leave you to your, uh . . . how should I put it? Just desserts seems too severe."

"Just leave. You can amuse yourself by searching for the *mot juste* on your way home." The Earl smiled thinly, saluted his son, and withdrew.

Clarice let out a long-held breath. "Is that man really your father?"

"Yes."

"He scares me to death."

"Then make sure you're not around when he gets really angry. He may be as thin as whipcord and as pale as a ghost, but the bloody bastard can get into a rage that would make a sailor quake. Unfortunately, I'm the one who usually puts him out of temper. I stay away from him as much as I can."

"Is that wise?" Clarice asked, thinking of the costly baubles Gavin had given her. "He does control your allowance."

"I don't have to depend on him to survive."

"I'm glad. He might force you to give me up."

"That's not within his power."

"He still frightens me," Clarice said with a pleasurable shudder. She sank back on the bed and pushed herself up against Gavin. "I'm glad you didn't get your body from him. I wouldn't find you nearly so attractive." She snuggled closer and let her hands begin to roam over his broad, muscled chest. "I hope you haven't forgotten where you were," she whispered seductively, as she drew his head down between her breasts.

Gavin swore to himself. It had taken Clarice *less* than five minutes to rekindle her passion. He had never wanted anything more of her than to be a satisfying bed partner, but to have her so accurately fulfill his father's prophecy destroyed all the enjoyment he found in her company; even his body refused to respond to her caresses.

"Damn, damn, and double damn!" he cursed, getting up from the bed so abruptly Clarice nearly tumbled onto the floor.

"What's wrong?" she asked, baffled.

"That bloody bastard has ruined it for me," Gavin shouted, knowing that Clarice would never divine the real reason for his fury.

"You can't let a little thing like a quarrel stop you," she said, attempting to draw him down close so she could rub her body against him. "This kind of thing is bound to happen lots of times after you're married," she said coyly. "You'll never have any fun if you let it throw you out of stride."

"Well, I'm *not* going to get married," Gavin declared, reaching for his coat. "There's nothing I want from a woman I can't get without it."

"How about children?" challenged Clarice mildly. She tried to take his coat away from him, and was not happy when he pushed her aside, but she didn't persist. The Earl wasn't the only one with a fierce temper. Gavin's hooded black eyes, down-turned mouth, powerful jaw, and deep sloping chin, gave him the appearance of a handsome bulldog.

Clarice was a little afraid of Gavin, yet that was part of his attraction. After a complacent and admiring husband, she wanted someone who would use her roughly. Gavin never did, but there was no doubt in her mind that he would use her very roughly indeed, if she dared cross him.

"It's cruel of you to leave me like this," Clarice said, pouting attractively. "Will I see you tomorrow?"

"I doubt it," Gavin replied with cruel honesty. "I'm not fit for human companionship after I've been with my father. I'm liable to bite your head off, or knock it off, just because you're within reach."

"Well, if you don't *want* to see me . . ."

"It's not that," Gavin assured her, yet he knew he wouldn't be back for several days, if at all. She hadn't changed, she was still the same lush, attractive woman he had found so desirable in the first place, but in some way he could not explain, his father's mockery had destroyed his pleasure in her company. He knew she was shallow and silly, even a little rapacious and untrustworthy—he certainly had no intention of marrying her—but all he had wanted was a few hours of unfettered pleasure.

He cursed his father for denying him that modest goal.

Chapter 2

Oliver Carlisle sat stiffly erect in a wing chair near the fire, his legs crossed and his fingers drumming restlessly on a nearby table. His translucent skin and fastidious dress gave him the appearance of an effete aristocrat, a misleading appearance which had caused more than one competitor to underestimate the steel-like determination and dispassionate judgement which had enabled him to accumulate an enormous fortune. Now he was about to bring these same qualities to bear on a problem whose solution had long evaded him.

Somehow, Gavin must be brought to realize it was time to marry, settle down, and raise a family.

Distant sounds of arrival reached the Earl's ear; at least the boy had enough force of mind to tear himself away from that overblown widow when duty called. Maybe there was hope for him yet.

Gavin burst into the library. His swift stride was a visible manifestation of his unwillingness to be present, and his dour expression an eloquent reflection of the effort he was exerting to hold his ill-humor in check.

The contrast between father and son was astonishing. Whereas the Earl was of medium height, slight build, and almost feminine in his movements, Gavin's tall, large-boned physique and athletic appearance gave him the look of a youthful Hercules. Both men shared a clear complexion unmarked by the shadow of a beard, but the Earl's thin, dark blond hair was in direct contrast to the thick, raven mane of which Gavin was so proud. A strong, broad nose and powerful sweeping jaw completed a face that could stop half the women of London in their tracks, but one so different from its sire that only the Earl's unwavering certainty of his wife's fidelity prevented him from questioning his son's paternity.

"I'm on time," Gavin said without a greeting. "Bear that in mind when you start in damning everything about me."

"I've always given you credit for punctuality," remarked his father languidly. "It's your unwillingness to come to this house under any except the most compelling circumstances that I complain of."

"Can you blame me?"

"I have, frequently." Gavin smiled without humor.

"That was a foolish question. I shall try to do better."

"If you would only make such a promise with respect to the manner in which you lead your life, I should be much more pleased."

"I don't propose to discuss my life with you."

"Did you and your ladylove part on less than cordial terms this morning?" the Earl taunted.

Gavin turned on his father with biting anger. "I spent the night in my own bed." The Earl's eyebrows rose questioningly. "You didn't expect me to be in an amorous mood after your intrusion, did you? I was sure putting me out of humor was your primary objective."

"It wasn't, but my interest in your welfare compels me to point out that though your companion appears to be a virtual cornucopia of erotic delight, even greedy children tire of sweets when they have gorged themselves too often."

"Is that why you maintain a virtual harem?"

"The fact that I do not share your taste for provincial widows is no excuse for crudity," declared the Earl.

"How do you explain them to mother?"

"Your mother is a lady—"

"Then treat her like one," Gavin exploded. "If I had a wife who accorded me half her forbearance, I wouldn't mortify her by keeping company with half the whores in London."

"Ladies do not inquire into such matters," the Earl stated in dour disapproval.

"This is a waste of time," Gavin said with a snort. He poured himself a glass of wine but didn't seem to enjoy it. "Don't you have some beer or ale? Bordeaux is hard to take before noon."

"I never try," remarked his father, as he rang a small bell that rested on the table next to him. Almost immediately a burly servant appeared from behind one of the several doors that led from the chamber.

"When did you start hiding servants behind doors?" Gavin asked sarcastically.

"There are those who believe it unwise for me to be alone with you."

"Don't be absurd," growled Gavin. "I might itch to choke the life out of you, but you're not worth being hung."

"Such filial concern."

"And you can drop the pretense of fatherly affection. You don't like me any more than I like you."

"Now that's where you are wrong. Though I most earnestly deplore nearly every action you have taken since you moved to London, on the whole I am quite pleased with you."

"I would have thought those attitudes incompatible."

"When you're a father, you will understand how easily two such contradictory emotions may coexist."

"Then I'll never understand. An heir isn't important enough for me to live a lie for thirty years."

"I hope you will reconsider," the Earl said quite calmly. "The Parkhaven estates have been handed down from father to son for over five hundred years. It is unthinkable that they should pass out of the family when there is a healthy son capable of siring heirs."

"How do you know I haven't sired several already?"

"I will not tolerate a pack of bastards sired from blowzy country sluts, fighting over a title that has been unsullied for half a millennium," decreed the Earl, suddenly losing some of his reserve.

"Is that all you care about, the title and the name?"

"I care about a great deal more, but you don't seem to care for anything at all."

"I do," Gavin assured his father with a mocking smile. "I care for my horses and my clothes, and I often worry whether the champagne will last out the night."

"I could cut off your allowance, and force you to accept my wishes in order to live."

"I'm lucky at cards," replied Gavin with a sudden grin. "And my horses win more than their share of races."

"It's inconceivable that a son of mine could actually consider supporting himself by gambling," the Earl intoned, much as if Gavin had just announced his intention of becoming a highwayman. "Does the Parkhaven name mean nothing to you?"

"Not a damned thing. And after I'm gone, anybody who wants it can have it."

"Lochknole will not leave my family," vowed the Earl, with such vehemence that Gavin was surprised into regarding him more closely.

"How are you going to manage that?" Gavin took a swallow from the mug of ale that had been set down before him.

"Do you care for your mother's happiness?" Gavin

stopped in mid-swallow. The Earl watched him closely, but Gavin finished his swallow and set the mug back on the tray before answering.

"I'm surprised you don't choke when you mention her," he replied, barely able to maintain his attitude of unconcern.

"If you won't consider marrying for the sake of the family name, perhaps you will consider it for her."

"She'd never ask it of me."

"I don't think you quite understand me," his father said very deliberately, watching Gavin intently all the while. "Your mother would very much like to see you surrounded by your children, but though she might urge you to take a wife, I'm convinced she's too kindhearted to require it of you. I, on the other hand, have no such reluctance." The Earl favored his son with an enigmatic smile. "Your willingness to accommodate me in this matter would insure your mother's comfort."

"Mother has survived nearly twenty years without your consideration. She sure as hell can get along without it now."

"You always were an unreasonable child," the Earl observed irritably, "but it is quite possible that I will find myself without the resources to provide for her care."

Gavin took an impatient swallow from his ale. "You can take care of mother out of her own fortune."

"I don't know when, or if, I will receive any more revenues from Scotland."

"Then use your own money."

"Most of my income derives from Edinburgh, which was captured in September. The rest is tied up in ventures supported by the money of an old friend who came with me from Scotland."

Gavin regarded his father cynically, unmoved and indifferent. "This is the first I've heard of that. How do I know you're not lying again?"

"Do you think I'm proud of having been born a pauper?" his father said quietly, his voice vibrating with unspoken rage. "Do you think I *want* it known that if the Raymond money were withdrawn, a business organization I have worked more than half my life to build would collapse tomorrow?" Carlisle breathed deeply and took a few seconds to calm himself.

Gavin was astonished. He was used to his father's anger, but he'd never seen him reveal this deeply buried rage; yet he'd done so twice in less than thirty minutes.

"But if this Raymond wants his money, my marrying won't make him change his mind."

"Raymond died ten years ago."

"So?"

"He left everything to his daughter, and he left his daughter in my care."

"I still don't see the problem."

"Sara Raymond will turn twenty-one in less than a month. When she does, the money may pass beyond my control."

"But your Scottish estate—"

"Don't you ever take your nose out of that female's bosom?" the Earl demanded with tightly controlled anger. "This upstart Stuart prince has conquered Edinburgh, invaded England, and is marching toward London at this very moment. Do you think he's going to allow me, a loyal follower of George II, or you, a boon companion to his sons, to hold estates virtually at his back gate?"

But Gavin wasn't listening. "Isn't she the female who used to spend Christmas with us?" he asked, casting his mind back in an effort to remember.

"I should have known that a female—*any* female—would always command your attention, even in the face of the impending fall of London."

Gavin flushed with hot anger, but he refused to be baited.

"*If* you are referring to Miss Raymond, I did invite her to spend a few holidays with us, before your mother's health became too fragile."

"That chit's as skinny as a starved chicken, and ugly into the bargain."

"She has grown into a lovely woman, very much like her mother."

"I'm still not going to marry her or any other female of your choosing." Gavin picked up his ale and stalked over to the fire; he stared into its depths for some moments.

"Mother seems to be better," he said at last. "I believe she's sorry she came to London."

"Georgiana has never once left Estameer without making me feel that I was tearing her away from her only child," stated the Earl, a hardness slipping into his voice. "She doesn't love anything so much as she loves those barren hills."

"She draws her strength from those hills," explained Gavin. "We both do."

"Then I trust you are both sufficiently fortified. I fear you shall need all your resources in the coming months."

"What are you talking about now?" demanded Gavin, weary of the duel of wills.

"Just of what may happen if you continue to disregard my warning."

"I might listen if you'd stop trying to make me believe you're worried about mother or your fortune slipping away. If England suffered rebellion, invasion, *and* a plague, you'd still come out with a profit."

"Then listen to this," the Earl said, in the deadly quiet voice his competitors had long since learned to fear. "Under no circumstances will I allow Lochknole to pass out of this family."

"So you said, but I won't marry your Miss Raymond."

"There is still one course of action open to me."

"What can you do? You can't disinherit me."

"No."

"Well?" Gavin inquired in frustration after a pause. "What in Hades are you going to do?" The Earl gave him a measuring look.

"You're supposed to be an intelligent man. Can't you figure it out?"

"No."

"You will, and when you do, remember I did everything in my power to keep from going to such an extreme."

Gavin turned away in annoyance, but long association with his father's determination to let nothing and no one stand in the way of his reaching his goal caused him to turn back and carefully study that parchmentlike face. It took only a few minutes before the awful idea sprang into Gavin's head.

"You wouldn't?" he ejaculated, slamming down his ale. "Not even *you* could be such a contemptible swine!"

"I wouldn't and couldn't *what?*" demanded the Earl. An intense light gleamed in his eyes, but his voice was as calm as ever.

"Divorce mother," Gavin said, his face a mask of incredulous rage.

"I find the idea wholly distasteful," his father replied deliberately, "but you have given me no other choice. It is quite impossible for your mother to bear any more children."

"But that would mean a trial in the House of Lords. It would kill her."

The Earl looked squarely into his son's eyes. "Then there would be no need for a divorce, would there?"

With an explosion of blind rage, Gavin attacked his father. His charge knocked the chair over backwards, sending them both onto the floor. Before the sound of the crash had stopped reverberating in the high-ceilinged room, before Gavin's hands had found a lethal grip on the Earl's throat, all the doors to the room flew open and a half-dozen sturdy men rushed forward to pull a nearly crazed Gavin off his father.

"You contemptible swine!" Gavin raged helplessly, now held securely by a dozen hands.

"Think of me as you please," panted his father as he attempted to put his person in some order, "but I will have an heir of my loins, be it through you or a son I have yet to sire. The decision is yours."

"You son-of-a-bitch!" Gavin roared. "I'll see you in hell for this!"

Chapter 3

"I don't know how she ever learned to play that dratted thing," Betty marveled to the downstairs parlor maid. "I couldn't hit that many keys unless I was to fall down on them."

"Miss Raymond is quite skilled at the harpsichord. Herr Bach says she is his best pupil."

"I'm not surprised, not as much as she works at it, but what else has the poor girl got to do with her time?"

"Not much, I'm afraid. But with her fortune, it won't matter. She's bound to marry soon, even though she is a little *old.*"

"Twenty is a perfect age for marrying," insisted Betty. "Though how she's to find a proper husband from this place I don't know." *This place* was Miss Adelaide Rachel's Seminary for Young Women, and the only unattached males allowed across the threshold were younger sons, boys in nearly every instance, who were forced to accompany their parents on one of the two painfully formal visits allowed each boarder per term. They were not the kind of males to attract the attention of a beautiful young heiress, who still dreamed of a fearless Adonis she had not seen in seven years.

"Surely her guardian will arrange a marriage for her."

"Not that one!" Betty sniffed. "He's not likely to put himself out unless it suits."

"Not many of them do," her companion observed with a sigh. "They're not brought up to consider any pleasure but their own."

"I guess I'd better stop worrying about what's none of my concern and tell Miss Raymond she's wanted in the parlor before Her Holiness has palpitations."

"You better not let anyone hear you talking about Miss Adelaide like that," warned the older woman. "She might turn you off."

"Being maid to a gaggle of hoity-toity females is no wonderful thing," Betty said with a shrug of indifference. "Besides, she wouldn't have hired me if the pox hadn't given the place a bad name." Betty chuckled at some private thought. "I don't think she trusts me."

"Why?"

"Too tall," explained Betty. "You'd better not let me keep you from your work. No need for us both to be out of a situation."

A short time later, Sara Raymond neared Miss Adelaide's sitting room with lagging steps. It seemed that her whole life had been dominated by this unbending tyrant, and even though she was almost twenty-one, she still couldn't approach this formidable woman without quaking inwardly. For months Betty had been telling Sara that she was richer, more beautiful, of higher social standing, and that she ought to stare right back at her. That was easy for Betty to say. She towered over every female in the academy, but Sara had never seen anyone who could intimidate Miss Adelaide, not even the most haughty of parents.

Sara paused long enough to make sure her plain blue serge dress was neat and straight, then she knocked firmly; the best way to handle an interview with Miss Adelaide was to get it over as quickly as possible. Her discreet knock brought a sharp summons to enter and seat herself in the straight, uncomfortable chair placed directly across from Miss Adelaide.

Right away Sara knew something was different. Miss Adelaide smiled. It wasn't an expression that would pass for a smile on the face of an ordinary person, actually it more closely resembled the puzzled grimace of someone suddenly encountering a pungent but not unpleasant odor, but for Miss Adelaide, it was unquestionably a sign of approval.

"I am the bearer of a message to you from the Earl of Parkhaven," she began without preamble.

"Is he ill?" Sara inquired anxiously. The Earl's visits were rare and never long, but she still remembered her vacations at Estameer with wistful pleasure.

"No, he is quite well," responded Miss Adelaide, with a frown that indicated she would like Sara to remain silent until invited to speak. "However, the Countess is quite unwell, and he is unable to leave her side."

"Oh," Sara said simply.

"He has asked me to speak to you in his place on a matter of great importance." Sara began to shake. She had the feeling that her only friends in the world were about to abandon her.

Miss Adelaide rose from her seat on the enormous sofa and took a chair closer to Sara; that was unusual, too, for Miss Adelaide used the size of the sofa to put her visitors at a disadvantage. Her mouth tightened, much like she'd tasted something sour, and her eyes grew intensely bright; if it had been anyone else, Sara would have said she was bursting with news, but Miss Adelaide would never allow herself to do anything so vulgarly commonplace as *burst*.

"The Earl has requested me to advise you that, unless you should be found to have an objection, you are to become the wife of his only son, Lord Gavin Carlisle."

Thinking that she had delivered some wondrous piece of news, Miss Adelaide was justifiably baffled when Sara didn't so much as blink. She paused briefly, but when Sara continued to stare at her as though hypnotized, she concealed her disappointment and proceeded in a brisk, businesslike manner. "Due to the Countess's illness, the Earl has deemed it expedient for you to be married as soon as possible. He has instructed me to have you ready exactly one week from today."

Sara did not speak, indeed, she *could* not speak, because the news had literally taken her breath away. She had idolized Gavin ever since she set eyes on him that first Christmas, but she was a sensible girl. She knew he had no partiality for her, that he actually disliked her and thought her rather plain and uninteresting. She had had no occasion to meet him since she was thirteen, but she had not forgotten his stubborn chin or his devil-may-care courage. Whenever she dreamed of being rescued from Miss Adelaide's by a handsome stranger, she thought of Gavin; whenever she dreamed of being kissed for the first time, she thought of Gavin; whenever she dreamed of nestling securely in the arms of her husband, she thought of Gavin. Yet never once had she actually believed it would happen. Being told point-blank that she was to marry the object of her fantasies at the end of one week left her dazed. She stared before her like an empty-eyed statue.

"I'm not surprised that you find yourself at a loss for words," said Miss Adelaide with a self-congratulatory smile. "It is a marvelous piece of good fortune. I know you are a considerable heiress and would naturally expect to contract a good marriage, but you are fortunate indeed to have achieved a brilliant one."

"Yes," agreed Sara numbly.

"There will be no time to send out invitations, but perhaps that is best. The unprecedented haste with which the whole is to be accomplished nearly takes my breath away." Miss Adelaide's disapproval was clear. "The death of the Countess would certainly postpone the wedding for as much as a year, but I would have thought such delay a small price to pay for the respect due a peeress. Nevertheless, I have been instructed to see that you are suitably provided with a wedding dress, every necessity to sustain life outside this school, and delivered to the chapel at St. George's, all within seven days. It is not an easy thing, but it shall be done." Sara didn't doubt it; Miss Adelaide never made promises she couldn't keep.

Miss Adelaide suddenly stared hard at Sara. "You don't object, do you? I am aware that Lord Carlisle's reputation is not spotless, but most young men are a little wild before they settle down."

"No, I don't object," Sara managed to mumble.

"Naturally you will be relieved of your duties at once. The dressmakers will be here within the hour to begin measuring you for your bride clothes and as many dresses as can reasonably be got ready in the time allotted. Is there anything else you need?" Sara stared back at her unable to think at all.

"I can see that you are wholly overcome by your good fortune," said Miss Adelaide with her grimace of a smile. "Perhaps a period of quiet reflection would help you become more accustomed to the prospect of someday becoming a countess."

I'll *never* get used to it, Sara muttered to herself as she hurried back to her room, her thoughts whirling out of control. She was going to marry Gavin! It seemed totally unbelievable, yet Miss Adelaide had told her so, and Miss Adelaide was never wrong.

"Did you know?" Sara asked Betty, when she found the maid dragging out trunks and valises and emptying drawers of all her belongings.

"No, Miss. Such tidings is not for the likes of me, but it couldn't be happening to a nicer young lady."

"But to marry Gavin!" Sara exclaimed, clasping her hands to her bosom, spinning about with a crazy smile on her face, and falling on the bed with such force that two of Betty's neat piles bounced onto the floor.

"I don't think I recall your mentioning the young gentleman before," said Betty, calmly picking up the clothes and placing them away from Sara.

"I've dreamed about him, ever since I saw him showing off for the coachman without knowing I was riding inside the coach. He was furious when he found out I'd told his parents," she said with a reminiscent laugh. "How was I to know he had taken a horse he was strictly forbidden to ride, had ridden over land claimed by a rival clan, and should have been with his tutor making up work he had failed to complete during the last term?" Sara laughed once again. "He probably never thinks of me without grinding his teeth." She stopped suddenly and sat up with an arrested expression. "I wonder if he ever *does* think of me?" she mused aloud. "He was forever calling me a scarecrow. I used to be quite painfully thin," she explained.

"Well, you aren't now," Betty stated emphatically. "Many's the time I've heard the girls, aye, and the teachers too, remark that you are *too* well filled out! If there were any young men about, some pretty nasty things would be said behind your back, or I'm no judge."

"Well, I *was* skinny then," said Sara, as she bounded up from the bed and ran over to the mirror to study her figure. She gazed at herself quite critically, taking notice of her full breasts, slim waist, and rounded hips. "Do you really think I'm well formed?" she asked.

"If the young gentlemen could see you right now, there'd be a line clear around the corner."

"No, there wouldn't," Sara said, unable to hide a smile

of satisfaction. "Miss Adelaide would lock the doors and call the constable. Besides, no man can admire a girl with freckles."

"You don't have freckles," argued Betty.

"Yes, I do," insisted Sara, pulling her over to the mirror and pointing to a spot on her creamy white skin. "See, a freckle."

"It's nothing you'd notice," declared Betty, who thought Sara the most beautiful girl at Miss Rachel's Seminary. "One look at your face and hair, and there's not a man alive who would notice an old freckle, even if you had one, which you don't."

"But I have *sandy* hair. And it's full of curls," lamented Sara, who had frequently bemoaned the fact that her magnificent head of hair wasn't stick-straight and didn't have more strength of color. "I look washed out and faded. How could anyone possibly admire me after seeing Symantha Eckkles?" Miss Eckkles was the resident *femme fatale*, pure white skin and flaming red hair; if Sara could have looked like anybody she wished, she would have been Symantha Eckkles.

"Ten to one he won't set eyes on Miss High-and-Mighty Eckkles," concluded Betty, who was not in the least fond of that imperious boarder. "And it wouldn't make any difference if he does, because he'll be married to you."

"But he won't love me."

"How do you know?" demanded Betty. "I'll wager there're not two men in a hundred who could look on your face and not fall in love with it."

"Not as long as it's covered with freckles."

"You don't have freckles, and your hair's a lovely strawberry blonde color," reiterated Betty. "From what Miss Adelaide says, this Lord Carlisle of yours is a great sportsman. I should think he'd be better pleased to find you've got a good seat in the saddle, than hair the precise color of flame. Besides, one look at your face, and he wouldn't give a fig if your hair was sandy and full of kinks. You have that good healthy look of the outdoors."

"He's looking for a wife, not a saddle horse," Sara declared disgustedly; nevertheless, she was pleased with Betty's compliment. Meribel Raymond had been an acknowledged beauty. She had bequeathed her high cheekbones, full lips, and slightly turned-up nose to her daughter, but Sara would have been the first to admit these features didn't look quite the same on her. She turned away and picked up her best dress which Betty had laid out to pack.

"I know this is the only face I'm ever going to have, but I shall insist upon more handsome clothes once I'm married," she announced, throwing the offending garment down in disgust. "All this grey and black makes me look positively haggard. I want vermillion red and emerald green and the deepest purple."

"Well, you won't get purple, for it's reserved for royalty," remarked the ever-practical Betty, "but I don't see any reason you can't have any other colors you fancy. In the meantime, I have to clear away this mess and get ready for the dressmakers. You can tell them about your vermillion reds and emerald greens, but the color you'd best be concerned with is pearl white. That is, unless you propose to get married in the dress you've got on."

"I want the most beautiful wedding dress that was ever made," rhapsodized Sara. "I want yards of lace, a train as long as the aisle, and a veil that reaches to the floor."

"Considering the time they have to cut and sew, you'll be lucky if it looks like a dress," Betty remarked prosaically. "For the life of me, I can't figure out why rich people are always in a hurry. What's the use of having money if you're forever rushing about like poor folks?"

"Miss Adelaide says the Countess is very sick. The

wedding would be put off a year if she died."

"Then again, there's no point in letting your young man run loose any longer than you have to. If he's half as wonderful as you believe, every female in London will be after him, and that includes the ones that already got husbands."

"I still can't believe I'm going to be gone from this place in just seven days," Sara said. Her gaze narrowed and became more intent. "It's just like a prison, and my visits to Estameer only made it seem worse. It was really beautiful there, and everyone was so nice," she continued with a touch of melancholy. "The Countess spoiled me wonderfully, but I've always longed for someplace I could *belong*, not just visit. And I'm tired of everybody always planning my life and telling me what to do. Just think," she added with a sudden eagerness, "I'll soon have my own house with my own servants and my own money. *I'll* be the one to decide when it's time for dinner or whether I go out and who I'll see." Suddenly Sara's face fell ludicrously. "I've never been taught how to run a house. I won't know what to do," she exclaimed, turning to Betty. "You'll have to come help me."

"Lordy, Miss, you won't be wanting a beanpole like me in your fancy house. You ought to have a French maid to pick out pretty dresses for you, show you the latest ways to fix your hair, and teach you things that will please your Lord."

"Are there special ways to please a man?" Sara asked innocently.

"Lawks, Miss, don't you know *anything?*"

"I've hardly seen a man since Daddy died. Not unless you count Aggie Peterson's brother, and I don't want to know how to please him."

"But you must have learned something from your father."

"Like teasing him, and sitting on his lap, and

demanding kisses?"

"Lord have mercy! I guess I'll *have* to go with you. There's no telling what kind of a fix you'd get into, unless somebody's there to keep an eye on you. You have no more sense of how to go on in the world than a baby."

"I *do* have sense," insisted Sara, stung. "It's just that I don't know much about men." Her brow creased, and then cleared almost at once. "Oh well, they can't be so very different from women," she said with a smile, dismissing her worries.

Betty could only stare.

"We're going to have a wonderful time together," Sara continued.

"The first thing you've got to learn is that I'm your maid, not your friend," Betty said, recovering quickly. "It's not proper for you to be talking to me like you are now."

"Why not?"

"You'll have lots of grand friends to talk to. And you can talk to your husband when he's home."

"But you're my friend."

"That may be," conceded Betty, "but it still doesn't change the way nobs are supposed to act. And you're going to have to make up your mind to like those fancy society folks. It's them you'll be seeing at parties and inviting to your balls. It's them, and your husband, you'll be studying to get along with, if you expect to have a happy life."

"I don't know much about how to behave in fashionable society," Sara admitted, as resolute as she was downcast, "but I won't be dictated to. People have been telling me what to do all my life, and I'm tired of it."

"Suppose your husband tells you what to do?" asked Betty.

"He won't," Sara replied instantly, but the proud face of Gavin intruded on her memory, and she was quite certain he would consider Betty an unsuitable maid and an unfit companion. Suddenly Sara realized that she knew very little about her future husband, and she ardently wished the Countess's illness had not ended her visits to Estameer. She wanted to marry Gavin, but she realized there were many important questions she couldn't answer, and that frightened her.

"I will engage a maid to choose my dresses and fix my hair if I have to," Sara stated firmly, "but I must have someone I can depend on."

"I was only a second maid when my last employer broke up household," Betty protested. "They were never very fashionable. I don't know anything about taking care of a countess."

"Well, I don't know anything about *being* one," Sara responded. "And I don't know anything about running a house, not even a small one. I expect the Earl would be terribly upset if things didn't go just right. You have to come with me."

"Sure I will," Betty consented cheerfully. "I don't suppose Miss Adelaide wants me anyhow."

"Now I don't feel nearly so nervous," Sara said with a grateful smile.

"Don't you go telling yourself that you're out of the woods yet," Betty counseled her young mistress, already assuming her role as mentor. "I'll do what I can, but there's many a step between here and your coronet. You're bound to have a few stumbles that'll give you a skinned knee."

Sara had little opportunity to ponder Betty's words during the remainder of that seemingly interminable day. She was almost immediately called into the reception room normally reserved for visitors. Miss Adelaide closed the doors against the curious, ordered Betty to fetch anything that was required, and then left Sara to the mercy of a stream of strangers who proceeded to poke, prod, and pommel her as heedlessly as if she were a straw-filled doll. Sara struggled to answer all the questions put to her, but long before the last person was ushered out the parlor, she had had numerous occasions to seek Betty's advice.

But now it was over until tomorrow, and as she snuggled down in her bed, there was a smile of pure happiness across her lips. It had been a wonderfully exciting day. She didn't have to concern herself with china, linen, and silver—Gavin's family would have more than enough, and then there was her mother's which was being kept in storage—but the wedding dress was beginning to take shape, and she was all aquiver that such a wonderful creation would be made just for her.

Sara had always known she was rich, but she had never *felt* rich until now. The other students went home during vacations where they could be pampered and spoiled, but Miss Adelaide treated all her girls like they were poor, and in the past eleven years, Sara had gradually forgotten what it was like to be the petted darling of her father and his household.

Consequently, she had hardly known what to do when Miss Adelaide came to her room, just as Sara was preparing to go to bed, and set down an enormous box in front of her.

"This was your mother's jewelry," she had said, opening the box so Sara could gaze at its contents. "It was given into my safekeeping when you came here. Until now you have had no need for anything more than a strand of pearls, but a married lady, especially a countess, will find a use for all these and more."

Sara was struck dumb by the number of jewels crammed into that box. "How can there be so much?" she asked without thinking. "Mama and Papa weren't married very long." A softened look came over Miss Adelaide's face.

"Your father never got over your mother's death. He continued to buy fine pieces and put them away in this great box. There's no telling how much would be here now, if he had lived to see this day."

Sara remembered the many hours her father had spent looking at the great portrait of her mother that hung in the library. That had been their sanctuary, a place where they could sit for hours, each alone with the other. She realized now that her father had spent those long hours with her mother and not with herself, and somehow she felt a little more lonely than before.

Chapter 4

Despite pain that grew more severe with every passing day, Georgiana Carlisle, Countess of Parkhaven, smiled bravely as her nurse placed extra pillows behind her back. She was about to receive a visit from her son, and she was determined he would not find her flat on her back.

"Ye have no business putting yourself about for anyone as young and healthy as Master Gavin," reproved Rose, the Countess's nurse and personal servant for more than twenty years.

"He should have come during the morning, when you were feeling stronger, but he had *things* to do," sniffed Olivia Tate, the Countess's equally long-term companion. "I'd own myself greatly surprised, if it was anything more pressing than a visit to his mistress or one of his horses."

"Don't be forgetting yer medicine," Rose said, handing the Countess a glass with a half-inch of liquid in the bottom. "Yer tae have a goodly dose this time, or ye'll not be able tae see anyone for the rest of the week."

Georgiana swallowed the bitter opiate without protest. She had swallowed so much in these last years, what difference could a little more make? Her malady, a strange and inexplicable deterioration of the muscles, had come upon her after the birth of her only child, and it had been nearly fifteen years since she had been out of her bed for as much as three days in a row. The doctors were constantly at her to remain in London, where they could watch her more closely, but despite the considerable suffering as her condition worsened, Georgiana insisted upon returning to Scotland every summer.

"Hand me my mirror, Olivia," the Countess requested, straightening her cap. "I don't want Gavin to know I haven't been well."

"It's about time he did," Olivia said. "The very idea of him roistering about town, while you lie tied to that bed, is shameful."

"What would you have him do, come sit and hold my hand?" The Countess laughed. "That would soon ruin both our dispositions. I'll not have my tiresome condition stand in his way. It's not as though he could do anything to help me."

"He should be here," Olivia insisted stubbornly.

"I prefer that he be where he likes."

"Do you plan to keep him in the dark right up to the end?"

"I don't know," Georgiana replied, unable to mask the pain of knowing that she was dying. "It depends on whether it will serve any purpose." She wiped away a tear and forced the smile back on her face. "Now don't either of you say anything to make me cry, while Gavin is here. I shall not forgive you if you do."

"Ye know we willna," Rose assured her roughly, wiping away her own tears. "Just lie back and enjoy yer visit."

"You can help me with the design of this quilt until Gavin arrives," offered Olivia. "I fear it will never be ready in time for Christmas."

Gavin's arrival unsettled the quiet of the room. He

examined his mother with loving but critical eyes, before bending over to give her a kiss. "Why didn't you tell me you weren't feeling well?"

"It's no more than what happens several times every winter," the Countess assured him, presenting her cheek for his salute. "I know I look a perfect hag, but I keep hoping you won't notice."

"You still look beautiful to me."

"So how come ye didna arrive this morning like you were supposed tae?" questioned Rose. She had been Gavin's nurse, and she had never relinquished her right to deal with him more harshly than his mother ever would.

"Go away, Rose. I didn't come to see you," Gavin said. "I make mother unhappy enough without you drawing attention to my misdeeds."

"You never make me unhappy," his mother was quick to assure him.

"Yes, I do." He put his hand gently over her lips to quiet her objections. "You never reproach me, but I know you're disappointed in me."

"Then why do you not give up your loose women and take a proper interest in lands that will be yours someday?" demanded Olivia. "You can't expect your father to live forever."

"If you two can't leave Gavin alone, I shall ask you to leave," the Countess warned as severely as she could. "This is *my* visit, and I won't let you ruin it by putting him into a temper, with questions which are really none of your concern."

"It's time they were asked," insisted Olivia.

"When I want them asked, I shall do so," Georgiana said gently, but with a tone that caused her companions to gather up their belongings and depart, Olivia with an offended air and Rose muttering dire predictions of disaster.

"They mean well. Unfortunately, they've forgotten what it was like to be young. But I want to talk about you, not them. Your father tells me you're about to be married," she said smiling. "I've waited so long for this news, I was afraid I would never hear it."

"I knew it would bring a gleam to your eye. I never knew a female yet who didn't get excited at the prospect of some man being clapped in irons for life."

"That's because we know what wretched creatures you are. Even the most admirable man is in need of a little polishing every now and again."

"According to my esteemed sire, I need a good deal more than polishing." Gavin could not keep the bitterness from his voice.

"There's nothing wrong with you that settling down and raising a family won't cure. Now tell me, who is the young lady? I hardly know anyone these days, and your father refused to say a word."

"You know this one. She used to visit us at Christmas."

"Do you mean Sara Raymond?" Georgiana exclaimed in surprise. "Poor child. I haven't seen her in years, but I think you've made an excellent choice."

"She wasn't my choice."

"I wish you would try to be more enthusiastic," Georgiana reproved her son gently. "She used to admire you so much. She would sit for hours talking about how well you rode, how handsome you looked, and how you never seemed to be afraid of anything. I think we females must be exceedingly timid creatures," she observed with a merry twinkle in her eyes. "Why should we otherwise admire a man who dashes about attacking all comers, when we know he's behaving quite foolishly?"

"What an unflattering picture, Mama."

"Men are the dearest creatures, but not even the silliest female would do half the things they do and think them something to be proud of."

"If that's how you feel, why do all women wish to be married?"

"I suppose it goes back to being timid. We need a man to protect us. In return, we work dreadfully hard to make something useful of him."

"How come you've never told me this before?"

"It's a trade secret," Georgiana whispered with a smile. "Now we've talked enough nonsense. Tell me, when are you to be married? I have so longed for the day when I could hold my first grandchild in my arms. You are going to live in Scotland, aren't you?"

"Of course."

"I know you're much fonder of London than I am, but I had hoped your children would grow up where you did."

"I hope Miss Raymond likes Scotland."

"I'm sure she will. She used to tell me how much she preferred the country to London. Poor girl, she hardly ever had a proper home. Her mother died soon after she was born, and then her father was carried off by some dreadful disease he contracted in India. I was distressed when your father discontinued her visits to Estameer, but this tiresome malady made it impossible for me to get out of bed."

"So father kept her locked away in some convent . . ."

"Miss Rachel's Seminary for Young Women."

". . . until it was time for me to gobble up her money, just like he did yours." Ordinarily the pained expression on his mother's face would have stopped Gavin, but he was still too full of the sense of his wrongs. "Rose and Olivia complain that I don't take an interest in the estates, but I'd rather be called a womanizer and a wastrel than to be forced into constant association with *him!*"

"You've never understood your father—"

"I understand him all too well."

"No, you don't," the Countess reaffirmed, showing a temper of her own. "Oliver did take my money, and there have been times when he has not treated any of us with compassion, but he suffers under the cruel necessity of having to be thankful for my fortune. No one can go on being grateful for years on end without choking on it sooner or later. I hope you and Sara manage better than we did. You never did get to know her, and you don't remember her kindly, but *try* to give her a chance to learn to love you. She has led a sheltered life, and is untutored in the ways of the world. Take care you don't frighten her so from the very first that she will have any difficulty coming to you willingly in the end."

"I don't want a terrified virgin who has to be coaxed into my bed," Gavin said, too angry to watch his words.

"Neither, I should hope, do you want some shameless tart for whom you have no use outside of it," retorted his mother. "Being gently born does not mean a woman is incapable of learning to please her husband," Georgiana pointed out more kindly. "It merely means she hasn't had the experience allowed men. I never wished for a lover, but I do think it unfair that men should be admired because they know so much about the world, while a woman with the same knowledge is shunned."

"What do you think we ought to do?" asked her unrepentant son with twinkling black eyes. "Set up schools of worldly knowledge?"

"I was thinking more of sending every boy to a monastery until he marries," answered his mother, returning his gleam of mischief. "Then both would start on an equal footing."

"Then nobody would know how to begin," Gavin responded. "You wouldn't have a dozen babies a year in all of England."

Shamelessly listening with her ear to the door, Rose was relieved to hear mother and son laughing naturally, but when she entered the room, the Countess was looking quite exhausted.

"I'm pleased ye had a nice visit with Master Gavin, milady, but it's time for yer rest."

Gavin stood immediately. "You have a good nap," he said, planting a kiss on his mother's soft, withered skin, "and be sure to tell me everything the doctor says."

"What do they ever say to purpose?" asked his mother with a weary sigh. "They poke and prod, ask questions and consult, then say they must go to make their decision. But they only come back with someone new, who must prod and ask more questions before *he* goes away to ponder a decision no one ever makes. I don't know why I bother."

"Because it pleases them that love ye," said Rose. "Now go away, yer lordship, or yer mother willna be strong enough tae see ye for a fortnight."

"Remember, have patience and be kind," Gavin's mother reminded him. "What you're trying to build has to last longer than one night."

"How ye do talk, milady! I blush to hear it," scolded Rose.

"You're an old maid. You blush at anything."

"Nevertheless, I know a thing or two," insisted Rose.

"Then maybe you can teach both of them to my future wife," Gavin said.

"Get along with ye," Rose admonished him severely. "I never did understand what a respectable woman wanted with a man. It seems tae me, they must always be hankering after what will give them a worse bellyache than green apples. Ye can get over green apples, but ye can no' get over a worthless man."

"How about a worthless woman?" countered Gavin.

"There's no such thing," replied Rose with her first full-mouthed smile. "Now be gone with ye before I have Miss Olivia chase ye off. 'Tis on a merry chase that boy shall be leading his wife," she prophesied after Gavin had gone.

"She adores him and thinks he can do no wrong," said the Countess.

"Then he'd better take her off to Scotland before she learns any better," announced Olivia, returning with the ever-present quilt.

Georgiana lay back, while the two women busied themselves settling her in for her nap.

"I want ye tae have a bonnie rest," Rose said. "Ye be looking a bit peeked tae me."

"I'm too excited to sleep," the Countess answered. "I've prayed for years he would find some nice girl who would love him in spite of his bitterness, but Sara is so innocent, she can have no idea of the things that sometimes drive him to act with great unkindness."

"Then let's hope she never finds out," observed Olivia, settling in with her needle and thread. "Now you go to sleep. I'm going to work here while I still have the sunlight. It's not half so good in my room." Rose took out some tatting that was to be her wedding gift.

For a while the Countess talked of Gavin's childhood, of her life in Scotland before she became too ill to leave her room, and of how much she looked forward to seeing Sara settled at Estameer and the mother of half a dozen strong sons. But she soon grew tired; her eyes closed and she fell into a light sleep. Rose and Olivia rose noiselessly.

"She'll never go back to Scotland, much less see any grandchild," Olivia said to Rose, after the bedroom door was closed behind them.

"She knows that," Rose said sadly. "The day we left Estameer, she said she wouldna see its walls again."

Chapter 5

"Stand still," Miss Adelaide commanded in her sternest voice. "How can anyone set your dress to rights with you bouncing about like a hoyden?"

Sara's limbs froze, but too much had happened to her in the last week for her to stand still very long. She could hardly believe she was really about to be married, yet here she was surrounded by seamstresses making last-minute adjustments to her wedding dress. Outside, the Earl's town coach waited to carry her to St. George's Church. A second coach—piled high with the boxes that had filled the parlor until an hour ago and which contained dresses, gowns, hats, shoes, and every other possible item of clothing a new bride could want—had already preceded her to Parkhaven House.

"The Earl will meet you at the chapel," Miss Adelaide was saying. "It's only natural that he should give you away, since none of your family has taken an interest in you all these years." Sara suspected that Miss Adelaide defined *interest* as willingness to defray her school fees. "It should be quite touching to see him hand you over to his own son," said the schoolmistress, revealing a streak of romanticism Sara had never suspected. "I wish I might see it."

"Aren't you coming?" Sara asked, surprise making her stand still at last.

"The Earl decided a private ceremony would be best," replied Miss Adelaide, recovering her austere demeanor. Sara was not really fond of Miss Adelaide, but she was genuinely disappointed that no one was going to be present to support her.

"You must come," she insisted. "You're as much my family as anyone else."

"I think it's best that I remain here," Miss Adelaide replied rather stiffly, in a vain effort to keep from showing how much Sara's invitation gratified her.

"Please," Sara begged. "I know the Earl wouldn't mind."

"But I'm not dressed," protested Miss Adelaide, thrown out of her habitual cool control by the obvious genuineness of Sara's invitation. But Sara noticed the older woman was wearing a gown of rich cobalt blue silk, a dress she normally reserved for special occasions.

"It won't matter. There'll be no one there to see you. Please, won't you come? I don't have anyone else."

Miss Adelaide's heart had remained steadfast against the importuning of young girls for more than thirty years, but it was not proof against the entreaty in Sara's light blue eyes. "All right, but you must explain to the Earl that I'm only coming at your insistence."

So the three of them climbed into the waiting coach, and Miss Adelaide passed the time in giving Sara good advice. Sara tried to listen, but found her concentration straying from Miss Adelaide's instructive homily to wondering what her future husband would look like. Betty's thoughts were also elsewhere, and from the nervous movement of her hands as she held the wedding veil, Sara could tell they were far from tranquil.

"And until you feel more comfortable, I would suggest that you depend heavily on the Earl's housekeeper. I don't know much about households of the nobility, my family being of merchant stock, but I imagine everyone will expect the Countess's arrangements to be maintained."

"Are you certain we are going to live with the Earl?" Sara had been dismayed to learn that her clothes were being sent to the Earl's town house.

"That was my impression, though naturally the Earl has not favored me with his confidence on that point. However, I expect that as long as the Countess is so very ill, Lord Carlisle shall wish to remain close by."

"I hadn't thought of that," Sara replied, but somehow her daydream lost a little bit of its luster.

"And, of course, you will take your lead from your husband in all social matters. I would not ordinarily presume to mention this to you," added Miss Adelaide, "except that you have no mother, and the Countess is far too ill to take your education in hand. There will be a great deal to be learned in the next several months, and it is extremely important that you learn it quickly. I may not belong to the aristocracy, but I've seen enough of them to know they rarely forgive mistakes. With you, an outsider, capturing the biggest matrimonial prize of the last ten years, there will be many only too happy to see you fail."

Sara's eyes hardened with determination. She vowed she would never embarrass Gavin or give him reason to be ashamed of her. Her eyes searched eagerly for him when they arrived at the church, but it was the Earl who met her.

"You will see Gavin at the altar. It's considered bad luck for the groom to see the bride on her wedding day." His bleak smile did little to bolster her confidence. Betty followed Sara out of the carriage, doggedly clutching the veil to her bosom. "I'm glad you came," the Earl said, turning to Miss Adelaide.

"Sara insisted," the lady explained.

"And well she should. Your unflagging attention to her well-being is something that cannot be repaid." The Earl's words were so devoid of warmth or feeling and his eyes so expressionless, that Sara wondered if he might not have opposed his son's marriage. Her uneasiness grew when the Earl showed Miss Rachel into the chapel, directed Betty to wait in an anteroom, and guided Sara into the priest's cubicle.

"I must apologize for not visiting you during the last few days, but the Countess had been quite ill."

"Will she be able to attend the wedding?" Sara asked anxiously.

"She cannot leave her bed," the Earl replied. "We still have hopes that the doctors will find a cure, but she suffers from constant pain."

"I remember her kindness whenever I visited Estameer. I hope I will be able to see her."

"She has commanded me to bring you to her straight way from the church, so she may give you her blessing. Now let me say a few words before we go to the chapel. When your father spoke to me of becoming your guardian, it was in the hopes that someday you would wed Gavin. As each of us had only one child, it was a natural aspiration. Your father did not foresee his tragic early death, and I did not foresee that my wife's illness would make it impossible for you to visit Estameer during these last years." Sara tried to interrupt, to protest that she had never expected to be taken into the Earl's home, but he continued without pause.

"I had expected that you and Gavin would grow to know each other in a natural way. As you are a gently bred young woman with no experience of the world, you may be shocked by some of his behavior. It will be your duty as his wife to pass no judgement. He will not expose you to his dissipation."

Sara's ignorance provided few clues as to the kind of dissipation the Earl might mean, and she could only stare tongue-tied as he continued.

"You must always bend your will to his. He is your husband and the only reason for your elevation. You must know you have been blessed beyond your just expectations. Few daughters, even of the nobility, are privileged to marry a peer." Sara stiffened. She didn't want to, but she couldn't help it. After all the years of being looked down on by the daughters of impoverished nobility, was her father's own partner going to do the same thing to her? She wasn't sure she could stand much more of it.

"You are young and inexperienced and will fall into many needless errors, if you go your own way without proper guidance. You must allow your husband to guide you in all things, but strive not to become a trial upon his good nature. Obey him in everything, great and small, and you may someday be a worthy addition to the Carlisle family."

Sara tried to listen humbly to the Earl's words, but his every utterance set her teeth on edge. She intended to work hard to become worthy of her position and to pay heed to Gavin's slightest wish, but to be *told* that she was fortunate to be marrying a peer made her angry. Her father might not have had a title and he might have made his money in trade, but her birth was just as good as any Carlisle, and she was a considerable heiress as well. Gavin ought to be grateful that *she* was marrying *him!* After all, she had led an exemplary life, was quite well educated, had perfect manners, and was a notable player on the harpsichord. She could also sing and draw quite well, and she did not regularly indulge in dissipation, whatever that might be. It was quite possible *he* should come to *her* for guidance.

"My wife has commanded me to tell you that she is

delighted you are to become a member of our family. She has long known of your partiality for Gavin. For my part, I have guarded you in the hope that Gavin might find with you the kind of happiness your father found with your mother. You greatly resemble her."

"But I'm not as beautiful," said Sara, unsure of how to respond to the Earl's kindness. "I have all the same parts, but they don't go together in the same way. And I have freckles." A ghost of a smile flitted across the Earl's face. This whole business of Gavin's marriage had tried his patience severely, but he was too much a connoisseur of women not to have some appreciation of Sara's beauty, her obvious intelligence, and this slender bit of female vanity.

"Will it make you feel better if I tell you Gavin has a mole on his cheek?"

Sara smiled. "Yes, it does. I remember him as being perfect."

"That was some years ago. Much has changed since then." A wintry coldness returned to the Earl's voice. "Now it is time I call your maid to put on your veil. If we don't appear soon, Miss Rachel may think I have abducted you."

"Nobody would ever think that," Sara said, brightening considerably. "I'm not pretty enough."

"I don't know who has been filling your head with such nonsense, but you are pretty enough to cause men to do foolish things."

"Will Gavin think me pretty?"

"If he doesn't, he's a bigger fool than I thought," said his father roughly. "Now let me summon your maid. Is that extraordinarily tall person *really* your servant?"

"Yes," Sara laughed nervously.

"I would have thought such a female would have been more likely to give you palpitations than inspire confidence."

Sara got butterflies in the pit of her stomach when Betty opened the door and the Earl led her out of the room. She closed her eyes, unable to stand the suspense, then opened them again, when the heavy doors to the chapel were thrown open. She heard the organ playing softly.

They entered a rather large and dark chapel, one of several built around St. James's Church. The thick stone walls were pierced by seven ornate stained glass windows, which would probably have admitted insufficent light even on a bright day, but the sun was not shining on this late November morning, and Sara felt as if she were entering a dark, gloomy tunnel. Seeing Miss Rachel seated primly in the disconcerting emptiness of the chapel helped to calm her nerves, and she was able to lift her gaze as she began her journey down the short aisle.

Two men waited at the altar. Ignoring the priest that was to marry them, Sara's eyes strained to see the man who would soon be her husband.

Ramrod straight and scowling heavily, Gavin towered over the priest. Yet in spite of the frown and the gathering gloom, Sara easily recognized him as an adult version of the boy she had last seen seven years before. His features had lost some of their youthful beauty, but they had matured in definition and gained in sheer masculine strength. His tight-fitting coat and breeches did nothing to conceal his powerful shoulders and muscled thighs, and Sara felt her knees grow weak with excitement.

Sara was not aware of walking down the aisle, only that she was drawing nearer to Gavin. How was it possible that this magnificent man was about to become her husband? He was even more handsome than she remembered! She ignored the brooding eyes and heavy scowl and saw only the heroic proportions of his body, his staggering good looks, and the powerful physical atttraction that communicated itself to her immediately. She didn't know why just looking at him should set her pulses racing, but her body seemed to understand all too well.

At last they reached the altar, and the priest began to speak. "Dearly beloved, we are gathered here today to join this man and this woman in holy matrimony."

The priest's voice droned on, but Sara didn't hear his words. The moment she had thought about continually for the last week was here, and she was incapable of doing anything more than holding on to the Earl's arm for fear she would swoon. For one dreadful moment the contents of the room did begin to swim before her eyes, but she resolutely forced herself to be calm. She had made a solemn vow that she would never do anything to embarrass Gavin or cause him shame. To faint at her own wedding would undoubtedly do both.

She focused her eyes on the small cross that hung from a black ribbon around the priest's neck, and concentrated intently. Slowly her vision cleared, and the objects before her eyes became stationary once more. The priest's voice came to her out of the mists as he turned to Gavin.

"Wilt thou have this woman to be thy lawfully wedded wife? Wilt thou love her, comfort her, honor, and keep her in sickness and in health, and, forsaking all others, keep thee only unto her, so long as ye both shall live?"

Sara had a sudden foreboding that if Gavin could have answered that question as he desired, he would have done so with a resounding negative. She didn't know why that presentiment should have come over her, yet it was unmistakable. A chill ran through her that had nothing to do with cold.

"I will." The voice was like a slashing sword edge, and involuntarily Sara drew closer to the Earl. There was no warmth in Gavin's voice, no invitation, no yielding, no desire, only the naked words themselves, forbidding and unwelcoming. It sounded more like the passing of a sentence. Fearfully, Sara raised her eyes to Gavin's face, and was startled by what she saw there. The look in his eyes was not reluctance or resistance; it was pure rage. He looked as though he would have preferred to leave her standing at the altar; he looked like he could have murdered her just as readily.

The twin sensations of alarm and anger flung their mantles over Sara. How could she be marrying a man who hated her, who at the very least hated having to marry her? This was not the wedding she had dreamed of. This was not what she had been led to expect by Miss Adelaide or the Earl. Why hadn't they told her? Why had they concealed his rage? But there was no time to think. The priest had turned toward her.

"Wilt thou have this man to be thy wedded husband, to live together after God's ordinance in the holy estate of matrimony? Wilt thou love him, comfort him, honor, and keep him in sickness as in health; and, forsaking all others, keep thee only unto him, so long as ye both shall live?"

Sara's tongue cleaved to the roof of her mouth. Why hadn't she had time to talk with Gavin, to find out how he felt? Why had he agreed to marry her, if he still disliked her so? The course of her whole life was to be decided in the next minute, and she didn't have time to ask a single question. How could she agree to marry Gavin after the look she had just seen in his eyes? But at this point, how could she do anything else? She had paused so long, the priest looked questioningly at her. Even Gavin turned those cold, anger-filled eyes on her. Her fear of what might happen in the future withered in the face of her terror of what would happen *now* if she didn't answer the question at once. She dared not even contemplate the consequences if she were to say no.

"I will," she managed to say in a barely audible whisper. The words were dragged unwillingly from her lips, and she guiltily averted her gaze.

"Who giveth this woman to be married to this man?"

"I do," responded the Earl in a cool, even voice. Then he placed Sara's hand in that of the priest and stepped back, leaving her alone beside Gavin. She was petrified. The Earl had been her only support, and now he was gone. Then the priest took her hand and placed it in Gavin's hand, and the electricity of his touch made her forget her fears.

Sara had never touched anything so dramatically alive. It was like holding on to something dangerously potent and quivering with barely contained power. The energy traveling from his hand made her fear she would be consumed. This was not the boy she remembered. That boy was gay and cheerful and reckless; there had been nothing threatening about him. He had frequently been angry with her, but she had never been frightened. She had been drawn to him because of his boundless energy, his questing spirit, and his ability to exact the greatest amount of pleasure from each day. How could he have turned into the man beside her?

A tremor ran through Sara. How could she marry someone whose mere touch frightened her? Did she still want to become his wife? Gavin was speaking to her, saying words that should have been sweet to her ears, but how could he mean any of them and look at her like that?

"I Gavin take thee Sara to my wedded wife, to have and to hold from this day forward, for better or worse, for richer or poorer, in sickness and in health, to love and to cherish, till death us do part."

Sara's eyes swam with tears. How many times had she dreamed of hearing these words spoken to her in loving accents? How many times had she imagined Gavin coming to her with his handsome face wreathed in smiles, welcoming her into his arms, eager for her to become his wife? How often had she told herself it would never happen, that she had to accustom herself to his marrying someone else? Yet somehow the impossible had happened. Gavin stood next to her saying the longed-for words without pause or stumble, and each pledge was like a fatal knife thrust in the very heart of her dream. She wanted to run away, to hide from everybody and everything, but there was nowhere to go. She *had* to stay here; she *had* to become his wife.

Sara mumbled her vows in a halting whisper, praying all the while that the service would end soon, but the priest's voice droned on and on.

"Bless, O Lord, this ring, that he who gives it and she who wears it may abide in Thy peace, and continue in Thy favor, until their life's end."

The golden band encircling her finger burned her skin so, Sara tried to withdraw her hand from Gavin's grasp. Every nerve in her body became numb until her entire concentration was welded to that gold band, that shining symbol of her bondage. There could be no drawing back now; she was forever bound to this rage-filled man. Banished were her dreams of happiness, of a lover who would long to take her into his arms, who would seek ways to please her, of a man whom she could trust with her person, her worldly possessions, and her love. All that was left was the grim reality of this scowling Adonis who terrified her.

"For as much as Sara and Gavin have consented together in holy wedlock, and thereto have given and pledged their troth, each to the other, and have declared the same by giving and receiving a ring, I pronounce that they are man and wife. Those whom God hath joined together, let no man put asunder. You may kiss the bride."

Sara's heart almost stopped beating. If his touch had

nearly been her undoing, how could she survive his kiss? She comforted herself with the certainty that he would do no more than brush her lips with his own, but she swayed ever so slightly when Gavin released her hand. She doubted she could stand unassisted, yet she remained immobile when he lifted the heavy veil. Then those searing, terrifying eyes encountered hers, and she felt like running from the church heedless of the consequences. They were hard, fierce, and challenging eyes, that defied her to love him, denied her right to anything that was his. They were angry and unforgiving, and there was no trace of warmth or tenderness in their black depths. It was like a sword thrust to her heart, and all remaining hope for her future collapsed.

Sara sensed rather than felt Gavin take her into his arms, in a way that didn't in the least resemble the chaste embrace expected in the hallowed precincts of St. James. Abruptly his lips descended on hers; they were hard, brutal, angry lips, and they hurt Sara's mouth, but the impact of the kiss was so shattering she didn't feel the pain. For one brief moment those forbidding eyes relented and something of a question entered them, but it was quickly routed by a suppressed fury; powerful arms encircled her and pressed her against his rigid body. Fear, wonder, and an odd assortment of emotions jostled each other in Sara's mind, but she was beyond being able to sort them out. She was just trying to survive until the next moment.

Then, as suddenly as it began, it was over. Gavin released her and turned away, as though she had never been there. After the savage kiss, this brutal rejection was too much for Sara, and she fainted.

Chapter 6

Gavin stared at the limp figure collapsed into the corner of the coach. She looked so young and helpless—she was nothing but an innocent pawn in his father's schemes—that some of the fury went out of his black eyes. At least his mother's future was secure, he told himself guiltily. Gavin had signed over control of Sara's fortune to his father. "I want no part of your blood money," he had stated furiously, but he knew even then his rage was half-directed toward himself.

As long as he could remember, Gavin had bridled at his father's treatment of his mother, but it was not until he entered Oxford that he realized the full extent of his father's ruthlessness. In a revulsion of feeling, he had turned away from everything his father stood for, in fear that he might have it in him to become the same kind of cruel, unfeeling man. He had even gone to the extent of choosing his mistresses in direct variance to his father's tastes. Yet he had just married a girl he didn't love—one he knew almost nothing about, a perfect stranger actually—and all for the sake of the fortune she brought with her. Nothing could have more effectively branded him his father's son, for that was exactly what the Earl had done nearly thirty years earlier, and Gavin cursed himself roundly.

He looked out the window, trying not to think of the girl across from him, or of the vows he had taken to love and cherish her. His mind rebelled at the very thought, and he cursed himself and his father once again. Why should he be forever bound to some girl with no knowledge of the world and no more gumption than to faint at her own wedding? What did she know about the life he enjoyed? How would she behave when faced with the cold, unforgiving curiosity of society? His friends would laugh at him, and Clarice would taunt and plague him, and with good reason, too. What could this thin, cringing girl offer him to compare with Clarice's ripe charms?

Still, he could not forget the feel of her lips when he kissed her. They had been very tantalizing, and that had been a surprise. He didn't know why he had handled her so roughly. He hadn't intended to kiss her at all, at most he meant to plant a chaste salute on her cheek, but instead he had kissed her with fierce intensity. He had done it more out of anger at being forced to marry, rage that he had been forced to do something he disliked because of his mother, rather than anger at having her for his wife. He also felt trapped; it was a new feeling for Gavin, and he didn't like it. He intended to make it plain to this frightened fledgling that though she shared his name and position she would never have any claim on him.

Still, as he looked at her slumped in the corner, miserably uncomfortable as the carriage bounced along, he couldn't help but feel more sympathy for her plight. What of *her* hopes and *her* feelings? Had she wanted to marry him, or had she been forced to wed him to escape her own confinement? If she was any happier to be espoused to him than he was to her, she didn't show it in the chapel. She looked like all she wanted to do was run away. He had been too angry these last few days to even think of her, much less think to ask his father about her wishes. Now it was too late for both of them.

Gavin found it difficult to believe that any girl, particularly one without parents and family, wouldn't welcome the chance to marry the son of a peer. In a single stroke, it provided her with money, a title, and social position, everything she needed to be a success in the eyes of the world. Yet the young girl Gavin remembered from those few visits to Estameer would unquestionably have preferred a husband who loved her rather than her money. As she had lived out of society most of her life, perhaps it was possible she didn't know the value they placed on money and a title.

But he was being ridiculous. No one, however sequestered or whimsically educated, could be without some understanding of the value of wealth and position. Her classmates would have taught her that lesson if no one else had.

Still, his memories of those few meetings were of a straightforward girl who could meet a man without coquettish flirting or youthful embarrassment. She had even had the courage to laugh at him and tell him that he had no business doing what he'd been forbidden to do if he didn't want it to come to his parents' ears. It had made him furious at the time, but now it made him wonder.

But speculation was useless now. Regardless of her feelings or of her situation, it didn't alter *his* feelings toward marriage. His anger had cooled and his resentment softened when he saw how helpless and vulnerable she was, but he refused to be imposed upon by a wife he neither wanted or cared for. He would be courteous—he had initially intended to be so cruel she would be only too glad to be spared his company—but he would make it plain he intended to be her husband in name only. He still had Clarice, and when his interest in her faded, there would be another to take her place. He had no intention of allowing himself to fall in love. He had seen what it did to his mother, and he had sworn a bitter vow it would never happen to him.

Sara opened her eyes. For a brief moment she was only aware of the uneven movement of the carriage as it lurched over the cobblestones, but then her eyes fell on Gavin seated across from her, and she sat up quickly, stiff with fright.

"How . . . When . . . ?" she began, desperately looking about for some support. But there was no one else in the carriage; she was alone with her husband.

"I carried you," he said, but there was a different quality in his voice now, one that lessened her fear.

"I fainted?"

"Quite completely."

"You must have been embarrassed. I'm sorry."

"Don't be. It was almost funny. For a moment I thought the priest was going to follow your example, but the fuss kicked up by that schoolmistress quite restored him. How did you manage to live under her control for eleven years without wanting to murder her?"

"She's really quite kind," Sara said, conveniently forgetting the many times she had quaked in fear or quivered with rage after one of Miss Adelaide's rebukes.

"I'm glad she wasn't head at my school. By the way, do you really intend to introduce that spindly female into my father's household? I should have thought you'd need stilts to talk with her." Sara managed a weak smile.

"Betty is the only friend I have. I won't feel quite so alone with her around." Gavin's feelings softened even more. "Besides, I don't know anything about being a countess, or any other kind of great lady, and if I asked you all the things I wanted to know, you would soon be out of patience with me."

Gavin was surprised to find himself smiling. "There will be lots of people to help you. My mother is too ill, but there's the housekeeper, her nurse, or Olivia Tate. She's mother's companion. She's a terrible busybody. She'll give you her opinion whether you want it or not."

"But I do," Sara insisted quite genuinely. "I know I should make the most awful mistakes by myself. I intend to study quite hard to see that I don't embarrass you, or the Earl, *or* the Countess," she added. "You've all been so kind to me."

Gavin wondered how grateful she would be if anyone had ever been *truly* kind to her, and he felt another pang of guilt.

"You won't have to worry about anything for a while. We won't go about much or hold entertainments while my mother is so ill. We always go to Scotland for the summer, but until then you will meet a very restricted circle." He smiled without warning. "You are not required to accompany me when I go out, and at times you are actually forbidden to do so. You will have more than enough time to become acquainted with the ways of *fashionable* London."

"It shouldn't be too hard with you to help me," she said more comfortably, having at last become almost at ease with Gavin. Maybe she had mistaken the look in his eyes in the church. He was certainly charming now.

But some of the warmth went out of Gavin's eyes at Sara's last words. "I doubt I will be home much," he said rather stiffly. "I have rooms on Jermyn Street. My father and I are unable to live under the same roof."

"How terrible for you," answered Sara, utterly at a loss to understand this latest disclosure. "My father and I were the very best of friends. I miss him quite dreadfully sometimes." She paused a moment then added, "Am I not to live with you?"

"That would not be advisable."

"Why not?" she asked, and Gavin cursed her inquisitiveness.

"Because the rooms are not set up to accommodate a female," he said, driven against the ropes.

"Couldn't you take new rooms or even hire a house?"

"That wouldn't make any sense, would it, not with Parkhaven House having fifty rooms and enough servants to handle a dozen new brides."

"But won't it cause talk if we live under separate roofs?"

She may have been closed up in a school half her life, Gavin thought, but she knows how to get to the center of an issue.

"I will only stay away when my father and I are on the worst of terms."

Sara attempted to digest this. It seemed a reasonable solution, particularly since the Countess's illness must be a great strain on both men's tempers, but she was still certain that something was not right.

"Do you still go to Scotland for Christmas?" she asked, changing to a less dangerous topic of conversation. "I've never forgotten my trips to Estameer." The rest of the ride was beguiled with small talk of visits Gavin barely remembered, and they arrived at Parkhaven House with Sara feeling much more relaxed with her new husband, and Gavin feeling less determined to ignore her existence.

The interview with the Countess nearly reduced Sara to tears; it was obvious, even to her inexperienced eyes, that the kind-hearted woman had only a short time to live. She required the support of both Rose and Olivia to sit up, but her indomitable spirit could not be contained.

"Come here child and give me a kiss," Georgiana said, beckoning Sara to her bedside. The frail hand grasped Sara's, and she could sense the weakness of the body. The Countess's sunken cheeks were incredibly soft, and she smelled faintly of jasmine.

"It's been such a long time," Georgiana said, letting her hand drop. "Stand back and let me look at you. Hold the light where I can see her, Rose." The old nurse held the lamp next to Sara's face, and Sara read the truth in the eyes around her. Only Gavin seemed unaware of the severity of his mother's condition.

"You look so much like Meribel, but you've got your father's smile. He was always such a cheerful man, even after your mother's death."

"It won't hurt my feelings if you say I can't hold a candle to Mama," Sara said. "I have all of Papa's likenesses of her, and I know I'm not nearly as pretty as she was."

"Maybe not in the classical sense, but you've got a smile that will mean more to you than the most perfect features. Remember that whenever things are going badly, and you'll be surprised what a difference it will make." The Countess beckoned Sara to come closer and lean her ear next to the invalid's mouth. "Especially with the men," she added with a faint smile. "Always smile at the men, and you'll get your way in just about everything."

The Countess paused for a moment, seeming to wait for her strength to return. Rose hovered anxiously at her side, but the Countess motioned for her to step back. "I want to talk with my daughter-in-law in private."

"I can't tell you how happy I am to see you married to Gavin," she continued after a moment. "I knew from that first day, when all you could see was a brave young man instead of a foolish little boy, that you would make him a perfect wife. Men don't like to be criticized, no matter how imprudently they behave, and Gavin's no different from other men in that respect. Love him, and try not to let the hurtful things that will happen destroy your contentment. You'll be much happier for it in the end." Sara hardly knew how to respond to the Countess's advice. She didn't have any idea what it was she was supposed to ignore, but the Countess saved her the trouble of making a reply.

"Now let me speak to my son," she said.

"If you don't talk secrets with me, I'm going to be jealous," Gavin said, as he took his mother's hand and knelt at her side. It was easy to see how deeply he loved his mother, and that caused Sara to love him all the more.

"Don't be absurd. I may love your bride, but you'll always have first place in my heart. However, a beautiful little grandchild might be a threat to your position." The Countess's eyes were too tired to see Gavin's eyes grow cold, but Sara did, and it frightened her a little.

"Then I'm safe for a while at least."

"You always will be," his mother smiled fondly, "but now you've got someone else to care for, and it's time you changed your ways. I don't mean for you to give up all your pleasures, but from now on you'll have to be thinking of two people instead of one." Georgiana lay back, breathing with difficulty. Rose glanced significantly at the Earl and he nodded.

"Maybe you will allow me to offer them the good advice they are bound to ignore," the Earl said to his wife. "Now I'm going to take them away so you can get some rest and Sara can get unpacked."

"Come again after dinner," said Georgiana without raising her head. "There's so much I want to talk to you about."

"Only if ye have a good nap," said Rose. "We all know ye get overtired when ye talk too much."

Georgiana nodded her head slightly and closed her eyes. "It seems all I ever do is rest, and still I'm so tired."

Rose jerked her head imperatively toward the door and the young people left the room.

"He'll be all right now," Georgiana said, addressing her husband without opening her eyes. "She'll see that he comes to no harm."

"Of course he'll be all right," her husband agreed reassuringly, but he remembered the anger in Gavin's eyes and wondered.

Sara sat before her mirror while Betty combed her hair. She could hardly believe this huge room was hers alone. She had spent years in a tiny cubicle that wasn't as large as the dressing room of this enormous apartment. The bed was even long enough for Betty. All of Sara's new clothes had virtually disappeared among the endless shelves of the vast closet. She could not imagine having enough clothes to occupy all the storage space, and if she had, she didn't know how she would possibly find time to wear them.

She had walked about in a daze, peering into corners and trying out chairs, while Betty had unpacked and put away her clothes. "It must be wonderful to be a countess, if you can have a room like this," she said to Betty, as she sank onto the bed, luxuriating in the deep, soft mattresses.

"It depends upon your lord," Betty pointed out. "It won't do you a particle bit of good to have a string of titles, if you don't have money and connections." Sara sat up with a puzzled frown.

"Do you mean if I had been poor, nobody would have

wanted to marry me?"

"Not with you as near to an orphan as makes no difference. What would they get by it?"

"But my husband would love me?"

"The upper class doesn't look for love where they marry."

"But I love Gavin."

"You're lucky. Most people marry where it will do them the most good, and look for love later."

"Is that why the girls at school never bothered with me?"

"That, and because your father made his money in trade."

"But Gavin married me, and he's important."

"His father and yours were in business together. You might say you're both tarred with the same brush."

"How do you know all this?"

"Miss Rachel told me. She said someone ought to know."

Sara chewed on her finger for a while, deep in thought. "Then people won't accept me."

"I don't know. I suppose if your husband is accepted, you will be, too. But you can never tell about women. Just imagine those snobbish young misses at Miss Rachel's all grown up, and you can see what you'll be up against."

Sara was thoughtful. "Then, if I do something they don't like, they might never accept me."

"Probably," said Betty noncommittally.

Sara did not mention the subject again, but it never left her mind during the rest of the afternoon.

Dinner was a strain. The Earl seemed to feel it was his responsibility to carry the weight of the conversation, but his cold, formal style of speaking inhibited Sara, and she barely said a word the whole time. Gavin's foul mood made the tension even worse. Being in his father's company had revived all the anger and rigidity in his temper, and by the time they rose from the table, Sara was almost afraid to address any remark to him.

She was relieved when she was allowed to remove to the drawing room. She noticed the harpsichord immediately, but as she expected the men to join her shortly, she busied herself with some needlework. After half an hour, boredom caused her to throw it aside and approach the harpsichord. It was a magnificent instrument, much more beautiful than the harpsichord at Miss Rachel's Seminary. Lovingly she stroked the polished wood, before gingerly lifting the cover to the keyboard. The gleaming ebony and ivory keys drew her fingers irresistibly, and she strummed a chord.

"Would ye like me tae open the instrument for ye?" Sara had not heard the footman enter, and she nearly jumped out of her skin.

"Yes, if you would, please. Does anyone play it?" she asked.

"Nay, excepting Miss Tate once in a great while. No one regular since the mistress has taken tae her bed." The man raised the top, and brought an embroidery-covered seat from where it stood against the wall. The inside of the top was most wondrously painted with a delightful hunting scene, at total variance with the heavy formality of the room.

"I dinna think there be any music for it," he said.

"I don't need any," Sara replied. She sat down at the instrument almost reverently, and then she began to play, slowly at first, and then with increasing confidence and speed, until her fingers were racing over the glossy keys in a blur. The majestic tones filled the huge salon, rushing to the far end of the room and back again. Sara had never played such a magnificent instrument, and she soon became lost in the glorious power of its two keyboards.

This was a world where she was in control, where she knew what would happen next. Gradually she forgot the terrors of the day and gave herself up to her music. For the moment at least, it was all that mattered.

Sara didn't know how long she had been playing when, during a pause, a voice from somewhere behind her drew her roughly out of her abstraction.

"I see you have been well instructed. If you perform as well in other endeavors, Gavin will indeed be a lucky man." Sara smiled nervously at the Earl.

"I couldn't resist," she explained, rising from the harpsichord. "It is such a lovely instrument."

"Play it as often as you like."

"But it belongs to the Countess."

"She is no longer able to use it herself. It might as well be yours."

"I could never accept anything so grand."

"Then it's a good thing I didn't offer it to you," observed the Earl dryly. He moved toward a chair, and waited until Sara had taken her seat before he took his.

"Will Gavin join us?" she asked nervously. The Earl's expression did not change, but Sara would have been ready to swear he flinched.

"Gavin has departed for what I fear can best be described as bachelor revels. It is a barbarous custom, but one which has lasted from my day."

"He will return?" She was barely able to form the words.

"Yes, no doubt in considerably worse condition than when he left, but strive to accustom yourself to it. He will regularly come to your bed the worse for drink." Sara struggled to keep her countenance. She had not had the courage, even in her own mind, to face the fact that this was her wedding night. The Earl rose.

"I regret that it is not possible for you to visit the Countess again this evening. She finds these interviews extremely fatiguing. I suggest you return to your chamber and prepare yourself to receive your husband."

Sara looked stricken.

"I shall have a footman escort you." Sara mumbled her thanks and sat numbed, like a lamb being led to the slaughter, until the servant came to take her to her room.

Chapter 7

Betty made Sara ready for bed, but the relaxed feeling that had always existed between them was absent tonight. This was an experience they could not share, and for the moment it stood between them like a high, stone wall. Sara felt tongue-tied, and she allowed Betty to undress her and brush out her hair in silence. Only when Betty had turned back the bed and was passing the warming pan between the sheets did Sara break the silence.

"Have you ever been with a man?" she asked, turning abruptly to Betty.

"Merciful heavens, Miss, I mean your ladyship," Betty corrected herself, "how can you ask a respectable girl a thing like that?" She was so startled by the question, she nearly turned the coals in the warming pan out onto the bed. "I'm a decent girl and always have been."

"That's what everybody says," muttered Sara. "The way the girls at Miss Adelaide's talked, you'd think being with a man was the most awful thing that could happen to a female. If it's so terrible before you're married, why is it all right afterwards?"

"It's all right as long as he's your husband."

"But suppose you married him later?"

"Didn't Miss Rachel tell you *anything?*" inquired Betty.

"Nobody did."

"I don't guess she knows," said Betty half to herself, "and you can bet those flighty young things don't know any more than fairy tales either. It's because of having babies."

"Having babies?" repeated Sara, completely lost.

"Being with a man causes you to have babies, and of course, that's a thing you wouldn't want to have happen without you were married."

"No," agreed Sara, struck. "But how does it happen?"

"I don't know," Betty said rather severely. "And don't you even think of asking the Countess such a question. It's not a fit thing for a lady to be talking about."

"But if it has to happen for me to have a baby . . ."

"I told you, it's not a fit thing for a lady to know, much less sit around discussing, like it was a new way to make preserves or pickle a ham. Men always know what to do, so you just leave it to his lordship," said the city-bred maid who was just as ignorant as her city-bred mistress.

"But will it hurt?" asked Sara, growing more fearful all the time.

"I can't rightly say, but nobody seems to like it much. Some scream and wail, and others lament over it for days afterwards. Most women just close their eyes and lie rigid until it's done. My old mistress used to say it was a trial all women had to endure, because somebody had to have the babies, and God, being a man himself, wouldn't think of putting it off on the husbands."

"If it's so terrible, why do men like it? The girls at Miss Adelaide's used to say that's why a man took a mistress."

"I can't say for certain, not being a man myself, but men are made different from females, and some of the things they get up to are downright shameful. They take to all kinds of unaccountable things like cockfighting, bearbaiting, and cutting each other up with those nasty swords. You can't go judging anything by what a man likes." She led Sara over to the bed and tucked her in.

"I heard some of the girls talking once," Sara said, sinking her voice into a low, timorous whisper, "when they thought no one was about. They said some women *like* it."

"There's females that will say anything for a new dress or a piece of jewelry," came Betty's scathing reply. "I'm happy to say that you'll have no call to know anything about *that* kind of abandoned hussy. Neither should you be listening to whispered secrets about them. Lordy, whatever will you be doing next?"

"But if some women don't find it so terrible—"

"Then they should!" said Betty without hesitation. "You're not to be judging yourself by low-born females. You're going to be a countess someday, and no countess I ever heard tell of went about talking about being with a man. As for *liking* it! Well, the idea is scandalous. Now, you just stay here all nice and warm, and put your mind to rest. It'll be over soon enough, and then you won't have to wonder about it anymore."

"But if it's so terrible . . ." Sara persisted.

Betty hunched an indifferent shoulder, as though the subject was beginning to bore her. "They all complain about it, but they're never any the worse for it the next morning. I don't suppose you'll be any different."

Sara had to be content with that. Betty finished tucking her in, banked the fire, blew out all the candles except the one by the bed, and left Sara to await her lord.

It was an awful wait. From the moment she had been told she was to marry Gavin, until Betty closed the door to her bedchamber, Sara had been too busy to do much more than try to understand and follow what was happening to her. Not once had she stopped long enough to wonder about her wedding night, but now it was here, and her husband could enter the room at any minute. She knew nothing of what was going to happen, and as the clock ticked inexorably on, she became more and more apprehensive. The difficulties ahead multiplied as the empty minutes piled up, until Sara was sure the ordeal itself could hardly be more awful than this waiting without knowing. Sara found herself picking at her skin, then chewing on her nails. If he doesn't come soon, she thought, I'll be nothing but sores and bleeding stubs.

But she did not have very long to wait.

The door was flung open without warning, and Gavin stood framed in the light. A double ripple of excitement made Sara sit straight up in the bed. The moment she'd been waiting for with fear and anticipation had arrived, but now that it was here, she wasn't at all sure she didn't want to postpone it a little longer. Yet the sight of Gavin's body—as he shed his coat and stood revealed in a sheer shirt and skintight pants—caused her own body to tingle in response. Even without understanding why, Sara felt drawn to that mighty, muscled physique. The long, clean lines of his legs and thighs made him seem graceful, the flowing shirt over hard-sinewed arms gave the impression of sinuousness, but his powerful chest and broad shoulders left her in no doubt as to the rugged strength of the man who was about to claim her. She was shaken by a quiver of pleasurable anticipation.

"The bride in her marriage bed," Gavin mocked as he advanced into the room.

Instinctively Sara drew the covers around her shoulders.

"What, no warm greeting for your new lord? I might get the idea you don't wish to lie with me."

"I am somewhat anxious about it," stammered Sara, holding on to the covers more tightly still, "but I am prepared to do my duty."

"Yeah, we must all do our duty," Gavin growled

fiercely, as he drew closer to the bed. He had drunk too much, in the hopes it would numb him to the innocence of his bride and the disgust he felt with himself for acting as his father's pawn. But now that he was face to face with the blameless victim of their struggle, he felt his resolution draining away. With a fiercely muttered oath, he steadied himself against the bedpost. The brandy hadn't been able to numb him to the shame he felt at the violation of his own principles either. He was preparing to deflower this innocent girl, a rite of passage she believed would truly make her his wife, but one he knew would only deprive her of something else irreplaceable, and he couldn't stop himself.

Hell, she married me for what she could get, he thought with a surge of rage. She can damned well take the consequences. "You just do your part," he muttered. "I'll do the rest."

"That's just it," admitted Sara sheepishly. "I'm not perfectly sure what my part is."

No man is ever too drunk not to be sobered by that statement, and Gavin directed his penetrating gaze to Sara's lovely, fearful face.

"Do you mean to tell me neither that Rachel woman, nor any of the dried-up prunes that infest the place, ever told you about laying with a man?"

"No."

"Goddamnit to hell!" moaned Gavin, swinging on the bedpost so that he dropped onto the bed. "The wench is not only a virgin, she's an *ignorant* virgin. She'll probably scream."

"Scream?" inquired Sara faintheartedly, her fear beginning to assume significant dimensions.

"They all do. Seems to be a law or something, that every gently bred female has to shout down the house."

"But you don't want me to scream!"

"Of course not. Puts a man out of the mood quicker

than a bucket of cold water. Besides, there's no call to be afraid. You'll soon learn to like it."

"Betty says no lady ever likes it."

"What would a bean pole like her know about men?" demanded Gavin. At that moment, his gaze focused on Sara for the first time, and he immediately became very still and quiet. He couldn't describe exactly how he had pictured her as he sat attempting to drink himself into a stupor, but the reality of her presence was a far different thing.

The skin which she stigmatized as freckled was rendered dead white by the deathly fear that filled her. Her long, slender throat, compressed lips, and apprehensive light blue eyes combined to present a picture of bemused innocence which her abundant strawberry blond hair, cascading over flawless shoulders in a riot of curls, did nothing to alter. Gavin suddenly realized that Sara looked damnably attractive, at least she would have if she could stop looking like she expected to be drawn and quartered. What could there be about this virginal girl that appealed so strongly to his jaded tastes?

Gavin quickly discarded his shirt. "Damn, it's hot in here. How can you stay under those covers? Come on out, so I can get a good look at you."

Sara didn't have to wonder what Gavin looked like. The light from the single candle fell directly on his disturbingly masculine body; he was within inches of her now and his aroused state was unmistakable. She wasn't entirely sure of what she was seeing, or why it should be in that uncharacteristic condition, but she had the distinct impression that it had something to do with what was about to happen to her. She did not let go of the covers, but when Gavin pulled them out of her hands, she sat perfectly still, rather than yield to her initial impulse to scramble to recover them. Her young, firm breasts rose and fell with her rapid breathing.

Betty had piled several comforters on the bed to insure that Sara would keep warm, but she had taken care to dress her mistress in a thin nightgown that did very little to hide the outlines of her body. In comparison to Clarice's opulent charms, Sara looked positively boyish. It was true that her breasts were firm and well raised, but they were demure little globes instead of huge pendulous gourds. And the scared, timorous look was definitely at variance with the coy invitation that characterized Clarice's approach to their times in bed. This was not what Gavin was accustomed to, and his ardor began to ebb.

But Gavin was honest enough to admit it was not just because she was different. He felt ashamed of himself. He had stormed out of the house and had taken his first drink because he was angry at his father, but he had kept drinking to postpone returning to this room, to blunt the sharp prick of his conscience. He had been able to force himself to marry Sara because he didn't know anything about her, but the few short hours they had spent together had already changed that. He could still make himself believe that she was marrying him because of his position in society, but he could not ignore the growing suspicion that he was about to destroy something much finer than anything he had ever known.

With a physical effort, he shrugged off his doubts. Pluck up, he told himself. There'll be plenty of time later to work something out, feed her on double rations maybe, but he had to go through with it tonight. Everybody expected it of him, even Sara.

"Don't be so standoffish," he said more kindly, reaching out his hand to her. "It's not so bad as you think." Sara couldn't move. The mere feel of his hand on her skin sent her mind into orbit, her inflamed senses interfering with rational thought. Her body was screaming messages at her brain, but it was speaking a new language, one her brain didn't know how to translate, so she continued to sit before him, immobile, mute, in a state bordering on shock as he trailed his fingers along her arm and up her shoulder. His touch was a match that ignited a trail of explosive powder that smoldered slowly, irresistibly, toward the powder keg that would soon cause the only existence she had ever known to explode into nothingness, and she was totally unable to do anything to prevent it.

She was unable to resist when he pulled her closer to him. His nearness, the intensity of his presence, the force of his attractiveness took her breath away. Why, when she had thought of him all those years, had she never realized what it would be like, *really* be like, to be with him? In her imagination, being with him had been a natural thing, something she did willingly, not waiting fearfully and apprehensively in the dark, wondering what would happen next. This was nothing like the wonder and magic she had dreamed of, nothing like the ecstasy she had looked forward to. She felt as though she were not a participant, merely an object to be used.

Sara was unable to resist when he reached over and roughly kissed her full on the lips, but she could not repress a tiny gasp of shock. The trepidation and fear was still there, but deep inside her a tiny kernel of pleasure began to unfold.

Gavin noted both her surprise and her lack of response, but the taste of her sweet lips reinvigorated his flagging ardor and he took her slender, trembling body into his arms. Sara thought she would disintegrate from the impact of her excitement. Her entire body was on alert, every nerve screaming that she was under attack, that something shockingly new was happening to her; she didn't know how to protect herself, or whether she even wanted to try.

Gavin kissed her again, hungrily this time, his lips

roughly crushing her mouth, and pressed her unresisting body against his chest. She was a skinny little thing, but curiously appealing nonetheless. There was a freshness about her, a feeling of newness that was unique in his experience, a sensation he found rather exciting. His tongue forced its way between her tightly compressed lips and plunged into her sweet mouth. At the same time his hands impatiently slipped the nightgown over her shoulders baring the breasts to his attack.

"I'm going to kiss your breasts now. There's no need to be afraid. I won't hurt you."

Sara had not resisted when Gavin's tongue ravaged her mouth even though she had wanted to. But now her body became rigid, and she gasped when his hot hands cupped her breasts; her breathing became shallow and rapid when his lips deserted her mouth for the rosy, mounding peak of her right breast. If her nervous system was in a panic before, it was having hysterics now. She hardly knew what she was feeling, but she was completely incapable of controlling her response. Everything was new, unsuspected, and affected her body so violently, her muscles rigidly refused to do anything she told them.

Her maidenly modesty, horrified by what was happening, encouraged her to resist, to brush away the hands and lips that were being so free with her body. These feelings were so insistent she was only marginally aware of the sensation of sensual pleasure that continued to flower, that was vainly trying to make its presence known; ignorance and fear were the twin drivers as her emotional carriage careened out of control.

Into *his* control, she realized. But was it so terrible a thing to surrender to him?

"Don't fight so hard," Gavin murmured without ceasing his attention to her breasts. "Relax, and you may find it as enjoyable as I do."

With a great effort, Sara forced herself to lie perfectly

still, not because Gavin told her she might enjoy it, but because she told herself it was her duty. She wasn't supposed to enjoy this night, and she wasn't. She wasn't supposed to know what was happening to her, and she didn't. But it frightened her. Gavin's actions were nothing like what she expected. His lips and tongue attacked her body like a starving man at his first meal and his hands were like those of a blind man determined to memorize every inch of her. To lie here half-naked was the final and almost unbearable indignity. She hoped it was almost over. She wasn't sure she could stand much more.

But there was much more. To her pleasure and horror, Gavin seemed to be tugging at her gown, trying to pull it further down her body. Caught between two powerful but totally opposite sets of feelings, she was helpless to resist at first. Fear was still urging her to violent resistance, but the other feeling was gathering strength, this new and unfamiliar sensation, this feeling of pleasure that sapped her energy and slew her will to resist. She lay immobile, unable to decide what to do, until she realized that he was *trying to take her clothes off!* Her whole being reacted in panic, and she clutched frantically at her gown. Gavin did not divert his attention from her breasts, and she was able to pull it back up just above her waist, but she had no time to enjoy her triumph.

"You really are quite lovely," he murmured, "much more than I expected." He spoke abstractly, as if he, too, were caught in this web of sensations.

His left hand was suddenly on her leg and moving with dispatch up her thigh. She was stunned. Betty had never hinted of this. Surely this could have no part of babies. But before Sara could attempt to think or reason, Gavin's hand reached the furry crescent between her legs, and her whole being exploded in rebellion.

"Don't!" The desperate protest burst from her lips as a plaintive, accusing wail.

"What in bloody hell?" Gavin exploded. He neither slackened his grip or arrested his actions, until he realized she was afraid of him.

"Don't touch me like that." Sara tried to roll away from Gavin's grasp, to draw her gown up over her violated body, but he continued to hold her captive.

"I'm going to do much more than touch you," he told her in a gentle, persuasive voice, as he paused to stroke her hair, "much, much more." Gavin's powerful grip, the tenderness in his voice, and her own feeling of helplessness held her prisoner, as he proceeded to explore her body with increasing intensity. "There may be pain at first when I take you. But never again, I swear."

Sara had no idea what he was talking about, but she made up her mind she didn't want to find out. "I want you to leave," she declared, desperation giving her courage.

"On our wedding night?" demanded Gavin, still too swayed by desire to realize that Sara was very badly frightened.

"I don't care what night it is. I just want you to go away and leave me alone."

"Easy," he whispered, doing his best to gentle her. "Your first time can be quite pleasant, I promise. If you like, I'll tell you everything before I do it."

"I don't want to know anything or do anything," Sara protested. "I just want this nightmare to end." Her protests became more shrill, but they had little effect on Gavin. His blood thundered in his veins, desire blotting out everything but his need for satisfaction. When Sara's gown became too tangled about her body for him to remove, he ripped it from seam to seam and cast it from him. Sara lay naked before him, trembling from head to toe. Her whole mind was filled with panic, but she was unable to move or protest any longer. Even when he paused to look at her unsullied perfection, she made no attempt to escape. She knew he would not be denied, and that it was her duty to submit. Dumbly she waited for the end to come.

Much to Gavin's surprise, he found he was highly excited by Sara's slim loveliness, and he shed his clothes quickly. If he had seen Sara's expression, he might have paused in his headlong rush to enjoy her. He might also have given some thought to what she must be experiencing on this, the most earth-shaking night in her life. But he only saw a flawless body whose appeal riveted every part of his attention.

Sara had never seen anyone naked, but she had already suffered so much from shock, she was unable to do more than unconsciously record the magnificent picture of manhood that Gavin presented to her gaze. All that pierced the haze of her panic was the image of his engorged manhood standing rigidly upright like an angry sentinel.

Gavin lay down beside her, impatient with having to lead her so slowly and carefully. Damn! This was one reason to stay away from virgins. He preferred a woman who welcomed the touch of his hands and lips on her body, one who could give him as much pleasure as he gave her. He felt almost as if he were manipulating Sara.

"I am going to take you now. Can you not try to share some of the pleasure with me?" In quick succession his hands and lips returned to caressing her body. Gently he braced his knee between her legs. "Open for me."

She tried to keep her knees together, but almost before she knew it, she felt his hot, insistent manhood pressing against her. When he entered her, she stopped breathing, her body opening to him in spite of herself.

"That's right, relax," Gavin coaxed. He cursed, but was not deterred when he encountered the resistance of her maidenhead. "It may hurt a little," he said, and before she could gather herself to resist, he thrust powerfully into her, driving deep. A knifing pain shot through Sara's body, and she cried out. Immediately she bit her lip; she would not scream no matter what happened.

The pain subsided quickly, and, to her amazement, Sara realized her body was responding instinctively to Gavin. It was a clumsy effort, to be sure, but with it came an awareness of pleasure and excitement that was building within her.

But her feeling of outrage caused her to deny those feelings, and the conflicting signals destroyed her pleasure. Suddenly, Gavin increased his movement, and then just as suddenly ceased altogether. He rolled over on his side, and the only sound in the room was the rasp of his heavy breathing. Sara lay still, utterly humiliated, without any desire to cover herself. What for? Surely it was over now. But her surprises were not yet at an end.

Gavin's desire was far from exhausted, and before she could summon the strength to fight him off, he entered her again.

"This time it won't hurt," he promised her.

She lay perfectly still. She knew what to expect and was no longer afraid, but she was so furious she didn't feel the swelling chorus of sensations in her body that urged her to respond to Gavin, to meet him in this physical manifestation of their union. All she could think of was her humiliation, and the thoughtless way he had taken his pleasure of her.

When Gavin prepared to mount her for a third time, she rolled away.

"No," she hissed between clenched teeth. "Don't touch me again. I feel *unclean.*"

Anger, black and fierce, slew Gavin's desire in an instant. Somewhere in the back of his mind, his conscience told him he should never have forced her, but his outrage at being accused of defiling her body—especially when he'd sacrificed some of his own pleasure to ease her fears—wouldn't allow him to consider that now.

"What's wrong?" he demanded.

"You dare to ask me that after what you've just done?" Sara exclaimed. She snatched at a comforter and wrapped it securely around her.

"What did you expect me to do, hold your hand?"

"I told you I was frightened and didn't know what to expect," Sara replied angrily.

"You can't blame me for that."

"Perhaps not, but I can blame you for the brutal way you used me."

"Brutal!" echoed Gavin, staggered that she couldn't see any of the trouble he had taken.

"Yes, brutal," reiterated Sara. "You knew I was ignorant and frightened, yet you ruthlessly ignored my protest and caused me pain."

"I won't hurt you again," Gavin told her irritably. "You'll feel nothing but pleasure from here on."

"If you think it's a pleasure to have my clothes ripped off and my body ravaged, you're demented," raged Sara. There was a nagging recollection that she *had* experienced some pleasure, but she swept the memory heedlessly aside. "I don't want you to ever enter my bedchamber again."

"This is *my* bedchamber," Gavin informed her, "and I'll enter it as often as I like."

"Then I will remove myself this instant," Sara declared. "And in future, my maid will sleep in my room. I will not be mauled and molested against my wishes."

Gavin threw himself from the bed and into his breeches with such force he almost ripped them open. "You need not disturb yourself," he shouted, affronted by her spurning him as a lover, and infuriated at her rejection of his attempts to ease her shock and salve his conscience. "I will *maul* and *molest* no female against her wishes."

Sara decided to ignore his last sentence. "And please tell your mother I'm sorry, but if this is the way one gets babies, I can't possibly give her a grandchild." There was enough sincere regret in her tone to penetrate Gavin's rage, and he experienced a moment of sympathy.

"She will pardon you, she already has me, but my father won't be so forgiving." He reached out to touch her, but Sara jerked herself back, the abhorrence in her eyes so unmistakable that a wave of guilt washed over Gavin. Immediately his anger was rekindled.

"I'll go, and I won't come back. I didn't want you when I first saw you years ago, I didn't want you when I met you at the altar, and by God, I don't want you now. I can satisfy my needs much more agreeably elsewhere." He snatched up his shirt. "Give my compliments to my father. He provided me with exactly the kind of wife I deserve." He laughed harshly. "But he overplayed his hand this time. Neither one of us will get what we want from you." He flung out of the room without looking back. The sound of the slamming door rang in Sara's ears for several minutes afterwards.

He had barely gone before Sara began to shake uncontrollably, and then she started to cry. She didn't understand why, but the outpouring of grief was just as violent as when her father died. Great sobs shook her body as she mourned the death of the dream that had sustained her through seven lonely years. There was a great, inchoate mass of thought that weighed on her brain, a seething turmoil she could neither understand or ignore. Tomorrow she would try to sort out what she had lost, what this night had cost her, but right now she only had the strength to mourn.

Chapter 8

Sara stood at her window and watched the cold dawn turn the sky to ice blue. Everything inside her felt the same way, only there was an emptiness there as well, a feeling of helplessness, a sense of having lost her way and having no idea how to find it again. And there was nowhere she could turn for help. She couldn't possibly tell anyone what had happened, not even Betty.

She could still feel the tremors of fear that had shaken her body as Gavin tore the gown from her, the flush of chagrin that had turned her skin to crimson as he ravaged her body, the surge of rage that he would, against her will, use her in such a manner. She couldn't decide whether she had been more embarrassed, afraid, or angry, but what did it matter now? Gavin was gone and unlikely to come back. She told herself she didn't care if he never came back, but she knew it was a lie. She cared very much, if for no other reason than that her marriage to Gavin was for the rest of her life. She couldn't just ignore last night and pretend it never happened, but neither did she know what to do to put it behind her. You've got to think of something, she told herself angrily. You're partly responsible. Your abysmal ignorance may not be your fault, but Gavin had a right to expect more from his bride.

She gathered her robe more tightly around her, to keep out the cold that pervaded the room.

She could almost laugh when she thought back to her behavior last night. Could she really blame Gavin for being upset with her complete lack of knowledge? Maybe not, but she could blame him for being drunk and inconsiderate. *Maybe you should have been drunk*, she thought wildly. *At least you might not have acted like a silly idiot*. God, what a fool he must have thought her. What a fool she *was* not to have persisted, until someone told her exactly what was going to happen. The mere fact that everyone avoided the subject so assiduously should have warned her there was something very important she didn't know. She was not used to thinking for herself—no one had ever allowed her to, much less encouraged it—but now she must. It was obvious she couldn't depend on Betty or anyone else to help her out of this awful mess.

She sighed and leaned against the windowsill. Assigning blame was not going to do the least bit of good, unless she could fix what was wrong. Besides, last night was behind her now. It would do no good to continue to dwell on it. She had been wrapped up in a daydream, convinced that everything would work out after the wedding, just as magically as it had before.

"For an intelligent woman, you have just given a convincing imitation of one of those foolish girls at Miss Rachel's," Sara castigated herself aloud. "You have a lot to do, and it will take all the intelligence you possess to accomplish it."

With energy born of frustration, she turned and strode across the room, only to be brought up short when her eyes fell on her wedding veil. With trembling hands, Sara picked it up. Sadly she looked at the wilted flowers. Yesterday they had been a symbol of joy; today they were as dead as her dreams of the future.

But one thing was unchanged: she still loved Gavin and wanted to preserve her marriage. She wasn't exactly sure how she felt about him now—her feelings were so tied in a tight knot she couldn't separate one from another—but she understood enough to know that her marriage was vitally important to her. Nothing would ever be the same after last night, but it hadn't changed the basic fact that she wanted to be Gavin's wife. She didn't know why that was so, she just knew it was.

Even though she didn't want to admit it, Sara knew there was no place for her in society outside of her marriage. If she wanted to be accepted, she had to stay married. If she were to stay married, she had to make their relationship work. And if she were to make it work, she had to have something to build on, even if it were no more than Gavin's reluctant desire for her body.

And now that some of the shock had worn off, she could admit that Gavin had not been as rough as she had thought at the time. He certainly had not been gentle, especially when she asked him to leave, but then she didn't understand much about men. She certainly couldn't understand what he could have liked about last night that would make him want to repeat the experience. She could vaguely remember some pleasurable sensations, but they came nowhere near compensating for the feelings of disgust and shame. But she would think about that later. Right now she had to figure out how to establish some kind of friendship between them. Nothing was going to work, until they could learn to like each other.

Sara let her finger caress the smooth silk of the headpiece. All her life she had dreamed of such a veil. It had seemed a symbol of the love her husband would shower on her. Now she realized that without the love it was intended to represent, this symbol was no more than a cold, plain piece of cloth.

She had to talk to Gavin. She didn't know what to say to him, but they had to clear away everything and start anew. She wasn't sure he could do that, she wasn't entirely sure *she* could, but there was no other choice, except to spend the rest of their lives blaming and avoiding each other. The picture of Gavin as he stood in the open door of her bedchamber flashed into Sara's mind, and she knew she couldn't live like that. She still loved him, at least she thought she did, but she also knew she felt an attraction to him that had not existed before, and that the attraction was physical. From the little she had learned about Gavin, she knew their physical relationship would be essential to any other relationship they had. After last night, she had a nagging suspicion that it could become true for herself as well.

But what if he wouldn't come back? What if he was content to enjoy his mistresses for the rest of his life? Hadn't he married her only to please his father and provide his mother with a grandchild? How was she going to recapture his interest? Recapture! How was she going to *gain* his interest when he had so emphatically stated he was not, never had been, and never would be interested in her?

Sara's eyes misted as she stared at her veil. It was so beautiful and had looked so pretty on her. Gingerly she settled the headpiece on her hair and smoothed the lace veil around her. She almost looked like a bride again. Now her eyes filled with tears. She would never be a bride again, but would she ever be a wife?

For a moment, Sara's back stiffened with pride. Why should she bother herself with a man who didn't want her, she asked? She had done nothing to deserve his scorn or earn rejection. If he didn't come to her, she would simply ignore him. But Sara rejected the thought almost before it was complete. She had too much to lose by turning her back on her marriage after just one bad experience, no matter how horrifying. There must be something she could do.

She felt an overwhelming sense of despair, but she couldn't cry. Her tears had run dry during the long hours of the black night. Now she sat dry-eyed, knowing her best weapon was the marriage contract. Gavin was tied to her just as firmly as she was to him; he could not ignore her forever. She would have to be patient, and if he didn't come back, she would have to go to him. Sara didn't want to think about that just yet. There were too many terrifying possibilities yawning before her timorous feet, but she was fighting for the rest of her life. It would be foolish to balk at anything that might save her marriage, when the only bar was fear of embarrassment, or fear itself.

Carefully she took off the veil. She would have Betty pack it away. One day she would put it on again, but not, she vowed, until her heart could swell with happiness at the memory of the years gone by.

Sara sat in her chair with stiff formality while the Earl responded to condolences from yet another pair of visitors. In the last two days, Sara had met more people than she had met in her eleven years at Miss Rachel's. Surely everyone in London had come to Parkhaven House to express their sorrow at the Countess's death, and extend their sympathy to her family.

As much as she was made unhappy by the Countess's death—she had looked upon her as her only friend and ally—Sara was relieved that the Earl had something else to occupy his mind besides her own failure as a wife. At least he would have if there hadn't been the continuing worry over Gavin's whereabouts. The Earl made no secret of the fact that he held Sara responsible for

Gavin's absence of nearly a fortnight.

"It looks bad," Olivia had remarked at dinner the night before.

"And it's damned hard to explain," added the Earl. He was endeavoring to do that very thing right now to a fawning mother and her simpering daughter. Sara might be naive and inexperienced, but she could tell they had nourished hopes of Gavin themselves. The knowledge that, even with her freckles and strawberry blonde hair, she was much more handsome than the haughty Miss Dorothea Burroughs gave her vanity a much-needed boost.

"It's so unfortunate that Lord Carlisle should be away from London at just this time," Lady Burroughs was saying.

"And him just married, too." This from Miss Dorothea who cast a smirking glance in Sara's direction.

"We have been experiencing some difficulties with our Scottish estates as a result of this unfortunate rebellion," explained the Earl. "He offered to spare me the necessity of traveling north in this season. Neither of us foresaw the Countess's untimely death."

"But the funeral is to be held tomorrow morning," tut-tutted Lady Burroughs. "I don't see how he can possibly return in time."

"I've sent someone after him," the Earl said. "That is all we can do."

Gavin had *not* been notified, because no one knew where he was. Every one of the Earl's attempts to locate his errant son had came to naught, another of the circumstances which had conspired to put him in a black rage. Between the stream of awe-inspiring visitors and the reports of yet another failure to locate Gavin, Sara had come to dread the sound of the knocker.

"It will certainly be a sad homecoming," stated Lady Burroughs with a suitably lachrymose expression.

"Everyone knows how extraordinarily fond Gavin was of the Countess. Are you sure there is nothing my son can do to help? He and Gavin are quite old friends."

The Earl's expression seemed unchanged, but Sara had learned that the color in his dark blue eyes turned almost black when he was angered. Now, in the face of Lady Burroughs's patent refusal to believe that Gavin had gone to Scotland and her determined effort to wrest information from him, the Earl's eyes were as black as onyx.

"It is most thoughtful of you to offer, but I expect we should see his arrival before we could get a new effort mounted."

Hardly had the words left the Earl's mouth when a disturbance was heard outside in the hall. Before anyone had time to wonder aloud at the cause of such an inexplicable commotion, the salon doors flew open with an ear-splitting crash, and Gavin stood on the threshold, Clarice Wynburn followed uneasily in his wake.

Sara's first impulse was to jump up from her chair and rush to Gavin's side. The expression on his face made her pause, but it was the woman at his side who kept her rooted to her chair. She was a beautiful woman, sophisticated and mature, and her body was expensively gowned in a way that made Sara feel like a blushing, ignorant, sexless girl. Who was this woman and why was she with Gavin instead of his wife?

"Poor, unhappy boy," gushed Lady Burroughs, the moment Gavin stepped through the door. She surged to her feet, her arms outstretched with the apparent intention of pressing the unfortunate "boy" to her very ample bosom. "Allow me to offer you my sincerest condolences." But Gavin stared past Lady Burroughs at his father, his own black eyes filled with pain and rage.

"Clarice tells me Mother is dead." He was unable to keep his voice from breaking on the last word. Sara was almost embarrassed to have to look upon the suffering in his face, but the Burroughs women hungrily devoured every detail, no doubt storing it up for retelling later.

The Earl rang a small bell before answering. "She died two days ago," he said, struggling to contain his feelings in the face of the inquisitive visitors.

"Why didn't you tell me she was so ill?" Gavin demanded.

Sara wondered if he could have endured watching his mother die. She wondered, too, if it might not have been the Countess's decision not to tell her beloved son that she had so little time left.

"Since you profess to love your mother so very greatly, I wonder that you did not see she was gravely ill."

"I didn't know." It was not offered as an excuse. It was an acceptance of guilt.

Two weeks of living in Parkhaven House had done a lot to disabuse Sara of her favorable opinion of the Earl's character, but the pointless cruelty of his words truly shocked her and she dug her nails into the arms of her chair as she watched Gavin turn white with shame. The accusation was cruelly unfair, but she could see Gavin thought he deserved it, and that he would never forgive himself for not being at his mother's side at the end.

But Sara knew it was his marriage to her which had driven concern for his mother from his mind. She could not evade the feeling of guilt that settled over her like a suffocating blanket, but even stronger was the feeling of anger at the Earl's brutal treatment of his son.

Couldn't he see how much Gavin was suffering? Couldn't he at least wait until these horrible women had left? The words of reproof popped out of her mouth before she had given them conscious thought.

"I'm certain Gavin would have remained here if everyone in the house, including the Countess, had not done their best to keep him from knowing just how ill she was," Sara said angrily. "Did you tell him she had very little time left, or did you leave him to guess?"

Gavin turned sharply in Sara's direction. His eyes scanned her face in search of an explanation for her unexpected defense of his conduct; the Earl completely ignored her outburst.

"Under the circumstances, I naturally supposed you would remain close at hand," he continued, driving the point of his verbal dagger deeper into Gavin's heart. "The fact that you were also newly married led me to expect that you would, for the meantime at least, maintain daily contact with this house."

"You can thank my blushing bride for that," declared Gavin angrily, still staring at Sara. "The reception she gave me was ample reason to take myself off." The Burroughs women, one seated and one still standing, were rooted to the spot, mouths and ears wide open.

Involuntarily Clarice's gaze shifted to Sara, as jealousy, then anger, flamed in her cheeks. So this was Gavin's wife. She nearly sniffed her scorn aloud. This shrinking Miss could never satisfy him. He would soon tire of this meager fare, if he hadn't already, and then he would come back to her bed.

No one saw Clarice's look, they were too busy staring at Sara, but Sara did. Even worse, she understood it.

"I can't think Lady Burroughs and her daughter wish to be burdened with the details of your domestic imbroglio," announced the Earl. "She would undoubtedly appreciate it if you would postpone this discussion until after their departure."

"I don't give a damn what Lady Burroughs wants," Gavin exploded, completely beyond caring for appearances. "If she doesn't like what she hears, she can leave."

The butler entered the salon on silent feet.

"Lady Burroughs and Miss Burroughs are ready to depart," the Earl announced. "See them to their carriage." Lady Burroughs made a determined attempt to prolong her visit, but the Earl would not be outmaneuvered, and his determined flow of small talk prevented Gavin from making any more ill-timed disclosures. When the door closed behind the visitors, however, he dropped the mask of politeness and turned swiftly back to his son, his face a deathly white from rage.

"You have not been backward of late in providing me with reasons to deplore your conduct, but never until today have you given me cause to be ashamed of you."

"Because I brought my mistress into your house, or because I gave that gossip-hungry witch something to prattle about?"

"Either would be sufficient to cause a person of ordinary sensibility to think before speaking."

"Why don't we invite them back, drop your pretense of paternal affection, and *really* give them something they can sink their teeth into? Or would you prefer I invite a hand-picked audience?"

"If this is the kind of behavior being with your mistress encourages—"

"What in hell makes you think Clarice determines my behavior? She's my *mistress*, not my *wife!*"

"I haven't noticed that your wife is able to exercise a restraining effect upon you either."

But Sara didn't hear the Earl's remark. The word mistress had exploded in her brain like a blinding flash of light, rendering her insensible to everything else. She was furious that Gavin would force her to meet this woman, especially in the presence of strangers, but she was more hurt than angry. She felt violated, much more so than on her wedding night.

"You have no one to blame but yourself," Gavin said to his father. "*You* chose her. But then it was the money and not the girl you wanted, wasn't it? The money and an heir, that is. That's why you didn't tell me mother was sick. You *knew* if she died, I would never set foot in this house again as long as you lived. It was the only way you could get me to marry the Raymond money and father an heir for your precious estate."

Sara turned toward the Earl, stunned that he would use the illness of his wife against his own son. Despite the anger in her own heart, she realized, at least for a moment, that Gavin had entered into this marriage with an even greater burden than she had.

"I have the misfortune to be your son and can claim no immunity from your evil," Gavin declared wrathfully, "but by all that's holy, this poor child shouldn't have to suffer because of your greed and cruelty."

"There is no need for such heat," replied the Earl impatiently, not in the least shaken. "I do not deny that I used your mother's illness to achieve my ends. The more usual tactics had already failed. I merely chose to employ an alternate means of persuasion."

"You mean you didn't care whether or not I loved Gavin?" gasped Sara. At last she understood the reason for her marriage, the haste, the secrecy, and she was angry at both Gavin and his father, but most particularly she was furious with the Earl.

"You were, and still are I might add, totally unimportant and unformed, without definition or value," the Earl stated contemptuously. "Since you would naturally take your fortune with you when you married, and since it was important to me to retain the use of your money, I saw no reason not to arrange a suitable marriage which would also enable me to maintain custody over the business I have worked so hard to create."

"Then you were never interested in my happiness?" asked Sara. This was all so incredible she could hardly believe it was happening.

"Not in the least," the Earl stated bluntly.

"You've got your fortune," announced Gavin, "but you won't have an heir. There is no power on earth that could force me to bed that . . . that *child!*"

Sara felt as though she was being brutalized from all sides. She didn't dare look at Clarice. She couldn't bear to know what she was thinking. But she vowed that no matter what she had to do, this would never *ever* happen to her again.

"What do you propose to do," demanded the Earl scornfully, "sulk about London with that milch cow in tow, providing the malicious with enough gossip to make them forget the imperfections of our coarse German king and his even coarser offspring?"

"I'm leaving for Scotland within the hour."

"What about your wife?"

"You picked her out. *You* keep her."

"So you're running away again, just like you did before."

"I went away to cool off and do some thinking. This time I'm *leaving.*"

"And I can see where you took yourself," replied the Earl shaking with rage. "How *dare* you bring that harlot to this house? If you have no respect for your wife and our guests, at least remember this was your mother's home as well."

"It was Clarice who brought me the news of mother's death. She seems to be the only person in London who gives a damn about me."

"Stop whining and get that slut out of here," commanded his father.

"Clarice will go when I ask her," shouted Gavin.

"Get her out, or I shall have the footmen throw her into the street," challenged his father. "This is my house, and I'll not have it disgraced by that whore."

"You can have your goddamned house," shouted Gavin turning on his heel.

"You know you can't leave before the funeral," the Earl taunted his son with a withering sneer.

"There's not going to be any funeral here," Gavin told his father, turning to face him with defiant, flashing black eyes. "I'm taking mother home to Scotland. You can have your house, your daughter-in-law, and everything else you've bought with your ill-gotten money, but you'll not have me or my mother ever again."

He turned from his father and strode from the room with enormous strides, his boots striking a rhythmic cadence on the marble floor, Clarice forgotten in his urgent need to be out of his father's presence.

"Gavin, wait!" she called out. "What about me?"

The loud slamming of the door was her answer, and she turned back to the room, stranded between fury at such a public rejection and fear of the Earl, who was even now instructing his footman to remove her, forcibly if necessary, from the room. Clarice faced the Earl with as much dignity as she could muster.

"You needn't put yourself out," she said fiercely. "I know you think it's fine for me to solace your son between the sheets, but I'm not good enough to be seen with him in public. You needn't deny it."

"I wasn't going to," replied the Earl in arctic tones.

"Look down your nose at me if you like, but I understand him better than you do, and that galls your soul. I *am* common, but I'm not stupid or selfish and deceitful. I never took anything from him when I wasn't willing to give something back in exchange. That's more than you can say."

"Get out of my house," commanded the Earl in a voice vibrant with loathing.

"I'll go, but not before I've said my piece. And you won't let your footman put his hands on me, because I'll set up a screech that will bring half the street to your door." She smiled complacently. "You wouldn't like that, would you?" The Earl regarded her in rigid silence, and Clarice chuckled. "I ought to do it just for the pleasure of seeing your face, but I'm a Christian woman and I won't do anything I wouldn't want done to me. I have one piece of advice for you, and if you ever want to get your son back, you'd better listen. Before you can have the man he has become, you're going to have to make peace with the boy he was." She turned to Sara and her expression softened, but only slightly. "And if you want him to be your husband, I mean a *real* husband, you're going to have to become a woman. Gavin lost interest in girls long ago." Having delivered herself of this Parthiare shot, Clarice gathered her cloak about her and marched through the door the footman was holding open for her with all the aplomb of a reigning monarch.

Sara, hardly able to function after the multiple disclosures of the last minutes, turned mute and anguished eyes toward the Earl.

"See what you've done, you frigid bitch!" he bellowed, rounding on her savagely. "I curse the day I decided you should be his wife. I wish to hell he had raped you."

"You almost got your wish," Sara cried, starting to her feet. "But you don't wish half as much as I do that I'd never set eyes on you. I don't know why my father ever thought you would make a suitable guardian. I wouldn't trust you with a half-breed dog."

"Then I guess I'm eminently suited to be your trustee," the Earl replied cruelly.

"You don't deserve to have had such a wonderful wife as the Countess," Sara continued, ignoring his insult. "And you don't deserve a son like Gavin. He only hurts others because he's hurting so much himself. But most of all, you don't deserve me, and I promise you I will find a way to escape this accursed house."

Sara thought she must begin screaming in loud, piercing wails if she stayed in that room one minute longer. Without excusing herself, she ran from the salon, raced down halls and up stairways, causing more than one servant to gape after her in open amazement, threw herself on her bed, and sobbed her heart out.

Chapter 9

A rapidly building crescendo of sound filled the salon and echoed down the broad hallway as Sara drove toward the climax of a Carl Philipp Emanuel Bach concerto, a composer made fashionable by the court of the German Emperor Frederick and now being popularized by England's own German monarch, George II. Music was Sara's solace, and she found herself turning more and more frequently to the harpsichord, to vent the anguish and longing locked up inside her. After being sheltered and protected her whole life, Sara was now beset on all sides by seemingly insoluble problems, and she was only gradually learning that she must begin to fight back.

It was hard to believe how differently she had viewed the world just a month ago. Then she had felt that to become Gavin's wife and escape Miss Adelaide's was all she needed to be happy. She had achieved both, only to realize she had achieved nothing. Love was of little value when it was not returned, and marriage was just another form of bondage. Becoming Gavin's wife hadn't given her love, hadn't given her freedom, and hadn't given her control of her own money. It *had* removed her from the safety of Miss Adelaide's seminary, shattered her childhood dream, destroyed her innocence, and made her the target of the Earl's brutal attacks.

She attacked the cadenza with more force than artistry, but then she wasn't playing for art.

At first she had hidden in her room, but she was too strong-willed to give up. By degrees she had come to realize that it might still be possible to achieve her dream of a loving marriage, but she wasn't going to do it as long as she remained a helpless pawn in the Earl's hands. She must have some leverage. After several days of soul-searching, she came to understand that it wouldn't just happen, and that no one was going to do it for her. Gavin and the Earl were part of a society which did not often concern itself with the fate of a powerless woman; in reality, neither did the rest of the world.

Along with this broadening of Sara's understanding came a change in her character. She began to see the need to act to change her situation, and to see herself as capable of this action. This change came in her slowly and reluctantly, much like a butterfly emerging from a cocoon, but she was a different and stronger woman now.

Sara finished her concerto and let her body sag from exhaustion, but the tension remained. She didn't have any answers yet; she had only just begun to search for a solution to her dilemma. She would have to discover a way to get around the Earl, and that wouldn't be easy. He was a cold and ruthless adversary. He had turned his back on her in cold rage when he had been informed that Gavin had removed his mother's coffin from the house.

"See what your squeamishness has done," said Olivia Tate, who had disliked Sara from the first. "If you hadn't been such a fool that first night, Gavin would still be in London, instead of subjecting his family to this public humiliation."

"You know his going to Scotland had nothing to do with me," retorted Sara, determined that she would not continue to flee from these attacks. "If you and the Earl are so worried about what everybody will think, why don't you go to Scotland with him? He only went to bury his mother."

"He doesn't mean to return."

"I don't see that as any of your concern." Olivia blinked at Sara's reproof but was silent. The Earl was not so easily quelled.

"Thanks to the Burroughs women, all of London knows why he was absent from his mother's bedside."

"If he had used me more kindly, I would not have withdrawn from him."

"Nonetheless, you're the only one capable of repairing the damage," the Earl pointed out acrimoniously.

"And how do you propose I do that at a distance of four hundred miles?" demanded Sara, getting up from her seat by the fire and walking over to the harpsichord. Somehow just standing by it, being able to touch it, gave her strength to fight back. "If you, who have known him all his life and can be said to have some call on his affections, cannot induce him to remain in London, how can I, who was in his company less than a day, possibly have any influence on him?"

"You're his wife."

"People don't love their wives just because of some words said over them. But then the real purpose of my wedding was the transfer of my fortune from one of your pockets to the other, wasn't it?"

"That would have happened no matter who you married."

"But if I had married someone else, I would have an allowance of my own."

"Your bills will be covered."

"That's not the same. I want to know how much money I have and how it shall be paid to me."

"You have none," said the Earl. "Your fortune is the property of your husband, and he made no provision for you to have a separate income."

"Then it must be changed."

"Nothing can be accomplished in Gavin's absence."

"I can't accept that."

"You are welcome to discuss it with my solicitor," said the Earl with hard, glittering eyes, "but he will tell you the same."

"You should be thankful the Earl doesn't throw you out," declared Olivia spitefully. "What good are you, if you can't prevent Gavin from disappearing or give the Earl a grandson?"

"Now that the Countess is dead, what good are *you?*" demanded Sara, turning on Olivia with a spurt of anger that surprised even herself.

"Remember that you're Gavin's wife and not his mistress," the Earl reprimanded her in his most contemptuous voice. "The manner of behavior expected of the two roles is really quite different."

"I'll behave like a wife when I'm treated like one," retorted Sara. "It's not my fault I was married in ignorance. *You* determined my education, so if your plans have fallen apart, you have only yourself to blame."

"None of this is of any consequence now," said the Earl, dismissing her words with a total lack of interest. "I will have to contrive another solution to this Gordian knot. In the meantime, I intend to join the retinue of the Duke of Cumberland when he goes to Scotland to put down this rebellion."

"What am I supposed to do?" demanded Sara, taken completely unawares.

"I don't care," said the Earl, rising to his feet. He walked toward the door, but turned back before he reached it. "The only justification you ever had for being here was to make Gavin a satisfactory wife. As far as I'm concerned, it still is."

"What can we do except go back to Miss Rachel's?" asked a dejected Betty. "She will be glad enough to have you, but I doubt she'll agree to take me on again."

"I'm not going back," Sara said quite positively. "I've already spent half my life under her thumb, and I don't mean to spend any more."

"But where can we go?"

"I don't know, but I'll think of something."

"Do you have any money?"

"No, but I mean to have an allowance."

But when Sara went to see the solicitor two days later, she found her fortune was no more accessible to her than to a total stranger.

"No provision was made for settling an income on you," the solicitor stated in a flat, noncommittal voice. "It was determined that you would live with the Earl and that your support should come from his personal funds."

"But I don't *want* to be dependent on the Earl."

The young solicitor was extremely uncomfortable. He was of the opinion that all women, and especially those possessed of great fortunes, should leave the handling of their money to their husbands or fathers.

"I can see there's nothing more to be gained here," said Sara, rising.

But she was at a stand. It was useless to approach the Earl, he rarely spoke to her now, and he was seldom at home. Olivia Tate was leaving the house tomorrow. The Countess's Scottish servants were going back home, and the others would soon be forced to seek new situations.

"I need a new situation myself," Sara mumbled to herself over the noise of the carriage. Betty met her at the door. "They won't give me a penny," she reported, and cast her wool cloak from her in disgust.

"What are we going to do?"

"I don't know, but I will not stay here," Sara observed tartly.

"But we can go nowhere without money."

"We shall have it, and the Earl will provide it."

"Milady, you know the Earl will never give you a shilling, much less a pound."

"I don't plan to ask him."

"But how—?" Betty's eyes widened. "You wouldn't!"

"Why not? It's my money."

"But that's *stealing*."

"He can take it out of my income." Sara leveled her determined gaze at Betty. "His strongbox must be in his bedroom. It shouldn't be too difficult to get in, if we wait until everybody's gone."

"I always did want to see inside one of them great money boxes," Betty said, her eyes gleaming with anticipation. "I've never seen more than a few pounds at one time."

"I imagine this box will have more money than you ever dreamed of, but we'll have a better chance to escape detection, if we only take a little."

Next morning they waited until after the bustle over Olivia Tate's departure had died down. The Earl left the house on some private business, and the servants were mostly getting themselves ready to leave. It was an easy matter for Sara and Betty to get inside the Earl's bedroom unseen.

"Jesu!" exclaimed Betty, who was the more nervous of the two. "You act like you break into rooms every day, and I'm shaking like a newborn lamb."

"What can he say that he hasn't said already?" was Sara's prosaic reply.

The chest was not hidden. It sat at the end of the Earl's bed, an impressive trunk made by one of the firms in

Nuremburg and elaborately decorated and bound with bands of iron. A great double lock insured that its contents would not be disturbed without the benefit of the keys that the Earl or his steward kept with them at all times.

"I've never seen anything like it," breathed Betty.

"I don't give a fig what it looks like. I just want it open. The Earl must keep a key here somewhere."

"I don't know," said Betty, inspecting the great double lock that protected the contents of the box. "I wouldn't leave the key lying about if it was mine."

"Let's start looking," hissed Sara. "I don't know how long the Earl will be gone."

"You'd better leave me to do it," advised Betty. "The way you leave a drawer, even a blind man could tell it had been gone through."

So Betty set to work systematically, going through every drawer and cupboard in the room, while Sara nervously guarded the door.

"Hurry up," she hissed. "What's taking so long?"

"I can't find the key," Betty hissed back. She turned over piles of clothes as rapidly as she could, but each passing minute wore at Sara's composure like dripping water on a sugar crystal. It wasn't long before she was dancing like a puppet on a string.

"It's his valet," Sara whispered urgently, when she saw the dour countenance of Skelton approaching down the hall.

"You can't hide there," Betty remonstrated, when Sara headed for the closet. "He's bound to have business with the Earl's clothes. Hide in the window alcove!"

Sara dashed behind the heavy curtains, hoping they hung low enough to hide her shoes. She had barely stilled their movement when the door opened.

She was unable to see the valet, but she could see the Earl's bed, and her heart nearly stopped. Betty had dived under the bed, but her feet were sticking out. Sara almost gave herself up for lost, but she heard Skelton go into one of the clothes cupboards and she hissed imperatively. Betty's feet remained visible, and Sara hissed again, too loudly this time, and Skelton came hurrying from the cupboard. For a moment she heard and saw nothing, even though she could have sworn she heard Skelton open the door, and then in a space between the two curtains, she saw him stealthily approaching the alcove, a broom raised above his head. Sara's body became rigid and she stopped breathing. Hurriedly she tried to think how she would explain her presence in the Earl's bedchamber. In almost the same instant, Skelton brought the broom down with a loud whack. His triumphant "Aha!" and the sudden onslaught of feline hissing and spitting covered Sara's muffled scream.

"And stay in the kitchen where you belong," Skelton called loudly, as he closed the door and returned to the cupboard. "I hope the cook takes that dratted cat off with her," he muttered grumpily.

When Sara was finally able to breath again, she saw that Betty's feet had disappeared. She let her breath go in a long, slow stream. If she ever got out of here without the Earl finding her, she'd starve to death before she tried to steal from him again, even if it *was* her own money.

Unable to see a thing from her position, it seemed to Sara that Skelton spent an unaccountably long time walking back and forth about the room, first to one closet and then to another cupboard. What can he possibly be doing, Sara demanded of herself, only to realize that he was packing. She tensed. That could keep her here for hours, and such a prolonged stay would undoubtedly lead to discovery by the Earl. Her palms began to sweat. Much of the time Skelton's tread was virtually inaudible from her hiding place, the heavy velvet muffling all sound except the opening and closing of the doors. She didn't know how long she had remained hidden when Betty suddenly pulled back the curtain.

"You scared me half to death," gasped Sara, looking around nervously. "I suppose we'll have to forget the money," she said, not entirely sorry to be leaving the apartment.

"Not on your life," said Betty cheerfully. "The last thing Skelton did was open the chest. See?" To demonstrate, she raised the heavy lid. Her eyes widened and her breathing stopped at the sight that met her eyes. The chest was nearly full of gold coins.

"I never knew there was so much money in the world," gasped Betty.

"How much do you think is here?" asked Sara, who had no experience of money except in small amounts.

"I don't know, but it must be thousands. How much should we take?"

"How about fifty pounds? Even that's bound to make an impression, and we don't want the Earl to know it's missing."

"I don't know," Betty said, wavering. "I'm sure the Earl would know if as much as a shilling was gone."

"No, he won't. Both he and his steward have keys to this box. Each will assume it was taken by the other. We can remove any reasonable sum without the slightest fear of detection."

They spent some minutes longer trying to arrive at a practical sum, and in the end settled on the fifty pounds Sara mentioned first. Having extracted that sum, they hurried away to their apartment. They breathed a deep sigh of relief once they had closed the door behind them.

"My agent in Scotland informs me that Gavin has arrived at Estameer," the Earl announced to Sara across the breakfast table the next morning.

Sara had made a deliberate attempt to avoid meeting her father-in-law since their last interview, but this morning she had come down to the breakfast parlor fully an hour before her usual time. She had done some more thinking, and she had a proposition to put to him.

"It appears your husband has wasted no time in providing himself with a mistress." The Earl lowered his letter and looked at Sara with a smile full of mockery. "Your charms seem to have made no lasting impression on him."

Up until now Sara had endured the Earl's numerous barbs in stoic silence, because fighting back only encouraged him to attack even more maliciously, but she would endure it no longer.

"I don't imagine he was looking forward to the winter without someone to warm his bed," she replied, trying to keep the hurt and chagrin from her voice.

"Madam, you speak very lightly of a serious matter," the Earl shot back.

"Am I to infer that you disapprove of the practice of keeping a mistress?" inquired Sara, determined not to back down.

"That is not the issue at all. You are his wife."

"Does that automatically make me deaf, dumb, and blind, or am I just supposed to act stupid?"

"You're supposed to be above such matters. Your purpose is to provide your husband with an heir, and that's impossible for you to accomplish with Gavin four hundred miles away."

"I can wait until he returns."

"*If* he returns," muttered the Earl, mostly to himself. For a moment, his gaze seemed to travel faraway, and Sara thought he was going to sink into an abstraction, but he roused himself and turned back to her.

"I shall join the Duke in two days." He didn't even pause to allow Sara to answer him. "I've made arrangements for you to have one hundred pounds for your personal needs, paid to you quarterly. However, my steward will remain in control of the house. Do not attempt to alter my arrangements. He has been instructed to ignore any requests to do so."

"I will not stay locked up in this great house with only the caretaker for company," Sara declared wrathfully.

"Suit yourself, though I doubt a hundred pounds will run to the lease of a house and hiring of servants." He rose to go. "Don't put my steward to a lot of unnecessary trouble. I would dislike it."

"Don't you care what *I* dislike?" Sara demanded. She didn't know why she continued to be surprised at his attitude.

"No," the Earl said, pausing on his way out. "I am only interested in you as a means of providing the family with an heir."

"And if I should succeed?" demanded Sara, coming at last to the reason she had wanted to see the Earl.

His cold eyes moved over her with contempt. "Then I suppose I should be forced to reorder my opinion of you."

"That's not enough. If you want an heir badly enough to force Gavin into marriage against his will, you ought to be willing to give up something important for it."

"Such as?"

"Control of my own fortune." The Earl regarded her more soberly for some time.

"And if I refuse?"

"Why should you? You can't hold on to my money forever, and even if you could, it won't give you an heir. Also, if you don't make more suitable provisions for me, I shall bring you into court, and that would create a scandal you won't like."

"You won't succeed."

"But then, neither will you." The two protagonists

faced each other, each trying to measure the other, each trying to fathom the other's strength. Sara's knees shook and her whole body felt weak with uncertainty, but her eyes did not fall.

"I can't give you control of your principal. Your father's will leaves it to your husband."

"But Gavin can turn it over to me."

"What makes you think he would?"

"He would if you asked him. He doesn't care about my money."

"Why do you think Gavin would do anything *I* wanted?"

"You forced him to marry me."

"Ah, but that was for his mother. I doubt I could persuade him to walk across the street to save my neck."

"You'll find some way," Sara insisted.

"I think I just might," said the Earl thoughtfully, intrigued by Sara's proposal. "I have the power to interfere with the property his mother left him. I think he would agree to almost anything, if I were to relinquish that right."

"Then you will give me my money if I succeed?" demanded Sara. The Earl studied her for a moment, and then brusquely prepared to take his departure.

"I don't suppose you will be able to do anything more than become a thorn in his side, but if you should succeed, I will transfer control of your principal and income to you. It will be worth anything to keep that bastard Hawley from stepping into my shoes."

"Put that in writing," Sara said, and produced a piece of writing paper from her pocket. The Earl regarded her with surprise, and then actually smiled.

"Certainly." He took up the paper, searched for and found pen and ink, and sat down to write. "I, Oliver Carlisle, Earl of Parkhaven, do agree to hand over to Lady Sara Carlisle control of her inheritance and its income on the day she becomes the mother of a healthy male heir to the Parkhaven title and estates. It is a further condition that she must be living under the same roof as her husband and be in good charity with him." The Earl read over his words, waved the paper in the air to dry the ink, and then handed it to Sara after signing and dating it.

"There's your agreement," he said standing. "Now please don't inflict yourself upon me, until you've fulfilled its conditions."

But for once his words had no power to hurt Sara. She had the promise she wanted, and the taste of success was sweet.

Chapter 10

Having cleared the first step, Sara was free to concentrate on Gavin, but she hardly knew how to begin. For years she had imagined him to be a slim boy with a merry laugh and dancing eyes, only to learn that he had grown into a tall man with a powerful body and an unforgettably handsome face. Yet before she could begin to assimilate the change, she found herself married to a morose and wrathful young man who had forced himself upon her in a drunken stupor, and kept a mistress besides.

Then, while she was still reeling from the shock of the Countess's death, she discovered he was haunted by the death of a mother he loved deeply, and the fear he might turn out to be like the father he despised. He was more tortured and unhappy than she had ever been.

But though her mind might not know what to think, her heart felt no indecision. Learning that Gavin suffered and bled like all other mortals somehow made him seem more real, more human, and that had the unforeseen effect of virtually wiping out the nightmare of her wedding night. Her stubbornly romantic heart gathered up all the sympathetic impressions and merged them into a portrait of a man who would someday welcome her into his arms with a kiss and a laugh, and make her feel warm and secure for the rest of her life.

She had no basis for this feeling, neither Gavin nor his father had given her reason to discount the ugliness she saw, but she was convinced that if she could only get past the barriers erected by anger, pain, and fear, her picture of Gavin would be the right one.

It hadn't taken Sara long to become jealous of the deep and unshakable love Gavin had for his mother. She longed to be the object of such fierce adoration. She chastised herself for being covetous of a son's love for his mother, but she was envious of it nonetheless. She was certain she could have lived the rest of her life in joyous contentment on just a tithe of the love, gentleness, sensitivity, and consideration he lavished on the Countess.

Almost as significant was Gavin's violent condemnation of his father. It must have taken great courage to oppose the Earl so openly. Not only did he risk being disinherited, he risked being cut off from the only society of which he could ever be a part. No, it didn't matter what the Earl said or what Gavin did, Sara was convinced that somewhere inside Gavin was the boy she remembered and the man who could love so generously, hate so intensely, and suffer so deeply.

It was a relief to have her mind made up at last. In the days immediately following their wedding, she had hidden in her bedchamber, horrified by the kind of man she had married, afraid he would come back, afraid he wouldn't, afraid of facing the Earl's anger, afraid of going back to Miss Adelaide. She had been helplessly caught between a past she didn't want and future that didn't want her, but the Countess's death had disclosed the pain and fear that knotted and confined Gavin's heart. Sara all but forgot her own misery in the face of his torment. Maybe he never would be the hero of her dreams, maybe he never would love her as much as she loved him, but there was a fine, honest, warm, and caring man hidden somewhere inside Gavin Carlisle, and she was determined to find him.

"We ought to go back to Miss Adelaide's," groaned Betty. "You have no business living in this great house alone."

"I will *never* go back," said Sara, her teeth clenched tight with determination. "We are going to Scotland and find my husband."

"B-but we can't," stammered Betty. "That must be hundreds of miles away!"

"If he can travel that far, so can we."

"He may not take you in.

"I'm his wife. He has to."

"We don't even know where he is."

"I can always ask the solicitor," Sara said, undaunted. "I have to see him about getting my money early."

But the solicitor would not agree to pay Sara any of the hundred pounds until the first of the year. Once again her proud spirit got her back up, and she marched back to Parkhaven House, a defiant look on her face.

"It's just as well we stole that money," she barked at Betty, as soon as she stepped inside the door. "That miserable little man won't give me a shilling until the first of the quarter. I refuse to sit around here another four weeks, but I don't know if our fifty pounds will be enough. Do we have anything we can sell?"

"There's all those clothes the Earl had made for you. Then there's always your wedding ring."

Sara looked down at the thin, gold band, and knew she could never part with her ring. There were times when it was the only thing that made her believe she was really married, that this whole terrible nightmare wasn't just a bad dream.

"You'll have to find something else," she said quietly, as she lovingly fingered the golden circle. "This ring will never leave my finger."

"A man!" echoed Sara, thunderstruck, when Betty told her she must travel in a disguise. "Why can't I be disguised as a maid? You should be the man. As tall as you are, no one will question you."

"But you're too pretty to travel as a female."

Sara was still so unaccustomed to hearing herself described as pretty, that she couldn't repress a smile of satisfaction. "Then we'll just have to travel as a lady and her maid."

"We can't," Betty told her. "We don't have enough money to hire a chaise and postilions. A real lady has to travel in a certain style, or nobody will believe she's a lady. Then there's the matter of accommodations. The best inns will turn us away, because a real lady never travels without male protection. I'm sorry, milady, but there's nothing for it but for you to go as a man. Inns and taverns are not safe for a gently bred woman."

"We can travel on the mail coach."

"There's still bound to be men who will take advantage of you," Betty continued. "You know I'll do my best to protect you, but his lordship wouldn't like it if we was to get into trouble and have to disclose your identity."

"Then his lordship should have seen to it that I was not put to the necessity of traveling alone," snapped Sara.

"Of course he should, but there's no sense blinking facts, and the fact is he ain't here. I've thought it all out, and you can be my younger brother. Everybody'll be so busy gawking at me, they won't have any time to be wondering at your fair complexion and slight figure."

Sara continued to object, but her protests grew more feeble as she perceived the truth of Betty's words, and Betty grew more firm as she noticed her mistress's waning resistance. But when Betty returned with a suit of men's clothes and a pair of scissors, Sara's acceptance was at an end.

"You can't expect to be taken for a young man unless you wear men's clothing," Betty pointed out sensibly, "and there's no way you can hide all that hair under a hat. The first good breeze will blow it off, and then we will be in the suds."

"I won't let you cut my hair, not even to protect my virtue."

"I won't have to cut much," Betty assured her. "The gentry wear their hair almost as long as ladies." But the twelve-inch lengths that lay on the carpet after Betty had finished the job seemed like a lot to Sara.

"I look like a sheep after the shearing," she said, staring gloomily at her reflection in the mirror.

"You won't even notice it with this hat." Betty handed her a three-cornered hat, and Sara laughed when she put it on, but she balked when Betty handed her the pants.

"It's indecent."

"Nobody will know it's you," Betty reasoned somewhat obscurely. "They'll think you're some schoolboy and pay no attention."

Sara wasn't convinced, and she was even less convinced when she saw herself in the shocking outfit. "I can't possibly be seen like this," she protested, cringing at the thought of appearing in public.

"You'll have to act like a man, too," Betty warned her. "That means no hiding in corners. Men aren't shy that way, and they never stay indoors unless they have to. And when they do, they always keep to the company of other men."

"But I don't know what men do," Sara protested, a

feeling of panic rising inside her. "I never even had a brother."

"That's true," admitted Betty, pausing to ponder this point.

But the thought of going back to Parkhaven House, or living in some cheap lodging until Gavin returned, stiffened Sara's resolve. Her bet with the Earl held out the promise of a freedom which looked sweeter every time she thought about it. And then there was Gavin. Pride might decree that she wait for him to come to her, but common sense told her it was a waste of time and a dangerous gamble.

"I'll think of something," she told Betty, with a confidence she didn't entirely feel. "I *will* reach Scotland."

Sara leaned back in the creaking, swaying coach and tried to ignore the fear that encircled her heart in a constricting band. The last few days had been a terrifying experience, and only the presence of a calm, placid Betty seated next to her kept Sara from bolting back to Parkhaven House.

Having endured the shock of appearing in public as a man, and surviving her first experience with all male companionship, she had been promptly faced with the fact that she would also have to share a bed with them. Only the certainty that she would have to slink back to London in disgrace, and the help of a friendly squire, had enabled her to endure that experience.

But the squire had left them early on the third day, and now Sara found herself seated next to a petty merchant of small means and even smaller interest in any person other than himself. He kept up a constant monologue about his tribulations, the injustice of the law, and the heaviness of the tax burden, until an exceedingly fat woman told him no one was interested in him or his troubles, even if they had been interesting, which they weren't, and if he didn't shut up, she was going to empty a jar of pickled cherries over him.

Indignant, the merchant did subside, but the atmosphere in the coach became so uncomfortable that Sara wished the lady had let him talk. Besides, Sara liked him more than the other male passengers, one of whom rode inside and the other outside on the roof. The man in the coach was quiet, looked rather furtive, and generally made Sara nervous.

She didn't feel any better when she learned the four of them were to share a huge four-poster bed. Spending two nights in perfect safety with the squire had given her some courage, and as Betty said, what can happen with four of them in the room?

The innocents found out next morning. Sometime during the night, two of the passengers broke into the merchant's and Sara's portmanteaux, stole their money, and disappeared. This time the merchant created a disturbance even the fat lady couldn't quell. He caused the sheriff, the constable, and the justice of the peace to be summoned to the inn, and demanded that the villains be apprehended at once.

When at length the officials were at liberty to turn to Sara, she made as little as possible of her loss, though the consequences were more serious for her than the merchant. She had a few shillings, Betty had a few more, and their ticket was paid up for two more days, but a check with the stage agent showed that their accumulated funds were insufficient to get them to Scotland. They would run out of money somewhere near the border.

"We don't even have enough to get back to London," Betty moaned.

"I won't go back," Sara said, stamping her foot.

"There must be a way to reach Scotland."

"Not without money."

"We can work."

"It would take more than I could earn to pay for our lodging."

"I can work, too," Sara insisted.

"It's not a fit thing. Besides, what could you do?"

Nothing, Sara admitted.

"Why don't you send his lordship a letter saying that you've been robbed, that you're continuing on to Scotland on foot, and if he wishes to avoid the shame of having his wife taken up as a vagrant, he should immediately dispatch enough money for us to reach Scotland."

"That ought to bring him hotfoot, or at least his steward," declared Sara, laughing in spite of the gravity of their situation. "Now let's see if we have overlooked any coins." A diligent search turned up a pound secreted in a pocket, and a few extra shillings fallen into the lining of her greatcoat, but there was hardly enough to keep them for more than a few days.

Suddenly Betty brightened. "I have an old aunt who lives below Carlisle, near the border."

"Do you think she would let us stay until Gavin could come for us?"

"Of course she would, and she wouldn't have you scrubbing pots to pay for your keep either," Betty added with a snort. "But we'll need more than these few shillings if we're to reach Carlisle."

At last the merchant's protests came to an end, and all the passengers boarded the coach to resume their journey. The merchant continued to complain loudly of his plight, and the fat lady not only allowed him to repeat, in excruciating detail, every word of the several lengthy discussions he had held with the representatives of the law during the course of the morning, but she went so far as to inquire into the nature of his business and his private situation. The merchant positively bloomed under her attention, until Sara was excessively thankful at the end of the day to be relieved of his droning voice.

"What more can you expect when invaders are allowed to march right into the country and molest honest citizens?" the innkeeper asked, when appraised of the robbery.

"What invaders?" Sara asked in some alarm. The merchant was displeased to have the conversation turn to a subject other than himself, but the fat lady had heard all she wanted about him and his troubles, and encouraged the landlord to answer Sara's question.

"Haven't you heard about the Scots?" he asked.

They had heard tales of a scavenging army and of rapine and outrage, but Sara could not fail to notice that the countryside looked as peaceful and undisturbed as that outside London. The citizens seemed to enjoy telling of the horrible Highland Scots, instead of actually being frightened of them. She wondered if they should turn back, but as they had no money, they had no choice but to go forward. Besides, there was nothing for her in London. Her only chance lay in reaching Scotland and winning her bet with the Earl.

Betty kept their small hoard of cash and guarded every penny with a stern eye. She argued with the innkeeper over the price and quality of the dinner, and refused to pay the sum demanded for their rooms.

"He'll never let us come here again," said Sara, when they were on the coach again.

"We won't need to," Betty replied, sniffing in contempt at the poor hostelry. "Once his lordship comes for us, we won't have anything to do with the likes of him." Sara noticed that the mention of Gavin had drawn the attention of the other passengers, and she signalled Betty to be silent. She didn't relish having to offer explanations no one would believe.

Gavin took an unsatisfying swallow of beer. He had drunk too much tonight. In fact, he had drunk too much every night. He told himself he was drinking to get over his mother's death, and because his father was an inhuman bastard, but he didn't tell himself he was drinking to forget the accusing blue eyes which haunted him whenever he was alone. That would have been too close to the truth, and he wasn't ready for the truth, not yet.

But no amount of beer could make him forget the hurt and shock in Sara's eyes, or how it had turned to fear and desolation. The only time he had been in her presence and *not* done something unforgivable was during the short ride from the church, and he knew it was that trip which had caused him to go to Sara on his wedding night instead of Clarice.

It would have been better if he'd kept to his original plan. Then he would only have to reproach himself for marrying her without regard for her feelings. And he couldn't justify what he'd done by using the argument that both his mother and father had assured him that Sara wanted the marriage. Whatever *her* reasons, *he* had married her for a coward's reasons—he could admit that now—and his conscience wouldn't let him forget it.

A crack of mirthless laughter drew curious stares.

Everyone thought he had gone straight from Sara's bed to Clarice, but that was a joke, on all three of them. All he had wanted to do was get away from the reminders of what he had done. Even when Clarice was standing on his stoop demanding entrance, he probably wouldn't have let her in if the look on her face hadn't told him that something other than desire had brought her to his door. Now he had turned his back on her, too; Sara's trim and lovely body had destroyed his taste for opulent widows.

Wouldn't his father love to know that. How did it happen the bastard was always right?

But the Earl had misjudged his son this time. He would not be part of a marriage that was a lie. Sara was welcome to live in London and enjoy the advantages of his title, as long as he could stay in Scotland, but if she wanted a divorce, he would give it to her. He saw no reason why she should be made to suffer for the rest of her life.

Gavin made a face. His mouth tasted like the outside of a fuzz ball, and he shoved his tankard away.

But Gavin still couldn't forget those haunting eyes, or escape the memory of Sara as she came down the aisle, her eyes shining with guileless love and unbounded hope. How could she be so innocent and unsuspecting? Didn't she know his title and social position weren't worth the deceit, lies, and the hurt? Or didn't she care? Her blindness had angered him, and he had let the fury flash from his eyes. It was then he had seen her happiness wither and die, like a lily cast into the fire. Her look of terror was more terrible than a shouted accusation, and he had kissed her in retaliation.

For the rest of his life, he would remember how she looked as she lay at his feet. Somehow it was worse than anything that had happened that night. It sounded inane when he put it into words, but it was a first betrayal, the first loss of innocence. He could still recall the moment that had shattered his image of his father, and the subsequent pain that had made him physically sick. He never thought anyone could be hurt as much as he had been, but the look in Sara's eyes when he released her had been one of utter desolation, and it was all his fault.

With a soul-wrenching moan, Gavin reached for his beer and drained the tankard. He didn't want it, but he didn't want to remember either.

Chapter 11

Sara and Betty's time on the coach came to an end sooner than they had anticipated. In Lancaster, more than ten miles from their destination, they found they could not pay for their ticket.

"Mayhap you can beg a ride with the Stuart Prince," the driver said derisively. "They say he's coming this way." Betty had some very sharp words to say, and she shook her fist at him with the promise of dire consequences if ever their paths should cross again, but he was not in the least sympathetic to their plight and put them out on the road, baggage and all.

The local innkeeper didn't regard them in a much kindlier light. His pocketbook had suffered from the Prince's first visit, and he wasn't looking forward to a second. True, the Highlanders had behaved well, but it was his loudly stated opinion that people who found themselves in the path of an army came off the worse for it sooner or later.

"Be off with you," he said rudely, when he found they could not pay for their accommodations, yet expected to occupy his best rooms until Gavin could come for them. "Lords and countesses!" he sniffed. "I've heard some brazen tales in my time, but none the likes of this."

Betty assumed a threatening stance, one the innkeeper eyed uneasily since she towered a full head above him, but Sara restrained her.

"Would you agree to keep our baggage until we can send for it?" she inquired with as much dignity as she could infuse into her voice. "If we don't claim it within a fortnight, you can sell it."

The innkeeper seemed disposed to refuse. He didn't want to get involved with *anybody* heading toward Scotland, but the baggage was obviously of the first quality. He stood to receive a handsome sum if he sold it, so he agreed to keep it for one week.

Sara and Betty took to the road. At first it was exhilarating; Sara had never walked through a town or the countryside, and now she was at leisure to gaze at everything they passed. The town, with its closely packed houses and cobbled streets, was soon left behind; the countryside appeared friendly in the warm sun, but it wasn't long before Sara's feet hurt and her shoulders ached from the weight of her small valise. Then it began to rain, and the cold and wet penetrated her bones. They had enough money to buy some bread and cheese at a farmhouse, but they were forced to enjoy it in the shelter of an empty barn set some distance from the road.

"We might as well sleep here," said Betty, noting that the rain had increased and the light was almost gone. Sara was sure she couldn't get a wink of sleep. She kept expecting someone to come along and throw them out, but Betty closed the door, propped a board against it, and made a bed for them in the straw.

The next day was the worst day of Sara's life. The rain was still falling when they woke, and by the time she had gone a mile, she was as wet and muddy as the road she traveled. They lunched on bread and cheese again, but as it was their third meal on the same fare, it was no longer very appetizing.

"We ought to reach my aunt's late tonight," Betty said, hoping to raise Sara's spirits.

"I don't know if I can last that long," Sara groaned, rising from the knoll where they had rested while they ate. "But if anything can keep me on my feet, it's the prospect of spending the night in a bed instead of a barn."

About an hour after lunch, they were overtaken by a small group of men. At first Sara thought they were going to join the Duke of Cumberland's army, but when they saw that several of them wore tartans, she realized they had been overtaken by the rebels themselves. This was the army of Bonny Prince Charlie.

"They *are* invading England!" Betty exclaimed.

"They're going in the same direction," Sara pointed out, "so they must be leaving." But Betty didn't seem to find any comfort in that.

The men appeared to be as downcast as Sara, and she hoped that in the gloom they would pass them by without notice. But Betty's great height attracted attention wherever they went, and from no one more readily than a group of soldiers, *none* of whom were as tall. It began with a few harmless remarks about Betty's height and some more concerning the wilted condition of the young dandy who trudged at her side. "Ignore them," Sara hissed under her breath, but when the remarks of one particular Scot, MacDonald by name, increased in abrasiveness, Betty's temper got the better of her judgement.

"Little men should be careful to play with naught but puppies." His companions' roar of laughter only served to make MacDonald angry. But Betty would not be bullied, and the increasingly spirited exchange captured the interest of more and more of his comrades until he was determined Betty should back down.

"Leave my sister alone," Sara said at last. "She suffers enough from her height without having to endure ridicule from men who should make it their duty to defend her."

"The wee dandy has a sharp tongue, too," one of the men called out. "Mayhap ye should hie tae the back until they turn off."

MacDonald might have abandoned his quarry if Sara had not spoken, but he was facing a man now, someone he could fight. His accumulated anger spilled over, and he planted himself squarely in front of Sara.

Sara didn't know what to do. She knew the male code required her to confront her challenger, but she cared nothing for a silly code formulated to guarantee a fight even when calmer thinking prevailed. She tried to walk around MacDonald, but he grabbed her by the shoulder and spun her around. Before the totally stunned gathering, Betty stepped in front of her mistress and delivered a punch to the soldier's jaw that sent him sprawling in the mud. It happened so fast MacDonald thought Sara had hit him, and he sprang to his feet, dirk in hand.

Two of his companions were quick to restrain him; it took two more to keep Betty from knocking him down again.

"Letting a wee bit o' blood sure enlivens a gloomy day," laughed one of the men, eying Sara speculatively, "but I be thinking there's a better way to amuse ourselves than carving up the bantam. He's bonnie enough, but he be the wrong sex." He ran his hand over Betty's bosom. "The lass is oversized, but a lass none the less."

"Don't you touch her," Sara commanded, suddenly so furious she forgot to lower her voice.

"Oich, are ye aiming tae stop us?" the man asked, sinister amusement glinting in his eyes.

"Yes," replied Sara, having not the faintest idea what she could do.

"Run away, get help," Betty urged, struggling so

valiantly two more Highlanders were needed to hold her. "You can do nothing alone."

"That's right, wee laddie. Run away. We'll be right here when ye return." He slipped his hand inside Betty's bosom. "I dinna foresee moving along quite yet."

A month earlier Sara would have fainted, but the last month, especially the last week, had toughened her, and she didn't consider leaving Betty for more than the second it took to realize what would happen before she could return. Without pausing to consider, she turned on Betty's assailant.

"Let her alone," she commanded, striking his hand from Betty's heaving breasts and putting herself in his path. Without so much as a pause, the soldier seized Sara by her clothes and flung her from his path. He was now more angry than MacDonald, and determined to have his pleasure.

"Mayhap we better move along, Gordie," began MacDonald, appalled at the turn of events.

"No' afore I'm done," he retorted.

"Behind ye!" someone shouted, but not before Sara had brought her sheathed sword down on Gordie's head. He staggered, but he kept his feet and turned to meet his assailant.

"I told you to leave her alone," Sara hissed, but she was firmly captured in the embrace of a handsome young Scot fully as large as Gordie, who now picked up her sword and jerked the blade from it sheath.

"If ye mean tae play with a man's weapon, me bonnie lad, ye ought tae learn how tae use it."

"I will," growled Sara, furious that she didn't know the sword was supposed to be taken out of the sheath before it was used. "I'm sorry I didn't run you through."

"No' sae fast," chuckled the handsome blond who still held her in his grip. "Wait till ye grow spurs afore ye commence ta crow."

"I'll show you my spurs," Sara flung at him, struggling with all her might to break his hold. Suddenly the laughter in her captor's eyes died, and a look of bewilderment took its place.

"There's something here that no' be right," he said. "From the feel o' him, this laddie be a lassie."

Betty had watched the soldiers' attention shift from herself to her mistress with growing alarm. Now her fear gave her the strength to break away from her bemused captors. She rushed upon the blond Scot and broke his hold on Sara before he could recover from his surprise. She knocked him down, and fell on top of him. "Run!" she urged Sara. "Get away while you can." Sara refused to leave Betty, but before she was able to do anything, she was captured by Gordie.

"Let's have a look at ye," he barked, grasping her by the hair and pulling her head back. He gazed at her closely. "I should ha known ye were too bonnie tae be a lad. Ye be worth a dozen o' the other." He impatiently ripped opened her greatcoat and tore at the lace that covered her chest. Almost at once his fingers closed on her tightly bound breasts. With a crow of triumph, he whipped about to face his comrades.

"Ye can have that long-necked quiz, but I lay claim tae this one. I'll lay ye a wager she's still a virgin."

"When my husband plunges his sword into your heart, you'll find that's one wager you've lost," Sara spat at him.

"By the time I'm done with ye, he won't want ye," laughed Gordie.

"You dare not lay a hand on a lady born and bred," disclosed Betty. "And wife of a Scottish lord into the bargain," Betty added in the pause that followed her stunning announcement.

"We'd best proceed no further," said the blond Scot, who had finally gotten from under Betty.

"Stick with your Amazon," declared Gordie, suddenly dangerously unfriendly. "This one be mine. And a mighty tempting morsel she be," he said, bringing his face close to Sara's.

"But one you'll never sample," Sara said defiantly, spitting straight in his eyes. She was almost able to break away, but he held on to her coat and both of them went down, tumbling in the mud of the road, the man determined to subdue the termagant who had excited his lust, and Sara just as determined to avoid it. The noise around them subsided quite unexpectedly, and Sara found herself being stared at in bewilderment by still another tall, handsome young man, this one astride a horse.

"Have you come to take your turn with us now that we're fairly caught?" she demanded, cold fury holding back the panic in her voice. A passageway opened and the handsome young man rode forward.

"What is the meaning of this?" he demanded.

"They be meaning to pleasure themselves upon us," Betty hotly informed him, breaking away from the men who held her and giving the one closest a resounding box on the ears for his trouble. "Her young lord will have their blood when he hears, even if they are in some foolish army."

"No maid has need of a husband to protect her from my army."

"And who are you to be talking so bold?" demanded Betty wrathfully.

"He is your true king, Charles Stuart," a young man next to the prince informed the young ladies.

"And it was my express command that no one be mistreated. Release them at once, and find me the men responsible for this outrage. I will not have my subjects terrorized by my own soldiers." For a moment there was some confusion while MacDonald and Gordie were thrust forward.

"Why should we believe a laird's wife would be traveling on foot like a common farmer?" asked the young man.

"We were trying to escape the notice of your army," snapped Sara, buttoning her coat to cover the torn lace over her bosom. Then added in a less strident tone, "And because our money was stolen. We are trying to reach the home of my maid's aunt, where we could remain until my husband is able to come for me."

"And who might your husband be?"

"Milady's husband is Lord Gavin Carlisle, son of the Earl of Parkhaven." The young man's lazy attention narrowed quite suddenly.

"I know Lord Carlisle, and he's not married," he said, coming closer and staring intently at Sara. He did not fail to notice that she wore a wedding band.

"We were married quite recently," Sara told him, suddenly embarrassed over the circumstances of her marriage. "He went off to Scotland to bury his mother, and I meant to join him. We were forced off the stage at Lancaster and had to leave our baggage."

"Then you shall travel with us," announced the Prince. "You," he said, pointing to the blond Scot, "see that her baggage is reclaimed."

"But Cumberland be behind us."

"Then see that he doesn't find you. Fraser, since you know her husband, I will leave them in your care."

Ian Fraser was off his horse and lifting Sara into the saddle before she could object. Betty soundly cuffed Gordie as a parting salutation, and hurried MacDonald on his way with the threat of similar treatment.

"There's no man alive I can't best," she announced. "Only bleeding cowards set upon a lone female like a swarm of bees."

No one disagreed with her.

They rode into Shap without further conversation, but after Fraser had garrisoned a house for Sara and had seen to it that she was comfortably situated, he went off to find the Prince. Not long afterwards he returned with their baggage.

"'Tis time ye were properly dressed," he said seriously. "Lord Carlisle wouldna want his wife tae be gawked at by an army of rough Scots."

"Then Lord Carlisle should take better care of his wife," Sara replied hotly. She hadn't intended to mention her differences with her husband to a virtual stranger, but her experiences over the last few days had destroyed the last of her reserve. She knew just how narrow was the line that separated the wife of a wealthy nobleman from an ordinary female left to the mercy of anyone strong enough to overpower her.

"I'm sorry I canna take ye directly tae Estameer," Fraser said, letting his eyes rest pleasurably on the now properly clothed Sara, "but Cumberland is at our heels, and we might have an engagement any moment now. I canna leave the Prince at such a juncture."

"Do you mean we might find ourselves in the middle of a battle?" exclaimed Sara, unable to believe the incredible things that continued to happen to her.

"No' a battle exactly," Fraser responded with a arrestingly warm masculine chuckle. "Something along the order of a fracas."

"I don't consider shooting pistols a fracas."

"Broadswords," Fraser corrected. "We Highlanders use the claymore almost exclusively."

"I don't find that any comfort, though it's certain the sword achieved no harm in *my* hands."

"Ye willna find it so with us," answered Fraser.

Sara found herself liking this man, but he couldn't compare to Gavin. None of them can, she thought, thinking of the Stuart prince and the handsome Scot who had imprisoned her arms. They might be as tall or as strong or as handsome, but her heart didn't leap when she thought of them or her pulses race when she looked upon them. Only Gavin had the power to overset her common sense; only Gavin could have caused her to undertake this insane journey.

Though she had no desire to stay with the army a minute longer than necessary, she realized it provided her with an unparalleled opportunity to study large numbers of men at close quarters. She had met very few men in her life, and her ideas had been dominated by her youthful memories of young Gavin. It hadn't taken her long to discover that men were quite a different matter from boys, regardless of how handsome and daring, and that if she was to understand her husband, she had better learn all she could about men. From the admiring look on Fraser's face, she guessed she would have ample opportunity to observe him.

She smiled to herself as she snuggled deeper into the bed. Fraser's friendliness and charm had already made one conquest.

"To my way of thinking, that young man is a proper kind of gentleman," Betty had told Sara as she prepared her for bed. "There'd be no carrying on with mistresses or dashing off to Scotland if you had *him* for your husband."

Sara steadfastly reminded herself that Gavin's rejection of their marriage had nothing to do with her, and that his rage was directed against his father. She had had plenty of time to think back on their wedding night, and she reminded herself that he *had* come to her bed, that he *had* slept with her, and that he *had* wanted to stay. Behind the bitterness and the fury there must have been some warmth of feeling for her. There *had* to be.

* * *

Sara was roused at dawn by the noise of the army readying itself to march. Men hitched horses to ammunition wagons, wheeled guns onto the road, and cooked what breakfast they could come by over open fires. It was a cold, damp morning, and the leaden sky promised more rain.

Sara and Betty hurried into their clothes, quickly swallowed the food prepared by their sullen hostess, and waited in front of the cottage for someone to come for them. But when the troops began to move away, Fraser still hadn't appeared. When it seemed they were going to be left behind, Sara ran into the road and stopped one of the wagons.

"Stand away," called the driver gruffly. "I havena room for lightskirts."

"Even a heathen Scot can tell my mistress is a lady!" Betty informed him, incensed that he should impugn Sara's character.

But the man's highland upbringing hadn't engendered any respect for the arrogant lowlanders or their proud ladies. "Ye'll have tae walk like the rest o' us, if ye want tae reach Glasgow."

"I don't mind walking if I must," said Sara, "but I can't carry these trunks."

"Then leave 'em behind. Ye can have little need for a lot o' fancy clothes." Sara planted herself in the wagon's path, prepared to block the progress of the entire army if necessary, but just then the Prince came riding briskly through the ranks, upsetting everyone and creating disorder around him on his way to the front. He pulled up next to Sara.

"Mr. Fraser has not come for us, and we have no means of reaching Penrith," she explained.

"Why have you not taken her up?" he demanded of the driver. "Put the ammunition in another wagon if you must, but make the ladies your first concern." The dour Scot was not pleased, but he could not disobey his Prince. So Sara and Betty were soon settled in the wagon and bouncing along the cut up road, much more uncomfortable than they had ever been on the stage.

It rained heavily all day. The bad roads became even worse, and tempers flared out of control. Sara was miserably cold. She huddled shivering inside her cloak, wondering how soldiers with their limbs exposed by their kilts could stand such misery. Lord George Murray, brother to the Duke of Atholl and commander of the Prince's army, went up and down the ranks shouting encouragement all during the miserable day.

But there was too much work to be done for the men to worry about the cold. The four-wheeled wagons began to mire in a road already churned up by thousands of horses and men, and before the middle of the day, the main body of the army had left the ammunition train behind.

Their progress came to a complete halt when they reached a stream where they had to make a sharp turn and climb a steep hill upon crossing. Wagon after wagon entered the stream, only to become firmly stuck. By the time Sara's wagon entered the stream, the banks were a deep morass and the men exhausted and irascible.

"Wait," she called to the driver. "We'll climb down."

"Milady, you're not going to drag your skirt through that muddy water?" exclaimed Betty, aghast.

"The wagon will never make it with us." Betty looked like she meant to argue, but the handsome blond Scot of the day before unexpectedly scooped Sara up in his arms, meaning to carry her ashore. Betty immediately blocked his path, a sword hastily snatched up from the wagon in her hands.

"I would like tae help," he offered apologetically.

"Like you helped yesterday, I suppose?" Betty growled, stabbing the sword point in his chest. "I can take care of my mistress without your help."

"But I have her already."

"You'll not have your breath if you don't put her down."

Sara felt foolish, dangling helplessly in the big man's arms, while he and Betty argued over who should carry her a distance of only a few feet.

"Put that sword down, Betty. I can't have you starting a war over me. I accept your offer and your apology," she told the Scot, "but I would much prefer to walk, even through water." However, the Scot carried Sara across the stream. It was with ill grace that Betty allowed it, and she didn't let him off without a dire warning. "Touch my mistress once more, and you'll not see Scotland again."

The little drama had momentarily obscured the fact that their wagon had become stuck in the stream. While exhausted soldiers rested against tree trunks or sank to the muddy ground, the driver whipped his tired horses to no avail. Without a word, Sara waded into the stream and put her shoulder to the wheel. Betty, loudly decrying the cruelty of a world which required such sacrifices from women, waded in after her.

That was too much for the men. Exhausted though they were, their pride would not allow women to do work they themselves could do. Silently they went into the water up to their middles; the wagon was out of the stream and up the steep incline in a matter of minutes.

"We can walk," Sara said, when the driver stopped for them to climb up again.

"Ye shall ride," commanded Lord George, coming up behind them unexpectedly. "We have no' time tae wait on ye."

They only made four miles that day. Darkness came upon them well before they reached Penrith, and they were forced to spend the night in open country in plain sight of enemy patrols. There was a farmhouse nearby, and in spite of the overt hostility of the inhabitants, Lord

George commandeered it for Sara.

"We can't take a bedroom," protested Sara.

"Ye have walked most o' the day, and ye must be exhausted," said Lord George.

"We can sleep in a barn," Sara offered heroically, but was unable to suppress a shiver at the thought.

"The men were there afore ye, and I doubt the Queen's arrival would cause them tae quit it afore morning. Ye and yer maid will take one room, and my staff will take the rest."

"I do have one request," Sara said, almost ashamed to ask for anything of this badly overworked man. "Is it possible to heat water for a bath?"

"I'll not have my girls carrying water for a damned Jacobite lightskirt," spat the farmer.

Betty stepped forward and dealt the man a ringing blow. "Take care how you speak of my mistress, or you'll be roasting over the very fire that heats her bath water. It's not for the likes of you to be questioning anything she does." Sara quickly mastered an impulse to come to the unfortunate man's defense. Betty's harsh treatment might be unwarranted, but Sara sorely wanted a bath.

The water was duly heated, and Sara was able to soak away the day's accumulation of mud and ease her aching muscles. In the soft light her pure white skin glowed like alabaster, without a single freckle to mar its perfection. Her soft blue eyes shone with contentment as Betty washed her hair. It would take some time to dry the luxuriant mass of strawberry blond tresses, but not nearly so long as when her hair was a foot longer.

Sara rose from the water and savored the luxury of having Betty pat her dry. She tried to catch a glimpse of herself in a small hand mirror, but Betty kept getting in the way. "Do you think my body is attractive?" she asked, remembering the feel of Gavin's lips on her skin.

"It's not my place to say," muttered Betty, drying her

with businesslike efficiency.

"But you must know something. *You* haven't spent your whole life within the walls of a girl's school."

"A man will take to just about any female that's prettier than his hunting dog and weighs less than a brood sow."

That was not the boost in confidence Sara was hoping for. "I mean a man like Lord Carlisle. After having lots of beautiful mistresses, wouldn't he expect more than an average female?" She looked at her trim body and pulled a face. "I'm too skinny," she said, remembering Clarice's opulent form and longing for just a few of the buxom widow's curves. "I look like a boy."

"Men don't go about choosing their wives the same way they choose their mistresses," Betty said reprovingly.

"But they must look for some of the same things in both." She didn't think she could stand it if every man needed a wife *and* a mistress. She couldn't share the man she loved with anyone, especially not a woman as beautiful as Clarice Wynburn.

"It's nothing you have to worry your head about," replied Betty, firmly ending the conversation. "You're his wife, and he has to take you the way he finds you. That's a husband's duty."

Sara allowed herself to be tucked in, but she had a feeling that however much other men might behave according to Betty's dictums, Lord Gavin Carlisle was different. Her curiosity was far from satisfied—she really wasn't sure Betty could satisfy it—but she was too exhausted to think about it anymore tonight. She drifted off to sleep and dreamed of Gavin, spurning an endless parade of voluptuous widows in favor of his slender, lissome wife.

"I don't want to see anyone, and I most particularly

don't want to see Colleen Fraser," Gavin barked at his valet. He didn't want to eat breakfast, not with his head pounding away like a piece of field artillery, but the news that Colleen had come to Estameer a second time killed what little appetite he had.

"What shall I tell the young lassie when she comes again, for ye know she will?" Lester demanded firmly, not the least bit deferential to his young lord. He remembered the day Gavin was born, and he could never bring himself to look upon him as anything but a boy.

"Tell her I've gone to Glasgow," Gavin thundered, throwing down his napkin and rising from the table, "because I have."

"Ye have no need tae travel all the way tae Glasgow, if ye're looking tae do business. Edinburgh canna be half so far."

"Where I go is none of your concern, you nosy old rascal. But for your information, I've already been to Edinburgh, and I don't like their prices. There must be more of the old man in me than I bargained for. It looks like I was born to haggle over the last penny."

But as he traveled the cold, wet roads across Scotland, he admitted it was just as well he was out of Colleen's way. He had first succumbed to her lusty ardor five summers back, but he had been at Estameer for nearly three weeks and had not had the slightest desire to quench the fires that raged in his loins in Colleen's embrace. It hadn't been necessary for him to dream about Sara every night to realize she was the only one who could satisfy the thirst which now bedeviled him, body and soul.

The more often he remembered the look on her face when he stormed out of his father's house, the more convinced he became that he had misjudged her. At the time he had been too enraged to care, but as the anger of that morning faded, a myriad of impressions began to emerge from the mist, providing him with a clear picture of his father's cold rage, the Burroughs women's incredulous disbelief, and Olivia Tate's chagrin. He didn't care about his father, and hadn't given more than a minute's thought to Olivia and the Burroughs, but he could not get Sara out of his mind.

It wasn't her shock or surprise. He'd been shocking and surprising people for years; it was their own fault if they expected something else of him. It wasn't even the hurt, though Gavin never intentionally hurt anyone who hadn't hurt him first. For the hundredth time he recalled the words he had flung at her. No, not at her—he hadn't even had the decency to speak directly to her—at his father, but meant for her. No, they *weren't* meant for her, but she thought they were, and he had done nothing to cause her to think otherwise.

It was as though some part of her, one of the intangible *somethings* that make a person an individual, had died. No, that wasn't it either. She had come face to face with something terrible, something that undermined the whole foundation of her beliefs, that literally threatened her existence, and she had drawn inward to protect herself. And he was that something.

She had come to him open and welcoming, expecting him to be the boy she remembered, and he had turned on her in a furious rage. She had somehow regained enough confidence to come to the marriage bed trusting that he would not hurt her, and he had shattered that hope as well. Then, as if that wasn't enough, he had said he didn't want her. During the day he could almost forget his infamous treatment of her, but the grinding weight of guilt seemed to grow heavier each night.

He knew he wanted her—God! His body grew rigid with desire every time he thought of her—but he felt an overwhelming need to make her hurt go away. He didn't know which he wanted to do first, or if he could do one and not the other. It was all tangled up in his mind at the moment, but it was probably too late either way. He couldn't believe he had rejected Clarice and Colleen for a skinny, virginal girl, and then abandoned her to the mercies of the Earl! "You are truly your father's son," he told himself furiously.

He cursed and dug his heels into his horse's side, driving the animal forward at a gallop.

Chapter 12

As they left Shap two days later, Sara saw troop after troop of enemy light horse on the hills beside the road, riding in pairs against the skyline.

"You think they mean to attack us?" Betty asked, her eyes wide with fear.

"I haven't the slightest idea," Sara said, not taking her own eyes off the following troops. "We never studied military tactics at Miss Adelaide's." A short time later, the sound of trumpets and kettledrums broke upon their ears so suddenly it surprised a scream of fright out of Betty. Certain that Cumberland's army would rush down in the next instant and slay them all without hesitation, Sara sat rigidly in her seat, and wondered why it had seemed important to leave London immediately. It was certainly foolhardy to continue on this ill-considered journey, when she was caught between two armies chasing each other across England.

Suddenly a man at the head of their column drew his sword and ran up the hill; he was immediately followed by others. The Highlanders arrived at the top of the hill, greatly to the consternation of a body of three hundred English light horse and chasseurs who found themselves mistaken for an army; they galloped off in haste, kettledrums and trumpets suddenly silent.

But Sara's relief was only temporary. Two miles farther on, the Macdonalds in the rear were suddenly attacked by two thousand of Cumberland's cavalry. Luckily the road was lined by thick hedges and ditches, so that the horsemen could not get round their flanks. The Macdonalds valiantly repulsed the attack with their swords, turned and ran down the road until they overtook the wagons, then turned and repulsed Cumberland's cavalry again. By constantly repeating these tactics, while the wagons before them fled as quickly as they could, the Scots came into Clifton with very little loss.

"Get the women into safe quarters and then join me," Lord George ordered Fraser. "I mean tae see how many men Cumberland has following us."

But Sara was not content to remain safely indoors. The experience of being outside with cheerful, energetic men had given her a strong distaste for a household containing a scolding housewife and two whining daughters. As there was no separate room where she and Betty could withdraw, she decided an hour's walk in the night air would be preferable to their company, and after a quick meal, she left the abode of her sullen hosts.

"You can't mean to go walking about like we were in London," Betty protested. "There are men out there with guns."

"They're to the south of town," Sara assured her. "We'll stay to the north."

What Sara couldn't know was that Lord George had taken his men out of Clifton in search of Cumberland's army, only to find four thousand of them approaching from north of the village. Lord George cunningly concealed his men behind the network of hedged enclosures along the very lane where Sara and Betty were walking.

The English couldn't get to the Highlanders because of the hedges and ditches, so five hundred of them dismounted and advanced in skirmishing order from ditch to ditch and hedge to hedge, keeping up an irregular fire. Sara and Betty found themselves caught between two advancing armies.

"Merciful Jesus!" cried Betty. "We'll be killed right here!"

"We've got to get through the hedge," Sara said, pushing her frantic maid toward the side of the road. They tumbled into the ditch and scrambled up the other side, but could find no opening in the hedge.

"We'll never push our way through without an ax," groaned Betty, giving herself up for dead.

"Keep looking," Sara whispered fiercely. "If we don't find an opening, we'll have to hide in the ditch."

"But it's full of water."

"Would you rather be wet or dead?"

But Betty wasn't required to decide whether she preferred to die of pneumonia or a musket ball. Sara found a weak place in the hedge, pushed Betty through, and followed herself just as the enemy came into view.

"There's someone behind us," Sara whispered moments later, when she heard sounds of stealthy movement through the hedges and enclosures behind them. Betty dropped to her knees and began praying, earnestly begging forgiveness for every sin she could remember committing.

"No one is going to harm us," Sara insisted. "One of those armies belongs to Lord George, and the other is supposed to defend English women."

Confident in their numbers and the superiority of their fire, and well-hidden in the wan, moonlit darkness, Lord George brought his men up to the road through the hedges behind Sara, allowing the enemy to draw closer. By now the light had faded, and the dragoons could scarcely see the sights on their muskets when the cry, "Claymore!" followed by a succession of wild yells coming from both sides of the road, warned them of a Highland charge. Jumping the hedges, swords held high in the air, the Highlanders were on top of them in a moment.

Sara couldn't stay hidden, and she squeezed back through the hedge. What she saw stunned her. This was no imaginary battle; men were being killed, swords plunged through their bodies, limbs severed from the trunk with a single swing of the broadsword. One man fell to the ground, his unprotected skull split to the teeth by a single blow. Suddenly it seemed to her that the whole world was smeared in blood.

Out of the melee Sara recognized Lord George, standing back to back with Fraser, fighting on foot. She watched fascinated as they parried sword thrusts with their targes (small, round wooden shields covered with leather) and drove their opponents back with powerful swings of their broadswords. Their alternate advances and retreats had the precision of choreographed movement; then unexpectedly one of them would vary the rhythm and a protagonist would step back with blood streaming from a fresh wound. Terrified, horrified, and fascinated, Sara watched the gory combat, the full meaning of war and what it could do to the human body coming home with crushing effect.

In that moment both Fraser and Lord George turned toward a fallen man, and Sara was jerked out of her trance by a sudden rush of a government dragoon against their unprotected backs.

"Look behind you!" she screamed, and clambered out of the hedge. She was unable to reach the dragoon, but the unexpected sight of a woman rushing out of the hedge caused him to falter. That was all Lord George and Fraser needed, and they converged on the unfortunate man.

The end came quickly. The dragoon turned to drive back a thrust from Fraser, and Lord George caught him from behind with a single, powerful swing of the broadsword. His severed head tumbled from his shoulders and rolled toward Sara. It came to a stop at her feet, his eyes still open and staring.

Sara screamed and fainted.

The Esk River separating England and Scotland was running high when they reached the border. Sara had been declared a heroine for her part in the battle outside Clifton, and the Prince had insisted that she ride with him. She appreciated the comfort of this favored position, but she was even more grateful for the companionship, which kept her mind from dwelling on the unforgettable horrors of the battle.

"Highlanders will cross a river where a horse will not," the Prince gaily informed Sara, as she watched column after column of men enter the river. Though the water rose to the men's shoulders, they crossed one hundred abreast, just as they marched, holding one another by the collars, until above two thousand were in the water at once. It was a thrilling sight, and Sara was proud to be part of such an intrepid band of men.

The Prince and all the men on horseback went in to break the force of the current, so it would not be as rapid for the soldiers on foot. Then he recrossed to escort Sara to the far side.

"We can cross on our own," Sara stated gallantly, as she watched the swirling water whip the men about like bobbing corks.

"Never will you insist, milady, if you have any feeling for my poor self," wailed Betty, petrified by the swift-running waters.

"You could cross on foot, and the water would reach

no higher than your waist," remarked the Prince, who had never accustomed himself to the size of the towering female. But before they reached the bank, the Prince caught sight of several infantry who had lost their footing and were being swept downstream towards them. He sprang forward into the river and caught one poor soldier by the hair, supporting him until he could receive assistance, then helped another to the bank. When he reentered the water to bring out a third man, the men cheered him warmly.

"The Prince and his Highlanders seem to be of the same intrepid spirit," Sara said to Fraser.

"'Tis a thousand pities his generals canna share his spirit," remarked Fraser bitterly.

But his sour mood evaporated quickly. Some of the men had waded into the water fully dressed, while others held their clothes above their heads to keep them dry. On reaching Scottish soil, the pipers began playing a reel, and all the Highlanders danced naked on the bank to dry themselves.

Sara didn't know where to look. She was surrounded on every side by an endless tide of men indulging in a display of unfettered natural exuberance. Betty was scandalized, and insisted that Sara close her eyes, but she stubbornly kept them open. It seemed foolish to be ashamed of something that thousands of men were doing without the least hint of embarrassment. Maybe that was part of the difference between men and women. Men could accept the sensual part of their nature, while so many women were determined to deny it.

Too, she found herself unconsciously comparing them to Gavin, and as always, they came off wanting. Among the thousands of men that surrounded her, there might be one who was as handsome, another with more powerful shoulders, and still another who was taller, but no one man combined all the attributes which made being held in Gavin's arms a shattering experience. In the days that had passed since she joined the army, her remembrance of Gavin had grown more vivid, and she found that nearly everything that happened made her think of him.

Sara's gaze fell upon some gaily dressed women who had preceded the army across the ford, and were now enjoying the nude dance with whoops and shrieks of delight. She didn't remember having seen them, and she was puzzled as to why they should have appeared now.

"Who are they?" she asked Fraser.

"You're never asking after *them*, milady," scolded Betty, maneuvering her horse until she had positioned herself between Sara and the women.

"But I've not seen them before. Where have they been?"

Fraser could barely contain his bottled-up amusement.

"No *lady* has any call to know of the likes of them," said Betty horrified.

"Are they respectable?" Sara asked Fraser, certain she wouldn't get an unprejudiced answer from Betty.

"I'm afraid your maid doesn't think so," he replied.

"I should say not," Betty snorted. "It is unfitting that milady should even know about them." Sara studied the women again. She, too, felt a slight sense of disgust, but there was also a flurry of excitement. These women were sought out by men because of the pleasure they gave. These were women who purported to *like* the same kind of things that men did, things that *nice* women merely endured. Memory of her own wedding night came flooding back, shorn of some of the fear and anger, and her curiosity increased.

"I would like to talk with one of them," Sara said, astounding Betty and Fraser alike.

"Milady," gasped Betty, "you would *never* disgrace yourself by passing words with those hussies!"

"If the officers deem them fit company, I don't see why I should not also," said Sara, unsure of herself, but unwilling to relinquish this chance to satisfy her curiosity.

"I think that wouldna be wise," said Fraser, agreeing with Betty. "None of the men brought along their wives."

"Then who's responsible for those women?" demanded Sara.

"Nobody has to hand around invitations to go where there's men," said Betty, condemnation in every word.

"There's never been an army without women," said Fraser with a half grin, "but the Prince willna allow them in his company." Sara reluctantly gave up the idea of being able to talk with the mysterious females, but she didn't forget them.

"It's just like men," she muttered as she turned away, "always ordering up pleasures for themselves, and then forbidding their wives to even be curious about it."

"That's because the sly beasts know they're disgusting, and want to protect you," said Betty.

"Is that the real reason?" Sara asked of Fraser.

"Pretty close," he replied, struggling not to break into a roar of laughter.

"Well, I'm not sure I believe you," she replied. "You're a man, too, and everyone of you is in league to keep your secrets to yourself. But I warn you, if there's something going on, I will find out."

"There's nothing going on with those hussies a lady would care to know," announced Betty loftily, but Sara had seen enough of men in one week to convince her that they rarely put up with anything they didn't like, particularly when all they had to do was turn their backs and walk away. There was some secret hidden from her sight, and she was sure she would have to find out what it was before she could ever understand men, particularly Gavin.

Five days later, the army halted, and the Prince went hunting in Hamilton Park. It was the custom that ladies were not included in these parties, so Sara was left on her own for the better part of a day. The Duke of Hamilton had placed his entire palace at the Prince's disposal, but there were no females present, and Sara was soon starved for company. After having wandered over the palace and rejected the only harpsichord as impossible to play, due to its being out of tune and damp to boot, she wrapped up carefully and went for a walk in the garden. She extended this to the park beyond, and it was while she was in the park that she came upon one of the women she remembered seeing at the Esk.

Sara's first impulse was to avoid such a meeting, but upon consideration, she continued her walk. This might be the only chance she would ever have to speak to one of these women, and she felt certain her future happiness depended on her understanding this woman and the attraction she had for men like Gavin.

The woman saw Sara coming and appeared to accept her hesitation, but when Sara came forward once again, unquestionably intending to meet her at the intersection of their paths, the woman became confused.

"Good day," Sara said by way of greeting. "Do you mind if I walk with you?" The woman stared at her. "I promise not to talk a great deal, but I feel the need for some company. My name is Sara Carlisle."

"Mine is Letty Brown, but 'tis no' for the likes o' me tae be talking tae ye, much less calling ye by yer Christian name."

"Well, you've got to call me something, and I would

much prefer Sara."

"Suit yourself, but don't blame me if ye get into a heap o' trouble," Letty replied. They walked in silence for a short space.

"I do think it's rather bad of the men to go off and leave us unattended," Sara said.

"They're always glad o' our company when they return," Letty replied, laughing a little too loud.

"I know, and that's what has me puzzled," Sara said, getting to the core of the issue immediately. "Why is it that men depend on their wives to run their household and raise their children, but as soon as they want a little fun, they go looking for some female their wives would blush to meet on the street?" Letty stopped in her tracks and turned to face Sara.

"What are ye doing, trying tae get me tae share confidences ye can laugh about over tea with your ladyfriends? Everybody knows men like their wives pretty, innocent, and stupid, and their ladyfriends painted, worldly, and up tae every trick in town."

"I don't have any ladyfriends, and I'm not trying to laugh at you," Sara answered. "My husband was driven away by my being just what you describe, innocent and stupid. I'm on my way to join him now, and I don't want to drive him away again. Obviously just loving him isn't enough. There must be something more." Letty stared at Sara like she couldn't credit a word she heard, then she suddenly burst out laughing.

"There's not a soul I know would believe a word o' what ye just said, even if I was tae swear it was true. Ladies don't want tae know what pleases a man."

"I do," insisted Sara. "I don't want to be married to a man who thinks of me only when he thinks of his dependents. I want to be the one he comes to when he wants to have fun."

"Ye are serious, aren't ye?" said Letty, still not sure

whether to trust Sara.

"Completely," replied Sara.

"The men I know don't want their wives tae be jolly and full of fun," said Letty after a space. "They like tae keep both parts o' their life separate, and from what their husbands say of them, the ladies are agreeable."

"But *I'm* not," insisted Sara.

"Their wives don't approve o' spirits. They turn up their noses at a little dirt and sweat, and refuse tae endure a man's amorous attention, except under the necessity o' wifely duty. Hrump!" Letty snorted. "If they'd give themselves half a chance, they might find it's no' so bad as they think."

"But is it pleasurable? I mean, do you *pretend*, just to please them?" questioned Sara.

"Are ye daft? Do ye think I would put up with traveling on a muddy road in the middle o' winter, sleeping in stinking hovels, and eating out o' a sauce pan for the sake o' a few dresses and a cheap trinket now and then?"

"Betty says women like you do."

"Then your Betty, whoever she might be . . ."

"She's my maid."

". . . is a fool. I'm as fond o' my man as any woman, no matter that our union hasna been blessed by a preacher, but I would no' set foot outside me own door tae follow him, if I dinna enjoy our little roll in the hay just as much as he does. I don't have a fondness for spirits—though there's many a lass I know that canna leave it alone—and I like a good time as well as anybody, but I can find a tankard of ale and a snug party at a dozen places back in Inverness. But tae a man, a cold bed is worse than no bed at all, and if a man doesna have his woman tae cuddle up tae, he'll find another. You can bet I willna stay home while he cavorts with some strange hussy. Now you hurry back before someone sees us. I don't think that good-looking Fraser would like it."

"Oh him," Sara said dismissing her guardian. "He takes care of me because the Prince told him to."

"The Lord knows ye need help, ma'am, but I'm no' the one tae give it. If that Fraser don't care who ye go about with, I'll lay my life that maid o' yers will throw a fit if she finds ye talking with the likes of me." Sara couldn't deny that.

"But there's so much I wanted to ask you."

"A lady like you shouldna be asking anything of me," said Letty with a kind smile. "We live in two different worlds."

"Well, my husband spends a lot of time in your world, and I'm determined to find out why. Whatever he finds there, I want him to find with me."

"If ye truly mean that, ye are one in a thousand," said Letty. "Why don't ye ask him what he wants? He'll probably be shocked, but he just might tell ye. Now ye must go. I hear the hunt returning."

Sara would have continued their talk despite the sound of approaching riders, but Letty turned off the path. She had barely disappeared into the wood when a troop of about thirty horsemen topped a rise a short distance away, and Sara recognized the Prince at their head.

There was much celebration of the hunt that evening, and many stories to be told, so it was several hours before Sara found the solitude to reflect on what she'd heard that afternoon, but she committed it all to memory. She didn't want to forget a single word. It was possible that something Letty said might hold the key to her future.

Chapter 13

The Prince entered Glasgow, a town of more than thirty thousand, on the twenty-sixth of December. Sara rode a little way behind, with Betty on one side and Ian Fraser on the other.

Glasgow was a town of cozy homes and lofty spires, framed in green meadows, and wealthy if not well-bred citizens who viewed the Prince's army with disgust. They jammed the street up to five and six deep on either side, but not one of them *uttered a single sound!* The army rolled through the town in dishevelled plaids and carrying the grime which accompanies any army on the march. They looked more like savages than soldiers, and appalled the fat Glasgow merchants and their self-satisfied wives.

At the very same moment, unbeknownst to Sara, Gavin, deep in thought and quite impatient with the crowds that blocked his path, was making his way to the home of a man he hoped would mine the coal that lay buried under his Scottish acres. The street was tightly packed with spectators, rich and poor alike, and not even for a horse would they give up their positions. From his vantage point in the saddle, he could see over the impenetrable crowds to the seemingly endless columns of kilted clansmen marching to the sound of pipes. He had just about decided it would be quicker to circle the town, when his attention was caught by two women riding close behind the Prince. The party had come to a halt before the imposing mansion of a Mr. Glassford—a man who had made his fortune in colonial trade—and was preparing to dismount.

What foolish creatures they are to ride openly at the Prince's side in a Whig city, he thought to himself. There won't be a respectable house that will open its door to them. But no sooner had the thought crossed his mind, than he sat up rigid in the saddle, his eyes starting from his head, his gaze fixed on the face of the smaller female who had just been helped down from the saddle; the female riding with brazen nonchalance at the Prince's side was Sara, *his wife.*

All thoughts of coal and mining costs were cast from his mind. Sliding from the saddle and giving the reins of his horse to a boy nearby, Gavin began to push his way through the throng that lined the street.

Though he had thought about Sara continually, he had never envisioned her in Scotland—it somehow seemed an invasion of his private domain—but now that she was here, he experienced a tremor of excitement, of anticipation. *Why* was she here? That question teased his wits until they were in a frenzy of perplexity. Had she come with his father? Had she come alone, and if so, had she followed him? But if that was true, and he could hardly allow himself to believe it was, what was she doing with the Prince's army? And what was she doing on the opposite side of Scotland from Estameer?

Gavin tried to sort through the emotions that clamored for his attention. He had no trouble identifying and understanding the immediate physical response to her presence. His body's need of her had continued to grow during these long weeks, and seeing her suddenly appear within reach sent his senses into chaos. As much as Gavin had been aware of his growing fascination with Sara, he was dismayed at the magnitude of his response to her presence. Only now did he realize how utterly uninterested he was in Clarice, Colleen, or any other woman who wasn't Sara.

But when he got to his emotional response to her presence, he lost his way. It seemed that the entire cabinet of his emotions had been emptied out into the Glaswegian streets, and every one of them was clamoring for his attention. Anger, frustration, irritation he could understand. But joy! He was acting like he was about to meet an old love after a long separation, not a woman who was a virtual stranger and had married him for his social position.

He realized he was becoming excited at the thought of being with her again, of holding her in his arms, and he told himself not to be a fool. She was no more experienced or sophisticated than she had been on their wedding day; things would be no different. They might even be worse, but still he pushed ahead vigorously, drawn by a kind of jealous possessiveness he did not yet understand.

But as he elbowed his way through the throng, Gavin became angry that she could have been so foolish, so completely without understanding of the rules and customs of war, as to be seen in the company of the Scottish rebels. But even more disastrous, it looked as if—even if it should somehow mercifully prove to be untrue—she had been traveling with the army. Setting aside the fact that having it known that his wife was a sympathizer of the Stuart Prince could endanger his life—if one *could* set aside such a consideration as that—didn't she realize what it would do to her reputation? Mercifully, Glasgow was miles away from Estameer and Edinburgh, and even farther from London. If she were fortunate, no one would ever hear of her mad escapade, but he had to remove her from the Prince's company, before he could introduce her to a Glaswegian merchant who just might happen to be doing business with his father.

"Have a heart!" "Find yer own place!" "Why does every big bleeder think he has the right tae step on us little people!" were but a few of the comments thrown at him as he rudely elbowed his way through the onlookers. Had he had time to think about it, Gavin would have remembered that he had never been good with words, that he was more likely to rub a person's feelings the wrong way by his terse replies than by his impolite silence, but even he was taken aback by the thoughtlessness of his first sentence. He would not have spoken to his mistress like that. Why did he do it to Sara?

"What the hell are you doing here?" he demanded, coming upon her so unexpectedly she uttered a gasp of fright.

Sara's heart leapt within her when she realized Gavin stood before her. Her memory had not lied; he *did* exceed every other man in the charms most likely to cause any resisting female heart to crumble. If there had been any remaining doubt as to why she had undertaken the perilous journey from London, it was gone now. Her heart beat so rapidly she was unable to form the words that rose to her lips, and her stupefied silence led Gavin into the error of believing she was speechless with contrition.

"You're supposed to be waiting for me in London, not following a ragtag army through the streets like a common doxy," he said, as he reached out and took her by the arm. "Come on. I'll have you on your way back to London in the first coach I can hire."

Sara came out of her daze with a jolt. It had taken his threat to send her back to London to break her trance, but now his other remarks also registered. His immediate, thoughtless censure overshadowed all her joy in their reunion, and she was instantaneously vibrant with cold anger. She would not be run roughshod over again, not by him or anyone else. She had come all this way in search of him, but she had not come crawling on her belly. She had come with shoulders squared and head erect, determined to fight for what she wanted.

"Let me go," said Sara, wrenching her elbow from his grip. "You have no right to send me anywhere."

"As your husband, I have every right."

"'Twould be a good idea for ye tae reconsider," suggested Ian Fraser, facing his old friend with a look that contained no sign of friendly greeting.

"Ian! I might have known you'd be up to your neck in this bloody mess, but did you have to drag my wife along with you as well?"

"He didn't drag me anywhere. In fact, he's done everything he could to insure that I received the kind of treatment that benefits *your* rank and station."

"We are waiting for you to join us," said the Prince, breaking into the circle gathered around Sara. He noticed Gavin and frowned. "Who is this man?"

Sara answered before Ian could reply. All the hurt and fury from her wedding night, of being left in London, of being forced to undertake a journey by herself, rushed to the surface. She would show him she was no longer a helpless, timid female, waiting quietly in a corner until he wanted her.

"I can not tell you, Sire, since he failed to introduce himself. However, it's clear he is possessed of Whig leanings and seems to have an unusual knowledge of the persons on your staff. I would never presume to instruct your Majesty, but it might not come amiss if he were detained until it could be determined how much he knows, where he gathered the information, and whether or not he might be injurious to your Majesty's cause."

The Prince had not actually heard their exchange, but he had seen enough to know that Gavin was no stranger to Sara or Ian Fraser. He glanced inquiringly at Ian who, after an initial moment of startled surprise, was clearly trying to conceal his amusement. When Ian winked at him, he was sure the man was not unknown to Sara.

"It's not my custom to imprison my subjects, even those who are so misguided as to support the Hanoverian usurper." Sara bowed her head in acceptance. "But since he has had the temerity to accost you in public, I would not feel comfortable leaving him to roam at large. Fraser, see that this man—who are you anyway?"

"I am Lord Gavin Carlisle of Estameer, and my father is the Earl of Parkhaven," Gavin announced in a clear, ringing voice. The Prince's gaze became extremely alert at the sound of that name.

"An aristocratic Whig is always dangerous, Fraser. See that he is closely guarded, but otherwise at his leisure. Now milady, if you are ready," the Prince said, offering Sara his arm. Sara cast Gavin a smile that succeeded in combining elements of triumph and regret, before ascending the steps to the house on the Prince's arm.

"I'll horsewhip her!" exclaimed Gavin. The smile on Ian's face froze.

"Ye shouldna say that in the presence o' the Prince, if ye cherish yer freedom."

"Don't act like an idiot," Gavin said wrathfully. "I might horsewhip my father for letting her run off unattended, I assume that my father is not also with the prince"—Ian shook his head—"but you know I wouldn't touch a female. You aren't actually going to detain me, are you?"

"Aye," grinned Ian. "A man who would publicly greet his wife like she was a servant, is in need of much time tae reconsider the wisdom o' his actions." Gavin stared incredulously at his friend.

"Even you must be aware that it can't become known that she has traveled with this army, or any other. It'll ruin her."

"Sara will be every bit a lady no matter where she be," said Ian, glaring peremptorily at his friend.

"Her name is Lady Carlisle," Gavin said stonily.

"Lord George says she saved his life," Fraser continued without pause. "And after more than a week o' her company, there isn't a single Highlander who doesna praise her courage and good cheer."

Gavin could only stare. This was a Sara he did not know, didn't even suspect, doubted could exist, but if she could capture the friendship of the Prince, and turn his own friend against him in less than ten days, there had to be more to her than the trembling young innocent he had seen.

"Ye can take me tae yer lodgings," Ian suggested. "It will ease matters if I bide with ye."

"You impudent dog," Gavin said with a laugh. "You dare to stand between me and my wife, and then you want to take my bed. Some friend you turned out to be."

"I'll always be yer friend, even though I canna share yer politics," Ian responded a little stiffly. "Now ye had better begin by telling me what ye have been up tae in Glasgow. It's a long way from Estameer, and the Prince will be wanting tae know why ye are here."

"Your damned pretend Prince had better concern himself with getting his hide out of England in one piece," snapped Gavin, a little of his friendliness wearing off.

"We left England quite at our leisure, thank you," replied Ian coldly.

"You know what I mean, and you might give some thought to your own safety."

"Ye seem tae forget that I am the one supposed tae ask the questions."

"All right, damn you," cursed Gavin, as he remounted his horse. "I'm here to see about mining the coal at Estameer. That, at least, is one thing I can do without my father's interference."

"And?"

"And nothing. I brought my mother home to bury her . . ."

"Oich, I'm sorry," Ian said, genuine sympathy thawing his reserve at once. "I know ye had a great fondness for the Countess."

"It's better this way." Gavin didn't want to talk about his mother. The wound was too fresh and too deep. "I told my father about the coal years ago, but he was sure nothing could make money except his trading. But Estameer's mine now, and I'm going to grub every piece of coal out of the ground. You know how miserably poor our people are. They need food, not war or a different king. This coal will bring enough prosperity to the estate that they won't have to raid their neighbors' herds to get a full belly."

"I dinna know ye had an interest in anything except horses and women, and no' in that order," observed Ian in cynical surprise.

"My father always kept everything in his hands, but the land is mine now, so you can see why I've got to send my wife back to London. With this war and all the work that must be done, I won't have time to see to her amusement."

"They why did ye marry her?"

Gavin's eyes blazed. "That's none of your damned business, Ian Fraser, and you know it. All you need to know is she was quite willing to become my wife."

"But where does being your wife leave Sara?"

"I intend to send *Lady Carlisle* back to London. She

knows nothing of country life. She'd be lost in Scotland."

"Don't ye want an heir?"

"What the hell kind of inquisition is this? Or do you think being fool enough to risk hanging for treason gives you the right to pry in my life?"

"I'm only interested in yer welfare, and that of yer wife," Ian answered, and his sincerity was so obvious Gavin felt ashamed of his outburst.

"I don't want anything or anybody to tie me down or get their claws into me." Gavin paused briefly. His voice was softer when he spoke again, but the layer of bitterness and self-scorn was deep. "Mother and I used to idolize Father. There was no good reason I guess, we just did. Anyway, he made her life a hell and nearly destroyed mine. I don't want anyone to ever have that much power over me again."

"I do no' think Sara wants tae do that tae ye."

"Dammit, man, you've no business calling my wife by her Christian name. I could call you out for that."

"I see ye still havena learned moderation," Ian said, but his eyes twinkled.

"You're supposed to lock me up, not preach to me," said Gavin sharply.

"From what she tells me, I've spent more time in Sara's company than ye have . . ."

"Ian!"

"Oich, all right, *Lady Carlisle's* company then, and I dinna think ye know her very well. She's a very resourceful lady and pluck tae the backbone."

"Then tell me how she got mixed up with this traveling troop of comedy actors?" All the friendliness in Ian's face vanished.

"'Tis better ye ask yourself what kind o' man she has married, that she should be abandoned by her husband and father-in-law, that she should have tae travel this far on her own."

"She married my title and social position." Ian studied the bitter look on Gavin's face.

"'Tis a good thing I became yer friend years ago. I do no' think I like ye now."

"You don't know me anymore."

"Nay, and I don't think I want tae." He paused. "Don't underestimate yer wife. Ye may wait too late tae discover what ye have thrown away."

"You dare to offer me advice about females?" Gavin asked in rough contempt.

"About females? Never," smiled Ian. "Ye be the expert there. I'm offering ye advice about ladies, especially yer wife. I don't think ye know anything at all about them."

"If you're through trying to tell me how much your opinion of me has deteriorated, then tell me when I shall be allowed to regain possession of my wife."

"Oich, I don't think there is any question of yer ever being allowed to *regain possession* of Lady Carlisle. I should think the most ye can hope for is tae be granted an audience of a few minutes."

"You can't keep me from my own wife," thundered Gavin angrily.

"I would never do such a thing," said Ian smoothly, "but the Prince has grown quite fond o' Lady Carlisle, and he was quite put out with yer treatment o' her this morning. He will be the one tae decide when, and if, ye can see her."

"This is intolerable. It's unlawful as well."

"What more can ye expect from a lawless rabble? Or was it 'comedy actors'?"

The Prince decided to stay in Glasgow, partly to obtain clothes and shoes for his now ragged army, and partly to punish its citizens for showing so much zeal in raising a militia regiment for the government and outfitting it at their own expense. He sent them a demand for six thousand cloth short coats, twelve thousand linen shirts, six thousand pairs of shoes, six thousand bonnets, and six thousand tartan hose and blue bonnets, in addition to fifty-five-hundred pounds sterling.

Glasgow had grown rich through trade in sugar and tobacco with the West Indies and the American colonies and could easily afford to pay, but this further demand on their pockets angered the citizens, particularly since the regiment they had outfitted had been withdrawn by Cumberland for the defense of Edinburgh, but fear of looting made them yield to all the Prince's demands.

Charles made a special effort to win over the Glaswegians. He took care to be elegantly dressed for his public appearances, and showed himself abroad four or five times without getting so much as the doffing of a cap from the meanest inhabitant. Twice a day he dined in public, accompanied by any ladies who would come, but most were from the narrow circle of Jacobite families who lived outside the city. It was at one of these dinners that Gavin was finally allowed to speak with Sara.

She saw him the moment he stepped through the arch into the great hall that served as the Prince's dining room. She felt herself swell with pride which could not be destroyed by the lingering anger she still felt toward him. It was impossible not to feel pleased when his appearance made everyone else—including the Prince who was himself over six feet tall and very handsome—pale by comparison.

"I see Fraser has brought your husband to dine with us," the Prince commented, following the direction of her gaze.

"My husband?" she faltered.

"I have not forgotten your title, nor did I miss the

manner in which you greeted each other. You might not be friends, but you are not strangers." Sara looked abashed, but the Prince smiled.

"I could not be unaware of the rough manner in which he used you. The man is a Whig and a fool not to value a wife such as you. Use him as you please. His imprisonment shall continue until you desire its end." Sara was almost too overcome to speak, but the Prince turned to some other guests, and she recovered her composure.

Ian brought Gavin to Sara. "Allow me to introduce Gavin Carlisle," he said with a grin. "He says he knows ye."

"It's *Lord* Carlisle, dammit, and she's my wife," Gavin said savagely. Gavin had meant to guard his tongue, but having to wait until it suited the Prince before he was allowed to join his wife, and then being introduced in an inconsequential way, rubbed his already bruised spirits, and his temper flared. Unfortunately, his inner devil prompted him to add, "You might even say I'm her lord and master."

"And I would reply as the Scots do," answered Sara, stung. "My Lord is in heaven. As for a master, I have none."

"Do you deny that we are married?" Gavin asked, realizing he had gone too far, but being too stubborn to admit it in front of Ian.

"I recall the making of quite a few promises, but as none of yours were kept, I saw no reason to be bound by mine."

Gavin made a tremendous effort and pulled his temper under control. Ian was grinning, just waiting for him to make another mistake. "I hoped you would wait in London until I returned."

"That's not the impression you gave me. As you

shouted at your father, and I repeat the exact words, *You wanted her, you can have her.* Well, he didn't want me either, so I suppose I belong to no one but myself now."

Gavin's instinctive response was to shout something rude and explosive, but he was certain they would be overheard, and he bit his tongue. No matter how angry he was, he would not admit perfect strangers into a knowledge of his innermost feelings. Also, Sara had caught him fair and square, and they both knew it. "You can't ignore our marriage contract," he replied with lowered voice.

"I think the Prince might be persuaded to set that aside. Since you're a Whig and a cousin to Cumberland's second in command, he might even decide you're too dangerous to live, and hang you."

Both Gavin and Ian's eyes grew large. "What do you mean, my cousin is Cumberland's second in command?"

"Your father told me just before he abandoned me. Oh dear, I hope the Prince doesn't find out," Sara said with spurious sympathy. "That would undoubtedly make your position more difficult."

Ian could not stifle the laughter that bubbled from his throat. An eruption of an entirely different sort threatened to explode from Gavin.

"I think ye must admit that Sara—I mean Lady Carlisle—has the upper hand," said Ian. "Whatever her political leanings, the Prince will allow her the freedom tae do as she will. Ye, on the other hand, are a prisoner, at least for the present. And if I told him about yer cousin—" Ian laughed again. "Well, 'tis no' exactly a position o' strength."

"Thank you, wife," growled Gavin.

"Maybe you'll take more care how you greet me next time," Sara replied spiritedly.

"I just said I thought you'd—"

"You're free to think what you wish," Sara interrupted, "but not to shout it at me, especially in the street, and *most* especially you are not to call me names."

"I didn't call you names."

"Am I to believe that *doxy* is a term you would have used for your mother?"

"If I dinna know ye were an only child, Gavin, I'd swear ye were fighting with yer sister," said Lord George coming up behind him. "Ye sound like two puppies squabbling over a bone."

"I should have known I'd find you here," said Gavin, shaking his head at a man who'd been his neighbor his whole life.

"Aye, ye should. Me family has always been loyal tae the Stuarts."

"What's your rank this time?"

"Lord George is Lieutenant-General in command of the whole army," said Sara.

"And the reason for our success so far," added Ian.

"That honor must be shared with the Prince," said Lord George diplomatically. "I would never have dared so much without his inspiration."

"You're all out of your minds," declared Gavin. "Do you seriously think those fat English merchants are going to hand the country over to a Catholic Stuart, after already fighting two wars to prevent it? You're living a fantasy."

"They havena stopped us yet," Lord George pointed out.

"They will soon. Hell, Cumberland can throw fifty thousand troops at you. How many men do you have? Five thousand?"

"We have enough."

"Where will they come from? The English won't rise for you, you've seen that already, and neither will lowland Scotland, even if they agreed with you. And when Cumberland does defeat you, he'll make you pay with your blood. I know him well, and he's not a pleasant fellow."

"I forgot, he's a horse breeder, isn't he?"

"And a damned good one, but that won't make any difference."

"The young lord doesn't seem to think much of our cause," said the Prince, coming up to claim Sara's company during dinner. "Why don't you give him a full account of our successes so far, Fraser. Then perhaps he will regard us with more respect." He turned from Gavin to Sara. "I hope you will honor me with your company, milady."

"I forbid her to parade about Glasgow on your arm," snapped Gavin.

Sara had wavered, wanting a chance to talk to Gavin alone, but his words made up her mind. "I'll be honored, your Majesty, unless you would prefer one of the local beauties. They've come just to see you."

"They come at their own convenience," answered the Prince sharply. "You are faithful at all times."

"I forbid it, I tell you," Gavin repeated, starting forward. The Prince stepped between him and Sara.

"I think it's time Lord Carlisle returned to his rooms," he said, before calmly escorting Sara to her place at the table.

"Ye never learn, do ye?" demanded Ian in disgust. "A wee bit more, and ye may *really* be a prisoner."

"You're only holding me because of Sara."

"Then take care no' to give the Prince reason tae hold ye on yer own. If ye don't treat yer wife with more respect, she may consider it good riddance tae bad rubbish. She will no' be taken for granted."

"You sound like you're in love with her."

"Then listen well, for 'tis how *you* should sound."

Chapter 14

Sara stood next to the Prince as he greeted his guests, but she had already forgotten the names of the more than two dozen people she'd been introduced to in the last half hour. She kept looking for Gavin, but he was nowhere in sight, and her interest in the ball had faded to almost nothing.

She had refused to communicate with Gavin for two days, and she wasn't sure but what she had been the one to suffer the most. She had returned his messages unopened and refused his requests to see her, but he had occupied her thoughts to the exclusion of all else. After the exhaustion of the march, she had been looking forward to a period of rest when they reached Glasgow, but oddly enough she didn't feel tired. Quite the reverse; she was brimming with energy, and time hung heavily on her hands.

She was keyed up, knowing that Gavin was just a few streets away, and all she had to do was ask and he would be brought to her. The feeling of power was wonderful, and it was all she could do not to use it, but she forced herself to wait. She wanted Gavin to come to her on his own, not be dragged from his room by a pair of burly Highlanders.

She hated to admit it, but his rude welcome hadn't made a bit of difference in her feelings for him; she loved him just as much as ever. But why should that surprise her? She had adored him when he was a boy, and he had been unkind to her even then. She was still angry with him, but one apologetic word would have sent her tumbling into his arms, begging for his forgiveness. But he hadn't spoken that word, and she refused to tumble before she was asked. She might be his wife, but she wasn't his slave, and he would have to learn that if he wanted his freedom.

"Do ye think ye could spare Lady Carlisle for a few moments?" Ian Fraser asked, coming up to the Prince. "I have someone who urgently begs the favor o' her company." Ian winked at the Prince, but Sara didn't need that wink to know that Ian was talking about Gavin, and her heart beat a little faster.

"Lady Carlisle is free to do as she pleases," the Prince replied graciously.

"Did Gavin really ask for the *favor* of my company?" Sara asked, as Ian guided her through the crowd.

"I canna recall if those were his exact words," he admitted with a beguiling smile, "but 'tis what he meant."

"I didn't think he had," replied Sara with a sigh of resignation. "And please don't tell me what he *did* say. I don't want to feel like flinging him under a runaway coach before I even speak to him." Sara didn't feel any more hopeful when she at last saw Gavin. That he was making an attempt to keep his temper in check was obvious. That the task was proving a great strain on his self-control was just as obvious.

"I brought her as ye requested," said Ian, without his usual smile, and immediately left them alone.

"I'm glad you could spare a few moments," Gavin said. greeting Sara quite formally.

That wasn't a very good sign, but she hoped he would become more friendly now that Ian was out of sight.

"I didn't mind being excused from the reception line. Those people are the Prince's friends, not mine."

"Then you shouldn't be here," Gavin said with suppressed wrath, unable to keep his tongue between his teeth.

"We've already touched on that subject," Sara said rather impatiently.

Gavin struggled visibly to restrain himself from uttering the blistering words that rose to his lips. "Why do you refuse to let me explain why I think you ought to go back to London?"

"As I recall, all you have done is shout orders at me. That virtually eliminates the possibility of any kind of explanation."

"You haven't given me much of a chance. I haven't been allowed to so much as set eyes on you for two days."

"You had more of a chance than I had on our wedding night." Involuntarily Sara turned crimson at the memory of that evening. She hadn't meant to mention it, but it just came out, along with the pent-up anger she had been saving for nearly a month. "You knew I was scared. And you were drunk."

"My friends toasted us," Gavin replied self-consciously. "I couldn't refuse to drink with them." Nor did you try, he reminded himself.

"You knew I was inexperienced," Sara continued, ignoring his excuse. "I told you so. Yet you treated me with great roughness."

"Every woman should know more than you did."

"Maybe the women you're accustomed to consorting with do," snapped Sara, "but I don't keep such company."

"Are you blaming me for your ignorance?" Sara was making him feel more guilty than he already did, and that made him angry.

"Not for my ignorance, but certainly for treating that ignorance as something for which I should be humiliated and punished."

"I told you what I was going to do."

"*As you were doing it!* Maybe you've forgotten your first time—possibly it is too far in the past—but to have your modesty stripped away and your privacy invaded in the space of ten minutes is a staggering experience."

Gavin did remember his own first time, and had the honesty to admit that Sara's words contained some truth.

"Then, to be attacked like I was an enemy, someone you didn't like in the least, made it all the worse."

"I didn't attack you," protested Gavin, his ire flaring instantly.

"Time doesn't seem to have calmed the rough waters that lie between you." The two combatants hadn't heard the Prince come up. "It's probably best that I've come to beg Lady Carlisle to help me begin the dancing." Sara looked a little embarrassed, but Gavin's face reflected only anger and vexation.

"You've done nothing but interfere between my wife and me since she reached Glasgow," he growled.

"Since it was my protection which enabled her to reach Glasgow in safety and some degree of dignity, I see it merely as a continuation of my role."

"She doesn't need your protection any longer. I'm here."

"I would say that she seems to need it more than ever. Would you favor me with the first dance, Lady Carlisle? You may continue your discussion with your husband if you wish, but I must ask you to see that it does not turn into a brawl."

"I would be honored. If you will excuse us?" she said, turning to Gavin.

"Do I have any choice?" he asked very ungallantly.

"No, I don't think you do," said the Prince with a pleasant smile, as he led Sara toward the head of the set that was forming.

"I hope ye do no' aspire tae become a diplomat," Ian observed caustically, as he stepped from behind a statue. "Ye are certain tae plunge the whole world into war inside a month."

"Oh, go to Hell!" exploded Gavin and stormed out of the hall.

It was two hours before Gavin was able to see Sara again, and then it was only for a country dance.

Even though Sara had received instruction from the best dance masters in London, she was only a moderate dancer, and since this was her first ball, she felt tense and unsure of herself. Gavin, on the other hand, was a natural athlete, and danced as though he were born to it. The movements of the dance kept them apart too often to permit rational conversation, but as soon as the last notes sounded, Gavin led her to a chair in an alcove, brought her some wine punch, and, directing a murderous glare at everyone who passed, dared anyone to join them.

"You never did tell me how you came to be in the west of England," he said, as politely as he could.

"You never stopped arguing long enough to ask me." Gavin's brow darkened. "Forgive me, I shouldn't have said that," Sara said, realizing it was pointless for them to continue finding fault with one another. If they were ever to begin a rapprochement, both of them would have to forget their wrongs.

"When your father said he was going to close the house, I had no choice but to follow you or go back to Miss Adelaide. I chose Scotland."

"But where did my father go?"

"You mean you haven't seen him?"

"No. Why should I?"

"He said he was going to join Cumberland, when he

came north to put down the rebellion."

"Something's wrong," Gavin said puzzled. "He's not at Estameer, and I doubt he's at Lochknole. The old bastard is up to something. He *never* makes a move without a purpose, and he never has any purpose except making money. Why didn't you hire a post chaise?" he asked abruptly, his thoughts returning to Sara.

"I don't have any money. All the income goes to your father."

"But he couldn't have left without giving you a considerable sum to live on."

"He offered to let me stay in the house with the caretaker."

"I know my father thinks of little else besides the making of money, but I've never known him to be so mean about its spending."

"He offered to give me an allowance of one hundred pounds a quarter starting with the new year, but I couldn't wait a month."

"Does he know where you are?"

"No."

Once more the Prince interrupted them. "Lady Carlisle, I have someone I most particularly want you to meet. She's a friend from my childhood in Rome." A tall, thin young woman stood at the Prince's side. Roughly the same age as the prince, she was attractive without being beautiful, with dark, hypnotic eyes. The Prince looked at her with obvious fondness, and the young lady smiled shyly.

"This is Clementina Walkinshaw," the Prince said. "She and I played together fifteen years ago."

"Twenty to be precise," said the young woman in a soft, deep voice. Clementina Walkinshaw was one of the Walkinshaws of Barrowfield, a family of strong Jacobite tradition, and it was obvious from the look in Clementina's eyes that she carried on the family tradition.

"You'll have to allow me to introduce you to some of the ladies of Glasgow," Clementina said to Sara. "It's not good for anyone to be exclusively in male company for very long."

"Why is that?" asked the Prince, displaying the first interest in a female that Sara had noticed.

"Everyone knows that men are terribly rough creatures. If a lady were to stay in your company for too long, she might begin to imitate your ways."

"Lady Carlisle already behaves quite differently from when she was in London," Gavin observed.

"Then I must take her away at once," laughed Clementina, and led Sara over to a group of young women, surrounded by a larger group of young men.

"I trust you had time to try and persuade your wife to your point of view."

"You interrupted before I had barely begun."

"I do apologize, but Lady Carlisle is much in demand. Now if you will excuse me, I must attend to my other guests."

The Prince left Gavin fuming.

Gavin spent the remainder of the evening trying to separate Sara from the press of people who wanted to dance with her, or meet the intrepid lady who had the courage to travel with the Prince and his army and win his unqualified approval. So great was her popularity that he was unable to speak to Sara alone, until the ball was almost over.

"If I ever get you back to London, I vow I'll not have to wait the entire evening just to be able to conduct an uninterrupted conversation with my own wife."

"Everyone is going home now. We can be free of interference."

"Hell and damnation," exploded Gavin. "Here comes your guardian angel. I will not be interrupted by him again, or be subjected to his sly insults. Good night, my wife, and maybe some day we will meet without every man in Scotland feeling he has more right to your attention than I do." He executed a quick, angry bow, and stalked off just as the Prince was coming up.

"Does he wish to go to bed so early?" inquired the Prince.

"He was upset at being interrupted again," Sara told him, trying to hide her own vexation at the Prince's constant attention, just when she would have liked to be forgotten for a few hours.

"But I was just coming to offer you both the use of the library. A pity, but there will be another day. Are you tired?"

"Yes. Are you pleased with the ball?"

"I'm afraid the evening has not been entirely successful. The ladies have unbent toward me, but their husbands are as adamant as before about adhering to their allegiance to the German."

"Maybe they fear Cumberland's vengeance."

"They don't care who sits on the throne as long as their ships continue to sail and their profits continue to grow." He breathed a sigh. "So different from their highland cousins." Sara could think of nothing to answer this, and they talked of other things until they parted for the night.

The cold, blustery wind whipped across the green with telling force, but the soldiers gathered in the open seemed oblivious to its icy coldness. The bright sun added to the festivity of the occasion, and the men milled about, too cold to stand still, too active to want to. Charles Stuart was reviewing his troops, and it seemed that all of Glasgow had come out to watch. The Highlanders were determined to make a good impression on the Glaswegian merchant princes, who had so little in common with their blood brothers from the hills.

At some distance away, Gavin sat astride his horse, impatiently awaiting Sara's arrival. He had not seen her since the night of the Prince's ball. Again she had refused to grant him any interview, and he had been reduced to the galling position of having to send polite notes through Ian, requesting that she take time from her growing friendship with Clementina Walkinshaw to see him. It was a new and unpleasant experience to have to repeatedly ask for a woman's time. It was an almost intolerable one when she continued to refuse him.

"'Tis good for ye tae be ignored," Ian had told him. "Yer women should have done it years ago. And they would have, too, if ye weren't always taking up with females so far below yer station they were overcome tae have an Earl's son showing them attention. But then, I hear that decent girls' parents lock them up when they see ye lurking about."

That was only one of several times that Gavin was sorely tempted to knock his old friend to the ground.

"She's agreed tae see ye, but only at the review."

"That's in the open. I can hardly discuss anything of a personal nature there."

"She suggested a private interview, but I vetoed it," Ian said coolly. For a moment, Ian thought Gavin *was* going to knock him down, but he contented himself with grabbing Ian by the throat and almost choking the life out of him.

"You Judas, you sneaking traitor," Gavin snarled when he decided to allow Ian to breath again. "I thought you were my friend."

"I am yer friend, at least I used to be," Ian said loosening his collar, "but I like yer wife better."

"You're not supposed to like my wife," growled Gavin.

"Why not? Ye don't, and the poor lassie needs some friends in this world."

"I *do* like her," Gavin protested, startled at the vehemence in his voice. "After all, I married her," he said sounding rather shaken.

"Ye will never get anybody to believe it from the way ye act tae her. 'Tis the reason I insisted she meet ye in public. At least if ye start tae shout, we can have ye back in jail before ye strike her."

"I'd never hit her!"

"Ye wouldn't live if ye tried." The two men's eyes locked. "Half the army would be ready tae cut ye tae pieces." Gavin entertained no doubts as to his old friend's feelings either.

"My wife seems to have acquired quite a new personality since I married her. I suppose I shall have to get to know her again."

"I doubt ye ever did know her," said Ian, but his eyes softened. "For years ye have been too angry tae pay attention tae anyone but yourself."

"I had reason."

"I suppose you did, but it shouldna be allowed tae destroy the rest o' yer life."

Gavin paused. "You wouldn't understand," he said, turning away.

"Maybe not, but then I could never understand anyone who would give up." Gavin's eyes blazed dangerously, but before he could assault Ian again, Sara came up accompanied by the Prince.

"Lady Carlisle tells me she is unable to review the troops with me, because she has to meet her husband. I suppose you do have a superior claim to her time, but it's rather hard on the rest of us." He turned to Ian. "If they fall into their usual imbroglio, bring her to me immediately. They can argue at any time." Sara looked embarrassed; Gavin held his tongue.

"Why wouldn't you see me?" he asked, when Ian and the Prince had gone.

"There didn't seem to be any point."

"Wasn't the fact that I'm your husband enough reason?"

"No."

"You didn't think that when we were married."

"That's true, but I was under several other misapprehensions then. Besides, both you and your father were too busy issuing ultimatums to listen to anything I might have said."

"Why did you marry me?"

"I wanted to."

"And now?"

"I don't know." Sara wanted to shout that he was a fool if he couldn't see the truth in her eyes, but she stilled her tongue.

"You'll have to make up your mind soon. The *citizens'* army can't last forever."

"I only agreed to travel with the Prince, because our money was stolen. I couldn't have had a more perfect escort."

"Then you will go to Estameer with me tomorrow?"

"You're still a prisoner. How can you leave?"

"The Prince will let me go, if you ask him."

Sara was in a panic. She didn't want to go to Estameer just yet. Here, she was in control of herself and of him. Once she reached Estameer, the reins of power would slip irretrievably into his hands.

She looked at him standing before her, his handsome face troubled, his powerful physical presence enough to tempt any girl to cast all her misgiving to the wind; she knew an overwhelming desire to end this whole charade and go off with him anywhere he wanted. She was tired of traveling like a gypsy, and being regarded by the people in whose homes she was billeted as a scourge upon the land. The warm regard of the prince and his staff was wonderful, but she knew it had to end. Why not end it now?

But would Gavin treat her any differently when they reached Estameer? He was *asking* her now to accompany him, but as recently as the ball, he was giving her orders. She doubted he would be any different at Estameer.

"Why don't you answer?" Gavin asked, his temper not quite under control.

"There are so many things to consider."

"There is only one."

"And what is that?" asked Sara, her own temper rising.

"A wife's place is at her husband's side."

"What should a man offer a woman for her to forsake all to be with him?"

"He offers his name and his protection. Isn't that enough?"

Sara tried again. "What should a woman ask herself before she agrees to follow a man?"

"I don't know," Gavin answered impatiently. "What?"

"She should ask herself if she would be happier with him than someplace else."

Gavin almost sputtered. He had never thought of that question, much less supplied an answer. "She should go with him because it's her *duty!*"

Sara's hopes plummeted. He clearly hadn't learned anything at all. She would be treated exactly as she had been treated before, and she couldn't go back to that. But if she refused, what would he *do?* What would *she* do if he never came back? She had already made up her mind to ask the Prince to release him. She wanted him with her, but not if he had to be imprisoned to keep him within reach.

"I don't think I should leave just yet."

"Why?" he demanded, his jaw hardening alarmingly.

Sara decided to be absolutely frank. "Because you still

regard me as a piece of property, and not very valuable property at that. You don't love me—I don't hold that against you—but I don't think you even like me."

"You won't go with me because you're not sure I *like* you, but you'd stay with Ian, poor lovesick puppy, and your blasted interfering Prince."

"At least they don't shout at me every time I disagree with them."

"I'm the only one you disagree with," Gavin shot back. "You can't wait to do anything they ask of you!"

Sara decided to change tack again. "Do you realize I have no money, no control over my property, and no right to decide what happens in my own life?"

"None of this has any bearing on whether you go or stay," said Gavin impatiently. "It's a wife's duty to give her life and her property into her husband's hands, and trust him to know what's best for her."

"Without any input from me?"

"My mother never wanted any."

"Your father left me with servants. You're trying to turn me into one," she almost shouted, but she realized he truly didn't understand.

"But I can't have my wife wandering all over the country like a gypsy."

"I thought you didn't care anything about your family name?"

"Maybe not, but I don't want to be made a fool of either."

"Well, you won't have to worry about that," stormed Sara. "I'm not going with you."

"You've got to go back with me sometime."

"The Prince may not want me to."

"You would stay because of him?"

"No," Sara answered firmly, looking him squarely in the eyes. "Because of you."

"Doesn't what I want matter to you?"

"Of course it does, but what *I* want doesn't make any difference to you. That's why I *can't*, not *won't*, go with you."

"Please?"

Gavin was even more shocked than Sara when the word came out of his mouth, but he let it stand. It had finally gotten through to him that the marital arrangement he saw as normal was not at all what Sara was willing to accept, and if he was going to have any success in dealing with her, he was going to have to start thinking of things in a whole new way. Frankly, he didn't know where to begin, but that one word had miraculously transformed Sara's whole appearance. Obviously, it was a good place to start.

"Do you *really* want me to go with you? I'm not talking about your wife, Lady Carlisle. I mean me, Sara Raymond."

Gavin knew exactly what she meant. He couldn't honestly say how he felt, but he answered, "Yes."

Sara didn't dare pause to think. She knew Gavin only dimly perceived what she was talking about, and that it might be years before they achieved a true understanding of each other, but she had to start sometime, and she couldn't remain in Glasgow depending on the Prince forever. "I'll go."

The exchange had been so simple, but they both knew these words were more important than the vows they had exchanged before the priest. Their marriage was only just beginning.

"Are you sure?" Ian asked, when Sara told him she was leaving with Gavin. "The Prince warned me no' tae allow him tae force ye to going with him."

"You would stop me if I attempted to take her by force?" Gavin asked, angered as always by Ian's obvious infatuation with his wife.

"I would call out the whole Highland army if necessary."

Involuntarily Gavin's eyes turned to where the thirty-five-hundred men were standing by clan before the Prince and Lord George.

"We won't be far away," Ian told Sara. "If you should need any help—"

"She can call on her husband," Gavin informed him angrily.

"If your husband should fail," persevered Ian in the face of Gavin's anger, "just send me word."

"I will, but it won't be necessary," Sara assured him. "I can't possibly repay your kindness during these two weeks. My maid tells me almost hourly what a wonderful man you are, and I never disagree with her. Thank you, and please express my appreciation to the Prince as well. In light of the enterprise he has undertaken, and the grave matters that hourly weigh him down, I feel honored he has deemed me worthy of so much of his time. I shall always remember his kindness."

"As we shall both remember ye." He bent down to give her a swift kiss on the cheek. "Remember, if ye need anything . . ."

"I will." Ian took one last look at Sara then swiftly departed without a single glance at his friend.

It was a severe struggle, but Gavin succeeded in not saying a word.

Chapter 15

Sara stared blindly out the window of the coach, hardly aware of the dreariness of the winter landscape. Her mind was much too taken up with being alone with Gavin—Betty was traveling in a second coach with their luggage—and wondering what would happen in the next few days, to notice whether the sky was grey or care if the landscape was cold and lifeless.

Almost from the moment she had agreed to go with him to Estameer, a nucleus of excitement had begun to grow within her, and it had continued to expand until it had become an uncomfortable feeling in the pit of her stomach. Gavin's presence always did that to her, and she wondered if she would ever grow accustomed to being in the same room with him. It clouded her judgement, and made it difficult for her to think. Even now, as she was trying to look ahead to the next few days, all she could think of was how unhappy he looked.

And that was such a shame. One of the things that had struck her most forcibly when she first saw him as a young man was his high spirits. No matter what punishment he had received, or how often it had been levied, he had always been cheerful, full of energy, and bursting with impatience to get on to something new.

There was the same energy about him now, only it was held under tight restraint. There was the same indifference to consequences, but it seemed to be almost a matter of angry defiance; and there was no joy, no exhilaration. Everything he did, he did because it was required of him; and everything seemed to bring him either pain or anger. Including marrying me, Sara thought to herself.

She sighed audibly. Could she change things for him? What did the future hold for her if she couldn't? He was a strong, self-contained man, and she wasn't sure he would let her inside him to heal the hurt. Even now, when he appeared to be asleep, his jaw was clenched and his lips pressed tightly together. She smiled. She remembered just such an expression once, after he had been punished. Then it had been a refusal to let her see that he cared in the least, but now it hid something more deep-seated, and Sara wondered if she would ever find out what it was.

She hadn't risked much when she left London. There had been nothing there for her. She had no family, no home, and no one who loved her. Everything she wanted and hoped for was in this coach, was centered entirely on Gavin, but something had caused him to build a barrier between himself and the rest of the world. The Countess had been the only person Gavin allowed inside his defenses, but even her love hadn't been able to free him. If he was ever again to experience the same joy in life he had exhibited as a boy, Sara must help him tear down that wall. And in order to do that, she had to find the doorway to his heart. She knew he would never accept help from an outsider.

She sighed again. What did she know about helping people understand themselves? She had been singularly unsuccessful at making friends with the girls at Miss Adelaide's, and she knew virtually nothing about men. She could tell herself it was because her father had made his money in trade, but she knew much of the fault rested with her. If she was to reach Gavin, she would need intuitive skills she wasn't certain she possessed, certainly skills she had never bothered to develop, and it wouldn't do any good to ask for Betty's help. Her henchwoman was bedazzled with Ian Fraser, and she lamented frequently upon the malignant twist of fortune that had caused Sara to be married to Gavin, when such an authentic gentleman as Ian Fraser was smitten with her. And it hadn't done Sara any good to tell Betty that she didn't want to be married to Ian, that she loved Gavin, and that it would all work out in the end. Betty would have it that, "Things is in a right fair mess this time, and it'll take some doing to sort them out again." Reluctantly, Sara agreed with her.

Gavin wasn't the least bit sleepy, but he didn't open his eyes. Sara would have expected him to carry on some kind of conversation, and until he got things sorted out in his head, he wasn't sure he could.

He was still stunned that he had begged Sara to leave the Prince and come with him, but what he understood even less was the feeling that he was glad he had done it. He could only interpret that to mean he felt drawn to her, but that went against every plan he had made, every vow he had taken during the last ten years. *All except your wedding vows,* he reminded himself.

He had felt guilty about those vows from the first, even though he had been too angry at the time to be aware of it. Guilt had prompted him to kiss Sara too hard, to drink too much, and to stay away from her for nearly a fortnight. Guilt had caused him to exert more control over his temper than ever before, in order to convince Sara to return to Estameer with him. Now he was feeling still more guilt, because he hadn't arranged for her to have the income from her own inheritance, hadn't sent her back to London, and hadn't told her to go on with her life without him. What did he have to offer her, but the residue of years of hate and the legacy of wasted opportunity?

Hell, he wasn't sure what he wanted to do, but something inside him was reaching out to that woman, and it grew stronger every day. And it wasn't her physical attraction, though the effect of that had been, and still was, quite strong enough. He hadn't realized until days later that he hadn't gone from Sara to Clarice because *he didn't want Clarice anymore!* The full significance of that hadn't hit him, until Colleen sent him a message at Estameer asking him to come see her. *He didn't want her either.* He didn't want anyone but Sara. All during the last month he had been haunted by the vision of Sara, waiting for him in bed, as he lurched through the door too drunk to know what havoc he was about to create.

He thought longingly of her slim body and pure white skin. He could still feel the firmness of her breasts, smell the warmth of her skin, taste the sweetness of her lips, and it made his body ache with desire. Knowing that she was within reach this very minute was agony, but he also knew she was afraid of him. She had lowered her eyes as she boarded the coach, sensing all of a sudden that she was alone with him, but not before he had seen the same fear in her eyes that he had seen that night, the same fear which had haunted him ever since. He could take her if he wanted, he had done it once before, but if she was ever to come to him willingly—and he realized quite suddenly that he very much wanted her to come to him willingly—he was going to have to begin all over again. He didn't know if he could restrain himself, he wasn't sure he knew how, but he knew he must.

He asked himself again what he wanted from a woman and he answered, "Nothing," but the contradiction to his answer was sitting across from him.

Gavin had hired the best bedroom in the inn, and they had dined in their own private parlor, but Sara had no thoughts to spare for her improved circumstances as her hands, hidden in her lap under the table, nervously clenched and unclenched. She had made up her mind to take Letty Brown's advice, but she was unaccountably anxious. She had been trying unsuccessfully for the last hour to summon the words, but it was getting late, and if she wanted an answer before Betty came to put her to bed, she couldn't wait any longer. She took a deep breath, and plunged in.

"I've been thinking about our marriage." A wary look came into Gavin's eye, but he didn't flinch. "We were married without knowing anything about each other. But possibly of still more importance, neither of us had any idea what the other wanted in a spouse."

"Very few people get married knowing any more than we did."

Sara sat as immobile as granite. "I think we should know a lot more. I want you to tell me quite honestly what you really want in a wife."

"What?" Gavin exclaimed, nearly choking on his brandy.

"And not just your wife," Sara added, while she had the courage. "What do you want from marriage itself?"

"You can't be serious."

"But I am."

Gavin looked quite uncomfortable. "Suppose you can't fill any of those needs?"

Sara felt like the bottom of the earth had dropped out from under her, and she took a moment to recover. "If I know what you want and still fail, at least I will have had a chance to succeed."

Gavin wanted to answer her, but he wasn't sure it was wise, for either of them. Suppose what he wanted was too unreasonable, even impossible. Was it fair to condemn Sara to defeat before she even started? And what of himself? Suppose he allowed himself to actually say it, to commit himself out loud to what he hoped to find in a wife. Could he accept failure after that? It was a dangerous gamble, one he might be paying for the rest of his life, but there was something about Sara's unwavering gaze that encouraged him to take the risk. But Gavin realized in that moment that he wasn't sure what he wanted. How could he tell Sara, if he didn't know himself?

"You deserve a straight answer, but I don't know that I can give you one. I've let myself be caught up in bitterness and anger for so long, it doesn't matter why, that I can't remember what I used to want. It's the reason I came to Scotland when mother died." Sara's expression grew perplexed. "But you didn't mean this, did you?" She shook her head. He paused while he took a swallow of brandy. Why was it so difficult to say the things that were most important to you?

"I want someone to love me as unconditionally as my mother loved my father," he said without looking up. "I don't say that I deserve it, or that I could return such a love in full measure, but I want it nevertheless. I want a wife who is willing to fill her day with toil because she knows it will please me. I want a wife who will not shrink from the marriage bed, one who can enjoy my body as much as I hope to enjoy hers. But most of all I want a friend, someone who can see all my faults and still want to share her life with me. It's hard to be alone all the time," Gavin raised his eyes until he met Sara's gaze, "but I guess you understand that better than I do."

Sara's voice wouldn't respond, and she was forced to nod.

Gavin drained his glass and poured out some more. "Well, you wanted to know."

"I'm glad you told me," Sara replied, her voice still feeling thick. "I wish I'd known before."

"Why?" demanded Gavin, irrationally angry at the compassion in her voice. "Would it have made my howling bad manners any more acceptable? Would it have made my drunken advances any more tolerable? Would it have made my brutal rejection any more palatable?"

"No, but I would have understood them better."

"What difference does that make?" he asked, still unplacated.

"I'm not perfectly sure, but I *think* it means that whenever you do something that hurts me very much, it's not because you dislike me, but rather because something is hurting you even more."

Gavin's anger and irritation evaporated. Even now, after all that had happened, she was still looking for the best in him. It made him feel more of a heel than ever.

"Now tell me what you want," he said, forcing himself to smile, though he didn't feel like it. "I should not be the only one to have his wishes considered."

"I don't think you will like it," Sara said, "but I suppose it's best that you know." She took only a minute to gather her thoughts before she looked up and met his gaze. "I want some control over my life. Ever since I can remember, people have been making decisions for me without asking me what I wanted. I want to be asked, and I want to be listened to. I want to belong somewhere that is mine. I don't want to live in your house or your father's house. I want to feel like I live in *my* house, even if I don't actually own it. And I want control of my money. I don't see why the income from my inheritance should go to you, just because you're my husband. There's no need for me to have to ask you for everything

I want, and there's no reason to think I don't know how to spend money, or save it, just because I'm not a man."

Gavin made no comment.

"The rest of what I want is not so different from you. I, too, long for a friend. I miss my father and the fun we had talking about everyday things that happened, making plans for special times, or the time we spent together without talking. I feel like I spent all those years at Miss Adelaide's alone.

"And, of course, I've dreamed of marrying a man who will love me. Every woman does. No matter how important his wealth or title may be to her, she wants to be loved for herself, not just her beauty or her dowry or her ability to provide an heir."

Sara broke off when Betty knocked on the door and then entered without waiting for permission. "I've waited as long as I can, milady, but it's time for me to put you to bed. Lord Carlisle can stay up drinking all night if he likes, but I won't have you staying up a minute longer."

"Thank you, Betty. I'll be ready in just a minute." Betty closed the door louder than necessary, and both Sara and Gavin could hear that her footsteps stopped outside the door.

"It is rather late," Sara said.

"She doesn't like me very much, does she?" Gavin said quietly. Sara blushed with embarrassment.

"You see, she . . . that is . . ."

"She doesn't think I'm nearly as much of a gentleman as Ian Fraser," Gavin finished for her.

"He found beds for us at night, emptied wagons so we wouldn't have to walk, and never let anyone forget I was a lady."

"And all I've done is mistreat you, abandon you, and force you to travel the length of England alone."

"I didn't mean to say . . ."

"You don't have to," Gavin replied bitterly. "I'm not so taken up with my own concerns that I can't face a few more unpleasant facts. I've been damned disagreeable, and I don't know why you didn't turn your back on me from the beginning."

Sara didn't know what to say, so she said nothing.

"Well, you can tell her I won't keep you up late tonight. That ought to make her happy."

It might please Betty, but it didn't please Sara. There was only one bedroom, with only one bed. Surely he didn't mean he wasn't coming to bed. Sara suddenly felt like her hopes had been blighted by a winter frost.

"To be sure it's nicer traveling in a coach and staying in a fancy inn, instead of one of those dratted cottages with the master and his missus scowling fit to put you off your dinner, but I was sorry to see the last of that Mr. Fraser. He is such a nice gentleman."

"Everyone treated us kindly," Sara answered her maid, "but we couldn't stay with them forever. It's time Lord Carlisle took us home to Estameer. That's what we came to Scotland for."

"Humph! I say handsome is as handsome does, and your lord doesn't look so good next to Mr. Fraser."

"Then it's a good thing I'm married to him and not you," Sara said, firmly dismissing her maid. "And I'd appreciate it, if you would try to make it less apparent to Lord Carlisle that you think I married the wrong man."

"You want me to hide my real feelings?" Betty asked in surprise.

"Yes, for my benefit, if not for his. He's not as bad as you think."

"Humph! If he's only half as bad as I think, he's still not worthy of you. Now if he were just more like Mr. Fraser—"

"Not everybody can be what you want them to be."

"Including myself," replied Betty, indicating her tall body. "It's hard to be thought of kindly by a man, when there's enough of you for two."

"As you said, handsome is as handsome does, and I wouldn't trade you for any little French maid in the whole kingdom. I don't know how I could have gotten through these last weeks without you."

"Or I without you, once we got started," Betty replied. She sniffed determinedly to ward off the threat of tears. "Do you remember that big Scot who captured you? The look on his face when he discovered you weren't a boy!" Betty started to laugh at the memory.

"I imagine he was considerably more astonished when you sat on top of him in the middle of the lane."

"How about that first night, when you found out you had to share a bed with that squire . . ."

"And spent half the night lying awake because he snored like thunder!"

They laughed heartily for a minute, then Betty wiped her eyes and said, "Well, you'll be sharing your bed with another man tonight. Let's hope he doesn't snore."

Sara sobered quickly. "If that were the worse thing that could happen, I wouldn't mind it too much."

"Are you sure you'll be all right, milady? If you want, I could—"

"I'll be fine. I admit I'm a little nervous, but it has more to do with being newly married and not yet sure what my husband wants. I used to think I knew all about Gavin, but those were just a young girl's daydreams. I woke up to find myself in a woman's world, and it was a bit of a shock. That's all."

"That's as may be, but if you want me, you only have to call. I'll be sleeping in the next room."

Sara allowed Betty to fuss over her some more while she put her to bed, but she steadfastly declined her maid's offers of protection. Instead, she tried to remember everything Letty Brown had told her that day in the garden, tried to convince herself there was no reason to be frightened. She could feel her body growing ever more tense, and she consciously tried to relax, yet every time she managed to ease the tension for a few moments, it would return again even stronger than before. She finally gave up. Nothing was going to erase her fear, except a very different experience from that first night.

But then a sudden thought struck her. Why should she like being with a man just because Letty did? If there were thousands of women who professed to dislike it, surely some of them must be telling the truth. A shudder of apprehension ran through Sara's body as she confronted the possibility that she might be one of those women. She tried to ease her fear by reminding herself that she did remember experiencing some slight pleasure before, but she knew that was like saying you experienced the pleasure of relief after your tooth had been pulled. Gavin wouldn't come to her very often, if she couldn't give him a warmer welcome than she would a tooth-drawer.

Sara realized that tension had been building up within her ever since she saw Gavin in Glasgow; tension that had its origin in their inability to understand each other. That pressure as now intensified several-fold by the memory of their failure to relate physically, and the certainty that she would have to make a second attempt very soon.

Sara decided that the first time with a man must be a difficult thing for all women of sheltered backgrounds. After years of being taught that a female must guard her modesty at all costs, and having the lesson repeated over and over again until it was ingrained in practically every fiber of her being, a woman was then expected to cast it all aside in one evening. Sara didn't see how it could possibly be anything but a terribly wrenching experience, and that discovery made her feel a little better. I'm sure it's much easier when two people care strongly for each other, she thought to herself a little wistfully, but it would have been much better for her if someone had at least told her what she would be expected to do. She wondered how many other marriages began badly because of ignorance.

But ignorance of the marriage bed was not the only reason she and Gavin had begun so badly. It seemed she had been unprepared for just about every aspect of marriage. She had learned a lot during this last month and a half; she hoped it would be enough, but she was already aware that the feelings she had for Gavin had been rooted in a fantasy. He might not know her at all, but then she didn't know him either, not the person he was now. She had married him and pursued him to Scotland because of the Gavin she remembered as a child, but she was married to Gavin the man. She had been able to see that he was an anger-filled man and that his cruelty to her had its roots in hatred that had nothing to do with her, but if she was to be happy in this marriage, it was not enough that she have sympathy for him. She had to learn to love him as he was now, and quite frankly she didn't know if she could.

Sara had tortured herself so worrying about every aspect of their relationship, that it was almost a relief when Gavin entered the bedchamber. Still, her body stiffened. He was silhouetted briefly in the doorway, then as he walked quickly to the bed, the disturbed air in the room caused the light from the candle Betty had left burning by the bedside to flicker, and shadows danced drunkenly about his face.

Sara almost held her breath. Would she ever grow accustomed to his handsomeness? His thick black hair was worn swept back from his forehead and temples. His eyes almost seemed to withdraw behind his brows, springing to life only in moments of unfettered joy. A broad, strong nose dominated the center of his face, but it was the firm lips and the massive jaw, so reminiscent of the Earl, which made his face almost unbearably handsome, and at the same time reflected the character of the man himself. Strong and determined was the message they sent out, but there was something in the eyes that said *There is more.*

Gavin discarded his robe, standing before her in his naked glory, and Sara's thoughts were immediately riveted to his body. Even though her memories of him that first night had neither faded nor lost any of their detail, the magnificence of his body overwhelmed her now, just as completely as it had then. There was nothing of his father here. Broad, well-muscled shoulders and chest, powerful arms, and muscle-ribbed stomach spoke eloquently of the heritage he received from his mother. It was her love of the highlands and the strenuous activity it took to live there which had given Gavin his body, and the love of exercise which had sculpted it into such perfect proportion. He reminded Sara of a prowling, wild animal, temporarily brought to live indoors, but unwilling to permanently forsake its natural environment.

She tried to control the tremors of excitement chasing each other up and down her body, but she shook like a leaf.

"You're cold."

"No."

"Frightened?"

"No."

"Worried?"

"Yes."

"You needn't be. There is nothing to hurt you this time." His voice had changed; it was like a caress, deep, rich, and velvety.

Sara started to tell him that physical pain was not the

worst of it, but abandoned the idea. Gavin sat down on the edge of the bed and turned toward her, and her mind could not grasp anything except the overwhelming fact of his nearness.

But Gavin didn't approach her right away. He sat quietly, looking into her eyes. "If there's anything that frightens you or you don't understand, tell me and I'll stop."

Sara nodded.

"I mean it. Anything at all."

Sara nodded again and was rewarded with a smile that briefly conquered the perpetual severity of Gavin's expression. If he could only be like this all the time, she thought, it would be impossible not to love him. He leaned over and traced the outlines of her cheek and jaw with his fingertip; Sara felt her body turn to jelly. How could a touch that was so soft and gentle burn her skin like a hot iron?

"My father told me you had turned into a beautiful young woman, but I was too angry to see it," he said, drawing that wandering fingertip lightly across her lips and causing her exulting senses to claim all of her conscious thought.

"Maybe pretty," Sara managed to whisper. "My mother was beautiful."

"I never saw your mother, but she would have had to be a goddess to be lovelier than you." If he says things like this all the time, no wonder his mistresses adore him, Sara thought to herself. His fingertip brushed her eyelids, and Sara melted further. Then he took her lower lip between his teeth and tugged gently, insistently, until she relaxed against him, far too weak to feel fear, anxiety, or anything else except expectant delight. She could hardly tell when his lips took over tantalizing her skin, and his fingertips moved to her neck, and then her shoulder.

"Did anyone ever tell you that you have wonderful skin?" he murmured in her ear, as his fingertips caressed her shoulders and fondled her throat. "It's soft and smooth and rich in texture and smells of roses."

Someday she would tell him about the rosewater she used in her bath and on her skin and the sachets of rose petals that Betty put in her drawers, but not now, not while his soft breath in her ear made nearly every thought disintegrate like morning mist in a hot sun, not while his touch ignited a flame of desire within her.

"I got drunk because I was ashamed of what I'd done," he whispered softly in her ear, "but I was a fool. It kept me from seeing what a truly lovely woman you are."

Sara almost gasped. Gavin was ashamed of his behavior even before that night! Tendrils of hope reached toward the terraces of her consciousness, but the wild sensations rocketing about her body pushed them back into the abyss of her subconscious. Tomorrow she could think; tonight she would experience.

Gavin's fingers skittered up the back of her neck, causing delicious shivers to race up and down her spine with lightning speed. He removed her nightcap and let her bountiful hair spill over the pillow, until it formed a halo of red gold in the soft candlelight.

"I had to cut it, to disguise myself as a boy," she murmured in apology, but he seemed heedless of her words as he ran his fingers through the rioting curls, arranging them about her face according to a design that he alone understood.

"I like it as it is," Gavin replied. His lips brushed hers, skimmed lightly over her eyelids, and returned to her mouth for several long, lingering kisses, each more insistent than the last.

Sara could taste the lingering sweetness of brandy as his tongue probed between her teeth, and she opened her mouth to him. Tentatively her own tongue responded, searching, seeking, until it probed his mouth and caused Gavin's body to tense with anticipation.

"You taste of mint," he said, as he kissed her nose. "I like it." Sara vowed to drink the same tea every night for the rest of her life.

As Gavin's lips sank to her neck and then her shoulders, Sara became aware for the first time of Gavin's own musky, masculine scent. She allowed her head to loll to one side, so that he could place his kisses unhindered. If the feel of his fingertips had excited her, the touch of his lips was electrifying. Her whole body was racked by uncontrollable tremors. The sensation was heightened still further when one hand slipped into the top of her gown and found her breast. Gently Gavin cupped the tender mound and rubbed her firming nipple, until it throbbed with a delicious ache. Sara's whole body arched rigidly, the aching, stinging pleasure causing her muscles to behave according to rules of their own choosing. She could only lie there, utterly helpless under the onslaught of his lips and hands, totally incapable of governing her body's response to his touch.

His other hand slid the loose gown over her shoulder and down her arms, until she felt it bunch at her waist. Half of her body was exposed to his attack!

But this gentle wooing was no attack. Sara felt like her body was being gradually released from its trammels, freed of inhibiting barriers, invited to immerse itself in a pool of warm and inviting sensual delight. Gavin's gentle hands captured her other breast, and even though she soon felt his lips take one achingly sensitive nipple into their hot grasp and tug and tease until she thought she would moan aloud, she felt her taut muscles relax and waves of unexpected contentment spread to every part of her body.

Sara had never felt like this. She had always been excited by Gavin's presence, and aware of unexplained sensations that disturbed her calm, but not even her wedding night had prepared her for this cornucopia of sensual pleasures. She felt like melting butter, her whole body was boneless, floating powerlessly on the undulating waves of pleasure which emanated from her teased and tortured breasts and ricocheted off her rib cage. A marvelous detachment came over her, an indescribable feeling of well-being, and she was almost unaware that Gavin had slipped her gown under her hips and dropped it silently to the floor.

Again it was Gavin's fingertips which explored new territory, setting more of her body aflame until she felt like a fiery sacrifice to his need. The muscles of her abdomen rolled and pitched as first his fingertips and then his lips played over her ultra-sensitive skin. Sara could feel herself sinking deeper and deeper into the welcoming embraces of this ecstasy, and not even the progress of one hand down her side and along her thigh had the power to draw her from the nimbus of pleasurable sensations which enveloped her.

She was aware only that the center of these delicious feelings had begun to shift, unconcerned that one hand had strayed to her inner thigh while the other, leaving her breasts to the ministrations of his lips and tongue, had taken a more direct route across her abdomen, both on a course which would cause them to meet at the apex of her thighs.

They met, and Sara's whole being was ablaze, a molten core erupting at last through the hard crust of fear and ignorance. Sara felt her body relax to welcome Gavin, enfold him, and draw him deep within her.

She could not have said what he did, what was happening to her, because she was incapable of thinking, of remembering. She knew only that she held in her arms the man she had dreamed about for half her life; she knew only that his incredible gentleness had slain the last vestiges of fear and distrust; she knew only that never before had she felt so alive, so wildly happy, so indescribably wonderful! The feeling continued to intensify until Sara clung to Gavin with all her strength, hoping never to let go, trying to absorb him within her, certain she would shatter into nothingness if they were ever separated.

Then it happened; she did shatter in the most exquisite burst of fireworks she could imagine. Her body was racked with an aching hunger which stretched every muscle to its breaking point, and turned every nerve into a shooting star of desire. Explosion after explosion battered Sara's newly responsive senses until she felt she was slipping into nothingness, her whole body incandescent with fulfillment.

Chapter 16

Sara woke to the sound of someone moving about her room.

"Drat!" Betty said, when she saw her mistress was awake. "You were sleeping so peaceful, I didn't want to wake you." She picked up a breakfast tray, meaning to bring it to Sara.

"Leave it on the table," Sara said, beginning to indulge in a pleasurable stretch. "I'm not hungry yet." But she had no sooner raised her arms from under the covers than she realized that she was completely naked. Instantly the whole of the previous night came flooding back to her, and she pulled the covers up to her chin.

"You all right?" Betty asked.

Sara nodded. "Why do you ask?"

"You look a little funny. Different somehow."

I *feel* different, Sara thought, but said, "I guess I'm still tired from all this traveling. It'll be nice to get home."

"That it will, but I don't mind telling, I wish home was London. This is cold country, milady, the kind that penetrates all the way to your bones."

I'm not a bit cold, Sara thought to herself. If Gavin continues to use me as he did last night, I may never be cold again. "You'll get used to it," she said, but she had already forgotten what Betty had complained of. She could only think of Gavin and last night.

"Perhaps," Betty said doubtfully, "but I'd better set about getting everything made of wool. You'll catch your death in a cotton chemise."

"What's in that pot?"

"Hot milk."

"I thought it might be. Ask the innkeeper for some cocoa instead, and wait until it's ready."

She hated to send Betty on a made-up errand, but she wanted to be left alone to take stock after last night, and Betty was distracting her thoughts. Last night had shaken the foundations of just about everything she believed about Gavin, the relationship between men and women, and the institution of marriage itself. She was going to have to start all over again, in her evaluation of what she wanted and how to go about getting it. She was pleased to know marriage offered her more than she had hoped for, but she could also see it was going to complicate matters a bit.

She had now seen another side of Gavin, one she knew was just as valid as all the others, and somehow she had to fit this new Gavin into the picture with all the rest. She had seen him young and carefree, she had seen him angry, bitter, and disillusioned, and she had seen him burdened by guilt. She had no difficulty accepting a Gavin who lustily enjoyed her body, but how was she to reconcile all this with the man who made love to her with exquisite tenderness, who treated her as if she were made of spun gold? Not even his behavior in the coach had prepared her for this worshipful gentleness.

Even though she had been certain she loved him and wanted to be with him, she had been afraid of him after their wedding night. The very fact that he had a mistress, that the Earl had them as well, convinced her that laying with a woman was an essential part of the relationship between a man and a woman. But after that night, she both dreaded and feared a repetition. The fact that all *nice* women were supposed to feel the same way was no consolation. Yet last night it felt as though something entirely different had taken place between them, something as far different from that first night as she was from Clarice. This was something she could participate in, something she *wanted* to be a part of, something she *had* to be a part of, if she wanted him for herself alone. It was not merely a means of binding Gavin to her; it was a means of separating him from every other woman who had ever been a part of his life. As long as he wanted to satisfy his need with her, he would have no reason to seek them out. Sara was inwardly pleased with her discovery. It not only gave her a weapon of immense power, it made her feel more important, more able to influence the course of her own life.

There was a much more difficult side of this physical relationship to be considered, because there was an important part of it that was *not* physical in its essential nature. Sara admitted she couldn't figure this out, at least not yet, but she knew it was pivotal. Otherwise, why would she feel so much closer to Gavin this morning? Why would she feel a part of him and not merely someone with whom he had experienced a few moments of passion? What had happened that enabled him to tug at her heartstrings in a way no one had since her father's death? Why did she see him less as a handsome young Adonis and more as a much-troubled man? Was it possible that one night together could do this for just anybody, or was there something special between them?

Betty came bustling back from her errand and scattered Sara's tenuous thoughts, but she felt much more optimistic than before. There *was* something special, something magical between them, and if that was so, there was something wonderful to be discovered, to be learned, and she could look forward to the coming days with eager anticipation.

Gavin strode through the streets of Edinburgh like the hounds of hell were at his heels. And indeed he felt they were. He was running to escape Sara, and the demons of love that had destroyed his mother's happiness and were waiting with gaping jaws to crush him as well.

He had awakened this morning feeling more at peace than he had in years; it had lasted precisely the length of time it took him to turn his head and see Sara's face on the pillow next to him. He had leapt from the bed as though it were aflame, and indeed it might as well have been, for all the comfort it gave him.

Why had he let Sara's loveliness lure him into making love to her? Why had he let her innocence make him forget why she had married him? Why did he think love would treat him any differently than it had his parents? How could he have been such a fool to forget every vow he had made, to forsake his chosen path?

The answer to all these questions was the thundering realization that, if he was fool enough to ignore the lessons of the past seven years, then he deserved whatever hell was reserved for those who will not learn from life's crucible of experience. He deserved that Sara think less of him than of her lovers, care less for his comfort than for her pleasure, care so little for his children as not to have them. He deserved to be made mock of by his friends for being under the sway of a wife who did not return his regard, even though he was sure Sara would do her best to be discreet.

But he didn't want discretion. He wanted all of her affection, all her loyalty, all her thoughts, or he wanted nothing at all from her. He told himself he was being unreasonable and unfair to both of them, but that didn't alter anything. He knew he would never find the kind of love he was looking for, he had accepted that, but he couldn't accept love on any other basis.

But a nagging doubt kept whispering in his ear. What if it *is* possible? What if you can have everything you want? Gavin didn't want to listen, but he couldn't stop himself. He barely knew Sara—he couldn't blame anyone but himself for that—but he already suspected she was not like other women he knew, that maybe there was less worldliness in her than in most females of his class. After all, he had never asked her why she married him, and he shouldn't have assumed he knew. Was it possible she *hadn't* married him for the title he would inherit? That's stupid, he told himself angrily. She couldn't have married you for any other reason. She wouldn't have known you from Adam if you hadn't been standing at the altar. She might have developed a regard for you, if you and your father had ever given her the chance, but you didn't. She married a perfect stranger for the same reason any other woman marries a perfect stranger, for the advantages the marriage would bring her.

Still, the nagging doubt would not be silent; it bedeviled his mind until, in near desperation, he uttered a scathing oath and started to run through the streets.

An old woman sweeping the steps in preparation for the coming of day was startled by his imprecations, and she quickly retreated indoors, certain he was mad.

Gavin stared furiously at the man seated across from him. "I have no intention of taking a hand in this rebellion, especially not against these poor misguided rebels."

"I do, and I always shall despise these rascals," Lt.-Gen. Henry Hawley said with arrogant disdain to his cousin. "It is your duty as a loyal Englishman to support the—"

"I'm a Scotsman, too," Gavin said, interrupting him abruptly. "I don't approve of the rebellion, but I'll not lift my sword against them."

"If you're not with us, then your loyalty must be suspect."

"Don't be a bigger fool than you already are," Gavin snapped angrily. "I'm not a soldier, and I'm not required to fight. I came back to Scotland to see if I could find some way to make my people more prosperous."

"I don't think His Grace will sympathize with your position."

"Then I know His Grace better than you, for all you're his second in command."

"Then the least you can do is put Estameer at the disposal of our troops."

"Are you mad? Do you think for one minute I'd voluntarily turn over my estate to be trampled by thousands of feet and hooves, the land gouged by your guns, and the larder and barns emptied when the government can amply provide for its own? Set one foot on Estameer, and I'll raise the whole countryside against you."

Gavin was livid. He had never met his cousin before, had only decided on the spur of the moment to see what he was like before he left Edinburgh. He was shocked by his senseless bigotry and then enraged by his stubborn arrogance.

"You seem to feel that being in command of the army gives you the right to trample over the rights of ordinary citizens."

"We're in enemy country."

"You are in England, even though some may want a different king on the throne. If you continue to treat Scotland as you have begun, you may find the whole of it in revolt. Does the Duke know what a buffoon he has on his staff?"

"You're insulting."

"And you're a fool," Gavin declared flatly, rising abruptly from his chair. "My father said it would be a tragedy for you to step into my shoes, but by God, I don't think he knows the half of it."

Gavin stormed out of the room, but paused in the outer room to regain some control over his temper. A tall young man of clear eye and smiling mein entered and regarded him quizzically for a moment.

"Your interview with the Lieutenant-General didn't go well?"

"My interview was a mistake," Gavin stated unequivocally. "If he doesn't raise the whole countryside against you, I'll be surprised. Why does Cumberland keep him?"

"He has rank and birth."

"I know he's descended from an Earl, but earls can sire imbeciles as well as anyone else."

The officer laughed easily, not discomfited by Gavin's anger or the obvious difference in class.

"Who are you?" Gavin asked.

"Brigade-Major James Wolfe."

"And what do *you* think of him?"

"He has a reputation as a savage disciplinarian, but he combines beastly ignorance and negligence, and embodies all the vices and stupidities of his class."

"You don't mince words, do you?"

"Neither do the soldiers. He's called *Lord Chief Justice* for his frequent and sudden executions. They hate him, dread his severity, and hold his military knowledge in contempt. He has some dangerous illusions about the lack of courage and resolution of Highlanders, particularly that they wouldn't stand up to cavalry, even though they have already done it at Prestonpans and Clifton."

"I must try and make Cumberland realize he's going to lose more than he will gain by keeping that man."

"His Grace has been called away to protect against a French invasion. Hawley is in sole command."

"Then God help you, because I won't."

Sara stared out the coach window, a tight ball of apprehension bouncing about in the pit of her stomach. They were approaching Estameer, and she didn't know what to do. She had hoped that she and Gavin could have established some kind of understanding while they were in Edinburgh, but Gavin had not come to her bed the second night, and she had found little opportunity to talk with him, because he was out on business most of each day. He had been unfailingly polite and considerate of her comfort, but there was a chasm between them she could not bridge.

And the gap grew wider when they boarded the coach for Estameer. With the passing of every mile that brought them closer to Gavin's home, he withdrew a little more from her. Sara felt confused and abandoned, but she was determined to discover the cause of this withdrawal. After four days of companionable coexistence, she found she liked being married to Gavin, and she was not going to give up because of some ancient problem with his father, or whatever ghost was haunting him now.

The coach slowed and turned into the gate of the avenue, which opened under an archway that was battlemented on top and adorned with two large weather-beaten pieces of upright stone. The avenue was straight and lined with ancient horse chestnuts and sycamores. Beyond were two high walls overgrown with ivy. Though it was half-hidden by the trees, Sara could see the high steep roofs and narrow gables of the mansion, and she felt herself tense. This was Gavin's home, and she doubted he was any more willing to let her inside its walls than he was to let her inside his heart.

The house, which seemed to consist of two or three high, narrow, and steep-roofed buildings projecting from each other at right angles, formed two sides of the enclosure. It had been built after the period when castles had ceased to be necessary, but before anyone had learned to design a domestic residence. The windows were numberless and very small; the roof had some nondescript projections and, displayed at each frequent angle, a small turret, more resembling a pepper box than a gothic watchtower. Nor did the front indicate absolute security from danger. There were loopholes for musketry, and iron stanchions on the lower windows, probably to repel predatory visits from their neighbors. Stables and other offices occupied another side of the square. The front court was spacious, well paved, and perfectly clean. The solitude and repose of the whole scene seemed almost monastic.

"Sure is a big place," Betty said in surprise. "I always thought Scottish lords were poor."

"They usually are, when compared to the English," Gavin told her. "Fortunately, I'm not."

They entered almost directly into the great hall, undoubtedly the largest room Sara had ever seen. The massive black oak beams that supported the ceiling were hardly less than whole trees hand-hewn and fitted into position with wooden pegs. A fire blazed in a hearth big enough for Sara to enter standing, but it seemed to have no effect on the icy cold of the room. The unrelieved whitewashed walls gave Sara the impression of a cold, winter landscape.

"Estameer used to belong to the laird of the clan. He built this hall so he could feed all his men at once," Gavin explained when he saw Sara's dismay. "It's never used now except in summer." A man and a woman of middle age hurried from one of the side doors to greet them with a warm welcome.

"This is Tom Campbell, my bailiff, and his wife, Mary, who acts as housekeeper," Gavin told Sara.

"And delighted I am tae see the young master has taken a wife at last," Mary said, beaming warmly at Sara. "It was the dearest wish o' his sainted mother for the last years o' her life."

"Mary has managed everything for years," Gavin said, a little stiffly. "You shouldn't have to do any more than come down for dinner."

Immediately Sara could tell that Gavin didn't want her to interfere with the household. She knew she couldn't let herself be managed by a housekeeper for the rest of her life, no matter how kindly, but she hadn't quite made up her mind how to respond, when Betty, who was in no such doubt, answered for her.

"Her ladyship can't be expected to live by anybody else's arrangements, though she's bound to be too tired from bouncing over those nasty roads to be thinking of anything but her bed right now."

"I am rather tired," Sara said, hoping to pacify Gavin before he could become angry, "but I would appreciate it, Mary, if you could wait on me in the morning."

"At what hour?" inquired the housekeeper, showing none of Gavin's stiff reluctance.

"Is nine convenient?" Sara asked. She would have preferred that Betty let her make the first step, but now that it had been made, she wasn't going to waste the opportunity.

"I'm sure you'll find that everything is being managed quite well," Gavin began.

"So am I," Sara agreed, cutting him off before he could actually forbid her to interfere, "but I must become familiar with the household routine."

"My yes," added Mary. "There must be dozens of changes ye shall want tae make."

"I doubt there'll be dozens, but there are bound to be some."

"They are my mother's arrangements," Gavin informed her ominously. He knew he shouldn't be responding this way, but he couldn't stop himself.

"And I'm sure they are quite excellent for a household set up for the care of an invalid," Betty struck in, "but her Ladyship is no such thing."

"I dare say I shall find them most suitable," said Sara, stepping in to prevent a quarrel. Betty had never liked Gavin, and only waited for any imagined slight to her mistress to flare up. Sara appreciated her help, she couldn't get along without it, but she didn't want to find herself fighting a battle not of her own making. "Now, if you will show me the way upstairs. It seems like years since I had a room of my own."

"Certainly, your Ladyship."

"Gavin?"

"I've business with the bailiff. I'll see you at dinner."

"When is that?"

"Dinner is always at half past four," Mary informed her.

"Four-thirty! Why that's in the middle of the afternoon!" exclaimed Betty.

"So it is," Sara said, giving her maid a fierce glance. "I must hurry if I'm to be ready in time."

"You can't be sitting down to dinner before you've had time to swallow your tea," Betty protested, aghast, as they reached a corridor out of Gavin's hearing. "That's heathenlike."

"Nor shall I, but it would be better to move the dinner hour back by degrees rather than all at once. The same goes for any other changes I might want to make."

"Aye," agreed Mary. "The young master is mighty loyal to anything his mother set up. It is wise to proceed slowly."

"But if—"

"No, Betty," Sara said firmly. "I don't intend to give up my rights, but I won't have my husband badgered by a lot of poorly considered changes, certainly not so soon after the Countess's death. But I'm afraid we must move dinner back to five-thirty. I doubt I can be ready quite so early."

"Certainly, your Ladyship. It's terrible late now."

Gavin didn't look pleased when she came down, and Sara decided to speak first.

"I'm sorry dinner's so late, but our arrival caught everyone by surprise. By the time everything was settled, it was impossible to have dinner ready on time. Please say something nice to Mary. She's upset, but I told her you'd rather have dinner late than ill-prepared." Sara settled herself into a chair. "How was your afternoon? Is it going to be difficult to extract the coal?"

Gavin regarded her with skepticism, but he began to tell her of his plans for the mines, and his displeasure vanished as he became caught up in his enthusiasm.

"It will be a real boost to the whole county," he said. "Scotland's extreme poverty is half the reason the clans are willing to fight for the Stuart prince. If you remember the villages we passed through, then you know how poor they are. The lairds can't help, because they have all they can do to provide for their tables. It's the custom in the Highlands, that the laird must feed anyone at his own table who comes to eat with him. Well, more and more are depending on him, because they can't feed themselves. The mines won't solve everyone's problems, but it's a start."

"You're more interested in Scotland than your

Father's trading empire, aren't you?"

"I've never had any interest in that." Gavin paused suddenly and looked at Sara, an arrested expression on his face. "I really don't know. I've never had anything to do with his business."

"Why?"

"My father keeps everything firmly in his own control. I couldn't work with him in any event, but I did enjoy planning the mining operation and working out the arrangements with contractors and agents in Glasgow and Edinburgh. I admit I wasn't always thinking just of the poor Scots." An unwelcome thought seemed to cheat him of his pleasure. "I seem to be growing more like my father every day."

"Not in the ways that count," Sara said, determined his old hobgoblins would not deprive him of his well-earned satisfaction.

"What do you mean?"

"You may enjoy the work for its own sake, but no matter how much it means to you, you always have the good of others as your reason for doing it. It's just like your relationship with me." Gavin immediately looked uncomfortable. "No matter how much you resent your father's forcing you to marry me, you've still managed to take my feelings into consideration. I know it hasn't been easy."

Sara's compliments made Gavin feel like a heel. He *had* been gentle with her, but he hadn't done it out of love; it was probably equal amounts of salving his own conscience and common consideration for another person caught in an awkward situation. Yet it was obvious in everything *she* did, in all she said, that his happiness was uppermost in her mind.

Now he had brought her to his home—*her* home, too—and had virtually ordered her not to touch anything. Yet here she was trying to convince him he wasn't like his father. Wasn't his treatment of her the worst indictment of all? Gavin swore under his breath. The least he could do would be to approach everything with the same open, uncondemning attitude she had toward him. If he wanted to prove himself different from his father, if he wanted to justify her faith in him, he must behave differently, and he could start by accepting the change in dinner time. After all, he had complained about it himself for years.

Mary announced dinner.

"Let's go in," Gavin said, offering his arm to Sara. "You've got a long day ahead of you tomorrow. By the time Mary gets through showing you over the whole place, you'll be too tired to suggest any changes, and I'll still be dining in full daylight come spring." An errant thought amused him. "Wouldn't Cousin Hawley be pleased to know that."

Sara took the arm offered and went into dinner, her feet almost floating on air. She understood that Gavin was giving her tacit approval to make any changes she wanted, and her heart beat with gladness. If he could accept her into his home and turn over its management to her, even though he knew she had no experience and might make an incredible muddle of things, then he must care for her after all.

But later that night, Sara wondered if anything had changed after all. She had waited up for Gavin until midnight, when she heard him enter his chamber next to hers. Hoping that his staying away from her bed the second night in Edinburgh meant nothing, she waited, her excitement building as she remembered every detail of that first night, the tension increasing as she experienced again the incredible revelation of his lovemaking, hope growing that he might someday learn to love her at least a little.

But he did not come. His valet left, the light coming from under the door went out, and all was quiet in his room. Sara didn't need to hear the soft sounds of his breathing to know that he would not come.

Sara cried herself to sleep.

But Gavin was not asleep. He lay awake until the grey dawn pierced the black night, his body stiff with desire, his mind a battlefield between raging, tumultuous passion and the iron manacles of rigid restraint. The struggle left him limp and dismayed, for he knew he was losing the struggle against physical desire and unquenchable hope. It took every ounce of willpower he could summon to remain in his bed, not to walk the short distance that separated his room from hers, not to give way before the memory of the wonderful fulfillment he found in her arms.

But he wouldn't give in. He *couldn't*. To do so would be to risk falling in love, and he was dangerously close already. He was being seduced by her kindness, her thoughtfulness, and her undeniably genuine caring. How could he *not* fall in love with a sensuous, beautiful, desirable woman, when it seemed that her every thought was for his happiness?

But to fall in love would be to render himself powerless, just as his mother had been powerless, and Gavin had sworn over and over again that he would never *ever* give anyone the capability of hurting him as his father had hurt his mother. It didn't matter that Sara said she loved him—he hadn't wanted her to fall in love with him, and in the beginning he had even tried to be so cruel she would hate him—he couldn't let that delude him into thinking he would be safe from the furies that would chain his soul to an altar of everlasting bondage. He must preserve his freedom at all costs, even if it cost him the only chance he would ever have to find the kind of love that could free his life of the hates and guilt that had hung over him like a perpetual cloud.

He told himself that Sara's love and kindness were only an enticement to lure him into the snare of love, that many a man had been deceived by a woman, only to end up losing his soul, but he knew it was only a matter of time before he passed through that door. No matter what bitter experience told him, as long as he was alive, he would dream, and Sara was at the heart of his dreams.

Chapter 17

"We'll never get this place running like a real English house," Betty complained, as she brushed Sara's hair, "not as long as you keep these dratted Scots about."

"We're in Scotland," Sara reminded her with an amused grin. "Who do you propose we use for servants?"

"Anybody would be better than these shifty-eyed rascals," Betty said sternly. "They look at me out of the corner of their eyes like they expect me to grow a second head any minute. And all the time they're jabbering away in a language no Christian can understand."

"It is a little hard to understand Gaelic."

"They could speak plain English, if they wanted. They just use it as an excuse to get out of anything they don't want to do."

"You must try to be more understanding," Sara said soothingly. "I imagine your size does intimidate them a little."

"They've had enough time to have gotten accustomed to Goliath himself," Betty said stringently. "They can't go on forever acting like I'm a freak."

"You are a little hard on them. You must try to have more patience."

"More patience!" Betty exclaimed, so indignant the brush stopped in mid-stroke. "How long is it going to take them to learn to act like god-fearing Englishmen?"

"Probably not half as long as it will take me to learn their ways," Sara said with a fatalistic sigh. "There are times I feel like I'm in a foreign country."

"It won't get any better, until you get rid of that Mary Campbell and take over things yourself."

"I can't do that. You know I depend on her."

"You'll never get the respect you deserve when they can go sneaking off to her, chattering away so nobody can tell what they're up to, and then before you know, it's done and can't be undone."

"Mary consults with me about everything she does. She even shows me the menus, though I'm not always perfectly sure what I'm going to see when I get to the table."

"Lord, yes, and I thought the Frenchies ate funny."

"I've got all the responsibility I want just now. The rest will come in its own time. And you must remember this is Lord Carlisle's home as well. He wouldn't like it if I changed everything all at once."

"But he's lived in London for years."

"True, but he loves Scotland for all its imperfections, and you have to remember that."

"That Mr. Fraser wouldn't have you living like they did a thousand years ago. *He* would tell you to do as you liked."

"Then you must be certain to tell his wife, whenever he chooses one," Sara said rising. "I'm sure she'll be glad of the information. I know," Sara said when Betty started to protest, "but I'm married to Lord Carlisle, not Mr. Fraser, and I'm happy about it."

Betty looked disgusted. "When I think—"

"Don't! Just remember that I'm happy and be glad for me."

But as Sara walked down the long corridor, her look of contentment faded and a crease settled on her brow. Gavin was joining her for dinner tonight, a circumstance which was rare, and she was nervous about meeting him. It seemed silly when she admitted it, but even though they were married and living in the same house, she saw so little of him she felt as if he were a stranger. The thought that she would have been more comfortable with someone she didn't know, and who had no claim on her affections, crossed her mind more than once.

She was happy as Gavin's wife, and she had enjoyed becoming familiar with the household routine and planning a few minor adjustments, but the barrier between them was still in place. Gavin was *allowing* her to enter his life, rather than *inviting* her to become part of it. The situation wouldn't have been much different if he had hired a new housekeeper instead of bringing home a wife. And he had become even more distant since they arrived at Estameer. He talked to her quite agreeably when they met, but they had dined together only twice in the past week and slept together not at all. If Sara had entertained any doubt about his reluctance to make her part of his life, the fact that he had not come to her room since they arrived at Estameer erased it.

There was no indication that she had angered him, but through a lot of little things—all probably unconscious on his part—he had made it clear that he did not expect her to understand anything about being Scottish or being in Scotland. It had taken Sara a few days to figure out what was happening, but when she spoke to Gavin, he reacted with surprise, protested that he hadn't meant to give her that impression, promised to be more forthcoming in the future, and then proceeded to act the same as before.

Sara decided something had to be done, but it was clear a direct attack would not work. It took her two days to decide what to do.

Gavin eyed Sara hungrily when she entered the parlor, and she smiled with inward satisfaction. She had given a lot of consideration to her gown tonight. If Gavin was going to stay away from her, whatever his reasons might be, she was determined he would suffer for it.

"You never got that at Miss Rachel's nunnery," he observed, the gleam in his eyes showing his appreciation.

"No," she replied with a demure laugh. "It was part of my bride clothes. My trunks arrived from London today. At least now I can look presentable."

"You always do."

"I mean for other women. They always expect more than men."

"Other women?" Gavin stumbled, only half-listening to her words. "Why would you worry about them?"

"I thought we could have a party, some kind of entertainment, probably with dinner and dancing, to introduce me to your neighbors."

"I should have thought of that," Gavin said instantly.

"Men never do," Sara said, with a smile which showed how relieved she was Gavin had accepted her idea.

"Still . . ."

"You can atone by helping me make out the guest list," Sara said, as they rose in response to the summons to dinner. "I don't know your neighbors, or really very much about Scotland."

They were dining at six-thirty—still too early by Sara's calculations—but Gavin said nothing, even though Sara knew he was aware of the change.

Sara was aware of Gavin's eyes on her all during the meal. She had decided after the first night to give up her place at the foot of the table, and had ordered her plate set on his right. It had been to no avail since he was absent most evenings, but she was glad of it tonight. Dinner was much more companionable and friendly, even if he would probably disappear immediately afterwards and seek his own bed well after midnight.

Sara wanted to ask him why he stayed away from her. He obviously wanted her, enough so that she could see it. She didn't know if her face showed it, but her body wanted him as well. She had enjoyed only one night in his arms, but that night had convinced her that everything Letty Brown had said was true. Having virtually forced her to this point, it seemed an unusually cruel twist of fate that Gavin should now eschew her bed.

Gavin did not know what he had just eaten. His entire concentration was on Sara and his own body, which virtually screamed for the release which only she could provide. It was all he could do to look at her and not choke on his food. Desire, naked and unleashed, rampaged through his body, causing his muscles to tense, his nerve endings to become acutely sensitive, and his limbs to tremble. He made a determined effort to appear at his ease and talk quite naturally, but he was utterly miserable, and he was sure it showed.

He had known from the beginning it would be a mistake to dine with Sara, but the hunger just to be in her company had grown almost beyond his ability to control it. No matter how much he busied himself with the estate, supervising the mining operations, or lobbying with the clans, Sara was never far from his thoughts. Neither the press of work nor the strain of physical exhaustion could long keep his thoughts from straying to her, and to that indescribable night in Edinburgh. He dreamed of her constantly, and would wake up in the middle of the night in a cold sweat of desire. She invaded every thought, every deed, every moment of his life. She was rapidly becoming an obsession.

"I must be going," Gavin said, rising abruptly from the table.

"You're going out again tonight?"

"It takes every minute I can spare to keep the undecided clans from joining the rebellion. I haven't been able to convince them that the prince's cause is hopeless, but if I can just keep them hesitating long enough, maybe the fighting will be over before they can get themselves killed." It *was* what he would do when he left, but he left because he couldn't remain in the same room with Sara and not make love to her.

"Why should you be the one to try to save Scotland? You'll wear yourself out. You've been gone every night for weeks." She could hardly tell him any more directly that she wanted him home with her, but he only withdrew all the more hurriedly.

"There's no one else they trust. Even though I've spent more time in England than I have at Estameer, they know my first loyalty is to Scotland."

"And they will listen to you?"

"Yes, but not willingly. Most suspect they can't win, but the prince has had nothing but victories so far. I've told them over and over they haven't met Cumberland and the full army, but they don't see that will make a difference. Cumberland is no less determined than Hawley to destroy the clan system, even though he may not be as cruel."

"Shall I wait up for you?" She asked that question every night, and the answer was always the same. She told herself not to humiliate herself over and over again, but it was important to her that Gavin know that she wanted to be with him. Besides, she couldn't help it. There was always the chance that he would say yes.

"No. I'll be late."

She gritted her teeth to keep from showing her disappointment. She refused to add to his burdens when he was doing everything he could to save as many men as possible from the bloodbath he foresaw, but she felt some of the energy go out of her body, and the smile on her lips became wooden.

"Ask Mary to help you with the list. I'll go over it with you later, but she knows as much about who to invite and what they would like to eat and drink as anyone," Gavin said. "You can depend on her."

I will not, Sara swore to herself. I'll do everything myself. Then at least I'll know whether I'm worthy to live in your beloved house in your beloved Scotland. Maybe Betty was right, she thought as she stumbled up the stairs, just as determined to keep the tears from her eyes in front of Betty as she was before Gavin. Maybe there was nothing under that crust but a cold unfeeling heart. Maybe she was doing all this for nothing. Maybe he wasn't capable of love.

But she remembered the night she had spent in his arms in Edinburgh, and knew that wasn't so. Something had cut him off from her, was blocking her approach to him. She knew that if only she could find the key, somewhere inside him there was an entirely different man with an infinite capacity for love. And she would find it some day, but she was beginning to wonder if she would still care.

Gavin surveyed the men gathered around him, their bodies torpid from feasting and their faces flushed with drink, and was almost tempted to leave and go back home to Sara. He could still see her as she had appeared at dinner, and he had to hold on to his chair to keep from leaping to his feet and calling for his horse. Even to sit with her, to be able to watch her as she worked her needlepoint, or listen as she played the harpsichord, would have been a balm to his lacerated soul. He knew that to spend a whole evening with Sara was inviting disaster, but he didn't care anymore. There were times when he thought he would willingly mortgage his soul for a few hours spent in her arms.

Gavin had been at his most persuasive this evening. He had come to the Fraser clan, to Ian's father to be precise, but his words had fallen on deaf ears. Donald Fraser, the old laird, was just as committed to the prince as his son, and nothing could sway him. Why did he keep trying? Why did he think he could change, in a few months, loyalties that went back hundreds, maybe even thousands, of years.

"It's no use being faithful to the Stuarts, when it's going to ruin your clan," he had argued in utter frustration.

"And 'tis no good yer telling me tae turn my back on my loyalties," Donald Fraser had replied. "'Tis the same as telling me tae turn my back on me own people."

"They may eat you out of house and home, but they won't get you killed. Why persist in a lost cause?"

"Who's tae say 'tis lost?"

"You know it is. No matter how many victories the Prince wins, he has nowhere to go for replacements when his troops are used up, no one has any proper military training, and he has no money to buy guns or ammunition. Cumberland has all three, and more besides. Hell, our men can't even hit a target with a gun."

"Ye canna understand that we're willing to die for our loyalty."

"You're right, I don't understand it. If you told me you were fighting for the good of your people, I would understand. If you told me you were fighting for independence from England, I might join you, and we might have a chance to win, but as long as you fight in the name of a pretender king, you'll only exchange one parasitic monarch for another. And I doubt you'll be any better off under your bonnie prince, for all his youth and charm. The Stuarts have always held to their divine right to be kings, and this young man has a full dose of the fever."

"But he *is* divinely ordained," insisted Donald Fraser. "He goes back to James I in an unbroken line!"

"You're forgetting that England has twice rid herself of Stuarts from this line, and at the third opportunity, they chose a German instead. England will never allow them back."

"We'll see."

"I'm afraid we shall."

There was a disturbance outside the room, and the door was opened to allow in a buxom young maid with flaming red hair spilling down her back who boldly scanned the gathering until her eyes settled on Gavin.

"Oich, I knew ye were here," she called, entering the room like a whirlwind and slapping Gavin with a huge kiss as he hastily rose to his feet. "My body always knows when ye are about."

Donald Fraser chuckled. "The lassie is nothing if no' direct. I'd beat her if she were mine, but I'll no' tell my brother how tae raise his child."

"I heard ye were back from London, but ye were off again before I could find ye."

"I had to go to Glasgow on business."

"And to bring back a wife," added Donald Fraser.

"Oich!" exclaimed Colleen, bounding up from where she had settled on Gavin's lap. "I heard ye were married tae a wheyfaced virgin who ran at the sight o' yer rod." She laughed lustily. "She ran the wrong way." She laughed again, but when Gavin didn't join her, she sobered quickly enough. "She'd better be Scottish," said Colleen, hand on her hips, a challenging look in her eye.

"She is, but she has lived in London all her life."

"Weren't nobody here good enough for ye? I'll bet she has white skin, no breasts, and lies rigid under you, holding her breath the whole time."

Gavin remembered Sara's far from cold response in

Edinburgh and flushed. Colleen took that for an admission, and he didn't tell her otherwise.

"Why could ye no' find yerself some Scottish lassie tae marry with ye?"

"Likely none *rich* enough," Fraser said, before Gavin could speak. "She's an heiress I heard."

"No thin-blooded heiress can keep a man like ye satisfied," Colleen said suggestively.

"Maybe not, but ye can't expect him tae admit it in front of a lot o' chattering witnesses, can ye?" asked Fraser with twinkling eyes, as Gavin removed Colleen's arms from around his neck, her lips from his mouth, and her buttocks from his lap.

"I still say you're making a mistake supporting the Prince," Gavin said, deciding to take his leave before Colleen could make any more advances.

"Only time will tell," Fraser replied.

"And I say be done with all this talk o' war and have some ale," Colleen encouraged them both. "'Tis all I ever hear, and I'm sick of it."

"You'll hear a lot more before it's over."

"I'll be here when you get tired of the ice maiden," Colleen whispered to Gavin as he started to leave.

"You might find yourself waiting a long time."

Colleen looked startled at Gavin's words, and then angry at Fraser's crack of laughter, but she quickly recovered her control.

"Are ye telling me she's as well-favored as I am?" she asked, rubbing her buxom figure suggestively against Gavin.

"No," Gavin replied, with a reminiscent smile that worried Colleen more than any of his words. "She's slender enough to please even my father."

But Gavin wasn't smiling as he climbed into the saddle, nor was it because of his father. He was stunned to realize that he hadn't been the least interested in Colleen. In fact, he hadn't even thought of her since he got back from Glasgow. It took a few minutes to absorb that shock, but it took the rest of the ride home to admit it was all because of Sara.

Colleen had not been his mistress exactly, but she was a lusty wench with a robust appetite and a great appreciation for Gavin's body. She had fallen into the habit of thinking of him as hers alone when he was in Scotland, and he had unthinkingly acquiesced. But now he was suddenly unmoved by her charms, so unmoved that he had not the slightest desire to seek her out, or allow her to seek him out.

His arrival at Estameer interrupted his train of thought, but it returned to Sara the moment his valet left his room. He had been haunted by her ever since that first night in London. At first it had been guilt—guilt had been one of the reasons he had slept with her in Edinburgh—but he had had time since to learn that guilt had been the least important reason of all. Now he was obsessed by an almost overmastering desire to experience her body once again. If that had been all, he wouldn't have hesitated any more than he would have with his mistresses, but he recognized a different quality in the feeling he felt for her, and he foresaw in that emotional response the strangling net of love. No matter what the sacrifice, he had sworn he would not allow himself to be caught in the same mesh that had made his mother's life a living hell.

Gavin drew the cord of his dressing gown with an oath and poured himself some brandy. More than once, he had almost persuaded himself he could enjoy Sara's body without endangering his soul, only to catch himself at the last minute. There was something about Sara that defied a limited involvement, and he had tried hard not to feel drawn to her, but once he had married her, once he had taken her into his home, it was impossible to remain indifferent. Even worse, he found he didn't want to.

Gavin sat down in his chair so abruptly he spilled some brandy, but he was too absorbed to notice. The defenses he had built over the years—defenses which had never been threatened until now—were in danger of being breached. His instincts told him to run, to escape before it was too late, but he could not, he would not. He would not because having married Sara and discovered she was in love with him, or at least thought she was, he could not desert her. She may have made a mistake, but she hadn't known it at the time. He had, and he owed her something for selfishly allowing her to link her future with his.

He would not turn his back on her because he simply *could not*. Struggle though he would, there was something that drew him to Sara, something of fascination, something of lust, and something more pure and exhilarating than anything he had ever experienced.

Gavin's eyes were drawn to the door that linked their rooms, and he could feel a force, physical in its strength, pulling him toward that door, to the unspoiled and loving woman who slept beyond, the woman who would undoubtedly welcome him into her arms. *His wife!* Gavin broke out in a cold sweat. He took another swallow of brandy, but it didn't help. With another oath, he surged out of his chair, grabbed up the candle at his bedside, and stumbled over to the door. It wasn't locked. He knew it wouldn't be. He forced himself to pause with his hand on the knob, but almost by itself, the handle turned and the door swung open.

Sara slept in a large bed on a raised dais in the center of the room. The room was plunged into stygian darkness, but the feeble shafts of light from his single candle found her, and drew Gavin to her bedside on silent feet.

The light fell on the bed, illuminating the deep shadows, revealing Sara lying on her side, her head resting in the crook of her arm. The light must have bothered her for she turned restlessly on her back and faced away from the flickering beams, one arm flung out from her. Gavin froze, the candle high above his head; she turned back toward him and was still.

Gavin stood transfixed by the serene loveliness before him, his body straining to reach out and touch her, his mind determined to keep to its vow to evade the clutches of her attractions. Her hair billowed away from her head in masses of red blond curls, framing the pale white of her skin. He had never known she had so much hair, or that it rioted in such a wealth of curls. She usually kept it confined under a cap, but he found he preferred it loose. It made her look younger, more innocent, more in need of his care.

His eyes studied her face, memorizing every detail. He longed to reach out and touch those lips. He remembered their sweetness, could feel the softness of her skin. One hand moved forward and hovered over her lips. Slowly and with great effort, he drew it back. She might wake to his touch, and hungry as he was to console himself with her body, the thought of having to explain why she should find him standing over her with a naked look of desire in his eyes gave him the resolution to draw back.

Even though it was winter, the neck of her gown was open, and he could see the column of her throat as it disappeared beyond the heavy cotton. A vivid picture of her body as it lay before him that night in Edinburgh sprang into his mind causing his body to ache and lurch in a spasm of desire. A drop of wax from the trembling candle fell on the pillow next to her hair, and Gavin hurriedly drew back.

He must leave, run out of the room before he lost control, or burn them both with a raging desire hotter even than the wax of the candle. Stiffly, with hesitant steps, Gavin backed away from the bed until he was across the room, through the door, and back into his own room. Then, desperately, like a man stumbling to reach his first water in days, Gavin staggered over to the chest, searched until he found the key, and locking the door, flung the key from him. It landed somewhere with a dull thud. The tension went out of his body and he sagged against the wall, breathing deeply. He drove from his mind the wailing voice that urged him to find the key and open the door once more; he ignored the heated blood that raced through his veins and burned like the fangs of a thousand serpents.

Agony worse than anything he had ever experienced or imagined, more than he could resist, racked his body. He took a deep breath and, walking unsteadily past his welcoming bed, threw open the casement windows. A raw January cold swept into the room; Gavin opened his dressing gown and let the freezing air pour over his body, until he shook uncontrollably. But he couldn't tell whether he trembled from the icy cold outside his body, or the scorching flame inside. With another oath, he flung himself on the bed, hoping sleep would give him at least a temporary release from his misery.

He had to do something soon. He couldn't stand to have Sara studying so hard to become the kind of wife he wanted, loving him without censure, looking more alluring than any female he knew, and continue to ignore her. It wasn't fair, and it wasn't right. Moreover, it wasn't possible. He felt his resistance waver more each day, and unless he was ready to take what she offered, without giving the promises she wanted in exchange, he had to get away.

He lay awake for most of the night thinking of her smile and the smell of roses, but never did he think of how to leave her.

Chapter 18

Gavin was waiting for Sara when she came down. Her breath caught in her throat when she saw him standing there in the candlelight staring up at her, and there was a perceptible pause before she continued down the staircase. Would she ever be able to look upon his handsome features or disturbing body without feeling the rush of adrenalin that made her pulse race? Even now, after weeks of living in the same house with him, he took her breath away each time she saw him. No wonder she still felt like a new bride.

Gavin was dressed in the Carlisle plaid, a bold combination of blue and green with thin stripes of red and yellow. Hat, coat, tartan, and kilt were a blaze of color against the pure white of his waistcoat. His muscled calves strained against dark blue socks that came to his knees and exposed the lower half of his powerful thighs below the hem of the kilt, leaving no doubt as to his masculinity or the power of his body.

It was a dazzling ensemble and Sara felt agog with excitement. This breath-taking man was her husband, and she renewed her vow to overcome whatever it was that still kept them apart.

"You have thrown down the gauntlet to the local

beauties right and proper," Gavin said, taking in the picture Sara presented with expert eyes. "They'll be reduced to biting their nails and blaming their dress-makers for making them look a dowd."

Sara knew her glow of happiness was too obvious, and she knew it was unsophisticated to long for her husband's approval, but she didn't care. She had spent a lot of time puzzling over what she should wear tonight, and she was pleased to have succeeded. It was worth any amount of work to have Gavin notice her like this.

She neither wore a wig nor had she powdered her hair, but everything else about her appearance was fashioned according to the latest Paris styles, and spoke eloquently of rich fabrics and expensive London modistes. Her gown was cut daringly low, but a ruffle in the bodice kept it from being provocative. The small waist over the enormous hoop emphasized the daintiness of her figure. An overskirt in deep blue velvet was pulled back to display a white silk underskirt, decorated with blue silk flowers that matched the color of her eyes.

"I hope I'm not overdressed, but I didn't want you to be ashamed of me either."

"Any man would take pride in having you for his wife."

Any man except you, Sara thought. Aloud she said, "You look rather splendid yourself."

Gavin laughed. "Let us agree that our clothes are a success. Shall we stun our guests with our magnificence?"

You don't need clothes to stun anyone, Sara thought, her body riveted by the electricity which flowed through her fingers when she touched his arm. He had hardly touched her since that night in Edinburgh, she had barely seen him, and the effect was sharper for the time spent waiting. She would have liked to lock the doors against the hordes of strangers and keep him all to herself, but she knew she couldn't. The next step in her campaign depended upon her success tonight. If the community began to see her as an inseparable and invaluable counterpart to Gavin, maybe he would, too.

Sara's excitement grew as the guests arrived and Gavin made them welcome. She knew he had come to accept her as his wife, but for the first time, he was presenting her with a note of pride in his voice. And pride of possession could be seen in his eyes when he looked at her. Her brain sang with happiness, and she had all she could do to pay attention to the guests as he introduced them to her.

Only one guest disturbed the decorum of the evening. Sara saw the flaming hair and heard the throaty laugh before she saw Colleen Fraser.

"Gavin, luv," she virtually shouted, breaking through the line instead of waiting for those ahead of her to move on. "The place doesn't look the same. You expecting a visit from Cumberland?"

"Just you," Gavin replied, no more troubled by the hated name than Colleen. "My wife decided you should not be allowed to outshine your surroundings." Colleen laughed in her seductive alto.

"Is this the blushing bride?"

I refuse to blush, Sara thought, wondering if she would ever escape from the shadow of flaming redheads. She pinned a smile to her lips, but her whole being reacted with pure antagonism. She didn't like Colleen, and it had nothing to do with her red hair.

"Yes, this is Lady Carlisle. Colleen Fraser."

"A skinny bit of a lass, isn't she?" Colleen said, squaring her shoulders, the better to contrast her ample figure with Sara's trim one.

"Gold is valued for its scarcity, coal for its abundance," Sara said, before she was even conscious of the thought. The atmosphere in the room, as well as Gavin's body, tensed as Colleen's eyes flashed in anger, but Sara refused to back down. She'd face Gavin's anger later, but she wouldn't be held in contempt by this redheaded hussy, and certainly not in her own home.

"My niece has never learned manners," Donald Fraser said, as he advanced toward Sara in his niece's wake. " 'Twould be a kindness tae me if ye would overlook her behavior. My sister died giving her birth, and I'm afraid the rest of us spoiled her, her being the only girl and pretty into the bargain."

Sara allowed Gavin to smooth over the awkward moment, which he did despite the exasperation that lurked in his eyes, but she didn't fail to notice that Colleen favored her with an interrogatory glance.

"I want the first reel," the redhead said, turning back to Gavin. "We always lead." It was more of a challenge to Sara than an explanation.

"I don't know the dance, so I'm glad Gavin will have a partner worthy of his skill. Your, uh, *amplitude* won't slow you down, will it?' Sara asked, staring meaningfully at Colleen's enormous bosom. Fraser's crack of laughter stalled Colleen's threatened outburst.

"We'd better move on, lassie. Ye have been bested in this encounter."

"I'll wait for ye," Colleen said seductively to Gavin. "It'll be nice tae feel yer arms about me again."

Sara said nothing, but her smile became more forced.

"Pay no attention to her," Fraser advised, following his niece with fond eyes. "She's a little high-spirited at times, but she is a bonnie lassie."

"I'm sure she is," Sara assured him. "I'm so glad she could come."

"Try to remember she's our guest," Gavin hissed under his breath.

"I will, when she remembers you are my husband," Sara hissed back. She didn't want to anger Gavin, not when the evening had started off so well, but she would not allow *any* woman to pursue her husband before her very eyes.

There were more guests to be greeted, and even though Sara felt Gavin's anger recede with the resumption of his duties, her high hopes for the evening began to fade.

The dancing had begun before the last guests arrived, but if Sara thought Colleen would wait until the end of the set to commandeer Gavin, she was mistaken. He had no sooner moved from his post then she uttered the heartfelt cry, "At last!" left her place in the line, and dragged him off to take the place of an accommodating young man who obligingly relinquished his place in the set.

"Looks as though we have both been deserted," Sara said to the rejected man, hoping she didn't sound as envious as she felt. She forced herself to move among her guests, speaking to the ladies, trying to fix their names in her memory, and keeping her thoughts off Gavin and the buxom redhead who was his partner. But her eyes continued to seek him out, and after her anger faded, she began to watch him in admiration. It was impossible not to be impressed by his looks or his skill at the dance.

Sara had never seen him in a kilt, but she decided she liked it. The glimpses of his powerful thighs as the steps of the dance lifted the skirt increased her body temperature. She could see why the Scots were a lusty race. They were dressed for it.

The dance came to an end, and Sara wondered where she could hide so that it wouldn't be noticed when Gavin danced with someone else, but to her utter amazement, he crossed the length of the room to reach her.

"Come," he beckoned to her. "We're going to lead the next set."

"But I don't know the figures," Sara protested, even though she would have been willing to risk life and limb in a totally unfamiliar dance just to be near Gavin.

"It's a country dance," he told her. "You could perform the steps in your sleep."

"If you're sure," but Sara had already headed toward the floor.

"You didn't take long to make up your mind," he said, an engaging look in his eyes.

"No, I didn't, did I?" she said, and the dimples appeared. Sara couldn't resist a glance at Colleen as she took her place at the head of the double line.

"We've been playmates since childhood," Gavin said, noticing the direction of her gaze.

"She's no longer a child, nor do I think she's thinking of children's games," Sara replied, the tartness of acid sounding in her voice.

"No, she's very much a woman," Gavin replied, irrationally annoyed at both women for catching him between them. This was something he didn't know how to handle, but he soon forgot Colleen and the tension her presence was creating. Sara looked unbelievably lovely, her charm and grace did him credit, and she was proving herself a most skillful dancer.

"I must congratulate you on the success of your party," Gavin said when the dance brought them together. "You seem to have emptied every house within miles."

"Mary tells me they've had few parties of late, what with the war and the scarcity of money. I decided it was a good chance to use some of your London wealth."

"You mean my father's," Gavin said bitterly.

"Or mine." Gavin's good humor fled completely at the reminder that he had turned Sara's fortune over to his father. He had been feeling increasingly guilty about that lately, but no mere letter to his father would alter the situation. Sooner or later he was going to have to journey to London, and force the Earl to hand back Sara's fortune. And quite frankly, Gavin didn't know how he was going to do that.

The dance came to an end and Colleen made a spirited attempt to regain Gavin as her partner, but Sara was relieved to see that he proceeded to dance with a series of ladies, even though Colleen's eyes unabashedly followed him around the floor. Sara's guests were treated to the amusing spectacle of Colleen dancing with one man and staring doggedly at another. No one present seemed to take it amiss, but Sara could not master the feeling of irritation every time she saw those green eyes hungrily fixed on her husband. Sara had begun to feel very possessive about Gavin, and she resented Colleen's proprietary attitude.

Sara's temper wasn't improved when Colleen finally snared Gavin for a Scottish reel. There was no possibility that Sara could have executed this intricate and highly complicated dance, but that was no reason why she had to enjoy watching Colleen dance her heart out, especially since her intent was obvious to everyone present. You shouldn't let your rancor ruin your enjoyment of seeing such a dance well executed, she told herself, but she decided right then that she didn't like the reel. It was vulgar. *She* wouldn't be seen in public with her hair falling down and sweat on her brow.

Sara watched the swirling dancers with mixed feelings. She had worked hard to make sure no one was left uninvited, to prepare the foods they would most enjoy, and provide the right entertainment. From the shouts of laughter, the wail of the pipes, and the exertions of the dancers, she felt she had succeeded, but she had also succeeded in making herself feel more of a stranger than ever before. Though the music might stir her blood, finding an answering chord somewhere among her ancestors, she was more familiar with Bach and Scarlatti and the decorous behavior of Miss Adelaide Rachel's Academy. The uninhibited drinking, dancing, and roistering good humor made her feel less a part of Scotland than ever before, and that was exactly the opposite of what she had intended.

She looked to where the bosomy redhead was leaning possessively on Gavin's arm, and felt her heart ache. True, Gavin had not given her any encouragement, and it was also true that he had not spent more time with her than with others, but they were so comfortable together, so natural, so at ease, that Sara found herself resenting and envying their spontaneity.

It was a struggle for her to say just the right thing, to see that everything was done just as it ought, to learn more of Scotland, but it was second nature for that brazen redhead.

Yes, that red hair was part of it. Colleen Fraser was Clarice Wynburn and Symantha Eckkles all rolled into one, and Sara felt more inferior than ever before. And it didn't matter how often Betty told her she was beautiful, or Mary told her she was making wonderful progress. She was doing it all for Gavin, and he seemed just as distant as ever.

"'Tis a wonderful evening ye have given us," Ian Fraser said, coming up to Sara's elbow. With an involuntary exclamation of pleasure, Sara turned and welcomed him like a long-lost friend.

"What are you doing here? I thought you were still with the Prince."

"I was, but we have just won a resounding victory over yer husband's cousin, and the army's moving North. I couldna pass without stopping."

"How are the Prince and Lord George?"

"They're no' speaking at all just now, mostly because of that accursed Irishman," Ian said furiously, "but they asked tae be remembered tae ye."

"Ian!" A single ear-splitting cry was all the warning they received before Colleen and her flaming hair catapulted themselves into their midst. Ian staggered under the force of her assault, but he had braced himself instinctively at the sound of his name, and he didn't end up on the floor as Sara fully expected.

"My dear cousin," Ian murmured, "still the shy, quiet wee lass ye always were." Colleen's rich laughter ricochetted off the ceiling.

"What are ye doing here? Where have ye been?"

"I was explaining that when yer arrival interrupted me." Colleen ignored his chastisement.

"Look, it's Ian," she called to Gavin as he approached his friend, a tepid smile of welcome on his lips. He had seen Sara's face light up when Ian appeared, and he was stunned at the feeling of jealousy that descended on him like a bucket of cold water.

"It didn't take you long to find us," Gavin said. Those were not the words he intended to say.

"I couldna stay away," Ian's eyes twinkled, and he looked meaningfully at Sara.

"Ye mean ye didna come tae see me?" Colleen demanded. "He's my cousin," she said, finally recognizing Sara.

"I came tae crow over Gavin. We have won another victory, this one at Falkirk, at yer cousin Hawley's expense."

"Hawley is a fool," Gavin said explosively, "and a cold, unfeeling brute."

"His men think so. He hanged several of them for desertion."

"What?" exclaimed Gavin.

"Claimed it was their fault he was defeated. Of course, he forgot tae mention he was warned twice and refused tae get up from the table until the charge had begun. He doesna have much opinion of Highlanders, ye see, and he didna think we could do him any harm.

"Ye still think we willna win?" Donald Fraser asked,

taunting Gavin.

"Cumberland is not Hawley. You'll see the difference much to your sorrow. He's bound to return now that the threat of a French landing is over."

"He willna find the Prince ready to do battle. He's been taken ill at Bannockburn House, and is being nursed by Clementina."

"Miss Walkinshaw?" asked Sara.

"The same," replied Ian, "and he's watched over like a child by O'Sullivan. None of us can come near him."

"Is he seriously ill?" asked Sara. "He was so kind to me."

"I'm afraid so, and his illness is making things difficult with the army. The clans pull in different ways, and only the Prince can untie them. It will be some time before he's able tae leave his bed."

"Then we can go back to dancing and forget politics," said Colleen, who didn't care who was king.

"I'm going tae ask Lady Carlisle tae play for us," Ian said. "She hasn't played already, has she? I most particularly wanted tae hear her."

There were several "No's" and a few "I didn't know she played." Ian would accept no denials from Sara. "She's a marvel on the harpsichord. Her fingers go so fast they disappear." At this the whole gathering insisted that Sara play for them.

Sara knew that as the hostess, she should play something modest, but she just couldn't. She sat down and tore into the showiest Scarlatti sonata she knew. She might not be able to dance a Scottish reel, but she *could* play a harpsichord. It wasn't the way she wanted to excel, but it looked like all she had. She had been pleased that Gavin's eyes seldom left her all evening, but it had not kept him at her side, nor brought him as quickly as one smile from her brought Ian. Well, she could do more than win smiles from Ian. She would show him.

Sara had her reward in the thunder of applause that greeted the end of her performance. With Ian in the lead and others seconding his requests, she shifted to some Scottish songs, and finally a spirited step dance. By the time she finished, the whole room was dancing and singing merrily, and everyone viewed her in a different light. This is just like being with the army after Clifton, she thought suddenly. Now they all knew she was more than just another woman, and it was a pleasant change.

Gavin was looking at her in an entirely new manner, one of admiration and of hunger. Sara suddenly felt giddy with happiness. She had forced him to see her as something other than a retiring female, who could draw attention in the army because she was the only female there. Tonight she was surrounded by every lovely and important woman within a radius of fifteen miles, and she was still the center of attention. She swore she would never be self-effacing again.

Gavin watched as Ian and the others crowded around Sara, and felt himself fall victim of the first jealous rage of his life. He was so surprised he almost didn't recognize what was happening. He had kept his eyes on her all night, he always did these days, but he had been proud of her and of the party. He didn't know how she managed it, but there was no name left off, and no one present who should have not been there. The choice of food was perfect, and her entertainment also well chosen. He found himself looking at her with increased admiration and respect. He had been pleased with her recently, you might even say complacent, but that had changed the moment Ian arrived.

Ian had brought Sara to life in a way he never had. He was shocked and jealous, and somehow felt excluded. Why couldn't he bring the smile to her face, the humor to her lips, the gleam to her eye?

He *knew* why. He didn't have to see Ian's unabashed

appreciation of her loveliness or his pleasure in her enjoyment of the evening. He, Gavin Carlisle, was the reason she thought before she acted, weighed each word before saying it, could not relax in his presence, and he cursed the fate which kept him on the horns of this dilemma. He cursed himself for his own distrust of love. But most of all, he cursed himself for being afraid of being vulnerable.

Someone asked her to sing a Scottish love song. "Sir," Sara replied, with playful downcast eyes, "surely it is not proper to sing such a song to any man except one's husband."

"Or one's lover," added Colleen.

Gavin roused himself abruptly from his reverie. "What if they are one and the same?"

"I doubt that's possible," Ian said, an infuriating smirk on his lips. "A lover must court his lady."

"Who ever heard of a husband doing such a thing?" said Colleen, adding her mite to the stinging wound of Ian's words. "What would be the fun in it?"

"That still doesn't answer the question about my song," complained the guest.

"Enough songs," Gavin heard himself say. "Ian, I challenge you to a sword dance." A roar of expectation went up from the crowd, and Sara saw a fleeting look of dismay scurry across Ian's features. "Are you still up to it, or has playing with real swords stiffened your muscles?"

"I'll match ye step for step as long as I can stand," Ian vowed.

Sara looked baffled when two swords were laid across each other in the middle of the floor. Donald Fraser explained what was happening.

"Both men must execute a series of complicated and extremely difficult steps as they dance over the swords *both at the same time.* If yer foot touches or dislodges the sword, ye are considered the loser."

"Ian 'tis the only man alive who can best Gavin," Colleen stated proudly. "I've seen him do this dance many a time, and never has he touched the swords."

But Sara didn't hear Colleen's words. She was beginning to realize the difficulty of what the men were about to do. She had also just realized that this was a kind of competition, and that in some way she was at the core of it. Colleen realized this as well, and she looked even less pleased than Sara.

The men danced in silence. The sight of them, dancing so closely they almost touched each other, feet moving silently as they moved rapidly through the steps, knees raised high, hands over their heads, was something Sara was sure she would not soon forget. Imperceptibly the tempo quickened, Ian stumbled slightly and bumped into Gavin, almost causing him to lose his balance. Only by a supreme effort did he recover without a misstep or loss of his place. Sara didn't fully understand it, but she knew she was witnessing a remarkable exhibition of coordination and physical endurance, as the men danced ever faster until they completed the dance without further mishap.

Their performance was greeted with piercing whistles and applause and loud stamping on the floor to the accompaniment of a wild tune played on the bagpipe at such volume that Sara winced in pain. It was a release of tension, a tension shared by the dancers and audience alike, and Sara could see they all felt a pride in what these men could do.

But it was nothing to the pride Sara felt for Gavin. It was not just that he was the best-looking man present, that his body caused Colleen to stray beyond the boundary of good taste, or that his performance represented a supreme achievement of skill and coordination. It was more than that. Somehow he and Ian had captured the spirit that was Scotland, had shown themselves to be leaders of men, and Sara was proud for them. This dance spoke of what it was to live in Scotland, to be Scottish, of a people proud of their heritage and determined to preserve it against all outsiders. It spoke of unbreakable loyalties, of unspoken allegiance, of the unalterable flow of Scottish history, much of it bloodied with tragedy. For the first time, Sara felt a part of the land that had given birth to and nurtured her parents, and she felt her eyes fill with tears of happiness. She wasn't home yet, but Gavin had helped her to build the first bridge toward understanding.

Chapter 19

Sara was on edge. The Frasers had been the last to leave, and now she was alone with Gavin. After the wild swing of emotions he had experienced during the evening, she was nervous about which one would surface now that they were by themselves.

"Tired?" he asked, and his voice was like a caress.

"I'm still too excited to be tired. It was a good party, wasn't it?"

"Superb," he said, smiling at her in a way that made the corners of his eyes crinkle and caused her bones to go soft. "You are a wonderful hostess. I imagine you'll be glad to get back to London."

Sara fought to keep her spirits from collapsing. She had *not* had this party to prove that she was a capable hostess, and she had *not* done it to convince Gavin to let her return to London. How could she persuade him that everything she did, she did for him, that she wouldn't care if she never saw London again?

"No," she replied, much more calmly than she thought possible. "I have no desire to return to London. If this is where you feel happiest, then it's where I want to live also."

Gavin's heart beat more quickly, and hopes he had

steadfastly refused to acknowledge soared within his breast, but he forced himself to respond carefully. He could feel the sand shifting beneath his feet and see the danger before him, but he could not overlook the chance that Sara might mean what she said, that she wasn't merely saying what she thought he wanted to hear. "But you've always lived in London. All your friends are there. You must feel uncomfortable with the strangeness of everything here."

"Yes. I do, but I'm Scottish nevertheless, and tonight I even began to *feel* a little Scottish. But that's not why I want to stay here. I would go to London if you wanted. It doesn't matter where we live. You remember that I said I wanted a home, to feel that I belonged somewhere. Well, I am your wife, and my home will be wherever you are."

"And children?"

Sara had not expected the question to be put to her so directly. She knew how he felt about the reason for their forced marriage, and she knew he had sworn never to satisfy his father's wish, but she felt she had to answer him truthfully. "I would like to have children," she replied, hoping he couldn't see the trepidation with which she answered.

"I suppose we must have at least one son," Gavin replied almost nonchalantly. "I don't think I could die in peace if I thought Hawley was going to inherit my title."

Sara clamped her jaw tight, to keep her mouth from falling open. It wasn't just the words Gavin had uttered, or the tone of voice he had used, though they signified clearly enough a change in his thinking. It was the way he looked at her when he spoke, his eyes sending a totally different message from his words. It was as though his tongue was speaking Sanskrit, and his eyes and the rest of his body were shouting in loud and very pithy English. He wanted her so much he was willing to break a promise that came as near to being an oath as was possible without swearing on the Bible; he wanted her so much his eyes looked at her with an intensity that burned her skin; he wanted her so much he had to clench his fists and set his teeth to keep from slipping her gown off her shoulders and covering her neck with kisses right there in the hall.

And she wanted him, too. After nights of hoping to hear his step at the door that separated their rooms, of remembering every minute of their night in Edinburgh, of comparing him to every man she saw and still finding him incomparable, her body trembled at the thought of being held in his arms and caressed until her sense of time and space was wholely suspended.

But she didn't want to be viewed solely as the mother of a son to displace Hawley, and she didn't want to think that Gavin was coming to her merely out of physical necessity. She would accept these as part of his reasons, but not all.

"It was nice to see Ian again. I had no idea he was coming. Was that your doing?" Her gambit succeeded more completely than she had hoped. Gavin's hot gaze focused even more intently on her face.

"I thought you had invited him. You seemed happy enough to see him."

"And I thought *you* had invited him. If he is your best friend, he must have been a childhood playmate as well."

A brief flicker of a smile acknowledged her hit. "He didn't spend the evening talking to me."

"That shouldn't surprise you." Gavin looked at her dangerously, but she replied with all the innocence she could muster. "After twenty years, there can't be much left for you two to say to each other. Besides, he wanted to tell me about the Prince and Lord George." They were walking up the stairs to the floor where their bedchambers were situated, and it was impossible for her to make out Gavin's expression in the flickering candlelight.

"I'd like it better if you weren't on speaking terms with half the men in Scotland," he said, trying to sound offhand and succeeding only in sounding jealous.

"I daresay I don't know any of them half as well as you know Miss Fraser."

"Oh, her. That's all right."

"Well, how was I to know that in Scotland it's perfectly acceptable for a woman to throw herself at a man? I wonder why it should be just the opposite in England? Oh dear," she said with an innocent fluttering of her eyelashes. "How very much I still have to learn about Scotland."

"You know Colleen's behavior is not acceptable. I heard Donald Fraser tell you so."

"Then I wonder why you put up with it so cheerfully."

"I told you . . ."

". . . we were childhood playmates," Sara finished for him. "It's a pity Ian and I weren't playmates as well. Then I could hang on his arm all evening, and it would be perfectly acceptable."

"It would be no such thing, and you know it," Gavin said, a rueful grin breaking the rigidity of his features. "I can't entirely avoid Colleen's attention without making an unpleasant scene, and possibly creating hard feelings."

Sara decided that, in all fairness, she was probably being too hard on Gavin. After all, it was Colleen who had been so obvious, and he had tried to divide his attentions among the other ladies.

"I promise I won't say anymore. It must be hard to readjust old friendships when you take a wife. Besides, it's probably just jealousy on my part. I've always wanted flaming red hair, and all I have is this pale stuff."

Gavin looked at her in surprise. He'd never realized her hair was any less vivid than Colleen's. "I like your hair," he decided. "It suits you, kind of dignified and elegant."

Sara decided that remark made amends for Colleen's pursuit. He could take her in his arms this very moment, and she wouldn't say him nay. Instead, he walked her to her door and waited patiently until Betty arrived to attend her mistress. Thrown temporarily off stride by Betty's scolding her for being up late and endangering her complexion, Sara allowed Gavin to leave before she knew whether she should wait up for him. For some reason, tonight she felt absolutely incapable of asking him.

Gavin proceeded to his room and poured himself a brandy, but the unhurried pace belied the tempest raging inside him. Whatever the reason for Sara's agreeing to marry him, it was not just for money, position, and freedom. He didn't begrudge her that, it would have been foolish for her to marry to her disadvantage, but she would not be willing to stay in Scotland, learn to understand his country, and bear his children, if those alone had been her goals. She *must* care for him. Oh, he knew what his father and mother had said, but it was a different thing to see proof, to have her volunteer to give up something she wanted for him, to try to become something because of him.

Nevertheless, he warned himself to proceed with caution. Many a laudable intent ran shallow, or lasted for only a short time. His mother had been fooled by a man she thought wanted her more than he wanted her money. He would not be taken in by a similar protestation, even if the protestor did have blue eyes, an eminently kissable mouth, and a waist he could circle with his two hands.

But reason no longer held the rein on his emotions. Simple desire, unseeing and unyielding, had gained the upper hand, and he was willing to dare anything, risk anything, to be with Sara. Tomorrow was soon enough to concern himself with the future. Tonight, for a few hours at least, he only wanted nothing more than to lie in her arms, feel the comfort of her body, and believe that someday she would come to him for himself rather than what he brought to her. A barely heard closing door told him that Betty had left Sara's room, and that she was alone.

He walked over to the door that separated them, aware that his heart was beating so rapidly he could feel it. He paused to take a few deep breaths and calm his racing pulse, but his hand could not wait, and the door opened before he was fully ready. A candle burned at Sara's bedside; she was sitting up, waiting for him, wearing nothing but a thin nightgown that barely concealed her shoulders.

"I hoped you would come."

"I couldn't stay away." He halted near the bed, content for the moment just to look at her. There was something very restful about her, something soothing and comforting. Odd that he should feel this way; it should be the other way around. She was such a slender thing, barely half his size, it almost seemed impossible that she could be a danger to him, but he felt the doubt drain away from him, leaving him prey only to the hunger which seemed to increase with every second he was in her presence.

He sat down on the bed and took her hand in his. "I didn't know if you wanted me to come."

"You're my husband."

"I'm not speaking of a duty," Gavin said, trying to keep his mind on his words rather than on her lips. They were pursed, moist, inviting, and he could feel them already touching his own, caressing his cheek, covering his face in a passionate outpouring of pent-up energy. "I wasn't sure you *wanted* me." He didn't know why he asked such a question, at least not why he should be asking it now. He didn't think he could leave her now, no matter what her reply.

"I've always wanted you," she replied simply. "I was afraid at first, but I'm not anymore." She took his hand and pressed it to her cheek. "I didn't know how wonderful it could be."

Gavin took her hands and pressed kisses into both palms, then held them in a tight grasp as he leaned forward and kissed Sara gently on the lips. Sara leaned toward him, meeting him eagerly, kissing him as hungrily as he kissed her. With a shuddering groan, Gavin dropped to the bed, pressed Sara's head tight against his chest, and dropped kisses on her hair.

"I don't know why you dislike your hair so much," he murmured. "I think it's beautiful."

"Then I don't care," Sara said, feeling a bubble of happiness forcing its way to the surface. "You're the one who has to look at it."

"And your eyes and your lips and your ears . . ."

"You can't like my ears," Sara said, sitting up in amazement, realizing it was the last thing she wanted to do, and sinking blissfully back into Gavin's embrace.

"I like everything about you. You're a very lovely woman. I'm sure Ian told you so."

"He would never be so indiscreet," Sara said, holding tightly to a shiver of delight. Jealousy was a wonderful thing, as long as it was Gavin who suffered from it and not herself.

"Then he's a fool," Gavin said, and kissed her hungrily on the lips. Sara wrapped her arms about him and pulled him down on the bed with her. She responded to his kisses with equal fervor, her tongue eagerly exploring his mouth, her body pressed tightly against him.

Minutes later, by means of some acrobatic expertise known only to Gavin, he had slipped out of his clothes from the waist up, and Sara happily let her hands wander over his torso, exploring the rippling muscles of his chest, the powerful curves of his arms, the firm plane of his stomach. She wondered if her hands gave him even one tenth the pleasure his hands gave her. His lips continued to scatter kisses on her eyelids, nose, ears, virtually every part of her face within reach, but each of his hands had captured a breast and they were methodically kneading them into a firm, excruciatingly sensitive state. Her gown had disappeared as mysteriously as his clothes.

Gavin's lips deserted her lips for her right breast, and with the freed hand he quickly slipped out of his remaining clothes and into the bed next to her. With a sigh of utter contentment, Sara snuggled up against him, until the whole length of her body was heated by his scalding flesh. She held his head tightly between her breasts, hoping to assure herself he would never leave her again. It felt so good, so natural to be with him. It frightened her to think of a future alone.

She thought of Betty's warnings, of the whispered cautions the schoolgirls had repeated, of Miss Rachel's veiled warning, and she could have laughed out loud. Only Letty Brown, a woman they would have refused to acknowledge, had known the truth and had dared to put it into words. What if she hadn't had the courage to go up to Letty that day, or to ask questions she was certain no respectable woman had ever asked a camp follower? Then she would have missed holding Gavin like this, of feeling a part of him in a way that was impossible to discover by any other method. There were no roles to play, no poses to maintain, no clothes to denote a false sense of personal importance, just a man and a woman sharing their bodies with each other within the blessed sacrament of marriage.

Sara wondered if this wonderful sense of belonging, of

feeling at one with Gavin, was why her father missed her mother so terribly all those years. But if this alliance of bodies could be so wonderful, what unimaginable joys must await those lucky enough to achieve a fusion of souls? And Sara was sure that her parents had felt as though they were merged into one. She wondered if she and Gavin would ever become so unified, but to achieve that she had to talk with him, find out what it was that was keeping them apart. After getting a glimpse of the rapture her parents found together, she knew she would never be satisfied with less.

But Gavin's need became more insistent and Sara yielded her body to him, joyfully and completely, welcoming him to join with her, encouraging him to do with her as he would.

Gavin gloried in the feel of Sara's body next to his. Her skin was soft and fragrant, the taste of her minty kisses lingered on his lips, and the fragrance of dusky roses in his nostrils. The soft sound of her rapid breathing made his heart beat a little faster. Never before had it meant so much to him to know that he was giving a woman pleasure. It made his blood sing in his ears, and his need to possess her fully blossomed like a morning glory at midday. He entered her slowly, fully, and felt his entire being quiver with unimagined sensual delight.

With practiced skill, Gavin moved within Sara, slowly building her pleasure, suddenly rushing forward, and just as suddenly holding back, keeping her off balance, keeping her wanting more, or overcome by the rush of feeling, until she was utterly incapable of doing anything except responding to his body, moving as he moved, breathing as he breathed. Then a moan of pleasure escaped her lips, and he rapidly drove her up to and over the crest of ecstatic release, and she subsided limply within his arms.

They lay next to each other for some time, only the

sound of their breathing breaking the silence, and Gavin wondered what it was about Sara that made being with her so different from Clarice. She was not as skilled in lovemaking, she did not participate as actively, and she hadn't yet learned how to seek out his pleasure, yet he felt more at peace, more fulfilled, than he had ever felt before. There was no longer this obsession to drive himself to exhaustion, in pursuit of some kind of sexual release he had never experienced until now. It was as though a demon had ridden his back for years, and for the first time he had been able to shake him off. It wouldn't last, it would begin all over again in the morning, but for tonight, at least, he could find succor in Sara's arms.

He wondered why he had found it at all, but more importantly, why had he found it with Sara? Oddly enough, he knew it didn't depend on the loveliness of her body; even less did it depend on her beauty. This wonderful quality flowed from some inner source he had not seen, but then he had not allowed himself to look outside himself or inside anyone else for years. He now realized that his preoccupation with himself had caused him to miss the most important part of the people around him. He didn't know Sara, he never had, and if he was going to get the answers to any of his questions, he had to start learning.

"Do you like me as much as the other women?" Sara asked unexpectedly, when her breathing returned to normal. She had been lying here wondering what was going on in Gavin's mind, torturing herself with doubts and teasing herself with hopes. It was a dangerous question to ask, but she had to know the answer. They couldn't go on fencing in the dark, each afraid to reach out to the other, each afraid that something would be wrong, or less than they had hoped for, and drawing back for fear of disappointment.

"More," Gavin murmured in her ear. Even though he

was half-drunk from gratified passion, his voice carried enough conviction to persuade Sara that he was telling the truth. "My father was right when he said I would tire of overripeness." And for once Gavin didn't care what his father thought. He seemed so content where he was, that Sara ventured another question.

"Why did you stay away from me after Edinburgh?" She felt Gavin tense, and wondered if she shouldn't have waited, but it was too late now.

"That's difficult to say," Gavin responded absently, too deeply satisfied to want to do anything except bask in the afterglow.

"Please try, for my sake," she asked softly. "It's important to both of us."

Gavin felt a stab of resentment as he pulled his mind from its state of blissful half-consciousness. He didn't want to have to think deeply, but more importantly he didn't want to take the edge off this moment by probing into areas of his soul that could only cause him pain. He had spent years building his defenses, hardening every sensitive spot, hoping he would never have to feel such pain again.

He had adored his father, and he could remember, as though it had just happened, the discovery that the father he thought he knew didn't exist, that he was a complete fabrication, that the man he had idolized was in reality a monster of selfishness and cruelty. It had been an even more bitter torment than the day he finally realized his mother would never again be the vital, splendid creature he remembered from his childhood, that she would remain frail and bedridden until she died. Life was treacherous; she would give generously of her bounty, and then snatch it all back after it had sunk deep roots. He could still feel the terrible agony of that ripping and tearing, as nearly everything he held dear was wrenched from his grasp, as the very foundations of his life disintegrated under his feet, and he instinctively veered away from opening the wounds again.

"You might say I don't trust things to last, or to be what they seem. The important things, the things that can make life something other than a living hell, never last. Never!"

Even though he continued to lie quietly by her side, Sara was startled by the vehemence in his voice. Its intensity frightened her, but it also warned her, that whatever was keeping them apart was no simple misunderstanding or idle prejudice, but something which had become as much a part of him as bones and sinew. A cold fear clutched at her heart, and she felt much of the glow of the evening evaporate. Would she ever bridge the chasm that separated them? Would she ever have the love she longed for?

Instinctively she moved closer to Gavin, and his hands began to roam over her body, awakening the feelings that had been only momentarily displaced by her fears. She tried to hold on to her thoughts, she *must* find an answer if she was to achieve happiness, but her body flooded her brain with a tidal wave of sensations that gradually blocked out all consciousness of anything other than the wonderful things that Gavin was doing to her. She gave herself up to him, and let herself be borne aloft until she felt completely detached from all earthly restraints. Tomorrow she could think about it, but tonight . . .

Sara woke slowly, gradually becoming aware of a wondrous feeling of contentment. She unfolded her body from its tight ball, stretched luxuriously in the cold bed, and then retracted quickly, until she occupied only the warm spot again, the covers tucked tightly under her chin. Gradually the memory of last night crystallized from the murkiness of her unfocused mind, and a smile spread across her face. Gavin had come to her, and everything felt right at last. She still had to discover what had kept him away from her bed, but as long as he was with her, she felt confident they could overcome any problem, no matter how terrible. Her hand reached out, but it encountered an empty pillow. Sara sat up with a start, than collapsed back on her pillow, her hopes dashed.

Gavin had not stayed the night. He was gone.

"And Mary said Lord Carlisle bid her strictly to tell you he might be away for several days," Betty told Sara, as she bustled about helping her get dressed. "He's gone to see about those coal mines of his, and doesn't know how long it will take. Seems there's some trouble about who's going to dig the stuff out." She helped Sara into her dress and twitched it into place. "They ought to leave it in the ground, if you ask me. It's nasty, dirty stuff. And it doesn't make nearly as nice a fire as wood."

"I believe Lord Carlisle is mining it primarily for sale," Sara said, her listless voice causing Betty's concern to grow. She had not failed to notice Sara's lack of spirits. At first she set it down to fatigue after the exertions of the party, but now she decided it was much deeper than that. Normally she would have asked her mistress straight out what was eating at her, but today Betty was reluctant to intrude. She had the feeling this was something Sara would not share.

"I think there are people coming to see me today," Sara said listlessly. "A poet if I remember correctly, and someone to play duets on the violin. Tell them I'm not feeling well, and to call again."

"When should I say?"

"I don't know, maybe in a few days . . ." But Sara stopped in her verbal tracks. She didn't know what was wrong with Gavin, and she was terribly disappointed he had chosen to disappear again, but she wasn't going to get anywhere by feeling sorry for herself. She certainly wasn't going to convince Gavin or anyone else she could handle adversity if she hid in her bedroom at the first hint of trouble. "I've changed my mind," she said to Betty, reaching down to summon every bit of determination she had to her aid. "And have my carriage ready after luncheon. One of my guests was unable to attend because of illness, and I want to call on her. If Lord Carlisle comes in, tell him dinner has been put back to half past seven. If he doesn't return, I shall dine alone at that hour."

"That'll show you, you old tyrant," Betty mumbled to herself later, as she carried the message to various persons in the household. "Milady is not going to curl up and die because of anything you do, so don't you think it. One of these days she's going to realize that Mr. Ian Fraser is worth ten of you, and then you'll be out in the cold, where you belong."

Chapter 20

"And we can run a rail down to the river along this ridge," Gavin was saying to his agent, Walter Kincaid.

"'Tis too shallow and rough tae take ships," Kincaid pointed out.

"Then we'll have to use barges. Without cheap transportation, we'll lose most of our profit."

Gavin had spent the last three days walking over every inch of his coal-bearing land, concerning himself with the most minute details of its mining and transportation, and working until he was ready to drop. All so he could keep from thinking about Sara. He had succeeded during the daytime hours, but at night she filled his dreams so completely he rose from his bed each morning more exhausted than when he laid down. Absence had only succeeded in making him think of her almost constantly and convincing him of his increasing vulnerability.

"As I remember, there are some caves around here," Gavin said, forcing his mind back to his work. "We can keep the equipment there when it's not in use. You can enlarge the openings if you have to." Gavin set off across the hillside, hardly aware that Kincaid was giving him a list of reasons why the caves wouldn't be suitable for the storage of valuable equipment.

"I know they're not ideal, but they'll do," Gavin said absently. He had already sighted one of the caves, and was more interested in seeing what had to be done before it would be made useable than in listening to Kincaid. As he neared the opening, he noticed that the ground had been cut up with hoofprints. Then he saw the imprint of wagon wheels leading up to the mouth of the cave.

"What's been going on around here?" he demanded, suddenly realizing that Kincaid's objections had been intended not only to discourage him from using the caves, but to dissuade him from visiting them at all. "Someone has been bringing wagons up here, and from the looks of these tracks, they were loaded with something heavy."

"This is lonely country," Kincaid offered nervously. "Anyone could be using these caves."

"Not anyone, just someone who is so well known no one would question him." Gavin leveled his unyielding gaze at his agent. "You know who it is, don't you?"

Kincaid fidgeted uneasily, but he nodded. "I did try tae stop them, yer Lordship, I surely did, but he wouldna listen. He said ye would understand."

"And who is *he?*"

"Yer friend, Mr. Fraser," Kincaid replied.

"What did he leave here?"

"I didna ask," Kincaid responded, with the bland innocence of one who thinks if he can't put a name to an evil, it can't hurt him.

"Then we shall find out. Do you have a torch?" Kincaid shook his head, but just inside the mouth of the cave, Gavin discovered several torches leaning against the wall, along with a flint to light them. "It looks as though they mean to come back," Gavin said, as he lighted one of the torches and motioned for Kincaid to light a second.

The light seemed pitifully insignificant when pitted

against the inky blackness of the cave, but they had no trouble following the tracks. About one hundred feet from the opening, they came upon several long wooden boxes piled against a wall in a dim recess. Gavin didn't need to open the boxes to know what they contained.

"These are rifles for the rebellion."

"Merciful God," Kincaid exclaimed, realizing the full implication of what they had found. "If the government was to find out . . ."

"We would all be hanged," Gavin finished for him.

"What are we to do?"

"Move everything *tonight*."

"Where to?"

Gavin was stumped. He couldn't keep the rifles on his property, couldn't hide them on anyone else's property without endangering them, couldn't return them to Fraser, and couldn't in good conscience turn them over to Cumberland.

"Dump them in the river," he decided suddenly, "and be sure to wipe out your tracks. I don't want anybody to know where to find them. And Kincaid, I want as few people to know about this as possible. Choose men not likely to get drunk and forget to guard their words. Your neck is even more vulnerable than mine."

Kincaid assured Gavin he would guard the secret with his life, a fact Gavin never doubted, and he turned his thoughts to Ian Fraser, or his father, whichever was really responsible for the rifles being hidden on his land. He was disappointed he couldn't convince the Frasers to withdraw their support from the Stuart prince, but if they insisted upon taking part in this rebellion, the least they could do was shoulder their own risks. He'd be damned if he'd allow them to endanger him and everyone at Estameer.

Instantly he visualized Sara, as she looked in the candlelight after they made love. My God, if they found the rifles, no one would believe she was innocent, not after traveling with the Prince for two weeks. Cold fear clutched his heart. No, not Sara! The thought of losing her, of knowing her smile would never welcome him again, almost unmanned him. In that moment, he knew he would do *anything* to protect her from the consequences of Fraser's folly.

That he should feel protective of her didn't surprise him very much, not after the agony he had endured to keep from going to her every night; that he should feel a murderous rage toward whoever placed the rifles in the cave did. Heretofore, he had been very tolerant of anyone taking part in the rebellion, but at this moment he was furious enough to have led Hawley's troops against them himself. That anyone should put Sara's life at risk was unforgivable, but that *Ian* should do it! Even the most pungent of oaths seemed inadequate.

He would go home immediately. He could trust Kincaid to see to the removal of the rifles, but he had to see Ian and make it clear that he wouldn't allow him to do anything that might endanger Sara's life. He'd already given her enough pain. He'd be damned if he'd have anybody else adding to it.

"'Tis that Miss Fraser, milady," Mary said, entering Sara's sitting room. "I didna think ye would want tae see her, but I couldna turn her off, no' without speaking tae ye first."

"Let me handle her," Betty said, starting up, a martial light in her eyes. She might favor Mr. Fraser over his lordship, but she wasn't about to have any redheaded hussy making eyes at her mistress's husband.

"Never mind, Betty," Sara said. "I will see her, and I will see her alone. Show her up, Mary."

"But milady—"

"I know, and I agree with you," Sara said, "but the Fraser clan is Gavin's ally, and the Fraser family his neighbors. I must try to remain friends with them. If I can't . . . well, I'll try first and worry about that later."

"Nobody can be friends with that hellcat, if they've got something she wants," Betty stated with uncompromising frankness. "You take care she doesn't try to make off with your husband, all the while she's giving you a great big smile."

"I will," Sara said, laughing more easily than she felt. "There are a lot of things I don't know much about, but I do know how to deal with women, even jealous ones. I've been doing it my whole life."

"I guess you have at that, but if you need any help, all you have to do—"

"If you hear me scream, come running. If you hear Miss Fraser scream, pretend you were at the other end of the castle." A conspiratorial wink passed between the two, just before Mary opened the door to Colleen Fraser. The impact of her entrance was equivalent to that of a strong gale, and Sara's composure was slightly ruffled in spite of herself.

Colleen paused just inside the door and glared openly at Sara, partly to take stock of the situation, Sara guessed, and partly to try and unsettle her rival by her boldness. Sara smiled inwardly, but preserved a calm and sedate exterior.

"Won't you be seated?" Sara invited. "Could I offer you some refreshment?"

"You're not much like him, are you?" Colleen asked, ignoring both of Sara's offers.

"Actually we're probably alike in as many ways as we differ. Did you have any particular difference in mind?"

"You're so ladylike," Colleen said, finally taking a seat.

"I hope so."

"But Gavin's rough, and he likes his women lusty. He may want a lady in his parlor, but he looks for a wanton in his bed. 'Tis exactly like a man tae be both boy and man at once, devil and saint."

"But don't you find that men look for different things in different women?" Sara suggested delicately. She couldn't really dislike Colleen for fighting for her man, at least not yet.

"Gavin always liked a woman o' spirit, one who could keep up with him, no matter how late he stayed up."

"But he'd never looked for a wife before." Colleen took a few seconds to digest this thought.

"Most men look tae marry a dull heiress who will stay home and bear his children, while he enjoys himself elsewhere." Colleen directed a particularly penetrating look at Sara. "But ye willna be doing that, will ye?"

"That's rather perceptive of you," Sara said, quite surprised.

"I can see ye will be a possessive female," Colleen said, rather belligerently.

"I hope not. I will certainly try hard not to be. A man doesn't like to feel confined."

"Good," Colleen said, brightening and relaxing a little. "Then ye willna expect Gavin tae be at yer beck and call every minute o' the day."

"Certainly not. I have servants for that."

Colleen relaxed even more and said, "I never dreamed ye would be so obliging. Half the women in the world only marry a man so they can try tae change him."

"I like Gavin the way he is."

"And ye willna set up a screech when he does something ye do no' like?"

"I didn't know Gavin very well before I married him, but to the best of my knowledge, he hasn't done anything since the wedding that I'm not perfectly content for him to continue doing for the rest of his life." Sara thought of the nights he had stayed away from her bed, and hoped she would be forgiven for this small lie.

"I think I will have some tea," Colleen said, becoming positively cheerful. "After the way ye looked at me during the party, I made sure ye would throw a fit if I ever came near Gavin again."

"I hope I will never *throw a fit,* as you put it, and I certainly have no intention of preventing Gavin from seeing anyone he likes or of hindering anyone from seeing him. I'm his wife, not his jailor."

"I must say, I never thought a proper set-up virgin out of a fancy London school would be ready tae turn a blind eye tae a man's mistresses." Colleen accepted the cup of tea Sara handed her. "I made sure ye would scream the house down and preach propriety at every turn."

"I don't mean to inquire about what Gavin does when he's not with me," replied Sara.

"Ye willna have tae," Colleen said with one of her lusty laughs. "Some gossipy female will give ye the name o' his next mistress practically the minute Gavin picks her out."

"No, they won't."

Colleen looked up from her tea so quickly she almost spilled it. Sara's words had surprised her, but her tone was even more unexpected. She had spoken in the same quiet voice, but there was an edge of steel in it now.

"Sure they will. Respectable females can't stop talking about a man's doings when he steps out."

"I don't think you understand me. I expect I shall hear a great deal about what Gavin does, but I won't hear anything about his mistresses."

"Well, I suppose yer friends wouldna tell ye, if ye really didna want them tae, but I wouldna be surprised if the lady herself spilled the beans."

"There won't be any beans to spill." Colleen's gaze became riveted.

"But ye just said . . . ye mean ye'll tell him he canna have a mistress?"

"Certainly not, but he will sleep in no bed but mine."

"Why . . . How?"

"Because I shall see that he doesn't want to."

"By gor, ye canna be in love with him!"

"I've loved Gavin since I was twelve." Colleen stared at her unbelieving for several moments. "Why is it so difficult to believe that a wife can love her husband, especially such a husband as Gavin?" Sara asked. "Surely his mistresses must find something attractive about him."

"Aye, his mistresses, but his wife . . ."

"Is there any reason why I can't like the same things? I'm a woman, too."

"But ye be his *wife*."

"We've established that. The sticking point seems to be that you can't believe a wife can enjoy the physical side of a relationship as much as the man."

Colleen's cup slipped out of her hand unnoticed. "Ye like bedding Gavin?"

Sara tried, but she couldn't suppress a blush. "I think it's the other way around, but yes, I like sharing a bed with my husband. Do you plan to turn your husband out of bed?"

"Not if he be a lusty lad," Colleen said forthrightly.

"Then you can understand how I feel about Gavin."

"Aye, and that be why I willna give him up. I dinna like ye when I came," Colleen confided suddenly. "I thought ye were a cold, hard woman, who would demand her man's faithfulness and then deny him the comfort of her bed. I dinna think ye loved him, no' like a *real* woman. This be a problem, aye, 'tis no' easy tae decide what tae do."

Sara took a sip of tea to keep the smile from her lips. The more she talked to Colleen, the more she liked her, but that didn't mean she liked her enough to offer her Gavin.

"I love Gavin," Colleen stated suddenly, "but ye love him too, even though ye are his wife. So, I will share him with ye."

"Wha—" Sara had just taken a swallow of tea, and she nearly choked, sending a spray of tea over her gown.

"Aye, we will share him," Colleen said, as she jumped up and helped Sara mop up the tea. "He won't mind."

"But I will," Sara stated emphatically, when she finally got back the normal use of her throat. "I will not share my husband with anybody."

Colleen gave her a hard stare. "I will fight ye for him."

"And I will fight you back," Sara said, calmly, implacably. "And if you persist in your pursuit of a man who is *my* husband, not yours, I will deny you entrance to this house."

"Ye must be daft. This be Scotland, not England. No woman tells a man who canna come into his home."

"I shall, and Gavin shall respect my wishes."

"He willna!" Colleen declared, outraged. "We will see what Gavin has tae say when he gets back."

"You can put your case to Gavin if you wish, but you will not do it here."

"Why not?" Colleen asked suspiciously.

"Because you will not be here. You will leave as soon as you've had your tea."

"I willna go."

"You may not think so yet, but you will."

"No, I willna." Colleen settled back into her chair, determined to show Sara that she could not be bullied, but Sara's air of calm certainty unsettled her. At last she would stand it no longer. "Why should I go?" she asked defiantly.

"Because if you don't, I shall scratch your eyes out."

Gavin heard the sound of the harpsichord and violin before he opened the door to the music room, but he was unprepared for the sight that met his eyes. Sara was accompanying a grossly fat man who played the violin badly, at least to Gavin's unappreciative ears, while a young exquisite Gavin didn't remember having seen before, was staring at her with a rapt gaze. Watching this group, and apparently amused by what he saw, Ian Fraser lounged at his ease across the room.

"What in thunder is going on?" Gavin demanded of Ian, raising his voice to make it heard over the scraping of the violin.

"Monsieur Frederic is performing a duet with Lady Carlisle. Had ye come earlier, ye would have heard the poem Eric Cameron dedicated tae yer wife's blue eyes." Ian's amused nod indicated the young exquisite.

"I'll strangle the puppy," Gavin growled, looking black. "How long has this been going on?"

"Only a few days, but if ye can judge by Lady Carlisle's effect on the men o' the district, 'tis only the beginning."

"The hell you say," Gavin said, his voice loud enough to bring a grimace from young Eric and a reproving frown from Monsieur Frederic. "I'll put a stop to this right now." He walked over and unceremoniously took the bow out of Monsieur Frederic's hand. "I must speak with my wife. Ian will show you out."

"Gavin!" Sara exclaimed, delight at his return mingled with reproof for his abominable treatment of her guests. "I didn't expect you back so soon."

"I finished sooner than I expected," he muttered, nearly swept beyond control by the warm welcome in Sara's eyes. He still had to confront Ian about those rifles, but he was almost tempted to tell him to go away with the others. "Don't leave, Ian. I must speak with you." Ian cast an enigmatic glance at his friend, then ushered the affronted artists out of the room.

"What in the name of hell was that about?" Gavin demanded the moment the door closed. "I turn my back for one minute, and I find you alone with three men, one of them a besotted puppy, staring at you like you were frosting on a cake."

"First, you turned your back on me for three *days*. Secondly, would you have preferred that I be with one man only?"

"No! You shouldn't be with any man when I'm not about."

"Were you never with a woman when I wasn't about?" Sara was delighted with this show of jealousy, and she decided it was the perfect time to tell him about Colleen.

"None," he said quietly.

"Not even Clarice?" Why was she always asking dangerous questions? Wasn't it much better to let the past remain in the past?

"No," he replied, and the tension between them seemed to evaporate. "My father assumed I went straight to Clarice, but I wanted to be alone. She only came to tell me of mother's death."

Sara had no idea how heavily that burden had weighed on her heart until it was lifted. Gavin had never been with anyone since he married her! She might not have captured his heart, but her hold was strong enough to keep him coming back to her even when he tried to stay away. She felt so happy she almost considered allowing Colleen back in the castle. Almost.

Sara took a deep breath and replied, "That's what I told Colleen." Gavin looked at her inquiringly. "She said she was quite fond of you and didn't want to give you up."

Sara would have been willing to bet that Gavin had never blushed in his whole life, but he did so now, and it did her heart almost as much good as it did to know he had not gone to Clarice. No matter what Gavin may have wanted to do or had done in the past, if he blushed like this, he was too ashamed ever to do it again.

"She actually told you that?"

"We had a very frank discussion," Sara said, pleased to see the incredulity in his eyes. "I told her I was also quite fond of you, and that since you were my husband, I felt I had the stronger claim. She was rather stunned to find that a wife would actually enjoy her husband's embraces, but once she had comprehended that notion—"

"You told her that?" Gavin asked in disbelief.

"I told you, we were quite candid."

"My god, if my father were only here now," Gavin said, starting toward the table where he snatched up a brandy decanter and poured himself out a large shot. "He thought you were practically a nun."

"I see no reason for a girl of restricted upbringing to be incapable to adjusting to the world," Sara said grandly. "But you've made me wander from the point."

"There's more?"

"Certainly. Colleen decided she couldn't give you up until she found someone as good . . ."

"Someone as good!" Gavin choked.

". . . but since she was forced to recognize the legitimacy of my claim, she offered to share you with me."

"Share me!"

"Gavin, dear, you're beginning to sound like an echo."

"My god, woman, I'm not a pie to be cut into slices and passed around."

"Colleen seems to think you've been passed around quite a bit already."

Gavin didn't know whether to be embarrassed or break out laughing. He compromised and poured himself another shot of brandy.

"Anyway, I told her I couldn't agree to share you. At that, she declared she would fight me for you."

Gavin couldn't help it. He went into a shout of laughter. He was still doubled up when Ian returned.

"Maybe I shouldna left. Yer two gentlemen were no' half as much fun."

"It's your cousin," Gavin told him when he could control his voice. "She offered to share me with my wife, and when Sara declined, she said she'd fight her for me just like I was a meat pie to be haggled over."

"So that's what Colleen meant when she said ye wouldna have her here again." Ian watched Gavin's changing expression with hopeful heart.

"What do you mean, Sara won't have her here?"

Sara couldn't help but be a little irritated with Ian. She had planned to tell Gavin herself, but she had wanted to prepare him a little first. "I told her she could not come here if she intended to embarrass you by her determined pursuit. I can't have my husband made the object of a determined pursuit in my own home."

"It would add considerably to the entertainment of the evening," Ian said, pure deviltry in his eyes.

"You stay out of this. I've got something to say to you later anyway." Gavin turned back to his wife. "Are you trying to make a fool out of me? What do you think people will say, when they learn my wife has to protect me from other women?"

"I don't imagine they will learn of it, and if not, they can't say anything."

"Aye, but they will. Colleen is already broadcasting it about tae all who will listen."

"Damn the bitch!" Gavin exploded, heedless of Sara's ears. "Why can't she keep her mouth shut for once. I'll be the laughingstock of the county."

"I didn't tell her she couldn't come here at all," Sara explained, "only that I wouldn't have her pursuing you under my nose."

"And what's to stop her?" Gavin demanded.

"I told her I'd scratch her eyes out."

"Aye," Ian added, "and she believed you."

Gavin's anger was stopped in its tracks. He didn't know if Sara would really throw Colleen out of the castle, but if she had made Colleen believe it, *Colleen Fraser*, a girl who had ridden bareback since she was two and wrestled anything in breeches since she was three, then she must have meant it. It was difficult for Gavin to picture Sara throwing Colleen out of any place she wanted to be—he found it impossible to imagine Sara losing her calm composure—but then he remembered the two nights they had been together, and realized there was much more to Sara than he knew. If she could talk openly with Colleen about sleeping with him, what couldn't she do?

"We'll finish this discussion later," Gavin said to Sara, not nearly as displeased as he appeared, but unsure of how to proceed in such an unprecedented situation. "I've got something to say to Ian." He turned abruptly to his friend to cover his confusion. "What in hell did you mean by hiding rifles on my land? Do you know what could have happened if the wrong people had found them?"

"I don't know what you mean," Ian said, feigning ignorance, but there was an ominous hardness about his eyes.

"The hell you don't," Gavin cursed, too wrought up to think of Sara's sensibilities. "If Cumberland, or my beloved cousin, had gotten their hands on them first, I could be swinging from a gallows right now."

Sara looked from one man to the other, horror and

incomprehension in her eyes.

"And what about Sara? After you let her go prancing over half of England with your Prince and the rest of those idealistic fools, not to mention marching into Glasgow at his side, do you think anyone would believe she knew nothing about it?"

Ian's cold gaze softened only slightly. "I didna mean to endanger Sara."

"Lady Carlisle to you!" Gavin thundered.

"I said tae hide them where they would no' be found."

"Well, I *found* them in a cave on my land, one hundred and fifty Dutch-made rifles. Quite enough to put my family in permanent eclipse."

"Ah well," Ian said, recovering some of his composure, "since there has been no harm—"

"Is that all you can say, there's been no harm? You and that damned foreigner—"

"I willna allow ye tae speak o' yer rightful prince in that manner." Ian's eyes were cold and angry.

"He's not my prince, and I'll speak of him any damned way I please," Gavin thundered back. "That man has no thought—and never has had any—for the lives he's putting at risk. What will happen to him if you fail? He goes back to Europe and continues to live in safety and luxury. And what will he leave behind? Thousands of men dead, a country needlessly torn apart, and Cumberland on our necks for the rest of our lives."

"I know ye canna see the justice o' our cause—"

"Justice be damned!" Gavin practically shouted. "It's suicide. I can't stop you from putting your own head on the chopping block, but I'll be damned if I'll allow you to endanger Sara. Not to mention me and everybody else at Estameer."

Ian's eyes softened to sadness. "I admit I didna think o' the danger. I told them tae use yer land, because I thought ye would at least be in sympathy with us."

"Sympathy! After I've talked myself blue in the face for—"

"Not the prince. My own family, the ones who were treacherously slaughtered in the '15."

"You know how I feel about that," Gavin said, in a much milder voice. "I will never lift a hand against you, and I've told Hawley and Cumberland the same, but I will not help you. You have no right to expect it of me."

"Nay, I willna ask it of ye. Now, if ye will tell me what ye have done with the rifles . . ."

"I destroyed them."

"Ye did *what!*" Ian cried, shock and fury turning him into a madman. He drew his dirk and sprang across the room toward Gavin, ready to strike. "Tell me ye lie. Tell me!" he shouted.

Utter panic clutched Sara's heart; she felt like she couldn't move, but she had to stop Ian. He would not hurt her, but in his madness, he might stab Gavin. Her body seemed immobile, then it moved too slowly, but somehow she managed to step between Gavin and Ian. The dirk came within inches of her throat.

In almost the same instant, Gavin pulled Sara aside with one hand and grasped Ian's wrist with the other, his fingers digging into the flesh with maniacal fury, until Ian's dirk clattered uselessly to the floor. All three of them froze, the horror of what had so nearly happened, locking them into position like so many mannequins.

"I destroyed them," Gavin said at last, speaking in a quiet voice. "That was my only choice. I could not give them to you or to Cumberland."

"I bought those rifles so the men would have some means of defending themselves," Ian said between clenched teeth, his hand sinking to his side, his face a mask of pain and defeat. "Some have nothing but a dirk, others not even that. They cost me everything I have."

"I'll give you the money, but I can't give you the rifles."

"I willna take money from a defender of the German usurper," Ian cried, unreasoning hatred turning his eyes a dark red. "I would kill you first."

"I think you'd better leave," Gavin said quietly. "And until you can think of something other than your fanatical loyalty to your prince, it would be better if you didn't come back."

Ian looked at him with dulled, listless eyes. "Ridding yerself of all yer dangerous baggage? Fat George would be proud of ye."

"I won't have you here, because you might harm Sara."

"I willna hurt her."

"You've already come too close. I can't risk it again."

"So that's it?" Ian asked, his eyes now empty.

Gavin could not put the excommunication into words, but his gaze never wavered. After a moment, Ian quietly turned and left the room.

Chapter 21

"Gavin, go after him. You can't let him leave thinking you hate him." Sara's shock at what had happened between Gavin and Ian far outweighed her joy in knowing that Gavin had been willing to jettison a lifelong friendship for her sake.

"He knows I don't. Both of us were fools to think this rebellion wouldn't come between us sooner or later, but I couldn't have him jeopardizing your safety."

"They really can't win?"

"No."

"What will happen?"

"I don't know, but I'm afraid it will be worse than anything that's come before. Hawley is out for revenge, because his own stupidity and arrogance made a fool of him, but I don't think Cumberland will be much better. This rebellion has posed a serious threat to his father's throne, and coming on top of the uprisings of '15 and '19, they've got to feel they must crush the power of the clans once and for all."

"Can't we help them?"

"No. I've already talked to everyone who'll listen. They've had one victory after another, and they think they can continue."

"Would Ian's rifles have made a difference?"

"No. In fact, losing them may actually save some lives."

Sara couldn't understand how that could happen, but that wasn't uppermost in her mind. Her coming to Scotland had caused Gavin to be separated from two of his oldest friends, and she couldn't help but feel guilty. She didn't mind too much about Colleen—though she liked Colleen, she couldn't tolerate the thought of her being with Gavin—but Ian's friendship was of a much higher order, and she knew that in spite of the wedge of jealousy her presence had created in their relationship, Gavin would soon regret the loss of this friendship.

"You didn't have to do this for me," Sara said, raising her eyes until she could look Gavin full in the face. "I could have gone back to London."

Gavin knew he hadn't done it *just* for Sara, but he also knew the threat of Sara's having to return to London would have been sufficient reason in itself for him to ban Ian from Estameer for life.

"It wasn't just for you. It was for everyone at Estameer, me included. And he would have endangered my father and possibly cast suspicion on Clarice and my friends. No, Ian had no right to jeopardize the lives of innocent people."

"Would you have done the same thing, if it had been just me?" She shouldn't push him, but she had to know what was in his heart. In the months since he had brought her to Estameer from Glasgow, her feelings for him had changed from youthful infatuation to a love built on trust and admiration. She *had* to know if there were a chance he would ever feel the same way about her.

"Yes, I would have done it just for you."

"Why?"

How could he tell her that in a matter of a few short weeks, the relationships of a lifetime had changed so completely, he no longer knew his own feelings? No one could have been more surprised than he that, when he found those rifles, his only thought was of the danger their discovery could mean to Sara. He had been so busy worrying that falling in love would make him vulnerable, that he hadn't realized he had *already fallen in love!*

"You're my wife, I'm supposed to take care of you," he said, trying to sidestep her question. "Besides, you were almost forced to marry me."

But Sara would not be sidetracked. He may have been coerced into marriage, but he was not one to bend to any man's will. He had opposed his father, the Stuart prince, Hawley and Cumberland, and the leaders of the rebelling clans—all men of great power and influence—and now he had turned his back on his best friend. His treatment of her had always been considerate, even though it wasn't heartwarming, but something had changed in their relationship, and she was going to make him tell her what it was. "Are those the only reasons, duty and guilt?" She didn't believe they were.

"Dammit, you know I didn't do it out of duty and guilt."

"No, I don't. You've never told me what you feel about me."

He hadn't told her, because things had happened so fast he wasn't sure himself. But now he was. "You have become very dear to me, even necessary," Gavin said, as he reached out and put his arms around her. "No matter what other reasons I might have for being angry with Ian, I couldn't let him do anything to hurt you."

Sara's eyes were so filled with tears of happiness she could hardly see, but she refused to blink, to miss even one sliver of this wonderful moment.

"At first, I was so busy hating my father, I was filled with hostility and distrust. I thought you only married me for my position in society, and I didn't *want* to like you. But when I saw you in Glasgow, and saw how everyone liked and respected you, I was forced to open my eyes and see what everyone else had been able to see from the first glance. I found I had married a beautiful woman of sufficient grace and courage to inspire admiration wherever she went. It didn't take me long to see that no matter what your reasons were for marrying a virtual stranger, you were determined to devote yourself to making me happy. I don't say you haven't given me a couple of shocks, like banning Colleen from Estameer, but I could never doubt you did it because you care for me."

"I love you," Sara said, barely able to articulate the words for the choking feeling in her throat. "I always have."

"I thought so, but I couldn't admit it until now. It made me feel even more guilty."

"But why should my love make you feel guilty?"

"Because I didn't love you, and I knew what that could do to a person's life. My mother loved my father utterly and blindly. He was punctilious in his attentions to her comfort, but he never cared for anything but her money and the empire it enabled him to build. You can't know what it's like to pour out unquestioning love year after year and receive nothing in return. I had to watch my mother literally die of emotional starvation. I've fought against my feelings for you, because I learned to equate love with suffering and betrayal."

"I will never betray you," Sara declared, her heart wrung at the thought of what he must have endured all those years. "*Never!*"

"I know you wouldn't intentionally."

"But I won't, not for any reason," Sara declared, hoping her earnestness would convince him of her sincerity.

"I believe you." Gavin's assurances were a little too

hurried; he didn't want to distress her, but he knew people's feelings could change. Nothing lasted forever.

Sara saw this distrust in his eyes, and her happiness lost some of its luster. I'll show him, she vowed to herself. I don't know how just yet, but I'll show him.

Gavin looked at her youth and her beauty, the body he could still visualize with aching clarity, and wondered if *his* feelings would last forever, or if he would tire of her as he had done of every other woman he had known. He was powerfully drawn to her—even now, just sitting next to her had thrown his blood in a fever—but he was just as powerfully drawn by her courage, determination, loyalty, and her willingness to accept people as she found them and like them anyway. He found his appreciation of these qualities affected him just as strongly as her physical attractions. He was a little surprised to realize that hadn't been true of anyone else. Maybe it *would* be different this time. He told himself not to hope too strongly, but he was learning a lesson that many had learned before him: when you want something badly enough, you never give up hope of finding it someday.

A wave of nausea swept up from Sara's stomach. This was the third morning in a row she had felt this way, but it was the first time she had been so strongly affected she couldn't eat. It was bothersome, but nothing could disturb her happiness. For two months she and Gavin had lived in utter contentment, and she was satisfied that though he still might not know he loved her, he did know he would never willingly let her go.

Sara pushed her breakfast away and settled back in bed with a pleasurable shiver. Though a recent warm spell had melted enough snow so that Gavin could go see how the mines were coming along, it was still bitterly cold, and she luxuriated in the warmth provided by the several down-filled comforters on her bed. It wasn't as warm as when Gavin lay next to her, but then she expected him home tonight. Not even once in the past two months had he failed to spend the night in her bed.

She thought of the glorious hours they had spent together, hours in which her expertise in and knowledge of lovemaking had been stretched beyond all conceivable bounds, and she smiled like a self-satisfied cat. She wondered if she would ever get a chance to thank Letty Brown for the knowledge that had helped her face this once-frightening aspect of her marriage and discover that it was not only an incredible experience in itself, but that it added a dimension to their marriage which would have been impossible without it. She was certain Gavin would never leave her bed for anyone else's, and she meant to rescind her ban on Colleen as soon as she had the opportunity.

She smiled a little guiltily. It wasn't just that she was trying to be fair, or that she was demonstrating to Gavin her complete trust. She had to admit she wanted to gloat a little over Colleen. After feeling second best for so long, it was wonderful to know that Gavin prized her slim figure and strawberry blond hair over Colleen's opulent curves and flaming tresses. She supposed if they were still in London, she'd have invited Clarice Wynburn to tea, even though it would have been shocking and not even Gavin would have understood. The longing to herald her triumph far and wide was irresistible, and she began to consider the possibilities of having another party. Just then, however, another wave of nausea rolled over her, sweeping away all thoughts of merrymaking.

"Take this away," she told Betty, the minute she stepped into the room. "The smell is making me ill."

"You're not taking sick, are you?" Betty demanded, giving Sara a careful look before she removed the tray. "Living in this terrible climate is enough to make a body go off with pneumonia. I never will understand why the men don't freeze right solid, especially wearing them disgraceful little dresses like they do."

"They're kilts," Sara said, "and you know it's their traditional form of dress."

"So I hear tell, but I never did hear what caused them to start doing such a nonsensical thing. You can't tell me they'd suffer a heat stroke from wearing proper breeches, not even in the dead of summer."

"I suppose every country has at least one custom nobody else can understand."

"Not those Frenchies. They've got *dozens* of them."

"Well, right now I'm not interested in the French, or anyone else. I just want this sick feeling to go away so I can get up. This is the third morning in a row, and I'm getting tired of it." That remark acted on Betty like a bolt of lightning.

"You mean you've been feeling sick every morning, and you didn't say anything to me?"

"It wasn't enough to bother me at first, but it's quite unpleasant today." Betty looked at Sara more closely, felt her temples, and looked at her eyes.

"I knew it," she exclaimed in triumph. "You're with child." Sara stared at her in disbelief. "We're both woolie heads not to remember you haven't had your flow since right after the New Year. Here it is nearly the last of March, and his lordship visiting you every night." Sara blushed. She didn't know why, but she did.

"Well, I hope I'm not going to feel like this the rest of the time," Sara said, making a determined effort to get out of the bed. "I'll be the most miserable person at Estameer."

"But the most cossetted," Betty said. "As long as you're carrying the heir, nobody will be able to do enough for you."

"I hope Gavin will be pleased," Sara said, remembering his loudly voiced determination not to provide his father with an heir.

"He'll bust his britches with pride," Betty assured her. "I must admit his lordship has changed a lot since you married him. You might be able to make something of him yet, though he won't never be the match of that nice Mr. Fraser."

Sara had given up trying to make Betty prefer Gavin to Ian. His gallant behavior, especially during the march north with the army, was Betty's idea of how a man should treat a woman. As a matter of fact, Sara thought pretty highly of it herself, but she had never been able to make Betty see that Gavin's own suffering and guilt had been at the root of his earlier mistreatment of her. As far as Betty was concerned, there was no such thing as extenuating circumstances.

"Well, it seems to have passed off," Sara said of the nausea after she was out of bed. "I don't think I want anything to eat, but I do feel better."

"Good. I'll dress you warm, and you can spend the day in the sitting room. You're going to have to take it easy until that baby comes."

"That will be months. You can't expect me to sit quietly on the shelf until then. I know Gavin won't."

"His lordship wouldn't dream of touching you," Betty stated confidently. "The urge is bound to leave him the minute he knows you're carrying his child." Sara thought she had a more realistic understanding of Gavin's *urges*, and she doubted they would be affected in the least.

"Oh, I almost forgot," Betty said, as she was laying out Sara's clothes. "This note was delivered all secretlike by one of the kitchen maids. She said it was most urgent that you had it." Sara took the note, but there was nothing on the envelope to tell her who sent it or what it was about. Betty made a pretense of going about her work, but she cast several curious glances at her mistress as she opened the note and read its contents.

Lady Carlisle,

I would like to offer my apologies for the unhappiness my behavior has caused you and Lord Carlisle. My cousin is equally sorry for the rude way in which she greeted your marriage, and she would now like to offer you her friendship.

We very much miss your company and beg that you and Gavin will rescind the ban against us. Since you are the more forgiving by nature, I beseech you to meet with us to formulate a way to bring Gavin to lay aside his distrust.

We will await you at the Lazy Sea Dog Inn at eleven this morning.

Your servant,
Ian Fraser

"Here," Sara said, handing the note to Betty. "I suppose I'll have to go, even though I don't much feel like going out today."

"Of course, you'll go. Just think of what that poor Mr. Fraser must have suffered all these months, from thinking you didn't like him anymore. Though I can't say I'll be pleased to see the likes of Colleen Fraser slinking about the place, making eyes at his lordship. I suppose you can't have one without the other, them being cousins and all."

"I do feel a little sorry for her."

"Pray tell why?" Betty asked, incensed that Sara should feel any sympathy for a female she considered barely short of a Jezebel.

"Well, she was hoping to marry Gavin herself, and if I hadn't married him, she might have succeeded."

"I don't believe it," Betty declared emphatically.

"Lord Carlisle is thoughtless, and his heart is about as tender as a piece of old goat meat, but he's got too much sense to tie himself up for life with that basket of curds."

For the last three hours, Sara had cursed herself for a fool, and she was still so angry with Ian Fraser she could have choked him with her own hands if she could just have gotten them around his traitorous throat. He and Colleen had met her just outside the gates of Estameer and talked her into riding in their carriage and sending hers home. They *had* talked of ways to induce Gavin to allow Ian to return to Estameer, even Colleen seemed to be genuinely sorry for her earlier behavior. Sara was conscientiously thinking of what approach to use on Gavin when she realized the carriage had not proceeded to the village as she expected but instead was stopping before an unfamiliar house. Upon being questioned, Ian had been unstinting in his apologies, but he had not hesitated to tell Sara that she had been kidnapped.

"But why?" Sara demanded. "What can you gain from kidnapping me?"

His reply was succinct and unflattering. "My rifles." Betty should be here now, thought Sara. She wouldn't think he's the most wonderful man since Sir Galahad anymore.

"Are they so important?"

"We cannot win without them."

"Gavin says you can't win no matter what you do."

"We haven't lost a battle yet."

"Gavin says you can win most of the battles, but you will still lose the war."

"I willna hear any more *Gavin says,*" snapped Ian. "I also do not want Gavin to fight on the side of Cumberland," he added after a slight pause.

"You know he wouldn't," Sara said indignantly.

"Gavin has already told Hawley and Cumberland he wouldn't lift a hand against his neighbors."

"I know. You can think o' yerself as a wee bit o' insurance."

"You don't need it," Sara snapped angrily. "Gavin has given you his word, and he is a man of honor. You, of all people, should know that. Why do you think he was so upset about those rifles?" Ian looked flushed, but he did not reply. "Where are you taking me?" Sara asked.

"Ye wouldna know if I told ye, but Colleen will stay with ye, until Gavin sends the rifles. We do not intend to mistreat ye."

"I didn't think you would. I'm merely a pawn, something to be exchanged for something else. Correct?"

"I wouldna want ye tae think so poorly o' yerself."

"But you do intend to exchange me for your rifles?"

"Aye."

"Then don't quibble over terms." Sara was angry, and she didn't care if he knew it. "What's *your* reason?" she demanded of Colleen. "Surely you're not hoping Gavin will be so grateful for your care for me, that he will take you as his mistress." Colleen's flush betrayed her intention. "This is unbelievable!" Sara exclaimed. "It's like a fairy tale, and just as intelligent!"

"We shall see," Ian said, then proceeded to ignore her.

"I don't know where she can be," Betty protested tearfully to Gavin. "She went to meet Mr. Fraser and his cousin before midday. She should have been back by mid-afternoon."

Gavin didn't hear Betty's tearful explanation. He was reading Ian's note, and every word stoked the rage that was building inside him. "This is an obvious ruse," he thundered at Betty. "Ian would never beg anyone's pardon, not even if they had a knife at his throat."

"But he was always so kind, such a gentleman," Betty protested.

"Ian has beautiful manners, much better than mine," Gavin admitted, "but it cloaks a will of iron. *Nothing* will stop him from getting what he wants."

"Not even the mistress?"

"Not even Lady Carlisle." Gavin strode to the door and gave a shout for his bailiff, while Betty gave this information some thought.

"Then he won't be bringing her back?"

"Not until he gets what he wants, no matter how long it takes."

Tom came at a run, and Gavin rapped out his orders without pause.

"Find Kincaid and have him dredge the rifles from the river bottom. They'll be full of mud, but they haven't been there long enough for corrosion to ruin them. I want you to have every man on the estate mounted and in the courtyard within the hour, armed and wearing the plaid. I don't care if they are five or a hundred and five and have to be tied to the saddle. Lady Carlisle has been kidnapped, and we're going after her."

Knowing nothing of the rifles, Tom had looked at his master like he had suddenly gone insane, but at that last sentence, the light of battle shone brightly in his eyes and all hesitation vanished. He was just as anxious as Gavin to take the battle to the offending clan.

"He must want you to do something," Betty said, frightened by the unexpected preparations for war. "Aren't you going to wait to find out what it is?"

"Ian knows it's something I won't do, or he wouldn't have captured my wife. He knows this means war."

By calling upon neighbors who did not support the Stuart prince, Gavin was able to gather almost two hundred men, and it was an impressive cavalcade that rode up to the Fraser stronghold three hours later. Armed with dirk, claymore, and Ian's rifles with fixed bayonets, they would have been a force to be reckoned with at any time. Against a clan whose ranks had been depleted to provide warriors for the rebel army, they were overwhelming. The sight of more than a hundred torches stretching far back over the hills as they blazed against the night sky sent chills through every Fraser heart, but old Donald Fraser came out in answer to Gavin's summons.

"Why have ye come in such a way against a friend?" the old man asked, facing Gavin courageously, but uneasy in the face of overwhelming odds.

"I want Ian and Colleen, but most of all, I want my wife."

"I know nothing of Lady Carlisle, but Ian has been called north to help with the siege of Blair Castle. He left this morning."

"*This morning* he was busy luring my wife outside the castle gates on the pretense that he and Colleen wanted to repair our friendship. It's nearly twelve hours later and she still has not returned. The innkeeper where she was supposed to meet them swore they never arrived." It was clear to Gavin that the old man knew nothing of this. The friendship between their families was of long standing and highly valued by both sides. He would not break it lightly.

"I will have a search made for Colleen and get to the truth. I do no' understand what reason Ian would have tae do such a thing," he said, after he had given the order.

"Rifles."

"Rifles?"

"You don't know about them either?" The old man shook his head. "Ian mortgaged his inheritance to buy them for the prince. He hid them in a cave at Estameer. I found them and destroyed them."

"Destroyed?" the old man queried, his skeptical gaze

indicating the rifles carried by the Estameer men.

"I meant to leave them in the river, but I needed them."

"And you would use them against us?"

"I will burn every house, barn, and croft on Fraser land to the ground, slaughter your livestock, and put every man to the sword if I must, but I will find my wife. Ian put everyone at Estameer at risk when he chose to hide those rifles on my land. Now he's endangered every Fraser life to get them back, and all for a prince who will desert you after he causes your best men to die. How long will you continue in this madness?"

"We canna desert our prince," Donald Fraser repeated stubbornly, but his declaration lacked the enthusiasm of earlier times. "However, I will have no part in kidnapping any man's wife. We will find Colleen and she will lead us to your wife." But when the search was completed, they could find no trace of Ian or Colleen.

"It is clear what ye say is true. We will search for them all night."

"My men will help you," Gavin said, and gave his men orders to prepare to make camp. The expected message from Ian reached Gavin less than an hour later.

"He paid one o' the lads tae keep it a day afore he delivered it tae the castle," Tom explained. "But with all the upset, the lad thought it best tae give it over now." Gavin read the note and handed it to Donald Fraser.

"It's what I expected," Gavin said. "We won't stop until we find them."

But though they searched the night through, they could find no trace of Sara or Colleen, the carriage, or the men who had driven it. They seemed to have dropped off the face of the earth.

Chapter 22

"Don't you want anything to eat?" Colleen asked, when Sara waved away her offer of breakfast.

"I can't eat anything. I'm sick every morning now."

Colleen gaped at Sara, the reality of her marriage to Gavin only just now sinking in. "Ye be carrying his bairn?"

"I hope so," Sara replied with a grimace, as a wave of nausea swept over her. "I'd hate to think I'm starving to death for nothing."

"Does Gavin know?"

"I didn't get a chance to tell him." Colleen's normally audacious gaze wavered before Sara's accusing eyes.

"I didna know, otherwise I wouldna help Ian steal ye."

"Why did you? What did you think you had to gain?"

"I want Gavin back. If it hadna been for ye, he would have married me."

Sara's gaze softened a little. "Do you love him?"

"Aye, I like him well enough."

"I asked if you *loved* him," Sara repeated, irritated at Colleen's lack of understanding. "Would you be faithful to him and strive to make him a good wife?"

"Aye, I would," Colleen answered angrily. "I am no rich, white-skinned virgin. 'Tis a big, healthy woman I am, and I would make him happy." She stared at Sara, and her belligerent gaze gave way to confusion. "What can he want with ye? Ye canna ride a horse like a man, ye dance like an old woman—I ken ye would faint at the sight o' blood—and ye havena the strength of a baby."

"You don't like me very much, do you?"

"I like ye a wee bit," Colleen admitted reluctantly, "but ye be no woman for a bonnie lad like Gavin."

"A man does not want the same thing in a wife that he likes in a mistress," Sara told her. "I think it's particularly unfair, but it's true."

"What do ye mean?"

"I haven't learned a great deal about men yet, but I do know that even though a mistress can be as bold as she likes, riding horses recklessly across the hills and dancing until she drops from fatigue, a man wants his wife to exercise decorum, ride in a carriage, and always be calm and composed."

"Nay, never a lusty lad like Gavin."

"Gavin is a man just like every other man, who wants his wife to stay home and see that his household is run properly, and that his guests and tenants are provided for. He wants sons to defend his lands, and daughters to comfort his old age. His wife must add to his dignity, but never become a burden. Above all, he demands that she be faithful to him, even though he may take her money and spend it on his mistresses. If she is all these things and brings him a substantial dowry as well, she can be as ugly as sin and shrink from his touch, but he will wed her, install her in his bed, and put her in control of his household. And he will defend her with his last breath."

"By gor!" Colleen exclaimed, shattered. "You would be all that for Gavin?"

Sara laughed softly. "That and more."

"What more can there be?" Colleen wondered, certain no woman could do that much.

"I will be his friend and his mistress, too." Colleen's jaw dropped. "I will let him bring me his troubles, listen to his tirades, and take his side in every issue. I will give him advice, but will not blame him if he doesn't take it, be at his side even when I disagree with him, and at night, whether he is tired or amorous, I will yield him the comfort of my body, taking as much pleasure from him as he draws from me."

"By gor," Colleen exclaimed, "how can I win against such a foe?"

"You can't, because I have the one weapon you will never have—his wedding ring."

"I have done a foolish thing," Colleen said after a bit. "Gavin will be so angry, he will never want tae be my friend."

"Forget Gavin, Colleen," Sara said earnestly. "You deserve more than any man's leftovers. You will make a good wife, if you find a man you can love and stick with him. Being a good wife is a lot like being an actress. You have to play every role, but you must remember not to mix them up or play them at the wrong time."

Gavin drove his tired horse up the steep hill, ignoring the darkness that made his reckless pace a dangerous one. It would soon be dawn, the beginning of a second day without knowing where Sara was or what had happened to her. All night long, over two hundred people had scoured the district without finding a trace of her. Gavin had racked his brain, threatened every Fraser unlucky enough to cross his path, and driven his men to the brink of exhaustion, but he could not stop. He must find Sara, but where could she be?

Twice he had started for Blair Castle, to find Ian and beat the truth out of him, and twice he had turned back, worried about what might happen to Sara during another night, fearful of what might have *already* happened. He had to think. His emotions had kept him in the saddle through the night, but while Sara might appreciate knowing how much he cared for her, right now she'd probably appreciate a little cool thinking on his part even more.

He had become wonderfully content during the past months, but he hadn't realized until now just how much she meant to him. He had become used to her company and used to her body, but he hadn't known how much he depended on her emotionally, how much he simply enjoyed being with her. And after so many years of bitterness and anger, it was an incredible relief to lay aside the terrible burden and let her goodness salve the wounds that had gone untended for so long.

She had brought a gaiety and happiness to Estameer, which had been missing since he was a small boy. Despite their distrust of the towering Betty, the staff had already taken Sara to their hearts, and he had gradually become used to finding his house invaded by poets, musicians, and several women who found the sounds of Bach and Scarlatti more appealing than the shriek of bagpipes. He had not yet accustomed himself to the warbling of Elizabeth Cameron, Eric's sister, but he could listen to Anne Grey's harp for as much as fifteen minutes before making a dash for the brandy. He didn't understand it, but he was proud that people seemed to naturally look to Sara for friendship and advice, as well as musical evenings and, God help him, poetry readings.

With an oath, Gavin pulled his horse to a halt, dismounted, and allowed the exhausted animal a drink of water and then a chance to graze. He decided he would not get back in the saddle until he had some concrete idea of where to look for Sara. What did he know and how much of Ian's thinking could he surmise?

He knew that they had met Sara outside the gate before

noon, but that no one in the village had seen the carriage go past, and it had not gone to the inn. Ian *had* left for Blair Castle before dusk, because he had been seen. So, where could they hide Sara that was only a few hours away by carriage? They had examined every building, cave, and crevasse on Fraser or Carlisle land, and had uncovered no trace of them, yet they had to be somewhere. They couldn't just vanish.

It was the carriage that baffled him. There were no cottages along the road, and it had not been seen by anyone. Of course, you fool, he told himself, it disappeared *before* it reached the village. Now the question was, where had it gone, but he knew the answer almost before he finished asking the question. An ancient aunt of Donald Fraser lived alone in a house in the hills several miles off the road between Estameer and the village. As she was undoubtedly the meanest woman in Scotland—she was also extremely hard of hearing and nearly blind—everyone stayed well clear of her. The only person she had ever shown any affection for was Ian. Somehow, she must have helped Ian hide Sara. Gavin leapt into the saddle and put his tired horse into a gallop. He thought vaguely that he ought to go back for Donald Fraser, but he didn't have time.

From his hiding place on the far side of the depression, which contained a small house and the several buildings surrounding it, Gavin watched Old Peg Fraser leave her home to feed and water her stock. She was accompanied by the largest staghound Gavin had ever seen. Obviously, his first task would be to reach the house without the dog catching his scent. He didn't know how he was going to get past the beast a second time, especially with Sara along, but he'd figure that out once he found her. Gavin was on his feet and heading toward the house, approaching the buttery—it was a small square building with a hole dug in the ground where Old Peg kept milk and butter cool in the summer—when the wind shifted, until it was coming directly from behind him. His scent! It would reach the hound in seconds. Would it attack?

Swiftly Gavin took stock of his position. Unaware earlier that Old Peg was guarded by a huge hound, and not thinking that he would need to defend himself against an old woman, he had left his sword on his horse. If the dog attacked him, he would have no choice but to use his dirk or take refuge in the buttery. But hiding wouldn't do him any good. He had to find some way to get to the house. Just at that moment, the air was split by a bone-chilling howl. The hound had caught his scent and was coming after him.

Quickly, Gavin rounded the buttery, flung wide the door, and positioned himself just inside. The hound could see him from a long way off, but that was what he was counting on. The buttery was a small building with steps leading down into a hole about six feet deep. He wanted the hound to attack at full speed. He would step aside just as the animal lunged for him, but the dog would be unable to stop before he tumbled into the hole. Gavin counted on being able to get out of the buttery before the hound could recover and climb the pitifully few steps.

Gavin had endured several experiences in his life which had tested his nerve, but none had been so difficult as to stand still before the galloping assault of a huge dog that measured nearly five feet at the head. His fangs would have done justice to the fabled tigers of India; his eyes were red with hate, and saliva dropped from his open mouth. Gavin thought of Sara locked up somewhere in Old Peg's house, and his nerve steadied. All he had to do was time his move so the fangs would miss him. Two hundred pounds of snarling fury would be hard to fight within the close confines of the buttery.

It all happened in a split second.

Gavin waited until he could feel the hot breath of the savage beast on his skin before he leapt aside from the doorway. The small ledge seemed insufficient purchase when the hound lunged into the darkness behind him. The animal struck the wall at the back. For a second Gavin feared he was going to go right through the ancient wood, but a startled yelp and a deeper thud told him the hound had struck the bottom of the pit. Already Gavin was moving through the door, and dropping the bar into the cradle. He just hoped it would hold.

He sprinted across the yard to reach the house, quickly entered the rear door, and in so doing, surprised Colleen in the kitchen. Gavin darted forward, intending to lay hands on her before she could escape, but Colleen was so shocked to find Gavin less than three feet away and glaring fiercely enough to cause an even more stalwart damsel to shrink in fear, she was unable to move. Gavin was on her in an instant.

"Where is Sara?" he demanded, his fury-twisted features only inches from Colleen's face. His hand gripped her wrist without regard for his strength, and the pain made it difficult for Colleen to think.

"What do you mean?" she asked, trying to gather her wits. "I'm visiting my aunt. I know nothing about your wife."

Gavin's hands immediately encircled Colleen's throat. His thumbs thrust up painfully under her chin, forcing her head back with his fingers pressed hard against the bones in the back of her neck. "I can break your neck with just a tiny bit of pressure," Gavin whispered fiercely, "then I can search the house at my leisure."

"She's upstairs," Colleen gasped. "She's taken no harm."

"You'd better be telling the truth," Gavin said, and

released her so suddenly Colleen staggered and nearly fell. "Show me. I have no time to waste." He forced Colleen to go before him, half-running and half-stumbling, until she opened one of the bedroom doors. Pushing her roughly in before him, Gavin's eyes had found Sara even before he entered the room. He crossed the space separating them in an instant, and swept her up into his arms before she could utter the cry of happiness that trembled on her lips.

"Are you all right?" he asked, as soon as he could trust his voice. "They didn't do anything to hurt you?"

"I'm fine," Sara assured him, unwilling to leave the comfort of his paralyzing embrace. "The only discomfort I suffered was having to sleep alone." She managed a smile. "No quantity of quilts can keep me warm like you can."

Then Gavin started kissing her all over again. She had become used to his kisses when they made love, but this was the first time he had kissed her with such fierce possessiveness, and it was the first time he had done so in front of anyone else. But Sara didn't think of any of that just then. She was too busy responding to Gavin's kisses, exulting in the knowledge that he had told her more with each kiss than any words.

"How did you find us?" Colleen asked, breaking the magic spell of their embrace.

"It was easy, once I started thinking with my head instead of my heart," Gavin said, putting his arms around Sara and holding her close. "I knew that old termagant would do anything for Ian."

"Where is old Peg?"

"Still feeding her chickens, I guess."

"She will turn that dog on you if she sees you! Even I can't leave here without her help."

"The dog is locked in the buttery, undoubtedly

upsetting everything inside. Do you have a horse?"

"There's the carriage horses."

"Then you'll have to wait until your uncle comes for you. I can't get to them without being seen."

"No," cried Colleen. "The old witch will kill me. She hates me as much as anyone else."

"My horse can't carry three people."

"Can't you try to get one of the horses?" Sara asked.

"She helped kidnap you. Why should you help her?"

"You can't leave her here, not if that woman will hurt her."

"I'll try," Gavin said, giving in, "but if that beast gets out, we may all be torn to bits."

Gavin helped Sara and Colleen mount his horse and made them swear to head for Estameer without waiting for him. He lingered until they had started down the lane, and then turned back toward the house.

The dog was still in the buttery, barking furiously at being closed in, and wild to get at the man who had imprisoned him. Old Peg had finished her chores and was heading toward the house. Gavin sprinted behind a low wall, climbed through a cow lot, stoically ignoring the squishing sound beneath his feet, and reached the barn unseen. He was putting halters on the two horses when he heard a rapid crescendo in the hysterical barking of the dog; it told him Old Peg was approaching the house. She probably couldn't hear the dog's barking, but it would be difficult to ignore the movement of the door. The huge dog virtually knocked the building off its foundations every time he threw his body against the door.

Gavin changed his mind about looking for saddles. The dog was hysterical now, and he expected it to be released any minute. He was leading the nervous horses out of the barn when a dramatic increase in the volume of the nerve-racking howls told him the dog was free. It would only be a matter of seconds before he would reach him. Gavin flung himself on the back of one of the horses and kicked it vigorously in the side, urging it to its utmost speed, but these were coach horses, bred for strength and stamina rather than speed, and they considered a fast trot fast enough. When the deer hound rounded the corner and bounded after them, they broke into a canter, but Gavin knew they could never outrace the dog. These hounds had been known to bring down deer and elk armed with a full rack of deadly antlers. He would have little trouble with these domesticated horses.

As the hound bounded nearer, Old Peg rounded the corner of her house, shouting encouragement, her hate-filled soul furious that Gavin had escaped her fury. The hound leapt for Gavin's leg as he pulled it atop the horse, but the hound's fangs left a bloody slash down the horse's side. The horse screamed in agony and bounded forward into a clumsy gallop, but not before the hound had slashed at its hindquarters, barely missing the hamstring.

Gavin was struggling to stay on the horse, determined not to let go of the second horse in case the hound brought the first one down, but he knew there was a good chance both horses would go down under him. He doubted he would be able to get to his feet *twice* before the dog was upon him. He dared not think what would happen then. He cursed himself for not being more heavily armed, but he had left most of his weapons behind when the Frasers agreed to help with the search. What he sorely needed was a pistol, but he had only his dirk. Driven by fear and the smell of blood, both coach horses were in full gallop now. Holding both reins as best he could with one hand and keeping his legs high, Gavin managed to take out his dirk; he was in the process of considering whether to chance a throw or save it in case he went down, when he saw his own stallion racing toward him, Sara and Colleen still on its back.

Gavin's blood ran cold.

"Go back!" he shouted, but they paid him no heed. Gavin knew that his stallion hated dogs so fiercely, he would attack the hound on sight. This might save him from a savage mauling, but Sara and Colleen were bound to be thrown from his back. On the ground they would be at the dog's mercy. Determined that Sara should not sacrifice herself for him, Gavin forced the terrified coach horses to race straight into the path of the oncoming stallion.

The horses came together with a terrible impact, and in the ensuing melee, the hound was unable to mount a lethal attack, but his slashing attacks at their hindquarters were cutting the carriage horses to ribbons. Colleen was able to slip onto the back of the second carriage horse, but they had to find some way to escape before fear drove the horses totally beyond control. Gavin also had to reach his own stallion, before the smell of the hound reached his nostrils and hate drove the huge animal beyond control. Even now, Sara was just barely managing to stay in the saddle.

Suddenly Gavin's stallion threw his head up; his nostrils distended, and his entire body started to shake. The next moment he whipped around until he saw the dog. Then with an ear-splitting scream of rage, he charged, teeth bared and enormous hooves ready to aim a killing blow. Sara clung to his mane with all her strength, but the bucking and whirling of the stallion unbalanced her, and she began to slide off. Without hesitation Gavin jumped from the back of his fear-crazed mount, just in time to reach Sara as she fell. Only the stallion's lightning whirl and attack with bared teeth prevented the hound from plunging his teeth into Sara's throat. Gavin thrust her behind him, and drawing his dirk, turned to face the hound.

The hound was vicious and cunning, but he was ponderous, and his great size was a handicap in close fighting; for Gavin's mammoth stallion, it was an advantage. The infuriated horse's teeth had grazed the hound's back when it had tried to attack Sara. Turning in snarling fury, the beast found himself scrambling frantically to avoid a lethal blow from a platter-sized iron-shod hoof. But the stallion was faster; turning with incredible speed for such a large horse, his front hoof struck the hound a glancing blow on the shoulder. Gavin doubted the blow did any great harm, but it stunned the hound long enough to give the stallion time to whirl and aim a mighty kick with both hind feet.

The thud of impact failed to mask the sickening sound of breaking bones as the hound went flying through the air. He had barely landed before Gavin's stallion was upon him. With a savage scream, the horse rose above the stricken hound. Even as the lethal hooves descended, the hound uttered a vicious growl and tried to rise once more, but he sank under the hammering hooves of the stallion.

A moment later, all was still.

Gavin turned to Sara, relieved that his broad back had hidden the terrible scene from her view. He closed his arms about her, holding her tightly in silence. He remembered the fear which had nearly paralyzed him when he saw Sara driving his stallion straight at the hound. His limbs trembled; his grip on her was vicelike.

"Why did you come back?"

"Colleen said the dog had been let out. She said the horses would never be fast enough to escape. Gavin, your sword was on your stallion. You couldn't defend yourself!"

"I had my dirk. You had nothing at all."

"I couldn't just leave you, not when Colleen said your horse hated dogs enough to attack the hound."

"Colleen talks too much."

"I'm sorry if you're angry, but it was all I could think of."

"You're safe, that's all that really counts, but don't *ever* do a thing like that again! You don't even know how to ride. How could you expect to stay on that stallion?"

"I didn't think. I just knew I couldn't leave you."

Colleen rode into view, Gavin's carriage horse in tow. Both horses were still wild with fear and bleeding from the hound's attack, but Colleen was a notable horsewoman, and she had them under control.

"I see what you mean," Colleen said, her eyes missing none of the significance of Gavin's hold on Sara. "They do prefer the one who must ride in a carriage."

"What is she talking about?" Gavin asked, his anger at Colleen deflected by the enigmatic statement.

"It's just woman's talk," Sara told him, hiding a bleak smile. "You wouldn't be interested."

"Well, I would be interested in knowing what possessed you to help Ian kidnap my wife?" Gavin demanded of Colleen, forgetting the women's cryptic exchange.

"That was a mistake," Sara intervened. "She was sorry almost from the first, weren't you?" Colleen had the good sense to nod unhesitatingly. "She did it to help Ian, but she took very good care of me."

"That crazy old woman—"

"She never came near me."

But Gavin wasn't mollified. "That note . . ."

"She does want to be friends with us again," Sara interrupted again. "She truly does, and we find that we like each other quite well."

Gavin could see that Sara was determined to defend Colleen, so he reluctantly abandoned that losing battle. "When I get my hands on Ian Fraser, I'll break his neck."

"You're perfectly free to do anything you want to him," Sara said, hoping his rage would have calmed down by the time he saw Ian again. "I don't think he was at all sorry about kidnapping me, and then he left us with that terrible old woman. He said he would be back in two or three days. He seemed to think you wouldn't find us."

"He didn't mean for the ransom note to reach me so soon, but I knew why he had kidnapped you. It was only because I was his closest friend that I even thought of Old Peg."

"Ian said no one would dare come here."

"Now you know why," Gavin said, and all their gazes silently turned to what was left of the hound.

It was a silent cavalcade that wound its way through the hills to Estameer. Each was occupied with their private thoughts, each aware that once they reached Estameer, there would be no time for thought for a long time. Colleen's thoughts were not happy, and her expression was a heavy one. Gavin's thoughts were of the revenge he would take from Ian, and his expression was ferocious.

Only Sara rode with some degree of contentment. She was still angry at Ian for kidnapping her, she might never forgive him for putting Gavin in danger, and she was still weak from shock, but she was also blissfully happy. She knew unquestionably that Gavin loved her. He still might not know it, but it would only be a matter of time, before he would discover it on his own. Everything she had dreamed of was within her reach at last, and knowing she carried Gavin's child within her womb added to her sense of fulfillment. They had come through a vale of trouble and had survived danger, but they *had* survived, and her dream was about to come true.

She suddenly thought of her father, and she longed to be able to tell him that she understood now what he had felt for her mother, and that she was sorry for her jealousy. She had sometimes thought that he didn't *try* to get well when he came down with the mysterious fever, but if that had been the case, she understood now. She would not have wanted to live without Gavin either.

Chapter 23

A week later Sara was stunned to receive an urgent message from Colleen Fraser to come down to the great hall. Ian had been seriously injured in the siege of Blair Castle, and she had brought him to Estameer.

"Why didn't you take him to his father?" she demanded, when she saw Ian lying upon the stretcher like a corpse.

"He willna take him in," Colleen replied, bitterness and anger in her voice. "Either of us. He says we have shamed him and disgraced the clan, and he willna have anything more tae do with us. He willna allow anyone tae help us either. Ye are the only one left."

"But Gavin . . . I don't know . . . Do you know Cumberland heard Gavin called his men into service? Only he thinks Gavin plans to join the rebellion. Gavin left for Aberdeen this morning, to explain that he was looking for me."

"I know Gavin's away, else I wouldna have come," Colleen said. There was a desperate quality to her voice. "I have nowhere tae go. He willna live unless ye help him."

"Then he'll be getting no more than he deserves," decreed Betty, who had just reached the hall. The chagrin of having championed Ian in preference to Gavin had caused her to feel very foolish, and she was willing to say just about anything in retribution. "I'll bet a lot of Frasers are going to look queer, when they learn the rifles his lordship's men carried were so full of mud they couldn't have fired a single shot."

"Let's get him upstairs," Sara said, making the only decision she could. She dared not think of what would happen if Ian was still in the house when Gavin returned, but she couldn't refuse him, not when he was so grievously wounded.

She had regretfully kissed Gavin good-bye less than two hours earlier, but she was still wrapped in an aura of contentment. The past six days had been almost perfect. Gavin had guarded her like a precious jewel, and couldn't seem to keep his eyes off her. Twice he had traveled back from the far reaches of the estate just to share the noon meal with her, and he hadn't once missed dinner. He still hadn't given up on talking some of the clans out of their support of the Stuart prince, but he never stayed away all evening, and he was never too tired to give Sara his undivided and energetic attention when he returned.

Not a day passed that Sara didn't give thanks for Letty Brown. If she thought she could have gotten away with it, she might even have named her first daughter after her. It scared her to think how close she had come to not speaking to her.

But even with Letty's help, she hadn't achieved her ultimate goal: Gavin still hadn't said that he loved her. But that didn't bother her very much anymore. He was just about the only person in Scotland who didn't know he loved her. Feeling secure in his love, Sara was perfectly content to let him discover it for himself.

She was also content to let him remain in ignorance of the fact that she had conceived an heir, a child she was certain would be a son. She wanted him to be able to love this child from the very first moment. But if he couldn't yet admit that he loved her, how could he love her child?

Sara was also afraid he might see this child as a victory for his father, rather than the fruit of their love. She knew that no matter how much Gavin had learned to trust her, his feelings for his father would never change. She prayed Gavin would come to see his child as a wonderful gift, not as the natural result of a marriage forced upon him specifically for the purpose of producing this child. Just knowing that she was going to have a baby made her happy, and she didn't want this wonderful experience to be denied Gavin. He had suffered enough already.

She was also a little selfish. She wasn't sure she was ready to share him with anyone just yet, even his own child. Gavin had opened up so little of himself, still held himself so privately. Sara wanted more time for just the two of them, time when he could slowly lower the barriers he had erected over the years, barriers that kept out his friends as well as his wife.

Not the least of her reasons was her fear that he would stop spending his nights in her bed. Sara could have stood it if he had ceased to make love to her—she wouldn't have liked it, but she could have stood it—but she was certain Gavin would lock himself in his own room until the child was born. Sara was honest enough to admit that she didn't want that. She was sure Gavin's physical desires were stronger than her own, but Letty Brown had been a better teacher than she knew. Sara was not willing to give up Gavin's embraces until she must.

Seven days later Ian sat up in the bed, as Sara came into the room carrying lint for more bandages. She stopped abruptly.

"I didn't know you were awake."

"I asked Colleen not tae tell ye." Sara's look asked why. "Ye have avoided me ever since I got here. I had tae think o' some way tae see ye."

"After what you did, you ought to be ashamed to look me in the eye."

"I was willing tae give my life for my prince," Ian said, pointing to the bandages that still covered his chest and one thigh. "Why should I balk at one little kidnapping?"

"Your *little* kidnapping could have cost Gavin his life. That hound might have killed him, if I hadn't gone back."

"Ah well, I hadna intended for Gavin tae receive my letter until I returned. I never thought he would find ye, nor succeed in getting into the house."

"I don't find anything laudable in what you did," Sara said, stubbornly refusing to unbend. "You gave no thought at all to how your actions might injure others."

"I plead guilty in the name of the Prince," Ian said with all the old charm Sara remembered. "In my own right, I wouldna risk a hair o' yer head."

"That's a fine thing to say, now that I'm safely rescued, but if Gavin's horse hadn't killed that dreadful dog, I could be cold in my grave by now."

"Sara, ye must believe me when I say I thought ye would be in the house and unharmed the whole while."

"Well, let's not talk about it anymore. It won't do any good. I might as well change your bandages, since I'm here. How are your wounds feeling?"

"'Tis still quite stiff I am, but they do no' pain me so much anymore."

"I thought you were dead when I saw you on that stretcher, but it was mostly exhaustion and loss of blood. You can go back to the Prince in a day or two."

"Could it be that ye are anxious tae be rid of me?"

"I admit I'd rather you weren't here when Gavin gets back. As it is, he's going to be angry when he finds out I took care of you."

"Gavin is always letting his anger get in the way of his being able tae see others for what they really are. No wonder he canna see yer worth."

"Gavin is quite pleased with me," she replied, determined to hear no criticism of Gavin from anyone.

"But he does no' appreciate ye as I do, or the Prince," Ian added, when he saw Sara's eyes widen in surprise. "He continues tae ask after ye, as does Miss Walkinshaw. She entreats me tae bring ye for a visit."

"I'm naturally grateful to the Prince for his consideration, and would dearly love to see Miss Walkinshaw again, but it isn't possible, not with Gavin supporting the King."

But she couldn't suppress a sigh. As much as she loved Gavin and enjoyed being with him, he was away a lot of the time, and she often found herself longing for company, especially females of her own class. Some of the local women would not visit her because they supported the Prince, and she had long ago reached the limits of Betty's and Mary's conversation. If it had not been for visitors coming for musical entertainments or to read an occasional poem, she would have been tempted to sneak off to the Prince's camp, in spite of Gavin's disapproval. She had to admit she missed the excitement of the army. It was impossible to be surrounded by five thousand vital men and not be affected by the sheer physical energy of their presence.

But she told herself to be patient. It wouldn't be long before she would have a family to care for. Her morning sickness was a regular thing now, and there was no question but that she could expect to give birth sometime in the fall. There was nothing in the world like a baby to bring women together, no matter what their political differences.

Ian misinterpreted Sara's hesitation, and assumed that

only persuading was needed to make her change her mind. He had wanted her for himself from the first moment he saw her, and he didn't intend to allow his friendship for Gavin to stand in his way. If he could just get her away from Gavin, even for a short while, he was sure she would get over her silly infatuation. But Ian was no fool, and he realized he could never cut as handsome a figure as Gavin. Neither could he forget the angry looks the couple had exchanged in Glasgow, nor the uncertainty he had seen in Sara's eyes when she left with Gavin for Edinburgh.

Ian exerted himself to talk Sara into going to Inverness with him—the Prince had been there for the last month—even if it was only for a short visit, but no matter how often he thought she might be changing her mind, she steadily refused.

"Surely Gavin wouldna forbid ye a short visit."

"Under the circumstances, I'm sure he would forbid any visit at all. You seem to forget that you have placed him in a difficult position with Cumberland."

"He is a coarse German lout."

"Possibly, but he's still the son of the king and the commander of the army. It's not easy to ignore a man in such a position."

"Can ye no' stop worrying about what Gavin would think and what would be best for Gavin, and think of yerself?" Ian demanded irritably. "Ye sound more like his mistress than his wife."

"His mistress was a very understanding woman," Sara answered, remembering Clarice's challenge to the earl.

"Then forget Gavin *and* his mistress," Ian snapped. "Think o' yerself for a change."

"Sit up so I can remove this bandage from around your chest, and stop trying to talk me into something you know I shouldn't do," Sara commanded. "Anything that's good for Gavin is good for me, too."

"What has he done tae make ye so loyal? Ye were certainly treated rough in Glasgow."

"Gavin has had many demons to overcome. He doesn't think a woman can love him for himself, and he's still afraid he may be betrayed, just like his mother was."

"Gavin has no heart tae lose tae a woman," Ian said impatiently. "I have known him for the best part of twenty years, and excepting his mother, he scorns the lot o' ye. He'll keep a mistress—even a woman-hater like Gavin needs the comfort of a woman's body—but he'll no' give ye his trust, nor his heart. He has none tae give."

"You don't understand," Sara began, but Ian cut her off.

"Ye wait until there is a crisis and see if I'm no' right. No matter what he's told ye, see if he does no' turn against ye."

"I thought you were his friend?"

"I would rather be yer friend."

"You are my friend. I would never have gotten to Scotland without your help."

"Then leave Gavin and come away with me."

Sara was so stunned, all she could think to say was, "But I'm married."

"It does no' matter. The Prince is Catholic, and his church does no' recognize a Protestant marriage."

"And if he loses?"

"They willna recognize yer marriage in France either."

"You're serious, aren't you?" asked Sara.

"Never more," Ian replied. "I've loved ye ever since I saw ye in those disgraceful clothes, and ye announced ye were Lady Carlisle and expected to be *protected* rather than assaulted by the Prince's army."

"But I didn't—You knew I was married—Gavin's your best friend!"

"A man has no best friend when it comes tae women."

Sara gave herself a mental shake. "You've got to stop talking nonsense and let me finish the bandage."

"I am no' talking nonsense," Ian assured her. "I was never more serious in my life. I love ye, Sara, and I want ye tae come away with me."

Sara could only stare at him. She realized that he really *was* telling the truth, and he *meant* every preposterous word he uttered!

"We can leave now and be in France in two days."

Sara's hands stopped in midair. This couldn't be happening to her. No one, especially Ian, could seriously ask her to leave Gavin. Surely Ian realized how completely she loved her husband and that she would never leave him. She was so bemused, she didn't stop him when he pulled her face down to his and kissed her hard. She just stood here, too shocked to move. She thought she heard someone in the hall, and the fear that Colleen should catch Ian kissing her brought her out of her trance.

But she didn't have to pull away. Ian already had. Sara's failure to respond to his kiss, her wooden acceptance of his lips, told him more clearly than words that his efforts were unavailing.

"Ye do no' love me." It was a statement, not a question.

"No. I love my husband."

"Did you ever?"

"I've always loved Gavin."

Sara couldn't read Ian's expression. It seemed to be a mixture of a fatalistic smile and a grimace, but his eyes were empty. "What has he ever done tae deserve tae have someone like ye tossed into his lap?"

"People aren't loved according to whether they deserve it or not," Sara said. "It just happens. It's not something you can plan."

"But marriages are."

"I was more fortunate than most. I loved my husband."

Ian looked angry, but he wasn't one to waste time lamenting over a lost gamble, and it wasn't long before a look of resignation settled over his face. He reached into his coat, pulled out an envelope, and handed it to Sara. "Here. I'll have no need o' this. Perhaps ye can find some use for it."

"What is it?"

"A letter signed by Gavin's father. I took it from the Prince's files, in case I might need it tae convince Gavin tae return the rifles, or tae let ye go."

"The Earl wrote the Prince?"

"I imagine it was in the nature of a hedge, in case the Prince won. This is the only copy."

"I don't want it," Sara protested.

"Keep it. You may find it useful some day. Having the Earl for a father-in-law is much worse than having Gavin for a husband."

"I don't think you're much of a friend, Ian Fraser, if that's the way you talk about Gavin."

"Where ye be concerned, I'm not."

Sara finished the bandage. "You've recovered most of your strength. I think you'd better go tomorrow."

"Aye, I'd better."

Gavin made himself slow his stallion. He had been riding at a breakneck pace for hours, and if he didn't take it easy, he might ruin the best horse in Scotland, if he hadn't already. He looked at the welts on the stallion's flanks and the trickle of blood from his mouth, and he felt ashamed of himself. He had no reason to rush home, not if he had any faith in his wife. Sara had never done anything to betray his trust or cause him to doubt the love she professed to feel for him. He believed her. He trusted her.

Then why in hell are you trying to kill your horse to get home two days early, he asked himself furiously, but he knew the answer to that question. Everybody in Aberdeen knew the answer. He had met his father at Cumberland's camp, and the Earl had wasted no time in telling him that Ian was at Estameer with Sara, in fact had been there for several days. He had taunted him with the rumor that she was going to run off to France with him.

Gavin had laughed at the accusation and steadfastly defended Sara's innocence, but he had been hard-pressed to keep up his show of confidence when the Earl cruelly produced one of Gavin's own men to bear witness to Ian's arrival. He still held out against his doubts, but then his father had sprung his next surprise.

"Did she tell you about the contract she made with me?"

"What trick are you trying to pull now?" Gavin asked, struggling hard to maintain his appearance of cold unconcern.

"The contract which will give her control of her fortune, if she can become pregnant with your child." Gavin's features were immobile, but he knew the shock must show plainly in his eyes. "She put her terms to me right after you left for Scotland, just before I left London."

A cold chill ran through Gavin's spine. He remembered the warmth of Sara's welcome every time he entered her bed, her inexhaustible ardor, the encouragement to sleep with her every night, and he doubted. He had often marveled that he should be fortunate enough to have a wife who enjoyed his embraces—he knew none of his friends were so fortunate—and it was impossible for doubt not to enter his mind. Was it reasonable for a woman who reacted as she had on their wedding night to be as different as she was in Edinburgh and all the nights since? Had she conquered her fear of the marriage bed because of her love for him, or because of the money?

Somehow he had managed to get out of his father's presence without losing his appearance of confidence, but he felt like a volcano about to erupt. He spent the rest of the evening demolishing the better part of a bottle of brandy, but it wasn't enough to make him drunk, and he couldn't sleep when he went to bed. All he could think about was Sara and Ian, *together*. That he couldn't doubt because his own man had seen them. There might be any number of explanations for such a thing, but neither his father nor the man had offered any; in fact, their reticence had pointed to the one explanation Gavin did not want to believe. Of all the women in the world, he could not believe that Sara could be guilty of such deception. She had spent months trying to convince him of the sincerity of her affection. But his father's parting words were a canker that was steadily eating away at his as yet unseasoned faith in his wife.

"I signed her paper," the Earl had admitted, "but I added the qualifier that she should be living with you in apparent harmony at the time."

Gavin fought against his father's interpretation—the Earl didn't know Sara, didn't know the openness of her gaze, the smoothness of her brow, the honesty that was a basic part of her. He was so corrupt and twisted, he couldn't believe that others could want to live in total honesty . . . but that would explain everything, the party, the welcome to her bed, her unceasing efforts to convince him of her love.

Gavin spent nearly the entire night going over everything he could remember of what Sara had said and done, hoping each further bit of evidence of her sincerity would bolster his sagging confidence, but instead of making him feel better, he actually felt worse by morning. He told himself he had sufficient proof that Sara loved him and had been faithful. Sure, she had been scared that first night, but she had known what to expect after that.

She couldn't have welcomed him to her bed because of the money. But no sooner had he said that, then he remembered that Sara herself had told him in Edinburgh that she wanted control of her fortune. True, she hadn't mentioned it since, and he thought she had forgotten it, but couldn't it be because she knew she was going to get control of her money another way? They had been sleeping together regularly for two months. She could be with child at this very moment.

He tried to tell himself that she wouldn't have followed him to Scotland if she hadn't loved him, but he realized immediately that she couldn't bear his child unless she did follow him. Too, she had spent weeks with Ian and the army, she had made no effort to hide her pleasure in his company either then or later, and she had refused to do more than mildly condemn Ian after she had been kidnapped.

Gavin tried to make his mind go blank, to stop his reason from dissecting Sara's actions and motives, but he couldn't. He felt in his heart that he was right, Sara was the best thing that had happened to him, she was honest and pure and meant every word she said, but the insidious skepticism which had plagued him most of his life would not leave him alone. He had always feared he would never find anyone to love, but even worse was the fear that the woman he loved would betray him, just as his father had betrayed his mother. He tried to tell himself Sara was different, that his father was only trying to make trouble, that the Earl's interpretation of the facts was wrong, but he couldn't make himself believe it. No, that wasn't it. He could believe it, but he couldn't make himself stop doubting, wondering if he might not be the one who was mistaken. After all the Earl *wanted* him to be married, *wanted* him to father an heir. What reason would he have for painting Sara's character black?

He had left Aberdeen at dawn.

But no sooner did he reach Estameer, than he began to feel foolish. The afternoon sun had settled over the great house, lending it the quality of liquid amber, and giving the whole a feeling of quiet and easy security. No one stirred, even the livestock on the hills seemed to be suspended in time, and Gavin could have believed that Estameer was in a world completely separate from that occupied by the Earl and Cumberland. He met no one in the great hall—it was the quiet time before preparations were begun for dinner—and he found no one in the sitting room. Maybe Sara had gone out for a walk. Maybe she wasn't even home.

She was not in her bedroom, and it was clear no one had been in there for some time. At almost the same moment that Gavin unconsciously heaved a sigh of relief, he heard voices coming from down the corridor, and stiffened when he realized one of them was masculine and it was now being answered by a feminine voice he knew equally well. Sara and Ian were in that room.

He moved as a sleepwalker in the direction of the sound. He didn't want to; he wanted to run from the castle and into eternal oblivion, but he couldn't stop himself. Every nerve was on end, and he knew he should turn around before everything inside him exploded. He could hear the words now. "Catholic church doesn't recognize Protestant marriages." "I love you, Sara." ". . . be in France in two days." Each word cut into his soul like a sharp knife. Why didn't Sara answer? Why didn't she tell Ian she loved Gavin?

Then Gavin was standing in the doorway, and he knew why. He didn't understand why Ian was so heavily bandaged, but he could understand that Sara was kissing him. Quickly he moved away from the door. He knew if he remained there a single instant longer, he would kill both of them.

Gavin wasn't sure how he found his way back to his own room. Even more, he didn't understand why he could not feel the pain that made his heart feel like a cold stone in his chest. Common sense told him he should feel something. Every hope that had taken root these past months had been wrenched up by the roots, roots that reached to the very core of his being. Why didn't he feel anything? Why did he feel like a disembodied spirit?

Then the pain struck, and Gavin wished he could have remained disembodied. He didn't know how it was possible for a soul, a spirit, something you couldn't see or touch, to hurt more than any physical part of him. He remembered that as a boy, he had suffered a long, deep gash in his leg, and it had to be sewn up. He had thought that nothing else in life could cause such pain, but now he would have willingly endured that pain twice over. The hurt he felt now could not be reached, could not be stitched up, would *never* heal. This wound would bleed for the rest of his life.

Gavin stumbled over to the table and poured out a glass of brandy. He swallowed three more before he sank into the chair. He didn't know how long he sat there, or when he knew he had to face them, to get them out of his house and his life, but he suddenly heaved himself out of the chair and lurched through the door and down the hall. Someone once said *Physician, heal thyself.* Well, he couldn't heal himself, but he could and would cut out the canker that festered in his soul. It might kill him, but he would be rid of it.

Everything seemed unreal when he entered the room. It was as though he were watching actors on a stage, but from so faraway, he could barely hear their words. Sara jumped up from where she sat next to Ian and hurried towards him. Her lips curved into a smile and moved with honied words of welcome. She was deceiving him again, the lying bitch; he would not listen. He refused her embrace and smiled at her confusion when he held her away from him. He saw Ian, too, lounging on the bed, only half-dressed, and rage flowed through him like molten iron.

He heard himself tell Sara to get out, take anything she wanted, but to go with Ian at once. He saw the look of stunned disbelief and heard her exclamations, but his heart was hardened against her pleas. He was not such a fool as to think she needed to be told *why* he wanted her to leave, but he told her anyway, told her that he knew she loved Ian, that she didn't have to pretend anymore. She could have her money, he would see that she got every cent of it, she could have all the freedom she wanted, she could belong to Ian and the Frasers if she wanted, but he never wanted to see her again.

It felt good to see her eyes fill with tears, to hear her cries of protest, to sense the pain in her heart, to see her face crumple with grief when she knew her game was over. He was glad she hurt. He *wanted* her to suffer. If she endured just a tithe of the agony he would suffer for the rest of his life, then he would be happy. She had made a fool of him. She had caused him to open his heart and to believe in love once again. She deserved the pain.

He called her a name, he didn't remember what, and saw Ian start up from the bed and demand an apology. He knew he laughed, because he heard the sound. He certainly didn't feel like laughing. Ian was furious at his slight to Sara's reputation. Now that *was* funny! He said so, and Ian responded oddly. He snatched up a sword and prepared to attack Gavin.

That was hard to believe, too, because even as boys, Ian had never been a match for Gavin in any physical contest. Gavin told him so, and Ian called *him* a name.

Before he could tell Ian his language wasn't suitable even for such ears as Sara's, he discovered he had his sword out and was attacking Ian. Odd that Ian didn't take the bandages off. He must have known they would hinder him. But then he didn't need to remove them. Sara threw herself between them, defying Gavin to touch Ian, calling him a base coward to attack a man in Ian's condition.

He would laugh if it weren't so absurd. Didn't she see she had just proved herself a liar, by protecting Ian instead of the husband she swore she loved? Did she think he was a fool to believe anything she said to him now? He would never believe anything she said again. He would never believe any woman.

Suddenly he was tired. He didn't want to hurt her anymore. He didn't want to hurt anybody anymore. He just wanted her to go away, to leave him in peace. He would do anything if he could just be left in peace, to never feel any emotion ever again. He told them he was going out—he didn't know where, nor did he care—but if they were not gone when he returned . . . well, he hoped they would be.

Suddenly a kind of madness seized him, and he rushed to Sara's room and began emptying every drawer he could find and throwing its contents into the corridor. He didn't know how long he rushed about like a lunatic, or how many times he thrust someone out of his way. He only knew he could not rest until he had emptied that room of everything she owned.

He thought he would feel purged, somehow relieved of the pain that continued to pierce his soul like an arrow, but he felt only a great emptiness, a loneliness more profound than anything he had ever experienced. With a moan of unutterable anguish, he rushed from the castle.

Chapter 24

"So ye have come back." Donald Fraser's angry voice cut through the quiet of the early evening.

"Aye," his son answered unhappily.

"Ye have disgraced us. I told ye that ye couldna return."

"I am no' asking for myself but for Lady Carlisle."

"Lady Carlisle!" Fraser repeated, sufficiently startled to forget his anger at his son and notice the figure of dejection standing in his wake. "What is she doing here? Has something happened at Estameer?"

"Gavin has thrown her out, and she needs somewhere to stay."

Donald Fraser's florid countenance flamed dangerously. "Tell me true, Ian Fraser, for I'll have no lie from ye. Are ye the cause o' this fresh calamity?"

Ian was too weak from the long ride to argue for his innocence. "Aye. If I had stayed at Blair Castle, this wouldna have happened."

"Then Lady Carlisle can stay, but ye shall no' darken this door until ye have repaired the damage ye have done with yer selfishness. Ye have brought shame on all the Frasers, that ye have, Ian. 'Tis a judgement on me for the way I brought ye up, aye, and my brother, too, for

Colleen. I do no' seek to avoid my share of the blame, but I willna shelter ye until ye dispel this cloud o' yer making."

Sara was aware that her horse had stopped, and she made a halfhearted attempt to gather her senses. She knew they had come to the Fraser home—she could hear Ian and his father arguing, and something told her she should pay attention to what was happening—but she didn't care about that, or much of anything else. In fact, she didn't much care about anything at all.

Gavin's attack had been such a complete shock, it had taken her several hours to convince herself she hadn't imagined it. At first she thought he must have gone completely mad; now she was certain *she* had. She didn't understand it, and she had no idea why he had told her to leave, but when he threw virtually everything she owned into the corridor, she knew she had to get away, to go somewhere until she could figure out what had gone wrong.

And something was definitely wrong. Gavin loved her, of that she was certain. They had behind them two months of almost perfect harmony, when he left for Aberdeen. Something had happened during that trip, something much more terrible than finding Ian at Estameer. She knew now that the noise she heard must have been his footsteps, that he must have seen Ian kiss her, must have seen that she didn't push him away. She would have expected him to fall into a furious rage, to strike her, threaten to kill Ian—well, he almost had done that—anything except stand there like a tailor's dummy telling her to leave.

She had known something was wrong when she looked into his eyes. There was nothing there, *nothing*, just two empty black holes. She knew it was useless to appeal to him. *There was no one inside to hear her!* He was like a shell, with all the inner being drained away by the poison which had destroyed her hope for the future; he was the charred remains left behind by the firestorm that had consumed her happiness. But she would find out what had gone wrong. Somewhere there was a key, and it had to do with Aberdeen and the Duke's camp. She didn't know how she would do it, she didn't care who or what stood in her path, but she must get to the English camp and talk to Cumberland. She didn't care about the war or whose side anybody was on. All she only cared about was Gavin, and she wasn't about to stand aside while someone attempted to destroy his love for her.

When Gavin returned to his senses two days later, he was sitting astride his horse on the ridge above the river where they had thrown Ian's rifles. For a moment he didn't know where he was or how he had come to be there, but gradually the numbness left his brain, the thick clouds began to evaporate from his memory, and the wall of pain descended upon him with annihilating force. A part of him wanted to return to that state of nonexistence, to that land of the living dead, but Nature would no longer shield him with her protective cocoon. From now on he would have to bear the full weight of the pain.

It was well past mid-afternoon, but he did not turn his horse toward home. There was no reason; there was nothing but emptiness at Estameer now. No, there was something worse. There was the memory of what he had almost captured, the memory of a dream nearly fulfilled, of paradise tasted but snatched too soon from his grasp. There was also bitterness and disappointment, and he could see no chance that there would ever be anything else.

He struggled to clear his mind of the fog that obliterated the better part of two days. He had to remember what had happened. He knew Sara was gone, the feeling of numbness in his heart told him that, but he had to remember why. Somehow he knew he was the cause, but he couldn't recall what he had done. Then he remembered the Earl.

Why had he decided to go to Aberdeen? If Cumberland was so worried about why Gavin had armed the men of Estameer, he could have come to see for himself. But it was too late to think of that now. He had gone, and his father had sown the seeds of doubt and disillusionment, seeds he knew would fall on fertile ground. Damn him! Would he never be free from the curse of being that man's son? *Only when you cease to believe everything he says,* a voice whispered to him. You have within yourself the power to break the shackles that bind you to him. Sara gave you the key, but you are the only one who can use it.

Sara! He hadn't meant to utter that name aloud, and he was shocked at the sound of his own voice. It was like a wild and untamed cry, like the wail of a wounded animal. What had he done? What had he said to her? He couldn't remember. It was as though a heavy veil was drawn across his mind shutting out everything that happened that afternoon.

The kiss. He remembered a kiss, but she wasn't kissing him; she was kissing Ian. Gavin shook his head, but the image wouldn't go away. But Sara wouldn't kiss another man, no matter how much she wanted to, not while she was married to him. But she *had* kissed Ian! He had seen it, and his father had warned him . . . he forced his mind to abandon the rest of the sentence. He would cast his father's accusations from his mind. He would never think of them again.

Why had she kissed Ian? She hadn't told him. You never asked her, never gave her a chance to explain, the accusing voice whispered as he remembered more and more of that afternoon. She was guilty, Guilty, GUILTY! Then why did she welcome you so joyfully? It was deceit. Then why did she look so shattered, when you told her to leave and promised to see that she got her money? If that was all she wanted why did she look as though she wished she could die? The closer Gavin came to Estameer and the more he remembered of that nightmare, the more his doubts grew.

Once again his father had played him like a harp. He had pulled the right strings, and Gavin's fear and his habit of cutting people off from himself had done the rest. Only this time, something inside Gavin would not let him believe Sara was the deceitful she-devil his father had painted. There was some truth to the accusations she had wanted control of her money, she must have made that pact with the Earl, Ian was at Estameer, and she was kissing him. But as damning as those facts seemed to be, Gavin could not put aside the feeling that he had missed the true meaning of all those things. He kept remembering Sara's spontaneous smile whenever she saw him, her unquestioning welcome of his embraces, her continuing effort to learn to please him, the fact that everyone she met liked her immediately, and he was certain that there was an explanation for all his questions, that if he would only listen to her, she would explain away all his doubts.

Then, just as suddenly, he knew he didn't care whether or not she could explain what she had done. He loved her, and that was all that mattered. It was the single most momentous moment of Gavin's life, even more so than when he finally unmasked his father's true character. That had almost destroyed him; now it was possible that he might someday be whole again.

For years he had lived in a virtual paranoiac fear of falling in love. He had expected something terrible to happen to him—he wasn't sure exactly what—but the rush of euphoria, of pure happiness, caught him completely by surprise. Then so many things happened at once, he started to feel so many things for the first time, it was like being an entirely different person. It was as though he had been seeing life in reverse; where there had been shadow, now there was gleaming light. Gavin could see that he had been backing away from everything he had ever wanted, and that only Sara's love had been able to change the direction of his life. He could only marvel at the tricks the mind could play on a person who let hate and fear rule his life.

Obviously he had loved Sara for a long time. Why couldn't he have seen it? Had he simply refused to see it? And she loved him. He had no doubt of that any longer. If she had been tempted by Ian, *if*, then it was partially his fault for taking so long to recognize and return her unselfish outpouring of love. It was possible she had grown tired of waiting, but after the way she greeted him, Gavin's heart wouldn't accept that. However, his brutal treatment of her when he found her with Ian may have achieved what his blindness could never achieve. It may have killed her love.

He must find her; he must tell her that he loved her more than life itself. He wanted to shout it to the whole world, to let them know what a fool he had been, but he contented himself with turning his horse for home.

Gavin was astounded at the way his heart leapt for joy, the moment he decided he had to find Sara. He cautioned himself to reserve his feelings. While he didn't believe Sara's actions were as black as they had been painted, he might find that neither was she wholly without blame. He didn't know if he could live with only part of her heart, but he knew he could not give her up. Not ever.

Mary and Tom were both in the great hall when he

returned. "Where is my wife?" he asked immediately, but their silence answered his question. They looked bereaved, like someone had died. "Where is she?"

"She went with Mr. Fraser and his cousin," Mary answered. There was accusation in her tone, but there was also fear and bewilderment. "They left before dinner two days ago."

Gavin turned to go, but Tom called after him, "There's a note."

"Why didn't you say so, man?" Gavin called, his habitual decisiveness returning at last. "Where is it?" Tom took a twisted piece of paper from a vest pocket, but Gavin's eagerness faded when he saw it was not Sara's handwriting.

Your Lordship,

I know I shouldn't be writing to you this way, especially not after what you did to my mistress, but I had to have my say. I never did think you were good enough for Miss Sara, but she could never see anything but good in you. No matter how wonderful everyone else was, including Mr. Fraser and that nice young Prince, they couldn't measure up to you in her eyes.

And look how you repaid her faith. She took care of Mr. Fraser out of the kindness of her heart, but you could only see bad in it. You ought to know she could never turn anyone away who was hurt. She never turned you away, did she? She was always insisting you was hurting inside when nobody else could see anything but meanness in the way you treated her. After all she did for you, couldn't you trust her even a little bit?

She's going away now, and if I have anything to do with it, she'll never come back. She still wishes you the best, but I wish old Peg's hound dog had got you.

Betty

Gavin didn't know how he could feel worse, but he did. Betty's letter seemed to point up all the things he had realized, only they seemed much more devastating when coming from someone else. He balled up the letter and shrugged off the extra burden of guilt as he tossed it into the fire. He knew more fully than Betty how badly he had mistreated Sara, but if he had learned one lesson during these months, it was that living with the past could very easily destroy the future.

"I'm going to bring Lady Carlisle home," he announced to Mary. "See that her rooms are gotten ready."

"She left orders that her things should be packed up and sent after her," Mary told him uneasily.

"Put everything back exactly as it was." He had almost reached the door before Mary's voice called him back.

"Is she really coming back?" Mary asked.

"I'll never set foot on Estameer again, unless she's at my side," Gavin assured her, and Mary broke into a smile of relief. She *knew* Sara was coming back now. The young master would sooner die than be banished from Estameer.

It was Colleen he saw when he reached the Fraser's home, and her greeting was anything but friendly.

"I suppose ye have come tae ask after yer wife?"

"Where is she?" Gavin demanded impatiently. The strains of the last few days were beginning to tell on him, and he had no time for Colleen.

"She's no' here. She's gone," Colleen said, eying him in a way Gavin found uncomfortable. "But I am." She drew closer, until she could rub her generous bosom against his chest, but her eyes held a dangerous challenge, one Gavin couldn't fathom.

"I want to see Sara," Gavin said, taking Colleen by the arms and putting her from him. "Where is she?"

"I said she's no' here." Colleen drew near and started to rub herself against Gavin once more. "There's nothing tae keep us from acting like we used tae." Again her body issued the invitation, but Gavin would have sworn her eyes defied him to accept. Well, he didn't have time to figure out what was wrong with Colleen. Let Ian or her uncle worry about it. He had to find Sara.

"I don't want anyone but my wife," Gavin said, once more taking Colleen by the arms and placing her at a distance. "Now tell me where she is, or I'll ask someone else."

"And what would ye be wanting with her this time, no' tae yell at her some more, I should hope? For I'm telling ye, Gavin Carlisle, I'll no' have ye treating that woman shabby again."

Gavin wondered if he was losing his grip on reality. Just a week before, Colleen had helped kidnap Sara. What was she trying to do now? "I want to talk to her," he said.

"Like ye did before?"

"No, not like before," Gavin replied angrily. What right did Colleen have to interrogate him? "I just want to ask her to explain why she—"

"Explain!" cried Colleen. "Why don't ye *explain* tae her why ye came storming into that room like a madman, ordering her out o' the house, tried tae kill poor Ian, and him with sword wounds just knitting, and then threw her clothes onto the floor. Why don't ye explain that?"

"I know I leaped to some stupid conclusions," he began, feeling himself getting angry at Colleen. He didn't have to explain anything to her. "I want to try to understand now."

"Ye have never understood anything about women, *any* kind o' women, Gavin Carlisle, and I doubt ye ever shall. All ye can see is the hair, the face, and what she will be like in bed."

"Dammit, Colleen, I haven't got time to stand here—"

"Ye had better take the time, or ye will never learn the whereabouts o' yer wife from me." Gavin was startled by that threat. "Do ye have any idea how hard she worked tae make herself into what ye wanted her tae be? Of course ye don't. Ye were too taken up with yer own worries. 'Tis a fool ye are, Gavin Carlisle. Ye don't deserve her. That's what I told her. I do no' doubt she will have ye back, poor lassie, but no' unless ye go crawling on yer belly, begging her forgiveness."

"I don't intend to—"

"I've no doubt ye don't, and I hope she shows ye the door," Colleen said forcefully. "And all the while she was doing her best tae keep ye from knowing she had the sickness, just because she didn't want ye tae be bothered."

"The sickness?" Gavin repeated, all at sea.

"The morning sickness, ye daft man. Lady Carlisle is carrying yer baby."

Gavin could have survived a blow from Colleen's fist better than he withstood the news that Sara was pregnant. He thought his legs were going to collapse under him at any moment, but he managed to pull himself together as Donald Fraser entered the room.

"Has Colleen told ye were tae find yer wife?" he asked.

"I was getting around tae it," she replied peevishly.

"I willna have this family causing any more trouble for the Carlisles," Donald roared at his niece, his anger formidable for such an old man. "Ye and yer cousin have done enough damage already. Tell him and be done with it."

"Ian has taken her tae Inverness. She plans tae seek asylum with the Prince."

Sara sat waiting for Prince Charles Edward Louis John Casimir Silvester Maria Stuart. She had been in Inverness since yesterday, securely lodged and carefully attended to, but her thoughts were many miles away at Estameer. She might as well have been in a mountain cave, for all she knew of her surroundings. Her whole mind was on Gavin, and what she could do to heal this breech. Many times during the last two days, she had relived those few terrifying minutes that had destroyed her peace and driven her from her home. All she had now was hope, and she held on to that with frantic desperation.

Gavin didn't understand, she kept telling herself. Something terrible must have happened, because she had never seen him like that, not even when his mother died. Once he understood, once she could *talk* to him, things would be different.

She would not allow herself to think of the consequences if he didn't. She had always loved Gavin, but she had realized in the last few weeks that what she had felt for him as she was growing into a young woman was merely a shadow of the love she held for him now. As she had come to know the extent of his love for Scotland, Estameer, and its people, and to understand his loyalty to his friends, even when they disagreed with him about the Prince, she began to see him as much more than a devastatingly handsome man whom fate had made her husband. Along with love and physical attraction came respect for his principles, and admiration for the way he held to them, even in the face of enormous pressures. This new prospective of her husband was given further impetus by the regard accorded him by both sides in the conflict. And if his work with the coal mines was any indication, he could become every bit as successful in business as his father.

And then there were those nights, those wonderful glorious nights, she had spent in his arms. Even now she would smile as she remembered little intimacies they had shared, the wonder of discovery as she became more familiar with her body and its reaction to his. It had made her feel warm and safe, had made her feel like she belonged, as nothing had done since her father's death. And he had been more than kind to her. He had *wanted* to come to her bed, wanted to please her.

Then there was the look she had seen growing in his eyes over these last weeks, a look of trust and love, a look she vowed she would see in his eyes once more, if she had to turn Scotland inside out to find the key to his wild behavior. She had almost despaired of anyone loving her as Gavin did, and now that she had seen his love for her come alive in his eyes, she would not rest until it lived there again. And it was for his sake as much as hers. She knew he felt cheated and betrayed, and that unless she could restore his faith in her love, he would have difficulty putting any meaning into his life. And as selfish as she was for her own happiness, she knew restoring Gavin's belief in her love would give him much more than love. It would give him back his life.

Then there was the baby, though how she could save it until last she didn't know. She was becoming accustomed to the sickness; it came every day, just as regularly as the sun, to remind her there was a life other than her own depending on Gavin. Whatever her feelings, she owed it to her unborn child to see that it was born into a family, with a father and a mother who loved each other, as well as the child. She had plenty of evidence in Gavin of what a selfish and manipulative parent could do to a child, and she was determined it would never happen to her baby.

"You've lost some of your bloom since I last saw you," the Prince said, as he entered the room where Sara waited for him.

"I carry my husband's child, and suffer from the sickness," Sara explained. "You do not look well yourself, your Majesty."

"Aye, I've been sick, too. In fact, Clementina gave me orders to remain in bed until she returned, but I could not let you arrive in Inverness without seeing you. It seems that both our causes have come upon disquieting times."

"I hope yours is only temporary."

"I greatly fear we shall have the answer to that question before I'm fully recovered. You know that Cumberland has left Aberdeen?" Sara nodded. "I'm told his army is more numerous than my faithful Highlanders. I know none of them have the heart of these courageous men who have risked everything for me, yet I know that heart and courage do not always carry the day. Is it not so?"

"I'm afraid it is. Truth and honesty often suffer badly at the hands of greed and guile."

"It sounds as though you have learned a difficult lesson."

"No, merely been forced to review one I had already studied. Now, tell me of yourself and Clementina since Glasgow. I have been told that you were gravely ill."

So they talked of many things, being careful to avoid the issues which touched them most closely. They talked with the ease and honesty of old friends, and it was thus that Gavin found them, when he burst in upon them unannounced.

"This is too bad," the Prince said, rising. "Am I never to enjoy a conversation with Lady Carlisle without your interrupting us?"

Gavin's eyes never left Sara. "Stay or go, I don't care,

but I must talk to my wife."

A single look, and Sara had the answer to the only question that mattered. It was all there in his face—the fear, the pain, the love. Whatever remained to be said could be left to some other time. She was out of the chair and into his arms almost before she knew it. Then she was trying to talk, trying to breathe; Gavin's grip was so tight she feared he would break her ribs.

"Don't say anything," Gavin said, covering her face with kisses. "I don't care what you did or why you did it, I only want you back at Estameer. I don't know what came over me—madness I suppose—but I didn't mean anything I said. I love you, Sara Carlisle. I love you so much I can't stand the thought of your not being wherever I am. I know the hell my mother went through, but I don't care, as long as I have you."

"When you hold me in your arms like this, it is pure heaven." Sara laughed aloud as the tears poured down her face. "It's only hell when your love is not returned." She didn't know why happiness had to be bought at the price of such bitter pain, but she decided not to question fate. For the moment, she was happy and that was all that mattered.

"There's one thing I have to tell you."

"You don't have to tell me anything. I don't care—"

Sara put her fingers over his lips. "I'm going to have a baby," she said. "You'll have to want both of us back."

After all he had gone through these last few days, Gavin was surprised that anything had the power to affect him, but he was amazed at the impact of Sara's words. Even though Colleen had warned him, there was something magical about hearing the news from his wife's lips.

"Aren't you going to say anything?"

"I don't know. I've said and done so much that was wrong, I'm afraid to do anything anymore."

"Just tell me you are pleased." She was afraid she had told him too abruptly. Maybe he still wasn't ready.

"I'm *very* pleased. That's what I don't understand. Maybe it's knowing that it will be your child, but it's not at all what I had thought it would be like. It's wonderful."

"Everything won't be wonderful. I will grow fat."

"I've always thought you were too thin."

"And I shall become very short of temper."

"Betty has always said you were far too reasonable and understanding."

"I shall demand all manner of strange foods."

"I shall hire a French chef."

Sara laughed joyously. "Is there nothing I can say that will make you regret your child?"

"Only that it will drive me from your bed."

"You will never leave my bed or my arms."

"I'm pleased to see that one of our ventures has reached a happy conclusion," remarked the Prince. They had forgotten about him. "I realize I should have withdrawn. I apologize, but I was determined to see that Lady Carlisle was not mistreated. I am very fond of her."

"No more than I."

"No, well, I should hope so. And now, if you would not scorn my counsel, I suggest that you either return to your home, or remove to Cumberland's camp immediately. There will be a reckoning very soon, and I doubt he would understand your being here."

"We shall remove to Cumberland's camp. My father travels with him, and I have much to say to him."

Betty entered the room at that moment. She took one look at her mistress firmly held in Gavin's arms, and charged down on them like a vengeful tigress protecting her only cub. "God almighty, milady," she snorted, her face a picture of disgust, "haven't you been injured enough by that man to know not to put yourself in his way again? You might as well lie down in front of a runaway wagon as to take up with him. At least the Fraser never made you cry."

"I'm crying with happiness, Betty."

"Nobody cries from happiness, unless they've cried from misery first," decreed Betty. "And this man is certainly a misery, but I suppose you're as determined as ever to have him."

"Aye," said Sara, smiling up into Gavin's eyes. "I am."

Chapter 25

Tuesday, April 15, 1746

Sara didn't like Cumberland; she liked Lt. Gen. Henry Hawley even less; she liked being with the English army as it readied itself for battle least of all. They had none of the high spirits and feeling of camaraderie that made the Highlanders a joy to be around, and very little of their manners either. Betty had more than once threatened to brain one of the soldiers, none of whom accorded her mistress the respect she felt was due a lady and a future peeress. Sara's most fervently expressed wish was to be back at Estameer, but she and Gavin were unable to leave. The Earl had been absent when they arrived, and Cumberland had asked them to remain for the celebration of his birthday.

"I never know where you're going to turn up next, dear boy," he told Gavin, "and I have even less idea what you're going to be doing. Not everyone has my faith in you."

Sara wondered just how much faith the Duke really had in his old acquaintance, but she made no comment. At twenty-three, William Augustus, Duke of Cumberland, was his father's second son and his greatest favorite. He was a tall, forceful man with a fleshy, porcine face, long nose, and sensual mouth.

"He has been brought up to be a soldier," Gavin had explained to Sara later. "He is brave, forthright, confident, aggressive, and quite brisk of manner. He never shirks danger, but faces it head on, thereby winning his men's respect and achieving a deserved reputation for heroism."

Privately Sara thought men were poor judges of character. Cumberland might be everything Gavin said, but she was certain he could be brutal and intentionally cruel as well. She did not enjoy his birthday celebrations, and she was relieved when the Earl finally arrived. She didn't look forward to the interview, but it meant she and Gavin were closer to being able to go home, together. Sara didn't intend to let Gavin out of her sight for a long time.

The Earl had not changed a bit since she had last seen him in London. He was just as thin, his eyes just as cruel, his mouth just as hard, and his words just as lacking in any kind of real kindness for his son.

"I see you have brought your wife with you," he remarked, as Gavin showed Sara to a chair. "Do you not care that you are seen with a woman of questionable reputation?"

"I will tell you this just once," Gavin said, facing his father with the same cold, remorseless eyes. "Speak of my wife in that manner again, and I shall knock you down. Do it a third time, and I shall break your neck."

The Earl regarded his son speculatively for a moment. "You know, I quite believe you would." Gavin made no reply. "Oh well, what you do is your own concern really, especially as long as you remain in Scotland. You could keep a harem, and I doubt anyone in London would know or care about it." Still Gavin did not answer; this irritated the Earl, and he shifted his attention to Sara.

"*You* seem to have accomplished quite a bit more than I anticipated," he said, glancing with pointed emphasis at his son. "There is much more of your father in you than I suspected."

"My father was a kind and generous man," Sara said, quick to defend her parent.

"So he was, too much so for my tastes," the Earl admitted, "but he was never one to let foolish sentimentality get in the way of achieving his ends. It appears you have been equally businesslike."

"I prefer to think that my success has been the result of genuine love and an honest heart."

"Pray, do not disgust me so early in the morning," the Earl protested, raising one white hand as though to ward off some offensive sight. "Being attached to this encampment of savages has already stretched my tolerance beyond all reasonable limits."

"You might as well save your breath," Gavin told Sara. "My father will never believe that a profit can be had from honest and plain dealing."

"It *can*," the Earl put in, "but it seldom is, and then in unacceptably small amounts. But then I doubt you sought me out for the purpose of discovering my business philosophies. Why did you trouble yourself to find me?"

"I came to ask you to honor your agreement," Gavin said, "The one you made with Sara."

"Are you aware of all its conditions?" Gavin nodded. "I take it then, that you agree they have been met?"

"Completely."

"Then how is it I see no heir? That is the one condition that is unalterable."

"I carry Gavin's child at this very moment," Sara told him.

"Suppose it should be a girl, or stillborn?"

"We will have others."

"And what assurances can you give me of that?"

"Dammit, there's no reason for Sara to wait around until you're satisfied about the child's sex and health. The money should rightly be in my control as it is. I want you to sign it back to me."

"I can't do that, not here, miles away from civilization."

"You know quite well all you have to do is sign a letter of intent. Your damned bankers are only too quick to do anything you ask of them."

"Your faith in my abilities is touching, it really is, but not even I can alter a contract with the wave of my hands."

"But we don't have a contract," Gavin said, the sharp edge of anger sounding in his voice. "It was merely an agreement. I took note of that before I signed it, and it can be voided by no more than a note to the solicitors with your signature."

"You have become observant," the Earl said, sounding not in the least pleased by his son's demonstration of this talent. "Since when did you begin to appreciate the intricacies of business?"

"I always have, but I said nothing, because it would have required that I too closely associate with you."

"Your devotion overwhelms me."

"Be done with your everlasting pretense and write that letter," Gavin directed, and turned to find paper and a pen.

"I don't think this is a good time."

"I don't care. Write it anyway."

"And if I don't?"

"I'll make you."

The Earl smiled, and Sara would have sworn it was a smile of amusement, if the subject of their conversation hadn't been so serious. "Now, just how might you achieve that? Surely you don't plan to use force, not right in the middle of the Duke's encampment?"

Gavin looked at him, and his eyes blazed with such fury it scared Sara. "A lot of people are going to die before this war is over. I don't think they'll question the disappearance of one more, one way or the other."

"You would harm your own father?"

"Not as readily as you've tried to destroy my happiness," Gavin told him, the red flame burning brighter still, "but I won't allow you to interfere in my life anymore, no matter what I have to do to prevent it."

Sara was nearly paralyzed with shock, but the two men stared at each other out of identical pairs of eyes, their expressions equally cold and equally determined.

"I believe you would. Would *try*, that is, but I've always been more clever than you."

"There's no need for Gavin to use force, or to have to prove that he is more clever," Sara said, intruding on the two men who were locked in a struggle for supremacy. "I have the letter you wrote to Charles Stuart, and if you don't do what Gavin asks, I'll give it to Cumberland."

The effect on Gavin was substantial, but the impact on the Earl was stunning. He staggered as though he had been struck a powerful blow, and his parchment complexion turned dead white.

"What letter?" he managed to ask, but his reaction had already convinced his surprised son that there was such a letter. What stunned him was that it should be in Sara's possession.

"I can read a part of it, if you would like."

The Earl made a desperate lunge at Sara, but even more quickly Gavin interposed himself between Sara and his father, the back of his hand sending the Earl to the floor. Before the older man could recover, Gavin dragged him to his feet. "Lay one hand on her, and I'll kill you now." From the look of unbridled fury on Gavin's face, Sara was afraid he was going to kill him anyway. "How did you come by that letter?" he asked Sara.

"Ian gave it to me," she admitted, then decided to tell Gavin everything. "He was going to use it to force you to let me go away with him, but when he kissed me and realized I did not love him, he gave it to me. He said he had no use for it, and being the Earl's daughter-in-law, I might need it someday."

"See what kind of Jezebel you've married," snarled the Earl. Gavin back-handed him again.

"I have reason to be grateful for the wife you gave me. You chose better than you knew." He turned back to Sara. "That was the kiss I saw?"

She nodded. "It was the only time I have ever been kissed by a man other than you and my father."

There was a plea for forgiveness in Gavin's eyes; Sara answered it with her own. Gavin swallowed, and turned back to his father.

"I think it's time you wrote your lawyers."

"What harm do you think you can do with that letter?" The Earl was bluffing, still trying to find a way to keep the money.

"Even if any promises or offers of assistance contained in the letter are vague and inconclusive, and I am quite certain they are, I doubt Cumberland will like finding a traitor in his camp. In his present mood, he would hang you. Your only chance of escape would be to leave England. And I imagine there is a good chance Hawley would be given your estates." The Earl blanched. "I would do what I could to see that you received a generous allowance, but someone would be needed to manage your business concerns in your absence, and I imagine your boards of directors would turn to me as the logical choice."

"*No one* will get their hands on my property as long as I live."

"Then write the letter. I'm not going to destroy this letter, until Sara's money is back in my hands."

The Earl dragged himself to a small table, picked up the paper and pen, and began to write. "You should take equal care that your wife is not suspect," he said maliciously, as he handed the sheet to Gavin for his inspection. "Everyone knows she traveled with the Prince when he left England, and she's just been to visit him again. She could be in danger of losing her own head."

"I'm sending Sara home as soon as I can arrange her transport," Gavin said. Sara looked up quickly, surprised. "I have to stay. Father's right. There's no way out of it. You must be gone before the battle. I want no one remembering and coming to ask questions. Tempers sometimes grow too heated under the stress of battle, and cause people to make decisions they later regret."

Sara could see the wisdom of Gavin's decision, but she dreaded being separated from him again, even though she had no doubt he would return to her as soon as possible. The misunderstanding over Ian had merely pointed out the danger of what could happen between two people, no matter how much they trusted each other. She didn't intend to give fate, in the guise of the Earl and any other malevolent person in the camp, a second chance to drive a wedge between them.

Sara still felt that way an hour later as she prepared to climb into their coach. Cumberland had almost refused them the use of their own horses and equipment, but reluctantly agreed when Gavin told him Sara was expecting a child.

"You must go straight home," Gavin reiterated. "By midday, I want you as far from Inverness as possible. This whole business will come to a head soon. When it's over, many people you know are going to be dead, and I don't want you to see that."

"You're going to fight?" Sara asked Gavin, cold fear making her feet pause on the steps.

"I told the Duke and Hawley that I would stay here as they wanted, but I would take no part in the battle. I can not lift a hand against neighbors and friends I've known since childhood."

"What will happen to Ian?" Gavin tried to suppress a surge of jealousy and was only partially successful.

"I don't know."

"Will you look for him, after the battle I mean? I don't mean just for me," Sara said when she saw him hesitate. "I know you two don't agree about the Prince, and I've seen jealousy drive a wedge between you, but he *was* your best friend. I think he still is."

"I'll find him," Gavin assured her, knowing it was virtually impossible to find any single individual in the gory aftermath of a battle.

They were interrupted by Betty's increasingly loud altercation with the soldier loading Sara's trunk.

"You turn Lady Carlisle's clothes out in the dirt, and you'll be picking yourself up as well," Betty told him, as the surly man started to lift the small trunk from where he had let it fall in the mud.

"Aw, shut up, you bleeding beanstalk. You're lucky the Duke ain't locked you and your bleeding ladyship up for being the traitors you are." Betty jerked the man to his feet, hit him squarely in the jaw with her fist, and *tossed* him out of the way. She then picked up the trunk with ease, fitted it into the boot of the carriage, and ordered a second soldier to load the remaining luggage. The soldier took one look at the crumpled heap that was his companion, and loaded the luggage without objection.

"I can handle any man one at a time," she explained to Sara. "It's only when they come at me in bunches that I have trouble."

"I'm glad she's in my service," Gavin said to Sara, the first gleam of amusement in his eyes she'd seen in days.

"I'm in Lady Carlisle's service," Betty informed him, "and if I had my way, what I did to this fella wouldn't be a ly on what I'd do to you."

"You just make sure to take good care of her until I get home," Gavin said, in an ill-advised attempt to intimidate the cheeky maid.

"You can bet I'll do it a damned sight better than you ever did," Betty told him. "You just make sure you get back without dragging any strange women along. My mistress has had enough to put up with in that Colleen Fraser, without you importing anything new."

"Betty!" Sara exclaimed, scandalized and embarrassed. "You shouldn't talk to my husband that way."

"When he starts acting like a proper husband, I'll look to changing my ways," replied Betty. "I always said you'd be better off with that Fraser. At least he puts up a show of caring for what you like, but you had to go and set your heart on this handsome rogue. Well, you got him, I guess, but I've yet to see any good to come of it."

"I'm soon to have his baby," Sara said, thinking that would soften Betty's attitude toward Gavin.

"Humph. Any man could do that, even that lump of a soldier," she said, pointing to the soldier who had finally gotten up off the ground where she had tossed him. "But I have to admit, the baby will look a sight better for having his lordship for a father."

Gavin went off into a peal of laughter that brought the camp to a near standstill. He was still laughing when the coach left the camp, and though he didn't realize it, he couldn't have done anything which would have come closer to making Betty accept him.

Several hours later, the Highland army was in full flight, and Gavin could find nothing to laugh about. The battle on Drummossie Moor had lasted less than an hour; it was over almost before it started. But as cruel as had been the slaughter of the outnumbered and outmaneuvered Scots, it was nothing when compared to the barbarism practiced on the wounded. As he wandered over the battlefield in search of Ian, Gavin was horrified to see Cumberland's soldiers, under the command of his cousin, searching through the acres of fallen Highlanders, systematically killing the wounded and bayonetting the dead. If he had not feared another killing party would find Ian first, Gavin thought he would have killed his cousin right then. As it was, desperation drove him forward in his search, but it was still only an accident that he found the spot where several Frasers had fallen together. Ian lay face down in the dirt.

It took a moment before Gavin could move forward. There were nine men—or what was left of them—in the clearing, and Gavin had known all nine. They were all dead, and Ian was so badly spattered by the blood of two maimed Highlanders who had fallen at his side, that Gavin was certain he was dead, too. Quickly he knelt beside the still figure and placed his hand against the side of his neck; he was relieved to find his old friend's heart still beat.

"Ian, can you hear me?" the cries and groans of the wounded lying helplessly on the battlefield rose to such a pitch, he couldn't have heard a reply had one been made. He was certain the tortured souls of hell couldn't cry out with greater anguish. It made him sick to think that Englishmen had done this to their own countrymen. He turned Ian over and was rewarded when his eyes fluttered open.

"My father said ye would find me, if I survived," he managed to gasp. "Ye never did know when tae stay at home."

"Don't waste your energy talking. I've got to get you way from here. Hawley and his men are killing the vounded."

"Then leave me. 'Tis no good I am tae ye now."

"How badly are you hurt? Can you walk?"

"I do no' think I can move. I have a terrible pain in my hest, and I canna feel my leg." A heart-stopping scream rom close by rivetted Gavin's attention, and he looked p to see Hawley approaching, his men cold-bloodedly riving their bayonets into every body they came to.

"Pretend you're dead," Gavin whispered urgently. "It nay be the only way to get you away alive." He turned an back on his stomach so quickly, he struck his injured houlder on a stone. Ian turned white, but uttered not a ingle sound. Gavin rose to his feet to meet his cousin.

He had never liked Hawley, but seeing him positively xult in the senseless murder of helpless soldiers who nly differed from him by being on the losing side, tterly sickened Gavin. Regardless of how many generaions back their different limbs might join the family ree, he was ashamed to belong to a family that could roduce such a monster of inhumanity. Gavin stoically vatched Hawley come toward him, rigidly determined hat his cousin would not see the nausea that threatened o overcome him. Hawley would interpret this as veakness, and Gavin refused to allow Hawley the leasure of feeling superior to him in any way.

"Well, if it isn't my squeamish cousin Carlisle."

"If by squeamish you mean I dislike the garrotting of vounded and helpless men, then I guess I am squeamish. prefer to meet *my* opponents on their feet, not with heir faces in their own blood."

The skin on Hawley's face grew taut with contained ury. "These are enemy soldiers, and I mean to kill them ll."

"All I see are dead soldiers. Is that the only kind of soldier you and your men are capable of defeating?"

"We defeated them today," he said.

"Ah yes, but then, the Duke was here today, wasn't he?"

Gavin knew Hawley would have traded everything he owned short of his command, to have been able to run him through. Gavin had refused to fight on the Duke's side, and in Hawley's eyes that made Gavin as responsible for the rebellion as any of the men who took the battlefield.

"What kind of satisfaction can a sane man derive from garrotting the dead?" Gavin demanded, pouring scorn into his voice to disguise the loathing.

"We have to make sure they're all dead."

"Then I'm pleased to be able to spare you some effort. These men are all dead," he said, gesturing to the group around Ian. "I've already checked."

"And why should you have done that?" demanded Hawley.

"I was looking for my friend. I had to turn some of them over. For others, there was no need." Hawley glanced around, and even in his mind there could be no question about all but three men.

"We'll bayonet them anyway," Hawley decided. "It serves the bastards right."

"You will not touch even one body," Gavin said, a dangerous flame in his eyes.

"I have my orders."

"You're a liar, Hawley. Cumberland may not lift a finger to stop this godless slaughter, but he never gave any such order." Hawley gaped at Gavin. His men had come up, and they had heard the accusation.

"What's wrong? Is your stomach too weak to stand it?"

"No, but my conscience is. I didn't share Ian's beliefs, but he was still my friend."

"If a man refuses to stand with me, he's my enemy," Hawley said, and ordered his men to begin the garrotting with a wave of his hand.

Gavin raised his own hand to halt the soldiers. "Why don't you garrote them yourself? Are you too squeamish?" Gavin guessed that Hawley was the kind of man who got the greatest pleasure from commanding others to perform atrocities, while he watched.

"Go ahead," Hawley directed his men.

"The first man who puts a sword into any of these bodies will find my sword in his belly." Gavin was half a foot taller than any of the soldiers, and much broader of shoulder. There could be no question who would suffer in a contest of arms.

"You can't stop the army in the performance of its duties," Hawley bellowed.

"And when did Parliament decree that desecration of the dead is part of the army's duty?"

"Parliament leaves fighting to those who know how to kill."

"In your case, I don't think that's such a good idea."

"Out of the way," Hawley shouted, goaded into action himself. "I'll stab them myself. You, take him back to the camp where all thin-blooded aristocrats belong."

In a series of lightning movements, Gavin unsheathed his sword, leapt across the space that separated them, and pointed his sword at Hawley's throat. "Not one of you is to move, or I'll drive this through your Lt. General's throat."

"You must be mad," Hawley raged. "You'd be hanged."

"But you'd be *dead!* I swear by all you hold sacred, Hawley, if there is any such thing, I will kill you before I let you touch one of these men. You," he shouted at the soldiers, "get out of here. Call the Duke if you wish, but leave me alone with my cousin." Hawley would have countermanded the order, but the sharp point of the sword in his throat warned him to repeat Gavin's command.

"Now," Gavin said, after the men disappeared, "you will allow me to remove my friend from this field, or I shall kill you."

"You would run me through?"

"I would allow you to fight me first, *then* I would run you through. Arm yourself or leave." Hawley knew that if he left he would be branded a coward, and though he was a great villain, he was not without courage or his own brand of honesty. He drew his sword and attacked.

It took Gavin less than ten seconds to realize that Hawley knew nothing about handling a sword, and he would have allowed him to utterly exhaust himself—thereby being unable to prevent him from removing Ian—had not Cumberland ridden up just as he was effortlessly evading another clumsy attempt by Hawley to drive his sword through Gavin's heart.

"Put up your sword, fool," Cumberland ordered. "Can't you see you'll never touch him?" Hawley nearly dropped his sword in shocked surprise, and spun about to greet his superior as Cumberland dismounted from his horse. "What is going on here, Carlisle? Why are you fighting one of my officers?"

"I requested that my cousin leave the bodies of my friends undisturbed and allow me to remove Ian's body unmolested. He refused, saying it was by your order that he was garrotting the dead and the wounded alike."

"I gave no such order, Hawley," said Cumberland, "but I wonder that you should be so anxious to remove a body, Carlisle."

"I have known all these men since I was a boy," Gavin said, emotion nearly choking him. "I tried to talk them out of this rebellion, but I can't turn my back on them because we disagreed. I want to give Ian a decent burial. We were raised together. He was my best friend."

"Which one is he?" asked Cumberland, apparently unmoved by Gavin's emotion.

"There," Gavin said, then barely kept from lifting his sword to Cumberland when the commander kicked Ian in the side. Gavin never did know how Ian lay there without making a sound, unless he had passed out from the pain. Gavin hoped he had.

"He seems dead to me," Cumberland observed indifferently. "Take him if you want."

"And the others?"

"Anybody can see they're dead, too. Leave them untouched." Cumberland gave Hawley a nod of dismissal.

"I don't normally allow civilians to interfere with my officers, even if I have known them almost as long as their best friends, so do not take this as a license to defend the rest of Scotland."

"I would never interfere with him in battle, but killing helpless wounded . . ."

"We've had too many uprisings and rebellions," Cumberland stated, showing none of the repugnance Gavin was certain he must feel. "We must teach these Highlanders a lesson they'll never forget. I mean to destroy the clans and drive their leaders into exile. Never again will England be threatened by a Stuart."

"Can't you moderate the cruelty of your soldiers?"

"I will if I see them," Cumberland replied, and Gavin knew he had his answer. Scotland would bleed unceasingly for this latest madness. "He's a Fraser, you said, a neighbor of yours?"

"Yes."

"Then I'll give you his lands. I'm confiscating the property of all the rebels, you know."

"No. I won't take it," Gavin replied, revolted at the idea.

"Would you prefer that I give them to Hawley?" Gavin shook his head, unable to speak. "I'm glad you agree. Now take your friend and be gone. I have much to do before this day is done."

Gavin gathered Ian in his arms as carefully as he dared under Cumberland's penetrating gaze, and began the walk back to camp. He did not look back. He couldn't.

Chapter 26

Gavin personally loaded Ian's *body* into the wagon that was to take him to Estameer. He didn't dare speak to him, but he had already whispered his instructions as he carried him from the battlefield. Gavin knew that if Ian could withstand Cumberland's kick without uttering a sound, he could survive the trip by wagon. Now it was up to Gavin to do his part.

Rather than trust to the silence of someone he didn't know, Gavin had his own valet drive the wagon to the inn where Sara would be staying that evening. Gavin's horse was saddled and ready. He would ride behind. He was in the act of mounting when a page reached him, with an urgent request from the Earl to come to his quarters immediately.

Gavin's first inclination was to ignore the message. He had suffered enough at the old bastard's hands, and he couldn't see him changing his colors at this point. It was important that he get Ian out of the English army's camp immediately. He doubted Cumberland would allow Hawley to kill Ian, even if they somehow discovered he was alive, but he would certainly be arrested, tried, and hanged for treason. If that was the fate in store for Ian, then Gavin might have served his friend better if he had left him on the battlefield. Discovery would also seriously compromise Gavin's own position. He was actually in the saddle and riding away when he changed his mind. Maybe it was habit, maybe it was filial duty, but he couldn't ride off and leave his father's summons unanswered. He sent the wagon on ahead and turned back.

"Be quick about it," Gavin announced rudely, when he entered his father's quarters. "I have Ian in the wagon, and every minute we're here endangers his life."

The Earl regarded his son coldly. "It would seem to me that you should think more of your own life. If Cumberland should find out—"

"If you called me here just to complain about my helping Ian—"

"I called you here to speak of your wife."

"Sara? She left camp early this morning."

"I know, and so does everyone else."

"Look, I haven't got time to go over the same discussion we had earlier."

"Then stop interrupting and listen."

Gavin's impatience evaporated, replaced instead by curiosity. His father was struggling with himself over something, and it was the first time Gavin had ever known him not to know exactly what he meant to do.

"I will confess that I find it extremely difficult to help you preserve your wife from danger. After the way that woman has thwarted and defied me—As I was saying," the Earl said when he had himself under control again, "everyone knows when your wife left, and where she was headed. They also know that she is quite friendly with the Stuart prince."

"So?"

"I have just come from headquarters. I was there when Hawley organized the detail that will pursue the Prince. He is known to have taken the same route as Lady

Carlisle. Hawley directed his men to pay particular attention to Lady Carlisle and her party. If there is any chance she may offer to help the Prince . . ." The Earl left his sentence unfinished, but Gavin understood. He knew there was *every* chance. In fact, he was quite certain that Sara would help the prince, if it were at all possible.

"I do not think Cumberland would go so far as to actually harm her," the Earl began.

"But she must not be found with the prince," Gavin finished for him. "Why did you tell me this?" he asked his father.

"It cost me a severe struggle before I could make up my mind, but there are many reasons."

"Many?"

"Actually yes, but I will give you one which I think you will believe. If anything were to happen to the child your wife is carrying, Hawley could inherit Lochknole. I would commit half the crimes of Christendom to prevent that."

Gavin let loose a crack of laughter. "Leave it to you to have a thoroughly hellish reason for doing something decent. We'll send you an announcement of the birth."

"Announcement be damned! I intend to be present at the baptism."

Gavin stared hard at his father for a moment, then shrugged indifferently. "In a way, I suppose this child means as much to you as it does to us. I guess it's only fair that you would be allowed to savor your success. Just don't plan to stay too long."

"I won't. Domestic felicity sickens me."

Sara could no longer hear the sounds of battle, but she knew what the deep boom of the big guns could mean to a human body, and her imagination continued to torture her with visions of what could be happening to the

Highlanders, to men she knew, to Ian. She had not wanted to be separated from Gavin again, but she knew it was best. She really *didn't* want to see the Prince's dream come to an end, but more than that, she didn't want to have to see what was happening to the people she knew. And she was certain their cause was lost. How often were wars started by the people least capable of winning them?

She tried to concentrate on Gavin and their future together, but for once her husband could not hold her thoughts. They were back on that terrible moor near Culloden.

"Are we going to reach Estameer tonight?" Betty asked. She was no more interested in the trip than Sara, but she seemed to be less upset about the battle.

"No. Gavin told me to spend tonight on the road." They were silent for a while longer.

"I wonder if the Fraser is all right?" Betty wondered aloud.

"You like him, don't you?" Sara asked. She tried to smile, but her face refused. "You should ask him to marry you."

"Marry *me!*" Betty squawked so suddenly, Sara did smile. "I'm not such a bold piece as that," exclaimed her maid. "Besides, what would a gentleman like him do with a female the likes of me?"

"Thank his lucky stars you agreed to marry him."

"No, I like him well enough but not to marry. It's just that he's such a charming gentleman."

"Not to mention handsome, loyal, and ruthless," said Sara. "Thank you, but I'm just as glad I fell in love with Gavin."

"I guess it is best, but . . ." Betty sighed and failed to finish her thought. Sara decided it would be useless to try and oust Ian in Betty's affections. If her anger over his kidnapping Sara could only last a few days, she doubted anything else would serve to turn Betty against Ian. She would always remember his courtly behavior and delightful smile, and never see the vein of selfishness that ran so close to the surface. Oh well, it wasn't necessary. Sara loved Gavin, and that was all that mattered.

They hadn't been on the road for much more than two hours when they suddenly became aware of the sound of several horses somewhere on the road behind them, coming toward them at a gallop. Sara and Betty looked at each other, unsure of what this could mean. Was Gavin coming after her for some reason? Could it be bandits? With so many men away from their homes with the Prince, there had been no one to keep the highwaymen in check all winter. Betty hung her head out the window.

"It's the Prince," she told Sara in surprise. "and he's coming this way as fast as he can."

"Tell the coachman to stop." Sara didn't have to wait long before the Prince reined in alongside them.

"All is lost," he declared dramatically. "There's a reward of thirty thousand pounds on my head, so I must get away quickly. Cumberland's men can't be far behind."

"Is there anywhere you can hide?" Sara asked.

"No. We must ride on and hope to find fresh horses before we are overtaken."

An idea suddenly sprang into Sara's mind. It seemed wild and improbable, but it might succeed for that very reason. "I can disguise you as my maid," she told the prince. "Then your men can ride off, and the soldiers will follow them. Everybody knows Betty is as tall as a man, and in the shadows of the carriage, they won't be able to see your features clearly."

The prince was naturally reluctant to adopt such a disguise, but his vanguard heartily approved of it, and in a short time they had him in Betty's clothes and seated opposite Sara. Betty was dressed as a man, given a hat and high collar which virtually covered her face, provided with a rifle, and told to ride in the box with the driver as a guard. Then the Prince's men rode off to the south, promising to leave his horse where he could find it later.

"This is a sad way to end our adventure," the Prince observed with a heavy sigh. "If I had known so many would lose their lives in my cause, I doubt I should have come."

"You had to come," Sara assured him. "It was your destiny, just as it was their choice to support your cause. They made the decision for themselves, so you must not reproach yourself with their deaths."

"You are such a comforting woman," the Prince said thankfully. "I wonder if your husband realizes what a treasure he has in you?"

"I'm not sure that treasure is the word Gavin would have chosen, but yes, I think he does know my worth."

"He is the most fortunate of men." The Prince lapsed into a period of introspection, only occasionally rousing himself to make a remark. Sara left him to his thoughts. She was worried about the soldiers she expected would soon follow them. They had turned to the east, away from the most logical route for the Prince to take, but she was certain Cumberland's men would follow her. She wondered what she would say to them.

She didn't have long to wait. Less than half an hour later, she heard the sound of thundering hooves again, and shortly afterwards Betty pounded on the roof with the butt of her rifle, the signal they had agreed upon to warn her the soldiers had come.

"Let me do all the talking," Sara told the prince. "You may pass for Betty in general shape, but not in voice."

A few moments later, the soldiers came alongside the coach, and Sara unfastened the window so she could talk to them.

"We're looking for the Stuart Prince," a soldier called

out to her.

"We haven't seen him. We left quite early this morning."

"I know, but we were told he had come this way."

"We did think we heard a troop of horses some time back, but they must have turned off. No one passed us."

"Who goes with you?" the soldier asked.

"My maid and a rather surly young man my husband hired to safeguard us from highwaymen." The soldier peered into the dim interior of the carriage. It was the man Betty had knocked down that very morning. "Surely you recognize my maid, or would you rather she got down, so you might inspect her more closely?"

"I remember her," the man replied, wanting to give Betty no further opportunity to assault his person. Lt. Gen. Hawley had told him the Prince was heading this way; he had also told him that Lady Carlisle would not be above helping him escape. Still, there was no doubt that this was her ladyship's maid. There couldn't be two women in the whole world that size, and he wasn't about to ask her to step out of the carriage. She might decide to fetch him another blow to the jaw in front of his men, and he would have to quit the army if they saw him bested by a woman twice in the same day, even if she was taller than he was. No, it had to be the maid, and that was all there was to it. "Would your driver have any idea where the horsemen turned off?"

"I don't know, but you may ask him." Sara waited patiently while the soldiers questioned the driver. At last they started back down the road at a gallop, and she was able to breath a sigh of relief.

"I congratulate you, Lady Carlisle," the prince said, "but weren't you afraid he would demand that I get out, so he might see me better."

"No. This morning Betty knocked that same soldier down. I was certain he wouldn't wish to give her the opportunity to do it again."

The prince laughed softly. "Now, what do we do next?"

"I was hoping you would have the answer to that question. I suppose we just now turn our thoughts to its solution." But neither of them had the opportunity to think for long. Within what seemed like minutes, they heard hooves approaching once again. The prince stiffened, and Sara turned white.

"Could they have returned?"

"But why? They couldn't have had time to find your vanguard."

"I have a pistol."

"That won't account for more than one, and you can't get away without a horse. Sit quietly. I'll think of something." But moments later Sara could have cried with relief when Gavin's beloved face came into view.

"I should have known I would find you here," Gavin said, as soon as he saw the prince sitting where Betty should have been.

"Your wife was kind enough to suggest the disguise."

"Foolish is the word I would have chosen," Gavin said, "but there's no time to worry about that now. We've got to get you out of those petticoats. If they should come back, they're bound to have you out of the coach."

"What did you tell them about Betty?"

"Just that she was a guard you had hired."

"Did they show any interest in her?"

"No."

"Then Betty and the Prince will exchange places."

"But why?"

"Betty was the only one they couldn't see, and she will be the only reason for them to come back. She must be Betty."

"Then what about the Prince?"

"Did your men leave a horse for you?"

"Yes."

"How long will it take you to reach it?"

"Under an hour."

"Then you're going to be the guard. I've caught up with my wife, and I've sent you back home. You'll point the soldiers in our direction, think of something slightly suspicious to tell them about my arrival, if you can, but make sure they're interested in us, not yourself. Once they're past, you can safely leave the road, find your horse, and rejoin your men. They won't follow you again."

"Will you be safe?"

"Yes. You're the only one in danger. Can you speak Gaelic?"

"After nine months' intimate acquaintance with Highlanders, I can speak it like a native."

"Good. Cumberland's soldiers can't, so they won't know if your accent is not exactly true. Make them have enough difficulty understanding you so they won't question you extensively, but be sure they understand well enough to know to come after us."

The Prince smiled. "If you had been on my side, we might not have lost today."

"If I had been on your side, you would never have left France," Gavin replied brutally. "You have cost Scotland more than you can know."

"I will do my best not to increase the price of her allegiance," promised the prince, as he alighted from the carriage. Minutes later, clothed in the shabby clothes Betty had worn, and his face smeared with enough grime to make him seem the peasant he claimed to be, the prince headed back down the road.

"Are you certain he will be all right?" Sara asked, as the coach resumed its journey. "He has no way to protect himself now."

"He has his wits and half the people of Scotland on his

side," Gavin replied. "He would do well enough with either, but with both, Cumberland will never catch him, even if it's months before he can find a way to get to France."

They had nearly reached the inn where they were to meet Ian, when the soldiers overtook them a second time. The men were tired and obviously out of temper.

"What are you doing here?" the soldier in charge demanded, when he saw Gavin seated next to his wife.

"What does it look like I'm doing?" demanded Gavin. "My wife and I are returning home."

"You weren't here before."

"You will notice my horse tied to the rear of the coach," Gavin said patiently. "I left after the battle and caught up with my wife and her maid."

"As to that maid, I'd be obliged if she would step down, so we could have a look at her."

"Betty? Surely you don't suspect *her* of helping the prince?"

"As to that, I can't say exactly, but he's somewhere along these roads."

"And you haven't been able to find him," Gavin finished for them.

"There's people only too ready to help him, even if there is a godless amount of money on his head."

"And just what do you expect my wife's maid to have to do with his escape?"

"Well, you see, sir, the Prince wasn't with that escaping party of Jacobites, and he wasn't on this road neither, but he must be somewhere."

"I can't fault your logic so far."

"Well, we met that guide you hired for your wife a ways back . . ."

"I sent him home because we didn't need him, now that I'm here."

". . . and he suggested there was some funny business

bout the maid."

"Funny business?"

"What he actually said was, that we ought to see about hat maid. He said it weren't natural for a female to be hat big."

"So you're thinking that we may have the Prince in ere, disguised as Lady Carlisle's maid."

"Begging your pardon, sir, but we have to check every ossibility."

"Certainly. Betty, would you like to speak to the oldier?"

"You bet I would," declared Betty, opening the door nd preparing to step down. "I may have grown a bit nore than was necessary, but I won't have any trouble onvincing this turnip there's nothing false about me."

The man needed no more than the sound of that vell-remembered voice to convince him this indeed was Betty, and not the prince.

"You don't need to get down, Miss," he said, before Betty's foot could touch the ground. "Anyone can see you're not the prince." Betty got down anyway.

"I want you to be sure this time," she said, pproaching the young man and towering above him ntimidatingly. "This is the second time you've stopped nilady's coach, which to my way of thinking is two times oo many. I don't want you messing about with us nymore. You can search under the seat and inside the runks if you must, but if I see you again, they're going to ave to carry you back to your captain."

"Now, Betty, he's just trying to do his job," Sara said, er voice unsteady with suppressed laughter.

"No more than I'm trying to do mine," Betty answered romptly.

Ian didn't arrive at the inn until quite late that

evening. Gavin had a doctor waiting to treat his wounds. Ian looked so bad the doctor immediately banished them from the room. After he had done all he could, the doctor gave Ian something to ease the pain and make him sleep, so it wasn't until they were on the road again the next day that Gavin and Sara had a chance to talk with him. Betty was once again riding in the box so Ian might be able to lie down on her seat.

"For a man who didna believe in the rebellion, ye have been put tae some shifts tae save the pair of us."

"I couldn't leave you to be butchered by Hawley's henchmen, but you'll have to thank Sara for helping the prince. I'd have told him to be on his way."

"Maybe," replied Ian, the pain of his wounds making it difficult for him to adjust his position so that he could see both Sara and Gavin, "but I thank ye none the less. Now, how do ye propose tae get me off yer hands? Ye can't be meaning tae hide me in yer cellars, and my father willna have me." He paused as a thought struck him. "I don't suppose he'll be able tae keep anybody now. No doubt yer precious Cumberland will give our land tae one of his German cronies."

"You must emigrate," Gavin said. "Many of your people have already done so."

"Aye. I wouldna mind it so much, if ye had the land," Ian said. "At least I would know 'twas in the hands of someone who loved it as much as I do."

"Then you didn't hear what Cumberland said on the battlefield?"

"No. I passed out when ye rolled me over."

"He did give me your land. I will send you some money, as soon as you get to America. Then, maybe in a few years, after everything is settled down again, you can come back."

"Nay, I'll no' be coming back," Ian said sadly. "It will never again be the Scotland I loved. Ye can change with the times, but I canna do aught but wish for the old days."

"But this is still your home," Sara said, unable to understand how Ian could turn his back on everything that until this morning he had been willing to give his life for.

"Not any longer. Some men can bend in the wind, adapt tae change, but I canna. 'Tis why I fought for the Stuart, and 'tis why I canna stay."

"We'll miss you."

"Aye, and that's another reason why I must go, lassie." Ian's gaze defied Gavin to refuse him the use of the endearment. "I might be tempted tae kidnap ye again."

"They don't approve of kidnapping, even in America," Gavin told him.

"Aye, but I willna be tempted in America, unless ye be meaning tae come for a visit."

They laughed at that and talked much more easily afterwards, but later, after Ian was settled in his room at Estameer, and they were preparing to leave him, Sara couldn't help but ask him again.

"Do you really have to stay away forever? Can't you come back someday?"

"It wouldna be wise. Gavin and I will part as friends, but too much lies between us. Besides, I canna face him day after day, knowing he possesses the two things in the world I hold most dear."

"Two things?"

"My land and you."

Chapter 27

As she waited for Gavin to come to bed, Sara allowed her mind to wander back through the most recent of the several turning points in their lives. Now that it was over, she could see that the last few days had cleared away all the remaining debris between them, and that their relationship would be the stronger for it, but it had been a painful purging, and she hoped they would never be forced to endure anything like it again. But Gavin was so much happier, so much more natural, she found herself unable to regret any of the suffering or unhappiness. After all, it's a lot like having a baby, she told herself. The discomfort is intense, but it's temporary, and is followed by a joy that will last forever.

The door between their rooms opened, and Sara felt sure her cup was full beyond holding. She could never look at Gavin without feeling almost overcome with wonder. That any of the events of the past several months should have happened to quiet, shy little Sara Raymond was incredible, but nothing was more unbelievable than that this gorgeous man was her husband. And he was her lover, too! Well, she still had trouble believing that.

"I have something for you," Gavin said, and handed

her a piece of paper. "It gives you absolute control of your fortune, the principal and the income. I've already signed it."

"But why?"

"Do you remember what you said in Glasgow? You said you wanted a home, a family to belong to, and control of your money. Well, Estameer is your home, and our child will be the beginning of a family. Now you have your money."

"And you said you wanted something you could do without interference from your father, and someone who could love you unconditionally."

"I have both." Gavin slipped into bed and took Sara into his arms. "But you are the more important of the two." His kiss was gentle at first, but then it became hard and insistent. "I thought I had lost you when I saw you with Ian. I don't know what happened to me, I'm not even sure I know what I did, but I felt like I was losing my mind." Sara tried to put her fingers to his lips to stop him, but he would not be quieted. "No, I must tell you. I must convince you it will never happen again. I don't know why I did it, but I guess it was the shock of thinking I was losing you, and that after finally falling in love, life was going to cheat me again."

"You never have completely stopped loving your father, have you?"

"No, which was why I hated him all the more. Does that make sense to you?"

"I think so."

"Well, I can accept him now. I still think he's a bloody beast, and I could kill him for what he did to my mother, if it would do any good, but I can accept that, too. And I could accept it if your love for me were to change."

"I will never—"

"I know," Gavin whispered, putting his fingers to her lips, "but I *could* accept it. I know now you have to take chances in life, and that you can't win every time, that you have to go on living. Ian risked everything he loved. He lost, but he will start over. You lost everything when your father died. I was blind to think I suffered more than others, or that my tragedy hadn't been acted out thousands of times before. If you hadn't been determined to force me to learn to love you, I might still be in the airless cocoon I built for myself, foolishly thinking I was protecting my life from hurt, even more stupidly thinking that what I had was worth protecting."

"And you have freed me from a limited view of life." Sara chuckled in spite of the lump in her throat. "I can't say I've *liked* everything that has happened to me over the last five months, but without them I would be a woman of very restricted experience, with little understanding of the world or her husband."

"You can't pretend that throwing you to the wolves was a virtue."

"No, but you didn't have to give me a chance to become your *real* wife. Even in Glasgow, you never turned your back on me."

"How could I, when Ian and the Prince were parading you all over town. I met you at every turn."

"I was always looking for you. Betty was disgusted with me."

"Do you know when I think I started to fall in love with you?" Gavin said.

"No."

"When we were returning from the church."

"But I had fainted."

"How could I be angry with a woman who had fainted?"

"You already know when I fell in love with you."

"When I was showing off for the coachman," Gavin said with a grimace. "I hope I've improved since then."

Sara let her hand run over his powerful shoulder and

then through the soft mat of hair on his chest. "Just a little. Now, if you could just not clench your jaw so hard when you get angry. It makes you look like you've got walnuts in your cheeks." Gavin tumbled her over and kissed her until she was breathless.

"Now look what you've done," complained Sara. "I've lost my paper."

"Here it is," Gavin said, fishing it out from where it had been crushed under him. It was badly wrinkled. "I'll give you another one."

"This is quite good enough for what I want," Sara said, and proceeded to rip the paper in half, turn it around, and rip it again several times more. She sprinkled the pieces all over Gavin.

"What did you do that for?"

"I remembered a line in the service that said you endowed me with all your worldly goods. I don't need a paper to give me what I already have."

"But I thought—"

"So did I, but I was wrong. But you can kiss me again. That's something I will never have enough of."

Gavin didn't require a second invitation. That he had found everything he wanted in a woman—in *one* woman—was a surprise. That she was his wife, was incredible.

And Sara welcomed his embraces. She was in awe of what had been given her, that Gavin should love her as much as she loved him. She thought of her father and smiled. *Now* she understood.

Author's Note

The Scottish army under Charles Stuart and Lord George Murray penetrated England as far south as Derby on December 6, 1745, roughly one hundred and twenty miles from London. There was a panic in the city, and George II ordered his private yacht ready to sail at a moment's notice.

Bonnie Prince Charlie never did forgive his clan chieftains for forcing him to retreat from Derby. There is considerable conjecture as to what might have happened if he had been allowed to proceed to London, and the promised help had come from France, but as it is only conjecture, it doesn't concern us here. He gradually removed his trust from the clan chieftains and Lord George, and placed it in the hands of a few hangers-on in his personal party. This had disastrous results during his long illness in the winter of 1746, and in the preparations for the battle of Culloden.

A reward of thirty thousand pounds, an incredible sum in 1746, was placed on the Prince's head by the English government, but it is even more remarkable that during the five months the Prince was in hiding, not a single person—and he was helped by many people during that time—attempted to claim the reward. He *did* elude capture by masquerading as the maid of Flora McDonald, but this did not take place where I have placed it in the book, or in the same manner.

Sara and Gavin are entirely fictional, as is their story, but the facts about the Highland army, its leaders and its battles, are accurate. I have used first hand accounts and, in so far as was possible, I have paraphrased the actual words of Bonnie Prince Charles, Lord George Murray, Lieutenant-General Henry Hawley, James Wolfe, and William Augustus, Duke of Cumberland.

The reprisals after Culloden were unbelievably cruel, the bayonetting of the wounded on the battlefield being only one of the gruesome acts intended to insure that such an uprising for the Stuart cause would never take place again. The clan system was systematically dismantled, the Highlanders were forbidden to render military service to their chief, the chief lost jurisdiction over his people—some also lost their lands—and wearing of the tartan was banned. The tartan and confiscated lands were restored after 1782, but the clan system was effectively destroyed, as much by changes in agriculture as government interference.

Emigration to America had been going on for many years prior to the rebellion, but it became a common way for survivors of the '45 to escape the brutal consequences of their loyalty to the last Stuart.